PENGUIN BOOKS

HOMO ZAPIENS

Victor Pelevin was born in 1962 in Moscow, where he lives today. His books include the novels *Omon Ra*, *The Life of Insects*, and *Buddha's Little Finger*, the novella *The Yellow Arrow*, and the story collections *A Werewolf Problem in Central Russia* and *The Blue Lantern*, which won the Russian "Little Booker" Prize in 1993.

Praise for *Homo Zapiens*

"[A] brilliant satire on the realities of post-Soviet Russia . . . there are a number of wonderfully comic and thoughtful assessments of the nature of things under emerging capitalism in *Homo Zapiens*, including a series of delicious take-offs on ad copywriting, exposes of the new corruption of 'black cash flow' into the arts as well as the commercial realm, and an amazingly outrageous explanation of the essence of Russian politics worthy of the imagination of Jorge Luis Borges or Italo Calvino."
—*The Washington Post*

"Tartarsky stands in for a whole generation trapped between a discredited Soviet past and a banal, Westernized future, and the absurdity of the situation sends him hunting through the seamy Muscovite underworld for some meaning at the bottom of it all. That he is coached on the way by the spirit of Che Guevara gives you the flavor of Pelevin's darkly anarchic imagination."
—*Time*

"Victor Pelevin, the enfant terrible of post-Soviet Russian literature, is a cultural magpie, borrowing the hip poses of MTV and disaffected argot of the Beat poets and combining them with elements reminiscent of his great countrymen: the ferocious satire of Mikhail Bulgakov and the phantasmagorical sense of the absurd purveyed by the dissident writer Andrei Sinyavsky."
—*The New York Times*

"One of the most energetic and imaginative voices to reach our Western antennas." —*Los Angeles Times*

HOMO ZAPIENS

VICTOR PELEVIN

Translated by Andrew Bromfield

PENGUIN BOOKS

PENGUIN BOOKS

Published by the Penguin Group

Penguin Group (USA) Inc., 375 Hudson Street, New York, New York 10014, U.S.A.
Penguin Group (Canada), 90 Eglinton Avenue East, Suite 700, Toronto, Ontario,
Canada M4P 2Y3 (a division of Pearson Penguin Canada Inc.)
Penguin Books Ltd, 80 Strand, London WC2R 0RL, England
Penguin Ireland, 25 St Stephen's Green, Dublin 2, Ireland (a division of Penguin Books Ltd)
Penguin Group (Australia), 250 Camberwell Road, Camberwell, Victoria 3124,
Australia (a division of Pearson Australia Group Pty Ltd)
Penguin Books India Pvt Ltd, 11 Community Centre, Panchsheel Park, New Delhi – 110 017, India
Penguin Group (NZ), 67 Apollo Drive, Mairangi Bay,
Auckland 1311, New Zealand (a division of Pearson New Zealand Ltd)
Penguin Books (South Africa) (Pty) Ltd, 24 Sturdee Avenue, Rosebank, Johannesburg 2196, South Africa

Penguin Books Ltd, Registered Offices: 80 Strand, London WC2R 0RL, England

First published in Great Britain as *Babylon* by Faber and Faber Limited 2000
First published in the United States of America by Viking Penguin,
a member of Penguin Putnam Inc. 2002
Published in Penguin Books 2003
This edition published in Penguin Books 2006

11

Originally published in Russian as *Generation II*

PUBLISHER'S NOTE

This is a work of fiction. Names, characters, places, and incidents either
are the product of the author's imagination or are used fictitiously, and any
resemblance to actual persons, living or dead, business establishments,
events, or locales is entirely coincidental.

THE LIBRARY OF CONGRESS HAS CATALOGED
THE AMERICAN HARDCOVER EDITION AS FOLLOWS:
Pelevin, Victor.
Homo zapiens / Victor Pelevin ; translated by Andrew Bromfield.
p. cm.
ISBN 0-670-03066-X (hc.)
ISBN 978-0-14-200181-3 (pbk.)
I. Bromfield, Andrew. II Title.
PG3485.E38 H66 2002
891.73'44—dc21 2001046967

Printed in the United States of America
Set in Palatino

To the Memory of the Middle Class

CHAPTER 1

Generation 'P'

Once upon a time in Russia there really was a carefree, youthful generation that smiled in joy at the summer, the sea and the sun, and chose Pepsi.

It's hard at this stage to figure out exactly how this situation came about. Most likely it involved more than just the remarkable taste of the drink in question. More than just the caffeine that keeps young kids demanding another dose, steering them securely out of childhood into the clear waters of the channel of cocaine. More, even, than a banal bribe: it would be nice to think that the Party bureaucrat who took the crucial decision to sign the contract simply fell in love with this dark, fizzy liquid with every fibre of a soul no longer sustained by faith in communism.

The most likely reason, though, is that the ideologists of the USSR believed there could only be one truth. So in fact Generation 'P' had no choice in the matter and children of the Soviet seventies chose Pepsi in precisely the same way as their parents chose Brezhnev.

No matter which way it was, as these children lounged on the seashore in the summer, gazing endlessly at a cloudless blue horizon, they drank warm Pepsi-Cola decanted into glass bottles in the city of Novorossiisk and dreamed that some day the distant forbidden world on the far side of the sea would be part of their own lives.

Babylen Tatarsky was by default a member of Generation 'P', although it was a long time before he had any inkling of the fact. If in those distant years someone had told him that when he grew up he would be a *copywriter*, he'd probably have dropped his bottle of Pepsi-Cola on the hot gravel of the pioneer-camp beach in his astonishment. In those distant years children were expected to direct their aspirations towards a gleaming fireman's helmet or a doctor's white coat. Even that peaceful word 'designer' seemed a dubious neologism only likely to be tolerated until the next serious worsening in the international situation.

In those days, however, language and life both abounded in the strange and the dubious. Take the very name 'Babylen', which was conferred on Tatarsky by his father, who managed to combine in his heart a faith in communism with the ideals of the sixties generation. He composed it from the title of Yevtushenko's famous poem 'Baby Yar' and Lenin. Tatarsky's father clearly found it easy to imagine a faithful disciple of Lenin moved by Yevtushenko's liberated verse to the grateful realisation that Marxism originally stood for free love, or a jazz-crazy aesthete suddenly convinced by an elaborately protracted saxophone riff that communism would inevitably triumph. It was not only Tatarsky's father who was like that – the entire Soviet generation of the fifties and sixties was the same. This was the generation that gave the world the amateur song and ejaculated the first sputnik – that four-tailed spermatozoon of the future that never began – into the dark void of cosmic space.

Tatarsky was sensitive about his name, and whenever possible he introduced himself as Vladimir or Vova. Then he began lying to his friends, saying that his father had given him a strange name because he was keen on Eastern mysticism, and he was thinking of the ancient city of Babylon, the secret lore of which was destined to be inherited by him, Babylen. His father had invented his alloy of Yevtushenko and Lenin because he was a follower of Manicheism and pantheism and regarded it as his duty to balance out the principle of light with the principle of darkness. Despite this brilliantly elaborated fable, at the age of eighteen Tatarsky was delighted to be able to lose his first passport and receive a new one in the name of Vladimir.

After that his life followed an entirely ordinary pattern. He went to a technical institute – not, of course, because he had any love for technology (he specialised in some kind of electric furnace), but because he didn't want to go into the army. However, at the age of twenty-one something happened to him that changed the course of his life for ever.

Out in the countryside during the summer he read a small volume of Boris Pasternak. The poems, which had previously left him entirely cold, had such a profound impact that for several weeks he could think of nothing else – and then he began writing verse himself. He would never forget the rusty carcass of a bus, sunk at a crooked angle into the ground on the edge of the forest outside Moscow at the precise spot where the very first line of his life came to him: 'The sardine-clouds swim onwards to the south.' (He later came to realise this poem had a distinctly fishy odour.) In short, his was an absolutely typical case, which ended in typical fashion when Tatarsky entered the Literary Institute. He couldn't get into the poetry department, though, and had to content himself with translations from the languages of the peoples of the USSR. Tatarsky pictured his future approximately as follows: during the day – an empty lecture hall in the Literary Institute, a word-for-word translation from the Uzbek or the Kirghiz that had to be set in rhyme by the next deadline; in the evenings – his creative labours for eternity.

Then, quite unobtrusively, an event of fundamental significance for his future occurred. The USSR, which they'd begun to renovate and improve at about the time when Tatarsky decided to change his profession, improved so much that it ceased to exist (if a state is capable of entering nirvana, that's what must have happened in this case); so any more translations from the languages of the peoples of the USSR were quite simply out of the question. It was a blow, but Tatarsky survived it. He still had his work for eternity, and that was enough for him.

Then events took an unforeseen turn. Something began happening to the very eternity to which he had decided to devote his labours and his days. Tatarsky couldn't understand this at all. After all, eternity – at least as he'd always thought of it – was something unchangeable, indestructible and entirely independent of the transient fortunes of this earthly realm. If, for instance, the small volume of Pasternak that had changed his life had already entered this eternity, then there was no power capable of ejecting it.

But this proved not to be entirely true. It turned out that eternity only existed for as long as Tatarsky sincerely believed in it, and was actually nowhere to be found beyond the bounds of this belief. In order for him to believe sincerely in eternity, others had to share in this belief, because a belief that no one else shares is called schizophrenia; and something strange had started happening to everyone else, including the very people who had taught Tatarsky to keep his eyes fixed firmly on eternity.

It wasn't as though they'd shifted their previous point of view, not that – just that the very space into which their gaze had been directed (after all, a point of view always implies gazing in some particular direction) began to curl back in on itself and disappear, until all that was left of it was a microscopic dot on the windscreen of the mind. Glimpses of entirely different landscapes began to fill in their surroundings.

Tatarsky tried to fight it and pretend that nothing was actually happening. At first he could manage it. By keeping close company with his friends, who were also pretending that nothing was happening, for a time he was able to believe it was true. The end came unexpectedly.

When Tatarsky was out walking one day, he stopped at a shoe shop that was closed for lunch. Swimming about in the summer heat behind the glass wall of the shop window was a fat, pretty salesgirl whom Tatarsky promptly dubbed Maggie, and there in the midst of a chaos of multicoloured Turkish handicrafts stood a pair of unmistakably Soviet-made shoes.

Tatarsky felt a sensation of instantaneous, piercing recognition. The shoes had pointed toes and high heels and were made of good leather. They were a light yellowish-brown, stitched with a light-blue thread and decorated with large gold buckles in the form of harps. It wasn't that they were simply in bad taste, or vulgar; they were the clear embodiment of what a certain drunken teacher of Soviet literature from the Literary Institute used to call 'our gestalt', and the sight was so pitiful, laughable and touching (especially the harp buckles) that tears sprang to Tatarsky's eyes. The shoes were covered by a thick layer of dust: the new era obviously had no use for them.

Tatarsky knew the new era had no use for him either, but he had managed to accustom himself to the idea and even take a certain bitter-sweet satisfaction in it. The feeling had been decoded for him by the words of Marina Tsvetaeva: 'Scattered along the dusty shelves of shops (No one has bought them and no one buys!) My poems, like precious wines, will have their day': if there was something humiliating in this feeling, then it was not he, but the world around him that was humiliated. But in front of that shop window his heart sank in the sudden realisation that the dust settling on him as he stood there beneath the vault of the heavens was not the dust that covered a vessel containing precious wine, but the same dust as covered the shoes with the harp buckles; and he realised something else too: the eternity he used to believe in could only exist on state subsidies, or else – which is just the same thing – as something forbidden by the state. Worse even than that, it could only exist in the form of the semi-conscious reminiscences of some girl called Maggie from the shoe shop. This dubious species of eternity had simply been inserted into her head, as it had into his, in the same packaging as natural history and inorganic chemistry. Eternity was contingent: if, say, Stalin had not killed Trotsky, but the other way round, then it would have been populated by entirely different individuals. But even that was not important, because Tatarsky understood quite clearly that no matter how things panned out, Maggie simply couldn't care less about eternity, and when she finally and completely stopped believing in it, there wouldn't be any more eternity, because where could it be then? Or, as he wrote in his notebook when he got home: 'When the subject of eternity disappears, then all of its objects also disappear, and the only subject of eternity is whoever happens to remember about it occasionally.'

He didn't write any more poems after that: with the collapse of Soviet power they had simply lost their meaning and value.

CHAPTER 2

Draft Podium

No sooner had eternity disappeared than Tatarsky found himself in the present, and it turned out that he knew absolutely nothing about the world that had sprung up around him during the last few years.

It was a very strange world. Externally it had not changed too much, except perhaps that there were more paupers on the streets, but everything in his surroundings – the houses, the trees, the benches on the streets – had somehow suddenly grown old and decrepit. It wasn't possible to say that the essential nature of the world had changed, either, because now it no longer had any essential nature. A frighteningly vague uncertainty dominated everything. Despite that, however, the streets were flooded with Mercedes and Toyotas carrying brawny types possessed of absolute confidence in themselves and in what was happening, and there was even, if one could believe the newspapers, some kind of foreign policy.

Meanwhile the television was still showing the same old repulsive physiognomies that had been sickening the viewers for the last twenty years. Now they were saying exactly the same things they used to jail other people for, except that they were far bolder, far more decisive and radical. Tatarsky often found himself imagining Germany in 1946, with Doktor Goebbels shrieking hysterically on the radio about the abyss into which fascism had led the nation, with the former Kommandant of Auschwitz heading the Commission for the Detention of Nazi Criminals, and SS generals explaining in clear and simple words the importance of liberal values, while the whole cabal was led by the newly enlightened Gauleiter of Eastern Prussia. Tatarsky, of course, hated most of the manifestations of Soviet power, but he still couldn't understand why it was worth exchanging an evil empire for an evil banana republic that imported its bananas from Finland.

But then, Tatarsky had never been a great moral thinker, so he was less concerned with the analysis of events (what was actually going on) than with the problem of surviving them. He had no contacts that could help him, so he dealt with things in the simplest way possible, by taking a job as a sales assistant in a trading kiosk not far from where he lived.

The work was simple enough, but quite hard on the nerves. Inside the kiosk it was half-dark and cool, like inside a tank; Tatarsky was connected with the world by a tiny little window, scarcely large enough to allow him to push a bottle of champagne through it. He was protected against possible unpleasantness by a grille of metal rods crudely welded to the walls. In the evening he handed over the takings to an elderly Chechen who wore a heavy gold ring; sometimes he might even manage to squeeze out a little bit for himself over and above his wages. From time to time novice bandits would come up to the kiosk and demand money for their protection in squeaky, still-breaking voices. Tatarsky wearily directed them to Hussein. Hussein was a short, skinny young guy whose eyes were always oily from the opiates he took; he usually lay on a mattress in a half-empty trailer at the end of the string of kiosks, listening to Sufi music. Apart from the mattress, the trailer contained a table, a safe that held a large amount of money and a complicated version of the Kalashnikov automatic rifle with a grenade-thrower mounted under the barrel.

While he was working in the kiosk (it went on for a little less than a year), Tatarsky acquired two new qualities. The first was a cynicism as boundless as the view from the Ostankino television tower; the second was something quite remarkable and inexplicable. Tatarsky only had to glance at a customer's hands to know whether he could short-change him and by exactly how much, whether he could be insulting to him, whether there was any likelihood of being passed a false banknote and whether he could pass on a false note himself. There was no definite system involved in all this. Sometimes a fist like a hairy water-melon would appear in the little window, but it was obvious that Tatarsky could quite safely send its owner to hell and beyond. Then sometimes Tatarsky's heart would skip a beat in fright at the sight of a slim female hand with manicured nails.

One day a customer asked Tatarsky for a pack of Davidoff. The hand that placed the crumpled hundred-thousand-rouble note on the counter was not very interesting. Tatarsky noted the slight, barely visible trembling of the fingers and realised his customer was a stimulant abuser. He could easily be, for instance, some middle-level bandit or businessman, or – as was often the case – something halfway between the two.

'What kind of Davidoff? Standard or lights?' Tatarsky asked.

'Lights,' the customer replied and leaned down to glance in through the little window.

Tatarsky started in surprise – the customer was a fellow student from his year at the Literary Institute, Sergei Morkovin, one of the outstanding characters of their year. He'd hardly changed at all, except that a neat parting had appeared in his hair, and a few grey hairs had appeared in the parting.

'Vova?' Morkovin asked in astonishment. 'What are you doing here?'

Tatarsky couldn't think of a good answer.

'I get it,' said Morkovin. 'Come on, you're out of this dump.'

It didn't take long for Tatarsky to be persuaded. He locked up the kiosk and, casting a fearful glance in the direction of Hussein's trailer, followed Morkovin to his car. They went to an expensive Chinese restaurant called The Shrine of the Moon, ate dinner and did some heavy drinking, and Morkovin told Tatarsky what he'd been up to recently. What he'd been up to was advertising.

'Vova,' he said, grabbing Tatarsky by the arm, his eyes gleaming, 'this is a very special time. There's never been a time like it and there never will be again. It's a gold-rush, just like the Klondyke. In another two years everything'll be all sewn up, but right now there's a real chance to get in on the ground floor straight off the street. You know, in New York they spend half a lifetime just trying to get to meet the right people over lunch, but here . . .'

There was a lot in what Morkovin said that Tatarsky simply didn't understand. The only thing that was really clear to him from the conversation was the outline of how business functioned in an era of primitive accumulation and the way it was interlinked with advertising.

'Most of the time,' said Morkovin, 'it goes like this: a guy borrows money on credit. He uses the credit to rent an office and buy a Jeep Cherokee and eight crates of Smirnoff. When the Smirnoff runs out, it turns out the jeep's wrecked, the office is awash with puke and the loan is due for repayment. So he borrows money again – three times more than before. He uses it to pay back the first loan, buys a Jeep Grand Cherokee and sixteen crates of Absolut vodka. When the Absolut . . .'

'OK, I get the picture,' Tatarsky interrupted. 'So what's the ending?'

'There's two endings. If the bank the guy owes to is one of the mafia banks, then some time or other he gets killed; and since there aren't any others, that's what usually happens. On the other hand, if the guy's in the mafia himself, then the last loan gets shifted on to the State Bank, and the guy declares himself bankrupt. The bailiffs come round to his office, inventorise the empty bottles and the puke-covered fax, and in a little while he starts up all over again. Nowadays, of course, the State Bank's got its own mafia, so the situation's a bit more complicated, but the basic picture's still the same.'

'Aha,' Tatarsky said thoughtfully. 'But I still don't see what all this has to do with advertising.'

'That's where we come to the most important part. When there's still about half the Smirnoff or Absolut left, the jeep's still on the road and death seems a distant and abstract prospect, a highly specific chemical reaction occurs inside the head of the guy who created the whole mess. He develops this totally boundless megalomania and orders himself an advertising clip. He insists his clip has to blow away all the other cretins' clips. The psychology of it's easy enough to understand. The guy's opened up some little company called Everest and he's so desperate to see his logo on Channel One, somewhere between BMW and Coca-Cola, that he could top himself. So just as soon as this reaction takes place in the client's head, we pop out of the bushes.'

Tatarsky liked the sound of that 'we' very much.

'The situation's like this,' Morkovin went on. 'There are only a few studios that make the videos, and they're desperate for writers with nous, because these days everything depends on the writer. The job itself works like this: the people from the studio find a client who wants to get himself on TV. You take a look at him. He tells you something. You listen to what he wants to say. Then you write the scenario. It's usually about a page long, because the clips are short. It might only take you a couple of minutes, but you don't go back to him for at least a week – he has to think you've spent all that time dashing backwards and forwards across your room, tearing your hair out and thinking, thinking, thinking. He reads what you've written and, depending on whether he likes the scenario or not, he orders a video from your people or gets in touch with someone else. That's why, as far as the studio you work for is concerned, you're the top man. The order depends on you. And if you can hypnotise the client, you take ten per cent of the total price of the video.'

'And how much does a video cost?'

'Usually from fifteen to thirty grand. Say twenty on average.'

'What?' Tatarsky asked in disbelief.

'O God, not roubles. Dollars.'

In a split second Tatarsky had calculated what ten per cent of twenty thousand would be. He swallowed hard and stared at Morkovin with dog-like eyes.

'Of course, it's not going to last,' said Morkovin. 'In a year or two, everything's going to look entirely different. Instead of all these pot-bellied nobodies taking loans for their petty little businesses, there'll be guys borrowing millions of bucks at a time. Instead of jeeps for crashing into lamp-posts there'll be castles in France and islands in the Pacific. Instead of five hundred grammes the former party secretaries will be demanding five hundred grand. But basically what's going on in this country of ours won't be any different, which means that the basic principle of our work will never change.'

'My God,' said Tatarsky. 'Money like that . . . It's kind of frightening.'

'It's Dostoievsky's old eternal question,' Morkovin said, laughing. 'Am I a timid cowering creature or have I got moral rights?'

'Seems to me you've already answered that question.'

'Yes,' said Morkovin, 'I reckon I have.'

'And what is your answer?'

'It's very simple. I'm a timid cowering creature with inalienable rights.'

The next day Morkovin took Tatarsky to a strange place called Draft Podium (after several minutes of intense mental effort Tatarsky abandoned the attempt to guess what that meant). It was located in the basement of an old brick-built house not far from the centre of town. Entry was via a heavy steel door, which led into a small office space crammed with equipment. Several young men were waiting there for Tatarsky. Their leader was a stubble-cheeked guy by the name of Sergei, who looked like Dracula in his younger days. He explained to Tatarsky that the small cube of blue plastic standing on an empty cardboard box was a Silicon Graphics computer that cost one hell of a lot of money, and the Soft Image program that was installed on it cost twice as much. The Silicon was the most important treasure in this subterranean cave. The room also contained a few more simple computers, scanners and some kind of VCR with lots of dials and lights. One detail that made a great impression on Tatarsky was that the VCR had a wheel on it with a handle, like the wheel on a sewing machine, and you could use it to wind on the frames on the tape by hand.

Draft Podium had a certain very promising client in its sights.

'The mark's about fifty,' said Sergei, dragging on a menthol cigarette. 'Used to work as a teacher of physics. Just when things started coming apart he set up a co-operative baking 'bird's milk' cakes and in two years made so much money that now he rents an entire confectionery plant in Lefortovo. Recently he took out a big loan. The day before yesterday he went on the sauce, and he usually stays on it about two weeks.'

'Where do you get that kind of information?' Tatarsky asked.

'His secretary,' said Sergei. 'So anyway, we have to get to him with the scenario now, before he has time to sober up. When he sobers up, he gets greedy. We're meeting tomorrow at one in his office.'

The next day Morkovin arrived at Tatarsky's place early. He brought with him a large, bright-yellow plastic bag containing a maroon jacket made of material that looked like the fabric they use for Russian army greatcoats. The intricate crest gleaming on the breast pocket was reminiscent of the emblem on a packet of Marlboro cigarettes. Morkovin said it was a 'club jacket'. Tatarsky didn't understand what he meant, but he did as he was told and put it on. Then Morkovin took a foppish notebook in a leather cover out of the bag, together with an incredibly thick ballpoint pen with the word 'Zoom' on it and a pager – at that time they'd only just appeared in Moscow.

'You have to hang this thing on your belt,' he said. 'You're meeting the client at one, and at twenty past one I'll give you a call on the pager. When it beeps, take it off your belt and look at it like it's something important. All the time the client's talking, keep making notes in the notebook.'

'What's it all for?' Tatarsky asked.

'It's obvious enough, isn't it? The client's paying big money for a sheet of paper and a few drops of black ink out of a printer. He has to be absolutely certain plenty of others have paid money for the same thing before him.'

'Seems to me,' said Tatarsky, 'all these jackets and pagers are just the thing to raise doubts in his mind.'

'Don't go complicating things,' said Morkovin with a dismissive wave of his hand. 'Life's simpler and stupider than that. And then there's this . . .'

He took a slim case out of his pocket, opened it and held it out to Tatarsky. It contained a heavy watch that was almost beautiful in a repulsive kind of way, made of gold and steel.

'It's a Rolex Oyster. Careful, you'll chip off the gold plate; it's a fake. I only take it out on business. When you're talking with the client, flash it around a bit, you know. It helps.'

Tatarsky felt inspired by all this support. At half past twelve he emerged from the metro. The guys from Draft

Podium were waiting for him not far from the entrance. They'd arrived in a long black Mercedes. Tatarsky had already learned enough about business to know the car had been hired for about two hours. Sergei was unshaven as ever, but now there was something sullenly stylish about his stubble – probably due to the dark jacket with the incredibly narrow lapels and the bow tie. Sitting beside him was Lena, who looked after contracts and kept the books. She was wearing a simple black dress (no jewellery and no make-up) and in her hand she was holding an attaché case with a golden lock. When Tatarsky climbed into the car, the three of them exchanged glances and Sergei spoke to the chauffeur.

'Drive on.'

Lena was nervous. All the way there she kept giggling as she told them about some guy called Azadovsky – apparently her friend's lover. This Azadovsky inspired her with an admiration that bordered on rapture: he'd arrived in Moscow from Ukraine and moved in with her friend, got himself registered in her flat, then invited his sister and her two children up from Dniepropetrovsk. He'd registered them in the flat and immediately, without the slightest pause, swapped the flat for a different one through the courts and dispatched Lena's sister to a room in a shared apartment.

'He's a man who'll really go far!' Lena kept repeating.

She was especially impressed by the fact that, once the operation had been completed, the sister and her children were immediately banished back to Dniepropetrovsk; there was so much detail in the way the tale was told that by the end of the journey Tatarsky began to feel as though he'd lived half his life in the flat with Azadovsky and his nearest and dearest; but then, Tatarsky was just as nervous as Lena.

The client (Tatarsky never did find out what his name was) looked remarkably like the image that had taken shape in Tatarsky's mind following the previous day's conversation. He was a short, thickset little man with a cunning face, from which the grimace of a hangover was only just beginning to fade – evidently he'd taken his first drink of the day not long before the meeting.

Following a brief exchange of pleasantries (Lena did most

of the talking; Sergei sat in the corner with his legs crossed, smoking) Tatarsky was introduced as the writer. He sat down facing the client, clanging the Rolex against the edge of the desk as he did so, and opened up his notebook. It immediately became clear that the client had nothing in particular to say. Without the assistance of a powerful hallucinogen it was hard to feel inspired by the details of his business – he droned on most of the time about some kind of oven-trays with a special non-stick coating. Tatarsky listened with his face half-turned away, nodding and doodling meaningless flourishes in his notebook. He surveyed the room out of the corner of his eye – there was nothing interesting to be seen there, either, if you didn't count the misty-blue reindeer-fur hat, obviously very expensive, that was lying on the upper shelf in an empty cupboard with glass doors.

As promised, after a few minutes the pager on his belt rang. Tatarsky unhooked the little black plastic box from his belt. The message on the display said: 'Welcome to route 666.'

'Some joker, eh?' thought Tatarsky.

'Is it from Video International?' Sergei asked from the corner.

'No,' Tatarsky replied, following his lead. 'Those blockheads don't bother me any more, thank God. It's Slava Zaitsev's design studio. It's all off for today.'

'Why's that?' Sergei asked, raising one eyebrow. 'Surely he doesn't think we're that desperate for his business . . .'

'Let's talk about that later,' said Tatarsky.

Meanwhile the client was scowling thoughtfully at his reindeer-fur hat in the glass-fronted cupboard. Tatarsky looked at his hands. They were locked together, and his thumbs were circling around each other as though he was winding in some invisible thread. This was the moment of truth.

'Aren't you afraid that it could all just come to a full stop?' Tatarsky asked. 'You know what kind of times these are. What if everything suddenly collapses?'

The client frowned and looked in puzzlement, first at Tatarsky and then at his companions. His thumbs stopped circling each other.

'I am afraid,' he answered, looking up. 'Who isn't? You ask some odd questions.'

'I'm sorry,' said Tatarsky. 'I didn't mean anything by it.'

Five minutes later the conversation was over. Sergei took a sheet of the client's headed notepaper with his logo – it was a stylised bun framed in an oval above the letters 'LCC'. They agreed to meet again in a week's time; Sergei promised the scenario for the video would be ready by then.

'Have you totally lost your marbles, or what?' Sergei asked Tatarsky, when they came out on to the street. 'Nobody asks questions like that.'

The Mercedes took all three of them to the nearest metro station.

When he got home, Tatarsky wrote the scenario in a few hours. It was a long time since he'd felt so inspired. The scenario didn't have any specific storyline. It consisted of a sequence of historical reminiscences and metaphors. The Tower of Babel rose and fell, the Nile flooded, Rome burned, ferocious Huns galloped in no particular direction across the steppes – and in the background the hands of an immense, transparent clock spun round.

'One generation passeth away and another generation cometh,' said a dull and demonic voice-over (Tatarsky actually wrote that in the scenario), 'but the Earth abideth for ever.' But eventually even the earth with its ruins of empires and civilisations sank from sight into a lead-coloured ocean; only a single rock remained projecting above its raging surface, its form somehow echoing the form of the Tower of Babel that the scenario began with. The camera zoomed in on the cliff, and there carved in stone was a bun and the letters 'LCC', and beneath them a motto that Tatarsky had found in a book called *Inspired Latin Sayings*:

MEDIIS TEMPESTATIBUS PLACIDUS
CALM IN THE MIDST OF STORMS
LEFORTOVO CONFECTIONERY COMBINE

In Draft Podium they reacted to Tatarsky's scenario with horror.

'Technically it's not complicated,' said Sergei. 'Rip off the image-sequence from a few old films, touch it up a bit, stretch it out. But it's totally off the wall. Even funny in a way.'

'So it's off the wall,' Tatarsky agreed. 'And funny. But you tell me what it is you want. A prize at Cannes or the order?'

A couple of days later Lena took the client several versions of a scenario written by somebody else. They involved a black Mercedes, a suitcase stuffed full of dollars and other archetypes of the collective unconscious. The client turned them all down without explaining why. In despair Lena showed him the scenario written by Tatarsky.

She came back to the studio with a contract for thirty-five thousand, with twenty to be paid in advance. It was a record. She said that when he read the scenario the client started behaving like a rat from Hamlin who'd heard an entire wind orchestra.

'I could have taken him for forty grand,' she said. 'I was just too slow on the uptake.'

The money arrived in their account five days later, and Tatarsky received his honestly earned two thousand. Sergei and his team were already planning to go to Yalta to film a suitable cliff, on which the bun carved in granite was supposed to appear in the final frames, when the client was found dead in his office. Someone had strangled him with a telephone cord. The traditional electric-iron marks were discovered on the body, and some merciless hand had stopped the victim's mouth with a Nocturne cake (sponge soaked in liqueur, bitter chocolate in a distinctly minor key, lightly sprinkled with a tragic hoar-frosting of coconut).

'One generation passeth away and another generation cometh,' Tatarsky thought philosophically, 'but thou lookest out always for number one.'

And so Tatarsky became a copywriter. He didn't bother to explain himself to any of his old bosses; he simply left the keys of the kiosk on the porch of the trailer where Hussein hung out: there were rumours that the Chechens demanded serious compensation when anyone left one of their businesses.

It didn't take him long to acquire new acquaintances and he started working for several studios at the same time. Big breaks like the one with Lefortovo's calm-amid-storms Confectionery Combine didn't come very often, unfortunately.

Tatarsky soon realised that if one in ten projects worked out well, that was already serious success. He didn't earn a really large amount of money, but even so it was more than he'd made in the retail trade. He would recall his first advertising job with dissatisfaction, discerning in it a certain hasty, shamefaced willingness to sell cheap everything that was most exalted in his soul. When the orders began coming in one after another, he realised that in this particular business it's always a mistake to be in a hurry, because that way you bring the price way down, and that's stupid: everything that is most sacred and exalted should only be sold for the highest price possible, because afterwards there'll be nothing left to trade in. Tatarsky realised, however, that this rule did not apply to everyone. The true virtuosos of the genre, whom he saw on TV, somehow managed to sell off all that was most exalted every day of the week, but in a way that provided no formal grounds for claiming they'd sold anything, so the next day they could start all over again with nothing to worry about. Tatarsky couldn't even begin to imagine how they managed that.

Gradually a very unpleasant tendency began to emerge: a client would be presented with a project conceived and developed by Tatarsky, politely explain that it was not exactly what was required, and then a month or two later Tatarsky would come across a clip that was quite clearly based on his idea. Trying to discover the truth in such cases was a waste of time.

After listening to his new acquaintances' advice, Tatarsky attempted to jump up a rung in the advertising hierarchy and began developing advertising concepts. The work was much the same as he had been doing before. There was a certain magic book, and once you'd read it there was no more need to feel shy of anyone at all or to have any kind of doubts. It was called *Positioning: A Battle for your Mind*, and it was written by two highly advanced American shamans. Its essential message was entirely inapplicable to Russia – as far as Tatarsky could judge, there was no battle being waged by trademarks for niches in befuddled Russian brains; the situation was more reminiscent of a smoking landscape after a nuclear explosion – but even so the book was useful. If was full of stylish expressions like 'line extension' that could be stuck into concepts and dropped into spiels for clients. Tatarsky realised what the difference was between the era of decaying imperialism and the era of primitive capital accumulation. In the West both the client who ordered advertising and the copywriter tried to brainwash the consumer, but in Russia the copywriter's job was to screw with the client's brains. Tatarsky realised in addition that Morkovin was right and this situation was never going to change. One day, after smoking some especially good grass, he uncovered by pure chance the basic economic law of post-socialist society: initial accumulation of capital is also final.

Before going to sleep Tatarsky would sometimes re-read the book on positioning. He regarded it as his little Bible; the comparison was all the more appropriate because it contained echoes of religious views that had an especially powerful impact on his chaste and unsullied soul: 'The romantic copywriters of the fifties, gone on ahead of us to that great advertising agency in the sky ...'

CHAPTER 3

Tikhamat-2

Lenin's statues were gradually carted out of town on military trucks (they said some colonel had thought up the idea of melting them down for the non-ferrous metal content and made a lot of money before he was rumbled), but his presence was merely replaced by a frightening murky greyness in which the Soviet soul simply continued rotting until it collapsed inwards on itself. The newspapers claimed the whole world had been living in this grey murk for absolutely ages, which was why it was so full of things and money, and the only reason people couldn't understand this was their 'Soviet mentality'.

Tatarsky didn't really understand completely what this Soviet mentality was, although he used the expression frequently enough and enjoyed using it; but as far as his new employer, Dmitry Pugin, was concerned, he wasn't supposed to understand anything anyway. He was merely required to possess this mentality. That was the whole point of what he did: adapt Western advertising concepts to the mentality of the Russian consumer. The work was 'freelance' – Tatarsky used the term as though it still had its original sense, having in mind first of all the level of his pay.

Pugin, a man with a black moustache and gleaming black eyes very like a pair of buttons, had turned up by chance among the guests at a mutual acquaintance's house. Hearing that Tatarsky was in advertising, he'd shown a moderate interest. Tatarsky, on the other hand, had immediately been fired with an irrational respect for Pugin – he was simply amazed to see him sitting there drinking tea still in his long black coat.

That was when the conversation had turned to the Soviet mentality. Pugin confessed that in the old days he had possessed it himself, but he'd lost it completely while working for a few years as a taxi-driver in New York. The salty winds of Brighton Beach had blown all those ramshackle Soviet constructs right out of his head and infected him with a compulsive yearning for success.

'In New York you realise especially clearly,' Pugin said over a glass of the vodka they moved on to after the tea, 'that you can spend your entire life in some foul-smelling little kitchen, staring out into some shit-dirty little yard and chewing on a lousy burger. You'll just stand there by the window, staring at all that shit, and life will pass you by.'

'That's interesting,' Tatarsky responded thoughtfully, 'but why go to New York for that? Surely—'

'Because in New York you understand it, and in Moscow you don't,' Pugin interrupted. 'You're right, there are far more of those stinking kitchens and shitty little yards over here. Only here there's no way you're going to understand that's where you're going to spend the rest of your life until it's already over. And that, by the way, is one of the main features of the Soviet mentality.'

Pugin's opinions were disputable in certain respects, but what he actually had to offer was simple, clear and logical. As far as Tatarsky was able to judge from the murky depths of his own Soviet mentality, the project was an absolutely textbook example of the American entrepreneurial approach.

'Look,' said Pugin, squinting intensely into the space above Tatarsky's head, 'the country hardly produces anything at all; but people have to have something to eat and wear, right? That means soon goods will start pouring in here from the West, and massive amounts of advertising will come flooding in with them. But it won't be possible simply to translate this advertising from English into Russian, because the . . . what d'you call them . . . the *cultural references* here are different . . . That means, the advertising will have to be adapted in short order for the Russian consumer. So now what do you and I do? You and I get straight on the job well in advance – get my point? Now, before it all starts, we prepare outline concepts for all the serious brand-names. Then, just as soon as the right moment comes, we turn up at their offices with a folder under our arms and do business. The most important thing is to get a few good brains together in good time!'

Pugin slapped his palm down hard on the table – he obviously thought he'd got a few together already – but Tatarsky suddenly had the vague feeling he was being taken for a ride again. The terms of employment on offer from Pugin were extremely vague – although the work itself was quite concrete, the prospects of being paid remained abstract.

For a test-piece Pugin set him the development of an outline concept for Sprite – at first he was going to give him Marlboro as well, but he suddenly changed his mind, saying it was too soon for Tatarsky to try that. This was the point – as Tatarsky realised later – at which the Soviet mentality for which he had been selected raised its head. All his scepticism about Pugin instantly dissolved in a feeling of resentment that Pugin wouldn't trust him with Marlboro, but this resentment was mingled with a feeling of delight at the fact that he still had Sprite. Swept away by the maelstrom created by these conflicting feelings, he never even paused to think why some taxi-driver from Brighton Beach, who still hadn't given him so much as a kopeck, was already deciding whether he was capable of applying his mind to a concept for Marlboro.

Tatarsky poured into his conception for Sprite every last drop of his insight into his homeland's bruised and battered history. Before sitting down to work, he re-read several selected chapters from the book *Positioning: A Battle for your Mind*, and a whole heap of newspapers of various tendencies. He hadn't read any newspapers for ages and what he read plunged him into a state of confusion; and that, naturally, had its effect on the fruit of his labours.

'*The first point that must be taken into consideration,*' he wrote in his concept,

is that the situation that exists at the present moment in Russia cannot continue for very long. In the very near future we must expect most of the essential branches of industry to come to a total standstill, the collapse of the financial system and serious social upheavals, which will all inevitably end in the establishment of a military dictatorship. Regardless of its political and economic programme, the future dictator-

ship will attempt to exploit nationalistic slogans: the dominant state aesthetic will be the pseudo-Slavonic style. (This term is not used here in any negative judgemental sense: as distinct from the Slavonic style, which does not exist anywhere in the real world, the pseudo-Slavonic style represents a carefully structured paradigm.) Within the space structured by the symbolic signifiers of this style, traditional Western advertising is inconceivable. Therefore it will either be banned completely or subjected to rigorous censorship. This all has to be taken into consideration in determining any kind of long-term strategy.

Let us take a classic positioning slogan: 'Sprite – the Uncola'. Its use in Russia would seem to us to be most appropriate, but for somewhat different reasons than in America. The term 'Uncola' (i.e. Non-Cola) positions Sprite very successfully against Pepsi-Cola and Coca-Cola, creating a special niche for this product in the consciousness of the Western consumer. But it is a well-known fact that in the countries of Eastern Europe Coca-Cola is more of an ideological fetish than a refreshing soft drink. If, for instance, Hershi drinks are positioned as possessing the 'taste of victory', then Coca-Cola possesses the 'taste of freedom', as declared in the seventies and eighties by a vast number of Eastern European defectors. For the Russian consumer, therefore, the term 'Uncola' has extensive anti-democratic and anti-liberal connotations, which makes it highly attractive and promising in conditions of military dictatorship.

Translated into Russian 'Uncola' would become 'Nye-Cola'. The sound of the word (similar to the old Russian name 'Nikola') and the associations aroused by it offer a perfect fit with the aesthetic required by the likely future scenario. A possible version of the slogan:

SPRITE. THE NYE-COLA FOR NIKOLA

(It might make sense to consider infiltrating into the consciousness of the consumer the character 'Nikola Spritov', an individual of the same type as Ronald McDonald, but profoundly national in spirit.)

In addition, some thought has to be given to changing the packaging format of the product as sold on the Russian market. Elements of the pseudo-Slavonic style need to be introduced here as well. The ideal symbol would seem to be the birch tree. It would be appropriate to change the colour of the can from green to white with black stripes like the trunk of a birch. A possible text for an advertising clip:

> *Deep in the spring-time forest*
> *I drank my birch-bright Sprite.*

After reading the print-out Tatarsky brought him, Pugin said: '"The Uncola" is Seven-Up's slogan, not Sprite's.'

After that he said nothing for a while, simply gazing at Tatarsky with his black-button eyes. Tatarsky didn't speak either.

'But that's OK,' Pugin said, eventually softening. 'We can use it. If not for Sprite, then for Seven-Up. So you can consider you've passed the test. Now try some other brand.'

'Which one?' Tatarsky asked in relief.

Pugin thought for a moment, then rummaged in his pockets and held out an opened pack of Parliament cigarettes. 'And think up a poster for them as well,' he said.

Dealing with Parliament turned out to be more complicated. For a start Tatarsky wrote the usual intro: 'It is quite clear that the first thing that has to be taken into consideration in the development of any half-serious advertising concept is . . .' But after that he just sat there for a long time without moving.

Exactly what was the first thing that had to be taken into consideration was entirely unclear. The only association the word 'Parliament' was able, with a struggle, to extract from his brain, was Cromwell's wars in England. The same thing would obviously apply to the average Russian consumer who had read Dumas as a child. After half an hour of the most intensive intellectual exertion had led to nothing, Tatarsky suddenly fancied a smoke. He searched the entire flat looking for something smokeable and eventually found an old pack of Soviet-time Yava. After just two drags he chucked the cigarette down the toilet and dashed over to the table. He'd come up with a text that at first glance looked to him as if it was the answer:

PARLIAMENT – THE NYE-YAVA

When he realised this was only a poor low-grade calque on the word 'uncola', he very nearly gave up. Then he had a sudden inspiration. The history dissertation he'd written in the Literary Institute was called: 'A brief outline of parliamentarianism in Russia'. He couldn't remember a thing about it any more, but he was absolutely certain it would contain enough material for three concepts, let alone one. Skipping up and down in his excitement, he set off along the corridor towards the built-in closet where he kept his old papers.

After searching for half an hour he realised he wasn't going to find the dissertation, but somehow that didn't worry him any more. While sorting through the accumulated strata deposited in the closet, up on the attic shelf he'd come across several objects that had been there since his schooldays: a bust of Lenin mutilated with a small camping axe (Tatarsky recalled how, in his fear of retribution following the execution, he'd hidden the bust in a place that was hard to reach), a notebook on social studies, filled with drawings of tanks and nuclear explosions, and several old books.

This all filled him with such aching nostalgia that his employer Pugin suddenly seemed repulsive and hateful, and was banished from consciousness, together with his Parliament.

Tatarsky remembered with a tender warmth how the books he had discovered had been selected from amongst the waste paper they used to be sent to collect after class. They included a volume of a left-wing French existentialist published in the sixties, a finely bound collection of articles on theoretical physics, *Infinity and the Universe*, and a loose-leaf binder with the word 'Tikhamat' written in large letters on the spine.

Tatarsky remembered the book *Infinity and the Universe*, but not the binder. He opened it and read the first page:

TIKHAMAT-2
The Earthly Sea
Chronological Tables and Notes

The papers bound into the folder obviously dated from a pre-computer age. Tatarsky could recall heaps of *samizdat* books that had circulated in this format – two typed pages reduced to half-size and copied on a single sheet of paper. What he was holding in his hands seemed to be an appendix to a dissertation on the history of the ancient world. Tatarsky began rememberin: in his childhood, he thought, he hadn't even opened the file, taking the word 'Tikhamat' to mean something like a mixture of diamat (dialectical materialism) with histmat (historical materialism). He'd only taken the work at all because of the beautiful folder, and then he'd forgotten all about it.

As it turned out, however, Tikhamat was the name either of an ancient deity or of an ocean, or perhaps both at the same time. Tatarsky learned from a footnote that the word could be translated approximately as 'Chaos'.

A lot of the space in the folder was taken up by tables of kings. They were pretty monotonous, with their listings of unpronounceable names and Roman numerals, and information about when they'd launched their campaigns or laid the foundations of a wall or taken some city, and so forth. In several places different sources were compared, and the conclusion drawn from the comparison was that several events that had been recorded in history as following each other were in fact one and the same event, which had so astounded contemporary and subsequent generations that its echo had been doubled and tripled, and then each echo had assumed a life of its own. It was clear from the apologetically triumphant tone adopted by the author that his discovery appeared to him to be quite revolutionary and even iconoclastic, which set Tatarsky pondering yet again on the vanity of all human endeavour. He didn't experience even the slightest sense of shock at the fact that Ashuretilshamersituballistu II had turned out actually to be Nebuchadnezzar III, and the nameless historian's depth of feeling really seemed rather laughable. The kings seemed rather laughable too: it wasn't even known for certain whether they were people or simply slips made by a scribe on his clay tablets, and the only traces remaining of them were on those same clay tablets.

The chronological tables were followed by extensive notes on some unknown text, and there were a lot of photographs of various antiquities pasted into the folder. The second or third article that Tatarsky came across was entitled: 'Babylon: The Three Chaldean Riddles'. Beneath the letter 'O' in the word 'Babylon' he could make out a letter 'E' that had been whited out and corrected – it was nothing more than a typing error, but the sight of it threw Tatarsky into a state of agitation. The name he'd been given at birth and had rejected on reaching the age of maturity had returned to haunt him just at the moment when he'd completely forgotten the story he'd told his childhood friends about the part the secret lore of Babylon was to play in his life.

Below the heading there was a photograph of the impression of a seal – a gate of iron bars on the top of either a mountain or a stepped pyramid, and standing beside it a man with a beard dressed in a skirt, with something that looked like a shawl thown over his shoulders. It seemed to Tatarsky that the man was holding two severed heads by their thin plaits of hair; but one of the heads had no facial features, while the second was smiling happily. Tatarsky read the inscription under the drawing: 'A Chaldean with a mask and a mirror on a ziggurat'. He squatted on a pile of books removed from the closet and began reading the text beneath the photograph.

P. 123. The mirror and the mask are the ritual requisites of Ishtar. The canonical representation, which expresses the sacramental symbolism of her cult more fully, is of Ishtar in a gold mask, gazing into a mirror. Gold is the body of the goddess and its negative projection is the light of the stars. This has led several researchers to assume that the third ritual requisite of the goddess is the fly-agaric mushroom, the cap of which is a natural map of the starry sky. If this is so, then we must regard the fly-agaric as the 'heavenly mushroom' referred to in various texts. This assumption is indirectly confirmed by the details of the myth of the three great ages, the ages of the red, blue and yellow skies. The red fly-agaric connects the Chaldean with the past; it provides access to the wisdom and strength of the age of the red sky. The brown fly-agaric ('brown' and 'yellow' were designated by the same word in Accadian), on the other hand, provides a link with the future and a means of taking possession all of its inexhaustible energy.

Turning over a few pages at random, Tatarsky came across the word 'fly-agaric' again.

P. 145. The three Chaldean riddles (the Three Riddles of Ishtar). According to the tradition of the Chaldean riddles, any inhabitant of Babylon could become the goddess's husband. In order to do this he had to drink a special beverage and ascend her ziggurat. It is not clear whether by this was intended the ceremonial ascent of a real structure in Babylon or a hallucinatory experience. The second assumption is supported by the fact that the potion was prepared according to a rather exotic recipe: it included 'the urine of a red ass' (possibly the cinnabar traditional in ancient alchemy) and 'heavenly mushrooms' (evidently fly-agaric, cf. 'The Mirror and the Mask').

According to tradition the path to the goddess and to supreme wisdom (the Babylonians did not differentiate these two concepts, which were seen as flowing naturally into one another and regarded as different aspects of the same reality) was via sexual union with a golden idol of the goddess, which was located in the upper chamber of the ziggurat. It was believed that at certain times the spirit of Ishtar descended into this idol.

In order to be granted access to the idol it was necessary to guess the Three Riddles of Ishtar. These riddles have not come down to us. Let us note the controversial opinion of Claude Greco (see 11, 12), who assumes that what is meant is a set of rhymed incantations in ancient Accadian discovered during the excavation of Nineveh, which are rendered highly polysemantic by means of their homonymic structure.

A far more convincing interpretation, however, is based on several sources taken together: the Three Riddles of Ishtar were three symbolic objects that were handed to a Babylonian who wished to become a Chaldean. He had to interpret the significance of these items (the motif of a symbolic message). On the spiral ascent of the ziggurat there were three gateways, where the future Chaldean was handed each of the objects in turn. Anybody who got even one of the riddles wrong was pushed over the edge of the ziggurat to certain death by the soldiers of the guard. (There is some reason to derive the later cult of Kybela, based on ritual self-castration, from the cult of Ishtar: the significance of the self-castration was evidently as a substitute sacrifice.)

Even so, there were a great many candidates, since the answers that would open the path to the summit of the ziggurat and union with the goddess actually did exist. Once in every few decades someone was successful. The man who answered all three riddles correctly would ascend to the summit and meet the goddess, following which he became a consecrated Chaldean and her ritual earthly husband (possibly there were several such simultaneously).

According to one interpretation, the answers to the Three Riddles of Ishtar also existed in written form. In certain special places in Babylon tablets were sold imprinted with the answers to the goddess's questions (another interpretation holds that what was meant was a magical seal on which the answers were carved). Producing these tablets and trading in them was the business of the priests of the central temple of Enkidu, the patron deity of the Lottery. It was believed that the goddess selected her next husband through the agency of Enkidu. This provides a resolution to the conflict, well known to the ancient Babylonians, between divine predetermination and free will. Therefore most of those who decided to ascend the ziggurat bought clay tablets bearing answers; it was believed the tablets could not be unsealed until after the ascent had begun.

This practice was known as the Great Lottery (the accepted term, for which we are indebted to numerous men of letters inspired by this legend, but a more precise rendering would be 'The Game without a Name'). Its only possible outcomes were success and death. Certain bold spirits actually decided to ascend the ziggurat without any tablet to prompt them.

Yet another interpretation has it that the three questions of Ishtar were not riddles, but rather symbolic reference points indicative of specific life-situations. The Babylonian had to pass through them and present proofs of his wisdom to the guard on the ziggurat in order to make it possible for him to meet the goddess. (In this case the ascent of the ziggurat described above is regarded rather as a metaphor.) There was a belief that the answers to the three questions of Ishtar were concealed in the words of the market songs that were sung every day in the bazaar at Babylon, but no information about these songs or this custom has survived.

Tatarsky wiped the dust off the folder and hid it away again in the closet, thinking that some time he would definitely read it all the way through.

He never did find his diploma dissertation on the history of Russian parliamentarianism in the closet; but by the time his search was over Tatarsky had realised quite clearly that the entire history of parliamentarianism in Russia amounted to one simple fact – the only thing the word was good for was advertising Parliament cigarettes, and even there you actually could get by quite well without any parliamentarianism at all.

CHAPTER 4

The Three Riddles of Ishtar

The following day Tatarsky, still absorbed in his thoughts about the cigarette concept, ran into his old classmate Andrei Gireiev at the beginning of Tverskaya Street. Tatarsky hadn't had any news of him for several years, and he was astounded at the style of the clothes he was wearing – a light-blue cassock with a Nepalese waistcoat covered in embroidery worn over the top of it. In his hands he had something that looked like a large coffee-mill, covered all over with Tibetan symbols and decorated with coloured ribbons. He was turning its handle. Despite the extreme exoticism of every element of his get-up, in combination they appeared so natural that they somehow neutralised each other. None of the passers-by paid any attention to Gireiev. Just like a fire hydrant or an advertisement for Pepsi-Cola, he failed to register in their field of perception because he conveyed absolutely no new visual information.

Tatarsky first recognised Gireiev's face and only afterwards began to pay attention to the rich details of his appearance. Looking attentively into Gireiev's eyes, he realised he was not quite himself, although he didn't seem to be drunk. In fact he was calm and in control, and he inspired confidence.

He said he was living just outside Moscow in the village of Rastorguevo and invited Tatarsky to visit him. Tatarsky agreed, and they went down into the metro, then changed to the suburban train. They travelled in silence; Tatarsky occasionally turned away from the view through the window to look at Gireiev. In his crazy gear he seemed like the final fragment of some lost universe – not the Soviet universe, because that didn't contain any wandering Tibetan astrologers, but some other world that had existed in parallel with the Soviet one, even in contradiction of it, and had perished together with it. Tatarsky felt regret at its passing, because a great deal of what he had liked and been moved by had come from that parallel universe, which everyone had been certain could never come to any harm; but it had been overtaken by the same fate as the Soviet eternity, and just as imperceptibly.

Gireiev lived in a crooked black house with the garden in front of it run wild, all overgrown with umbrellas of giant dill half as tall again as a man. In terms of amenities his house was somewhere between village and town: looking down through the hole in the hut of the outside lavatory he could see wet and slimy sewage pipes that ran across the top of the cesspit, but where they ran from or to wasn't clear. On the other hand, the house had a gas cooker and a telephone.

Gireiev seated Tatarsky at the table on the verandah and tipped a coarsely ground powder into the teapot from a red tin box with something Estonian written on it in white letters.

'What's that?' Tatarsky asked.

'Fly-agarics,' answered Gireiev, and began pouring boiling water into the teapot. The smell of mushroom soup wafted round the room.

'What, are you going to drink that?'

'Don't worry,' said Gireiev, 'there aren't any brown ones.'

He said it as though it was the answer to every conceivable objection, and Tatarsky couldn't think of anything to say in reply. He hesitated for a moment, until he recalled that only yesterday he'd been reading about fly-agarics, and he over-came his misgivings. The mushroom tea actually tasted quite pleasant.

'And what will it do for me?'

'You'll see soon enough,' replied Gireiev. 'You'll be drying them for winter yourself.'

'Then what do I do now?'

'Whatever you like.'

'Is it OK to talk?'

'Try it.'

Half an hour passed in rather inconsequential conversation about people they both knew. As was only to be expected, nothing very interesting had happened to any of them in the meantime. Only one of them, Lyosha Chikunov, had distinguished himself – by drinking several bottles of Finlandia vodka and then freezing to death one starry January night in the toy house on a children's playground.

'Gone to Valhalla,' was Gireiev's terse comment.

'Why are you so sure?' Tatarsky asked; then he suddenly remembered the running deer and the crimson sun on the vodka label and assented internally. He reached for his notebook and wrote: 'An ad for Finlandia. Based on their slogan: "In my previous life I was clear, crystal spring water". Variant/complement: a snowdrift with a frozen puddle of puke on top. Text: "In my previous life I was Finlandia vodka".'

Meanwhile a scarcely perceptible sensation of happy relaxation had developed in his body. A pleasant quivering rose in his chest, ran in waves through his trunk and his arms and faded away without quite reaching his fingers. And for some reason Tatarsky very much wanted the quivering to reach his fingers. He realised he hadn't drunk enough; but the teapot was already empty.

'Is there any more?' he asked.

'There, you see,' said Gireiev, 'what did I tell you?'

He stood up, left the room and came back with an open newspaper scattered with dry pieces of sliced fly-agaric mushrooms. Some of them still had scraps of red skin with little white blots, while others had shreds of newspaper with the mirror-images of letters clinging to them.

Tatarsky tossed a few pieces into his mouth, chewed them and swallowed. The taste of the dried fly-agarics reminded him a little of potato flakes, except that it was nicer – it occurred to him that they could be sold in packets like potato chips, and this must be one of the secret routes to a bank loan, Grand Cherokee jeep, advertisement clip and violent death. He started pondering what the clip might be like, tossed another portion into his mouth and looked around him. It was only at this stage that he actually noticed several of the objects decorating the room. For instance, that sheet of paper hanging in the obvious place on the wall – there was a letter written on it, maybe Sanskrit, maybe Tibetan, resembling a dragon with a curved tail.

'What's that?' he asked Gireiev.

Gireiev glanced up at the wall. 'Hum,' he said.

'What d'you need it for?'

'That's how I travel.'

'Where to?' asked Tatarsky.

Gireiev shrugged. 'It's hard to explain,' he said. 'Hum. When you don't think, lots of things become clear.'

But Tatarsky had already forgotten his own question. He was overwhelmed by a feeling of gratitude to Gireiev for inviting him here. 'You know,' he said,' I'm going through a difficult period right now. Most of the time I associate with bankers and other scum who want advertising. The stress is just incredible. But out here with you . . . I feel just as though I've come back home.'

Gireiev seemed to understand what he was feeling. 'It's nothing,' he said, 'Don't even think about it. A couple of those bankers came to see me last winter. Wanted to expand their consciousness. Afterwards they ran off barefoot across the snow. Why don't we go for a walk?'

Tatarsky was happy to agree. Once outside the garden gate, they set off across a field criss-crossed by freshly dug ditches. The path led them to a forest and began winding between the trees. The itching and trembling in Tatarsky's hands was getting stronger, but it still wasn't reaching his fingers. Noticing there were lots of fly-agarics growing on the ground among the trees, he dropped behind Gireiev and picked several of them. They weren't red, but dark brown and very beautiful. He ate them quickly and then caught up with Gireiev, who hadn't noticed anything.

Soon the forest came to an end and they came out into a large open space, a collective farm field bounded on its far side by the river. Tatarsky looked upwards to where motionless clouds towered up into the sky above the field in the last orange rays of one of those inexpressibly sad sunsets that autumn sometimes produces outside Moscow. They walked on for a while down the track along the edge of the field and sat down on a fallen tree.

Tatarsky suddenly thought of a potential advertising concept for fly-agarics. It was based on the startling realisation that the supreme form of self-realisation for fly-agarics is an atomic explosion – something like the glowing non-material body that certain advanced mystics acquire. Human beings were simply a subsidiary form of life that the fly-agarics exploited in order to achieve their supreme goal, in the same way as human beings exploited mould for making cheese. Tatarsky raised his eyes towards the orange rays of the sunset and the flow of his thoughts was abruptly broken off.

'Listen,' Gireiev said after a few more minutes' silence, 'I just thought about Lyosha Chikunov again. Sad about him, isn't it?'

'Yeah, it is,' Tatarsky replied.

'Weird, that – he's dead, and we're alive . . . Only I suspect that every time we lie down and sleep, we die just the same way. And the sun disappears for ever, and all history comes to an end. And then non-existence just gets sick of itself and we wake up. And the world comes into existence all over again.'

'How can non-existence get sick of itself?'

'Every time you wake up, you appear again out of nowhere. And so does everything else. Death just means the replacement of the usual morning wakening with something else, something quite impossible even to think about. We don't even have the instrument to do it, because our mind and our world are the same thing.'

Tatarsky tried to understand what this meant. He noticed that thinking had became difficult and even dangerous, because his thoughts had acquired such freedom and power that he could no longer control them. The answer appeared to him immediately in the form of a three-dimensional geometrical figure. Tatarsky saw his own mind: it was a white sphere, like a sun but absolutely calm and motionless. Dark, twisted fibrous threads extended from the centre of the sphere to its periphery. Tatarsky realised that they were his five senses. The fibres that were a little thicker were sight, the ones a bit thinner than those were hearing, and the others were almost invisible. Dancing and meandering around these motionless fibres was a winding spiral, like the filament of an electric-light bulb. Sometimes it would align itself for a moment with one of them; sometimes it would curl up around itself to form a glowing circle of light like the one left by the lighted tip of a cigarette swirled rapidly in the dark. This was the thought with which his mind was occupied.

'That means there is no death,' Tatarsky thought happily. 'Why? Because the threads disappear, but the sphere remains!'

He was filled with happiness at having managed to formulate the answer to a question that had tormented humanity for the last several thousand years in terms so simple anyone could understand them. He wanted to share his discovery with Gireiev, and taking him by the shoulder he tried to pronounce this final phrase out loud. But his mouth spoke something else, something meaningless – all the syllables that made up the words were still there, but they were jumbled up chaotically. Tatarsky thought he needed a drink of water, and so he said to Gireiev, who was staring at him in fright:

'Li'd winker drike I watof!'

Gireiev obviously didn't understand what was going on; but it was clear that whatever it was, he didn't like it.

'Li'd dratinker wike of wit!' Tatarsky repeated meekly and tried to smile.

He really wanted Gireiev to smile back at him; but Gireiev did something strange – he got to his feet and backed away from Tatarsky, who understood for the first time what was meant by the phrase 'a mask of horror'. His friend's face was distorted into the most distinct possible mask of precisely that kind. Gireiev took several faltering steps backwards, then turned and ran. Tatarsky was offended to the depths of his soul.

Meanwhile the evening twilight had begun to thicken. As it flitted through the blue haze between the trees, Gireiev's Nepalese waistcoat looked like a large butterfly. Tatarsky found the idea of pursuit exciting. He launched himself after Gireiev, bounding high in the air in order not to stumble over some root or hummock. It was soon clear that he was running a lot faster that Gireiev, quite incomparably faster, in fact. He overtook him and turned back several times before he realised that he wasn't running around Gireiev, but around the remnant of a dry tree-trunk the same height as a man. That sobered him up a little, and he set off down the path in what he thought was the direction of the railway station.

Along the way he ate several more fly-agarics that attracted his attention among the trees, and soon he found himself on a wide dirt road with a fence of barbed wire running along one edge of it.

Someone appeared ahead of him, walking along. Tatarsky went up to him and asked politely: 'Stan gou thecation totet yell he mow? There trun rewains?'

Glancing sharply at Tatarsky, the stranger took a quick step backwards, then took to his heels. Everybody seemed to be reacting to him in the same way today. Tatarsky remembered his Chechen employer and thought cheerfully to himself: 'What if I met Hussein now, I wonder if he'd be scared?'

When Hussein promptly appeared at the edge of the road, it was Tatarsky who was scared. Hussein was standing there silently in the grass and not reacting in any way to Tatarsky's approach. But Tatarsky slowed his pace, walked across to Hussein with meek, childish steps and stood there paralysed with guilt.

'What did you want?' Hussein asked.

Tatarsky said something extremely inappropriate: 'I just need a second. I wanted to ask you, as a representative of the target group: what associations does the word "parliament" have for you?' In his fright he didn't even notice whether he was speaking normally or not.

Hussein wasn't surprised at all. He thought for a moment and answered: 'Al-Ghazavi had this poem called "The Parliament of Birds". It's about how thirty birds flew off in search of the bird that is called Semurg – the king of all birds and a great master.'

'But why did they fly off in search of a king, if they had a parliament?'

'You ask them that. And then, Semurg was not just a king, he was a fount of great knowledge. That's more than you can say for a parliament.'

'How did it all end?' asked Tatarsky.

'When they had endureded thirty trials, they learned that the word "Semurg" means "thirty birds".'

'Who from?'

'The voice of God told them.'

Tatarsky sneezed. Hussein immediately fell silent and

turned away his glowering face. Tatarsky waited for a continuation for quite a long time before he realised that Hussein was actually a post with a sign nailed to it saying: 'Campfires forbidden!' that he could scarcely make out in the semi-darkness. That upset him – so Gireiev and Hussein were in league now! He'd liked Hussein's story, but now it was clear that he'd never learn all the details, and in the form he'd heard it, it wasn't even fit for a cigarette concept. Tatarsky walked on, wondering what it was that had made him stop in such a cowardly fashion by a Hussein-post that hadn't even asked him to.

The explanation was not a very pleasant one: it was a relict of the Soviet era, the slave mentality he still hadn't completely squeezed out of himself. Tatarsky thought for a while and came to the conclusion that the slave in the soul of Soviet man was not concentrated in any particular sector, but rather tinged everything that happened in its twilit expanses in a shade of chronic psychological peritonitis, which meant there was no way to squeeze this slave out drop by drop without damaging precious spiritual qualities. This thought seemed important to Tatarsky in the light of his forthcoming collaboration with Pugin, and he rummaged in his pockets for a long time to find a pen to note it down, but couldn't find one.

Another passer-by appeared, coming towards him; this time it was definitely no hallucination. That much became clear after Tatarsky's attempt to borrow a pen – the passer-by took to his heels, running with genuine speed and not looking back.

Tatarsky simply couldn't figure out what it was in his behaviour that had such a terrifying effect on the people he met. Perhaps they were frightened by the strange disorder of his speech, the way the words he tried to pronounce fell apart into syllables that then re-attached themselves to each other in a random order. Even so, there was something rather flattering in such an extreme reaction.

Tatarsky was suddenly struck so forcibly by a certain thought that he stopped dead and slapped his palm against his forehead. 'Why, of course, it's the Tower of Babel!' he thought. 'They probably drank that mushroom tea and the words began to break apart in their mouths, just like mine.

Later they began to call it a confusion of tongues. It would be better to call it a confusion of language . . .'

Tatarsky could sense that his thoughts were filled with such power that each one was a stratum of reality, just as important in every respect as the forest he was walking through this evening. The difference was that the forest was a thought he couldn't stop thinking, no matter how much he wanted to. On the other hand, there was almost no will whatsoever involved in what was going on in his mind. As soon as he had the thought about the confusion of tongues, it became clear to him that the memory of Babylon was the only possible Babylon: by thinking about it, he had summoned it to life; and the thoughts in his head were like trucks loaded with building materials, rushing towards Babylon, making it more and more substantial.

'They called the confusion of tongues the Tower of Babel,' he thought. 'But just what is the Tower of Babel?'

He swayed on his feet, feeling the earth swing round smoothly beneath him. He only stayed upright because the axis of the earth's rotation ran precisely through the top of his head.

The confusion of tongues coincides in time with the creation of the tower. When there is a confusion of tongues, then the Tower of Babel starts to rise. Or maybe it doesn't rise; maybe it's just that the entrance to the ziggurat opens up. Yes, of course. There's the entrance right there.

A pair of large gates decorated with three-dimensional red stars had appeared in the barbed-wire fence along which Tatarsky was walking. Above them blazed a powerful lamp surmounted by a cowl, and the bright-blue light illuminated the numerous graffiti covering the green sheet-metal of the gates. Tatarsky stopped.

For a minute or two he studied the traditional mid-Russian attempts to write the names of the surrounding villages in Latin script, various names surmounted by crude crowns, symbolic representations of a penis and a vulva, the English verbs 'to fuck' and 'to suck' in the third person singular of the present tense, but all peppered with incomprehensible apostrophes and abundant logos from the music business. Then his gaze fell on something strange.

It was a large inscription – significantly larger than all the rest, stretching right across the gates – written in fluorescent orange paint (it gleamed brightly in the rays of the electric lamp): THIS GAME HAS NO NAME.

The moment Tatarsky read it, all the other ethnographic material ceased to register in his awareness; his consciousness held nothing but these glittering words. He seemed to understand their meaning at a very deep level, and although he could hardly have explained it to anyone else, that meaning undoubtedly required him to climb over the gates. It proved not to be difficult.

Behind the gates was an abandoned building site, a wide area of waste ground with only sparse indications of any human presence. At the centre of the site stood an unfinished building – either the foundations of some intergalactic radio telescope or a strangely designed multi-storey parking lot: the construction work had been broken off at a stage when only the load-bearing structures and walls were in place. The structure looked like a stepped cylinder made up of several concrete boxes standing one on top of another. Round them wound a spiral roadway on reinforced concrete supports, which ended at the top box, surmounted by a small cubic tower with a red signal lamp.

Tatarsky thought it must be one of those military construction projects begun in the seventies that had failed to save the empire, but had shaped the aesthetic of 'Star Wars'. He recalled Darth Vader and his asthmatic wheezing and marvelled at what a wonderful metaphor he was for the career communist: probably somewhere on his starship he had a dialysis machine and two teams of cardiologists, and Tatarsky recalled vaguely that there had been hints at something of the kind in the film. But in his present state thinking about Darth Vader was dangerous.

The unfinished building was illuminated by three or four floodlights that plucked patches of it out of the gloom – sections of the concrete wall, the spiral road and the upper tower with its winking signal light. If not for that red beacon, the building's incompleteness could have been taken in the darkness for the dilapidation of age, and it might have been a thousand or even a full ten thousand years old. But then, thought Tatarsky, the beacon could be powered by some unimaginable ancient electricity transmitted under the ground from Egypt or Babylon.

Recent traces of man were only visible by the gates, where he was standing. There was something like the branch office of a military unit here – several living trailers, a boom, a board with a fire bucket and a crowbar, and a stand with a poster showing identical soldiers with a strange self-absorption imprinted on their faces demonstrating various training formations. Tatarsky was not in the least bit surprised when he saw an immense mushroom with a tin-sheet cap and a telephone hanging on its stalk-post – he realised it must be the sentry post. At first he was sure there was no sentry on duty, but then he saw that the mushroom's conical cap was painted red and decorated with symmetrical white spots.

'Nothing's quite as simple as it seems,' he whispered.

That very moment a quiet, mocking voice spoke somewhere close beside him: 'This game has no name. It will never be the same.'

Tatarsky swung round. There was no one anywhere near him, and he realised it was an auditory hallucination. He felt a bit scared, but despite everything, what was taking place held a strangely delightful promise.

'Onwards,' he whispered, leaning forward and slipping quickly through the murk towards the road that led to the ziggurat. 'After all,' he thought, 'it's just a multi-storey car-park.'

'With hanging gardens,' the voice in his head added quietly.

The fact that the voice spoke in Russian convinced Tatarsky it was a hallucination, but it reminded him once again of the confusion of tongues. As though in response to his thought the voice pronounced a long phrase in a strange language with a large number of sibilants. Tatarsky decided to ignore it, especially since he had already set foot on the spiral ascent.

From the distance he had failed to appreciate the true dimensions of the building. The road was wide enough for two trucks to pass each other ('Or chariots,' the voice added gleefully, 'chariots with four-in-hand! Now those were chariots!').

It was constructed of concrete slabs, with the the joints between them left unsealed. Tall plants protruded from the joints – Tatarsky didn't know what they were called, but he had known since he was a child that he could use their tough stems in his shoes instead of shoe laces. From time to time wide gaps appeared in the wall to his right, leading into the body of the ziggurat. Inside there were wide open spaces littered with building waste. The road constantly disappeared round the corner ahead, seeming to break off in mid-air, and Tatarsky walked carefully, clinging to the wall with one hand. On one side the tower was illuminated by the floodlights from the building site, and on the other by the moon, suspended in a gap in a high cloud. He could hear an open door banging in the wind somewhere up above, and the same wind brought the distant sound of dogs barking. Tatarsky slackened his pace until he was walking really slowly.

Something crunched under his foot. It was an empty cigarette pack. When he picked it up and moved into a patch of light, he saw it was a pack of Parliament Menthol. But there was something else much more surprising about it: on the front of the pack there was an advertising hologram showing three palm trees.

'It all fits,' he whispered and carried on, keeping a careful eye on the ground beneath his feet.

The next discovery was waiting one tier higher – he spotted the coin gleaming in the moonlight from a distance. He'd never seen one like it before: a Republic of Cuba three-peso piece with a portrait of Che Guevara. Tatarsky was not at all surprised that a Cuban coin should be lying on a military construction site – he remembered the final sequence of the film *Golden Eye*, with that immense Soviet-made antenna rising up out of the water somewhere on the Isle of Freedom. This was obviously the payment received for its construction. He replaced the coin in the empty Parliament pack and put it in his pocket, completely confident that there was something else waiting for him.

He wasn't mistaken. The road was approaching its end at the very top box, in front of which lay a heap of building waste and broken crates. Tatarsky noticed a strange little cube lying in among the waste and picked it up. It was a pencil sharpener in the shape of a television, and someone had drawn a large eye on its plastic screen with a ballpoint pen. The sharpener was old – they used to make them like that in the seventies – and it was remarkable that it was so well preserved.

Cleaning off the mud clinging to the sharpener, Tatarsky slipped it into his inside pocket and looked round, wondering what to do next. He was afraid to go into the box: it was dark in there and he could easily break his neck if he fell into some hole or other. Somewhere up above, a door banged once again in the wind, and Tatarsky remembered there was a small tower on the summit of the building, with a red beacon lamp. He couldn't see the tower from where he was standing, but there was a short fire-ladder leading upwards.

The small tower turned out to be the housing where the lift motors should have been. The door was open. On the wall right inside the door there was a light-switch. When Tatarsky turned on the light he saw the lingering traces of a soldier's harsh life: a wooden table, two stools and and empty beer bottles in the corner. It was obvious that these were the traces of a soldier's life, and not any other, from the magazine photographs of women stuck to the walls. Tatarsky studied them for a while. He thought that one of them, running across the sand of a tropical beach entirely naked and with a golden suntan, looked very beautiful. It wasn't even so much her face and figure, but the incredible, indefinable freedom of her movement, which the photographer had managed to capture. The sand, the sea and the leaves of the palm trees on the photograph were all so vivid that Tatarsky heaved a heavy sigh – the meagre Moscow summer was already over. He closed his eyes and for a few seconds he fancied he could hear the distant murmur of the sea.

He sat down at the table, laid out his trophies on it and looked them over once again. The palms on the empty Parliament pack and on the photograph were very similar, and he thought they must grow in the same place, in a part of the world he would never get to see – not even in the Russian style, from inside a tank – and if he ever did, it would only be when he no longer needed anything from this woman or this sand or this sea or even from himself. The dark melancholy into which he was plunged by this thought was so profound that at its very deepest point he unexpectedly discovered light: the slogan and the poster for Parliament that he had been searching for suddenly came to him. He hastily pulled out his notebook – the pen turned out to be inside it – and jotted the ideas down:

The poster consists of a photograph of the embankment of the river Moscow taken from the bridge on which the historic tanks stood in October '93. On the site of the Parliament building we see a huge pack of Parliament (digital editing). Palms are growing profusely all around it. The slogan is a quotation from the nineteenth-century poet Griboedov:

> Sweet and dear
> Is the smoke of our Motherland

Parliament slogan:

THE MOTHERLAND'S #1 SMOKE!

'Thou lookest out always for number one,' he thought gloomily.

Putting the notebook back into his pocket, he gathered up his prizes from the table and took a final glance around the room. The thought flashed through his mind that he could take the beautiful woman running across the sand as a souvenir, but he decided against it. He turned out the light, went out on to the roof and stopped to allow his eyes to grow accustomed to the darkness.

'What now?' he thought. 'To the station.'

CHAPTER 5

Poor Folk

The adventure in the forest outside Moscow proved posi-
tively stimulating to Tatarsky's professional abilities. Scenarios and concepts now came to him far more easily, and Pugin
even paid him a small advance for his slogan for Parliament:
he said Tatarsky had hit the bull's-eye, because until '93 a
pack of Parliament had cost the same as a pack of Marlboro,
but after those famous events Parliament had rapidly become
the most popular cigarette in Moscow, and now they cost
twice as much. Subsequently, however, 'the smoke of the
Motherland' was dispersed without a trace into the thick
gloom of a winter that arrived unexpectedly early. The only
dubious echo of the slogan left in the snowbound advertising
space of Moscow was the phrase: 'From ship to ball', another
borrowing – by an unknown colleague of Tatarsky's – from
the poet Griboedov. It was to be glimpsed at one time on large
hoarding advertisements for menthol cigarettes – a yacht,
blue sea and sky, a peaked cap with a sunburst and a pair of
long legs. Tatarsky felt a pang of jealousy at this, but not a
very powerful one – the girl in the menthol advert had been
chosen to suit the taste of such a wide target group that the
text seemed spontaneously to read as: 'From ship to balls'.

For some reason the wave of fly-agaric energy that had
swept through his nervous system found its finest outlet in
texts for cigarettes – probably for the same reason that the first
truly successful experience of love or narcotics determines
your preferences for the rest of your life. His next great success (not only in his own opinion, but in the opinion of Pugin,
who surprised him once again by paying him) was a text written for Davidoff cigarettes, which was symbolic, because his
career had started with them. The text was based on an advertisement for Davidoff Classic that was on all the hoardings

in the city centre: dark tones, a close-up of a wasting face with the burden of unbearable knowledge glinting in the eyes, and the inscription:

THE MORE YOU KNOW: DAVIDOFF CLASSIC

At the first sight of the wise, wrinkled face, Tatarsky immediately began wondering just what it was that this foreign smoker knew. The first explanation to come to mind was rather sombre: a visit to the cancer clinic, an X-ray and a dreadful diagnosis.

Tatarsky's project was in total contrast: a light background, a youthful face expressive of ignorant happiness, a white pack with slim gold letters and the text:

'FOR IN MUCH WISDOM IS MUCH SORROW
AND HE WHO INCREASES KNOWLEDGE
INCREASES GRIEF.' DAVIDOFF LIGHTS

Pugin said Davidoff's agent would be unlikely to be interested, but some other cigarette market leader might very well take it. 'I'll have a word with Azadovsky,' he said casually. 'He's got an exclusive on sixteen brands.' It seemed to Tatarsky he'd heard that name before. He jotted the phrase down in his notebook and casually dropped it into several conversations with clients, but his natural shyness found expression in the fact that he usually halved the number of brands.

At the beginning of winter Tatarsky had his one-room flat redecorated after a fashion (against the background of cornflower-blue Soviet-era tiles that were coming away from the wall, the expensive Italian mixer-tap looked like a gold tooth in the mouth of a leper, but he had no money for major renovations). He also bought a new computer, although he had no particular need for it – he'd simply begun to have difficulties getting texts printed out that he'd typed in his favourite word-processing program: one more muffled groan under the iron boot of Microsoft. Tatarsky didn't feel seriously aggrieved, although he did note the profoundly symbolic nature of the event: his interface program – a medium by its very nature – was becoming the most important message, taking over an incredible amount of computer memory space and resources, and that reminded him very much of a brazen new Russian running the funds for teachers' salaries through the accounts in his bank.

The further he penetrated into the jungles of the advertising business, the more questions he had to which he couldn't find the answer, neither in Al Rice's *Positioning: a Battle for your Mind*, nor even in the latest book on the same topic, *The Final Positioning*. One colleague swore to Tatarsky that all the themes that Al Rice hadn't touched on were analysed in *Confessions of an Advertising Man* by David Ogilvy. In his heart of hearts Tatarsky suspected Ogilvy was really the same character who appeared for a second in George Orwell's *1984* in the consciousness of the hero in order to perform an imaginary feat of heroism and then disappear into the ocean of oblivion. The fact that comrade Ogilvy, despite his double unreality, had nonetheless made it to the shore, lit his pipe, donned his tweed jacket and become a world-famous advertising guru filled Tatarsky with a mystical, rapturous admiration for his own profession.

But the book he found particularly helpful was by Rosser Reeves: he discovered two terms in it – 'penetration' and 'involvement' – that proved very useful when it came to throwing curves. The first project he managed to design on the basis of these two concepts was for Nescafé Gold.

'*It has long been recognised*,' Tatarsky wrote just twenty minutes after he first learned about it,

that there are two basic indicators of the effectiveness of an advertising campaign: penetration and involvement. 'Penetration' is the percentage of people who remember the advertisement. 'Involvement' is the percentage of people the advertisement has persuaded to consume the product. The problem is, however, that a brilliantly scandalous advertisement, capable of producing high-level penetration, is absolutely no guarantee of high levels of involvement. Likewise a campaign that cleverly demonstrates the virtues of a product and is capable of producing high levels of involvement is no guarantee of high-level penetration. Which is why we propose taking a new approach and creating a kind of binary advertising, in which the functions of penetration and in-

45

volvement will be performed by different sets of information. Let's examine how this approach would work in an advertising campaign for Nescafé Gold coffee.

The first step in the campaign is directed exclusively at implanting the brand name 'Nescafé Gold' in the consciousness of the largest possible number of people (we start from the assumption that any means are justified to this end). For example, we organise the planting of fake bombs in several large shops and railway stations – there should be as many of them as possible. The Ministry of the Interior and the Federal Security Services receive calls from an anonymous terrorist organisation informing them that explosive devices have been planted. But the searches carried out by the police at the sites named by the terrorists produce nothing but a large number of jars of Nescafé Gold packed in plastic bags. Next morning this is reported in all the magazines and newspapers and on television, following which we can regard the penetration phase as complete (its success is directly dependent on the scale of the operation). Immediately after this comes phase two – involvement. At this stage the campaign is waged according to the classical rules: the only thing linking it with phase one is the basic slogan: 'Nescafé Gold: The Taste Explosion!' Here is the scenario for the advertising clip:

A bench in a small city square. A young man in a red tracksuit sitting on it, with a serious expression on his face. Across the road from the square a Mercedes-600 and two jeeps are parked outside a chic town house. The young man glances at his watch. Change of camera angle: several men in severe dark suits and dark glasses emerge from the mansion – the security guards. They surround the Mercedes from all sides and one of them gives a command over his walkie-talkie. A small fat man with a depraved face emerges from the mansion and looks around in a frightened manner, then he runs down the steps to the Mercedes and disappears behind the dark-tinted glass of the car, and the guards get into the jeeps. The Mercedes starts to move off and suddenly there are three powerful explosions in rapid succession. The cars are scattered in flying debris; the street where they have just been standing is hidden by smoke. New camera angle: the young man on the bench takes a thermos flask and a red mug with a gold band out of his sports bag. He pours some coffee into the mug, takes a sip and closes his eyes in ecstasy. Voice-over: 'He brewed it rough and dark. Nescafé Gold. The real taste explosion.'

The term 'involvement' didn't only come in useful at work. It also forced Tatarsky to start thinking about just who he was involving in what and, most importantly of all, just who was involving him in what.

He first began thinking about it when he was reading an article devoted to cult porn films. The author of the article was called Sasha Blo. To judge from the text, he should have been a cold and world-weary being of indeterminate sex, writing in the breaks between orgies in order to convey his opinions to a dozen or so similar fallen supermen/women. The tone adopted by Sasha Blo made it clear that de Sade and Sacher-Masoch wouldn't even have made it as doormen in his circle, and the best Charles Manson could have hoped for would have been to hold the candlesticks. In short, Blo's article was a perfectly formed apple of sin, worm-eaten, beyond a shadow of a doubt, personally by the ancient serpent himself.

But Tatarsky had been around in the advertising business for a long time now. In the first place, he knew that the only thing these apples were good for was to tempt suburban Moscow's kids out of the Eden of childhood. In the second place, he doubted the very existence of cult porn films, and was only prepared to believe in them if he was presented with living members of the cult. In the third place, and most importantly, he knew Sasha Blo himself very well.

He was a fat, bald, sad, middle-aged father of three, and his name was Ed. In order to pay the rent on their flat, he wrote simultaneoulsy under three or four pseudonyms for several magazines on any topic. He and Tatarsky had invented the name 'Blo' together, borrowing the title of a bottle of bright-blue glass-cleaning fluid they'd found under the bath (they were looking for the vodka Ed's wife had hidden). The word 'Blo' summoned up the idea of inexhaustible reserves of vital energy and at the same time something non-humanoid, which was why Ed used it carefully. He only used it for signing articles imbued with such boundless freedom and ambivalence, so to speak, that a common signature such as 'Ivanov' or 'Petrov' would have been absurd. There was a great demand for this ambivalence in Moscow's glossy magazines, so great indeed that it posed the question of just who was controlling its penetration. To be honest, even thinking about the topic was a bit frightening, but after reading Sasha Blo's article, Tatarsky suddenly realised that it wasn't being implanted by some demonic spy or some fallen spirit who had assumed human form, but by Ed and himself.

Of course, not just by them alone – Moscow probably had two or three hundred Eds, universal minds choking on the fumes of the home hearth and crushed under the weight of their children. Their lives were not one long sequence of lines of coke, orgies and disputes about Burroughs and Warhol, as you might have concluded from their writings, but an endless battle with nappies and Moscow's own omnipresent cock-roaches. They weren't obsessed with arrogant snobbery, or possessed by serpentine carnal lust or cold dandyism: they demonstrated no tendencies to devil worship, or even any real readiness to drop a tab of acid occasionally – despite their ca-sual use of the term 'acid' every day of the week. What they did have were problems with digestion, money and housing, and in appearance they resembled not Gary Oldman, as the first acquaintance with their writing led you to believe, but Danny de Vito.

Tatarsky could not gaze trustingly into the distant ex-panses sketched for him by Sasha Blo, because he understood the physiological genesis of those expanses in the bald head of downtrodden Ed, who was chained to his computer in just the same way as they used to chain Austrian soldiers to their machine-guns during the First World War. Believing in his product was harder than achieving arousal from telephone sex, when you knew that the voice hoarse with passion speak-ing to you didn't belong to the blonde promised by the pho-tograph, but to an old woman with a cold who was knitting a sock as she read off a set of standard phrases from a crib soaked by the drops falling from her running nose.

'But how do we – that is, Ed and me – know what to involve other people in?' wrote Tatarsky in his notebook.

From one point of view, of course, it's obvious: intuition. No need to inquire about what to do and how to do it – when you reach a certain degree of despair, you just start to intuit things for yourself. You sense the dominant tendency, so to speak, with your empty stomach. But

where does the tendency come from? Who thinks it up, if – as I'm con-
vinced – everyone in the world is simply trying to catch it and sell it,
like Ed and me, or to guess what it is and print it, like the editors of
those glossy magazines?

His thoughts on this theme were morose and they were reflected in his scenario for a clip for the washing powder Ariel,
written soon after this event.

The scenario is based on motifs from Shakespeare. Loud music, solemn
and menacing. The opening shot shows a cliff on the seashore. Night.
Down below, menacing waves rear up in the dim moonlight. In the dis-
tance is an ancient castle, also illuminated by the moon. Standing on the
top of the cliff is a girl of incredible beauty. She is Miranda. She is
wearing a medieval dress of red velvet and a tall pointed cap with a
trailing veil. She raises her arms towards the moon and utters a strange
incantation three times. When she pronounces it for the third time there
is a rumble of distant thunder. The music grows louder and more men-
acing. A wide beam of light emerges from the moon, which is visible in a
break in the clouds, and extends until it reaches the rocks at Miranda's
feet. Her face expresses confusion – she is clearly afraid of what is about
to happen, and yet she wants it. A shadow slides down the beam of light,
coming closer, and as the melody reaches its climax, we see a proud
spirit in all his evil beauty – his robes are flowing in the wind and his
long hair is silvered by the moonlight. On his head is a slim wreath set
with diamonds. He is Ariel. He flies close to Miranda, halts in mid-air
and holds out his hand to her. After a moment's struggle Miranda
reaches out her own hand to his. Next frame: close-up of two hands ap-
proaching each other. Lower left – Miranda's pale weak hand: upper
right – the spirit's hand, transparent and glowing. They touch each
other, the spirit instantly transforms into a box of Ariel and everything
is flooded in blinding light. Next frame: two boxes of washing powder.
On one it says Ariel. On the other, in pale-grey letters, it says Ordinary
Caliban. Miranda's voice-over: 'Ariel. Temptingly tempestuous'.

Possibly the specific elements in this clip were inspired by a
black and white photograph that hung above Tatarsky's desk.
It was an advertisement for some boutique, showing a young
man with long hair and carefully tended stubble in a luxurious
wide-cut coat carelessly hung across his shoulders – the wind
filled out the form of the coat so that it echoed the sail of a boat

visible on the horizon. The waves breaking against the rocks and splashing up on to the shore fell just short of his shiny shoes. His face was set in a harsh, sullen grimace, and somehow he resembled the birds with outstretched wings (maybe eagles, maybe seagulls) soaring into the twilit sky from a supplement to the latest version of *Photoshop* (after taking a closer look at the photograph, Tatarsky decided that the boat on the horizon must have come sailing in from there too).

After contemplating it for days Tatarsky finally understood: all the clichés to which the photograph was alluding had been born together with romanticism in the nineteenth century; their remains, together with those of the Count of Monte Cristo, had survived into the twentieth, but on the threshold of the twenty-first the count's legacy had already been completely squandered. The human mind had sold this romanticism to itself far too many times to be able to do any more business on it. Now, no matter how sincerely you wished to deceive yourself, it was virtually impossible to believe in any correspondence between the image that was being sold and its implied inner content. It was an empty form that had long ago ceased to mean what it should have meant. Everything was moth-eaten: the thoughts provoked by the sight of the conventional *Niebelung* in the studio photograph were not about the proud Gothic spirit implied by the frothing waves and sideburns, but about whether the photographer charged a lot, how much the model got paid and whether the model had to pay a fine when his personal lubricant stained the seat of the trousers from the company's spring collection.

Tatarsky's deductions led him into a state of total and utter confusion. On the one hand, it seemed that he and Ed crafted a false panorama of life for others (like a battle scene in a museum, where the floor in front of the spectator is scattered with sand and worn-out boots and shells, but the tanks and the explosions are only drawn on the wall), guided solely by their intuition as to what the punters would swallow. On the other hand, his own life was a frustrating attempt to move a bit closer to the contents of this panorama. In essence it was an attempt to run into the picture drawn on the wall. Being a co-author of this picture made the attempt more than grotesque. Of course – or so it seemed to Tatarsky – a rich man could escape the bounds of false reality. He could move beyond the limits of the panorama that was compulsory for the poor. Tatarsky didn't actually know much about what the world of the rich was like. There were only vague images circling around in his consciousness, clichés from advertising, which he himself had been rebroadcasting for such a long time he couldn't possibly believe in them. What was clear to him was that you could only find out what prospects opened up to a man with a substantial bank account from the rich themselves, and on one occasion – by pure chance – Tatarsky managed to do just that.

While he was drinking away a small fee in the Poor Folk bar, he eavesdropped on a conversation between two TV chat-show hosts – it was after midnight and they were continuing a drinking spree begun earlier somewhere else. Tatarsky was sitting just a couple of metres away from them, but they paid no more attention to him than if he'd been a stuffed model of a copywriter nailed to the counter in order to brighten up the decor.

Although both of the showmen were thoroughly drunk, they'd lost none of that strange holographic gleam in every fold of their clothes, as though their physical bodies were not actually sitting at the next table but were simply being shown on a huge television standing next to Tatarsky. When he noticed this inexplicable but undoubtedly real effect, Tatarsky found himself thinking how long it would take them in limbo to scrape away all the human attention that had eaten into the pores of their souls. The showmen were talking shop, and Tatarsky gathered that one of them was having problems with his contract.

'If they'd just extend it for next year,' he said, clenching his fists.

'Say they do,' the other replied. 'At the end of the year it'll be the same thing all over again. And you'll be living on tranquillizers again . . . And then what?'

'Then what? Then I've got a serious plan.' He slumped over the table and poured himself some vodka. 'I'm just five hundred thousand short,' he said. 'That's what I've got to make.'

'What plan?'

'You won't tell anyone? Listen . . .'

He reached into the inside pocket of his jacket, rummaged around for a long while and finally pulled out a sheet of glossy paper folded into four.

'There,' he said, 'it says it on here . . . The kingdom of Bhutan. The only country in the world where television is forbidden. Unnerstand? Completely forbidden. It says here that not far from the capital they have an entire colony where big TV moguls live. If you spend all your life working in television, the very coolest thing you can do when you retire is move to Bhutan.'

'Is that what you need the five hundred grand for?'

'No, I need the five hundred grand so no one will come looking for me in Bhutan afterwards. Can you just imagine it? Forbidden. Not a single television set anywhere except in counter-espionage! And the embassies!'

His companion took the sheet of paper from him, unfolded it and started reading.

'You unnerstand?' – the first showman carried on speaking regardless – 'If anyone is keeping a television at home and the authorities find out about it, the police come round, unnerstand? And they cart the queer fucker off to prison. Or maybe they even shoot him.'

He pronounced the word 'queer' with that sabre-whistle intake of breath you only ever hear from latent homosexuals who have deprived themselves of the joys of love in the name of a perverse misinterpretation of the social contract. His companion understood everything and didn't take offence – he was looking through the article.

'Ah,' he said, 'out of a magazine. It's interesting all right . . . So who wrote it? Where is it now . . . Some guy called Edward Debirsian . . .'

Tatarsky almost knocked over his table as he stood up to go to the toilet. He wasn't surprised that TV personalities should feel that way about their work, although the degree of these people's spiritual degradation did make it possible to allow that some of them might actually like their jobs. It was something else that had finally finished him off. Sasha Blo had a particular foible: any material that he liked, he would sign with his own real name. And what he liked more than anything else on earth was to pass off the products of his own untrammelled imagination as a narrative of real events – but it was a luxury he allowed himself only very rarely.

Tatarsky laid down a line of cocaine on the cold white cheek of the toilet tank and, without even bothering to crush the lumps, snorted it through a rolled-up hundred-rouble bill (he was already out of dollars), then took out his notebook and wrote:

In itself a wall on which a panoramic view of a non-existent world is drawn does not change. But for a great deal of money you can buy a view from the window with a painted sun, a sky-blue bay and a calm evening. Unfortunately, the author of this fragment will again be Ed – but even that is not important, because the very window the view is bought for is also only drawn in. Then perhaps the wall on which it is drawn is a drawing too? But drawn by whom and on what?

He raised his eyes to the wall of the toilet as though in hopes of an answer there. Traced on the tiles in red felt-tip pen were the jolly, rounded letters of a brief slogan: 'Trapped? Masturbate!'

Going back to the bar, he sat further away from the TV personalities and attempted to lean back and enjoy it. But it didn't work for him – it never did. The repulsive Moscow cocaine, cut almost to nothing by the unwashed hands of a long chain of dealers, deposited an entire bouquet of medicinal smells in his nasopharynx – everything from streptocide to aspirin – and triggered an intense, stressful trembling in his body. They did say the powder they took a hundred and fifty dollars a gramme for in Moscow was not cocaine at all, but a mixture of Estonian speed with an assortment of Russian pharmaceuticals. As if that wasn't enough, for some reason half of the dealers always wrapped the powder in a glossy advertisement for the Toyota Camry cut out of some magazine, and Tatarsky was tormented by the unbearable suspicion that they made a fat living not just at the expense of other people's health, but by providing a PR service as well. Every time Tatarsky asked himself why he and others paid all that money in order to subject themselves once again to a humiliating and unhygienic procedure, the only explanation he could come up with went as follows: people weren't sniffing cocaine, they were sniffing money, and the rolled-up hundred-dollar bill required by the unwritten order of ritual was actually more important than the powder itself. If cocaine was sold in chemists' shops for twenty kopecks a gramme as a mouthwash for toothache, he thought, then nobody but punks would sniff it – the way it was, in fact, at the beginning of the century. But if some ether-based glue sniffed by juvenile junkies cost a thousand dollars a bottle, all the gilded youth of Moscow would be delighted to sniff it, and at presentations and buffet luncheons it would be *très chic* to waft the volatile chemical vapours around yourself, complain about your brain neurons dying off and disappear for long periods into the toilet. Youth fashion magazines would devote revelatory cover stories (written, of course, by Sasha Blo) to the aesthetics of the plastic bag that was placed over the head for this procedure.

'Oho!' Tatarsky exclaimed, smacked himself on the forehead, took out his notebook, opened it at the letter 'C', and noted down:

Youth market colognes (all manufacturers). Link them with money and the Roman emperor Vespasian (tax on lavatories, the saying 'Money doesn't smell'). Example:

> ### MONEY DOES SMELL!
> ### "BENJAMIN"
> ### THE NEW COLOGNE FROM HUGO BOSS

Putting away his notebook, he felt that the peak of the loathsome sensation had passed and he was quite strong enough to walk as far as the bar and get himself a drink. He wanted tequila, but when he reached the barman for some reason he ordered Smirnoff, which he normally couldn't stand. He downed one shot right there at the bar, then took another and went back to his table. In the meantime he'd acquired a companion, a man of about forty with long, greasy hair and a wild beard, dressed in a crazy kind of embroidered jacket – in appearance he was a typical former hippy, one of those who had failed to find a place for themselves either in the past or in the present. Hanging round his neck was a large bronze cross.

'Excuse me,' said Tatarsky, 'I was sitting here.'

'So be my guest,' said his new neighbour. 'Don't need the entire table, do you?'

Tatarsky shrugged and sat facing him.

'My name's Grigory,' his neighbour said affably.

Tatarsky raised his weary eyes to look at him. 'Vova,' he said.

Catching his glance, Grigory frowned and shook his head in sympathy.

'You've got the shakes bad,' he said. 'Snorting?'

'A bit,' said Tatarsky. 'Just now and again.'

'Fool,' said Grigory. 'Just think about it: the mucous membrane of the nose – it's as good as the exposed surface of the brain . . . And did you ever think about where that powder came from and who's been sticking his body parts in it?'

'Just this moment,' Tatarsky confessed. 'But what's all this about body parts? What other body parts can you stick in it except your nose?'

Grigory glanced around, pulled out a bottle of vodka from under the table and took a quick swallow from it.

'Maybe you've heard of an American writer called Harold Robbins?' he asked, hiding the bottle away.

'No,' answered Tatarsky.

'A total arsehole. But all the English teachers read him. That's why there are so many of his books in Moscow, and the children's knowledge of the language is so bad. In one of his novels there was this black guy, a professional fucker who pulled rich white dames. So before the procedure this black dude sprinkled his . . .'

'OK, I get it,' said Tatarsky. 'I'm going to be sick now.'

' . . . his massive black dong with pure cocaine,' Grigory concluded with satisfaction. 'You might ask: what's this black dude got to do with anything? I'll tell you. I was re-reading Andreiev's "Rosa Mundi" recently, the part about the soul of the nation. Andreiev says it's a woman and she's called Navna. Then afterwards I had this vision – she's lying there like she's sleeping on this white rock, and leaning over her there's this vague black figure, with short little wings, you can't see his face, and he's just giving her it . . .'

Grigory pulled an invisible control column in towards his stomach with his hands.

'You want to know what it is you're all using?' he whispered, leaning his leering face close to Tatarsky. 'Exactly. What he sprinkles on himself. And at the moment he sticks it in, you're all shooting up and snorting. When he pulls it out, you all go running off trying to find more . . . And he just keeps on sticking it in and pulling it out, sticking it in and pulling it out . . .'

Tatarsky leaned down into the gap between the table and the counter and puked. He glanced up cautiously at the barman: he was engaged in conversation with some customers and didn't seem to have noticed anything. Looking around, Tatarsky noticed an advertising poster on the wall. It showed the nineteenth-century poet Tyutchev wearing a pince-nez, with a glass in his hand and a rug across his knees. His piercingly sad gaze was directed out of the window, and with his free hand he was stroking a dog sitting beside him. The strange thing was, though, that Tyutchev's chair wasn't standing on the floor, but on the ceiling. Tatarsky looked a little lower and read the slogan:

RUSSIA – NO WAY IS THERE TO UNDERSTAND HER
NO WAY HER SECRET SOUL TO RENDER
SMIRNOFF

Everything was calm. Tatarsky straightened up. He was feeling significantly better.

Grigory leaned back in his chair and took another swig from his bottle. 'It's disgusting,' he asserted. 'Life should be lived cleanly.'

'Oh, yes? And how's that done?' Tatarsky asked, wiping his mouth with a paper napkin.

'Nothing but LSD. Only via the gut and always with a prayer.'

Tatarsky shook his head like a dog that has just clambered out of the water. 'Where can you get it?'

'What do you mean?' Grigory was offended. 'Just you come round here.'

Tatarsky obediently got up , walked round the table and sat beside him.

'I've been collecting for eight years,' said Grigory, taking a stamp album out from under his jacket. 'Take a look at that.'

Tatarsky opened the album. 'Well I'll be damned,' he said. 'Look at all those different ones.'

'That's nothing,' said Grigory. 'What I've got here's just for swapping and selling. I've got two shelves of these albums back at home.'

'And you mean they all have different effects?'

Grigory nodded.

'But why?'

'In the first place, because the formula's different. I've not gone into it too deeply myself, but there's always something added to the acid – phenamine maybe, maybe barbiturate or something else – and when it all works together, the effect's cumulative. But apart from that, the most important thing is the drawing. There's no getting away from the fact that you're swallowing Mel Gibson or Mitsubishi, get it? Your mind remembers it; and when the acid reaches it, everything follows a set path. It's hard to explain . . . have you ever tried it once at least?'

'No,' said Tatarsky. 'Fly-agarics are more in my line.'

Grigory shuddered and crossed himself.

'Then what am I doing telling you about it?' he said, glancing mistrustfully up at Tatarsky. 'You should understand well enough.'

'Yes, I understand, I understand,' said Tatarsky casually. 'And these here, with the skull and cross-bones – does anyone take those? Are there people who like those?'

'They take all sorts. People come in all sorts, too, you know.'

Tatarsky turned over the page. 'Hey, those are pretty,' he said. 'Is that Alice in Wonderland?'

'Aha. Only that's a block. Twenty-five tabs. Expensive. This one here's good, with the crucifixion. Only I don't know how it'd go down on top of your fly-agarics. I wouldn't recommend the one with Hitler. It's euphoric for a couple of hours, but afterwards there's bound to be a few seconds of eternal torment in hell.'

'How can you have a few seconds of eternal torment? If it's only a few seconds, how come they're eternal?'

'You just have to go through it. Yeah. And you might not make it through.'

'I get you,' said Tatarsky, turning the page. 'And that glitch of yours about "Rosa Mundi" – which one was that from? Is it in here?'

'Not a glitch, it was a vision,' Grigory corrected him. 'There's none in here. It was a rare tab with a dragon defeating St George. From the German series: "John the Evangelist's Bad Trip". I wouldn't recommend that one either. They're a bit longer and narrower than usual, and hard too. Less like a tab than a tablet with a label on it. A lot of stuff. You know what, I'd recommend you to try this one, with the blue Rajneesh. It's kind and gentle. And it'll sit well on top of the booze.'

Tatarsky's attention was caught by three identical lilac rectangles set between a tab with a picture of the *Titanic* and a tab with some laughing eastern deity.

'These three here all the same, what are they?' he asked. 'Who's this drawn on them? With the beard and the cap? I can't tell whether it's Lenin or Uncle Sam.'

Grigory chuckled in approval.

'There's instinct for you,' he said. 'Who it is that's drawn on them I don't know. But it's really wild stuff. The difference is the acid's mixed with a metabolic. So it cuts in really sharp and sudden, in about twenty minutes. And the dose in them is enough for a whole platoon of soldiers. I wouldn't give stuff like that to you, but if you've been eating fly-agarics . . .'

Tatarsky noticed the security guard looking at them attentively.

'I'll take them,' he said. 'How much?'

'Twenty-five dollars,' said Grigory.

'All I've got left is a hundred roubles.'

Grigory thought for a second and nodded.

Tatarsky held out the banknote rolled into a narrow tube, took a stamp out of the album and tucked it into his breast pocket.

'There you go,' said Grigory, putting his album away. 'And

don't you go snorting that garbage any more. It's never done anybody any good. Just makes you tired and ashamed about yesterday and makes your nose bleed.'

'Do you know what comparative positioning is?' Tatarsky asked.

'No,' said Grigory. 'What is it?'

'It's an advertising technique you're an absolute master of.'

CHAPTER 6

The Path to Your Self

Next morning Tatarsky was woken by the phone. His first reaction was annoyance – the phone had interrupted a very strange and beautiful dream, in which Tatarsky was taking an examination. The dream had started with him drawing three question tickets one after the other, and then setting off up a long spiral staircase like there used to be in one of the blocks of his first institute, where he studied electric furnaces. It was up to him to find the examiners himself, but every time he opened one of the doors, instead of an examination hall he found himself gazing into the sunset-lit field outside Moscow where he and Gireiev had gone walking on that memorable evening. This was very strange, because his search had already taken him up several floors above ground level.

When he was fully awake he suddenly remembered Grigory and his stamp album. 'I bought it,' he thought in horror, 'and I ate it . . .' He leapt out of bed, went over to the desk, pulled out the top drawer and saw the stamp with the smiling lilac face looking up at him. 'No,' he thought, 'thank God for that . . .' Placing the stamp in the very farthest corner of the drawer, he covered it with a box of pencils.

Meanwhile the phone was still ringing. 'Pugin,' Tatarsky thought to himself and picked up the receiver.

'Hello,' said an unfamiliar voice, 'can I speak to Mr Tatarsky, please?'

'Speaking.'

'Good morning. This is Vladimir Khanin from the Privy Counsellor agency. I was left your number by Dima Pugin. Could we maybe get together some time today? Right away would be best.'

'What's happened?' Tatarsky asked, realising immediately

from the verb 'left' that something bad must have happened to Pugin.

'Dima's no longer with us. I know you worked with him, and he worked with me. So indirectly we're acquainted. In any case, I have several of your works we were waiting for an answer on lying here on my desk.'

'But how did it happen?'

'When we meet,' said his new acquaintance. 'Write down the address.'

An hour and a half later Tatarsky walked into the immense building of the Pravda complex, the building that had once housed the editorial offices of almost all the Soviet newspapers. A pass was ready and waiting for him at the duty desk. He went up to the eighth floor and found the room with the number he needed; there was a metal plate on the door bearing the words: 'Ideological Department' – apparently a leftover from Soviet times. 'Or maybe not,' thought Tatarsky.

Khanin was alone in the room. He was a middle-aged man with a pleasant, bearded face, and he was sitting at a desk, hastily writing something down.

'Come in and sit down,' he said, without looking up. 'I won't be a moment.'

Tatarsky took two steps into the room, saw the advertising poster sellotaped to the wall and almost choked on the spot. According to the text under the photograph, it was an advertisement for a new type of holiday involving the alternate use of jointly rented apartments – Tatarsky had already heard talk that it was just another big rip-off, like everything else. But that wasn't the problem. The metre-wide photograph showed three palm trees on some paradise island, and those three palms were a point-for-point copy of the holographic image from the packet of Parliament cigarettes he'd found on the ziggurat. Even that was nothing compared with the slogan. Written in large black letters under the photograph were the words:

IT WILL NEVER BE THE SAME!

'I told you to sit down! There's a chair over here.'

Khanin's voice roused Tatarsky from his trance. He sat

61

down and awkwardly shook the hand that was extended towards him over the desk.

'What's the problem over there?' Khanin asked, squinting across at the poster.

'Oh, nothing,' said Tatarsky. 'Déjà vu.'

'Ah! I understand,' said Khanin in a tone of voice that suggested he really had understood something. 'Right, then. First of all about Pugin . . .'

Gradually recovering his composure, Tatarsky began to listen.

The robbery had obviously been an inside job and, taking everything into consideration, the thief must have known that Pugin had worked as a taxi-driver in New York. It was a horrible and rather improbable story: while Pugin was warming up the motor of his car, two guys had climbed into the back seat and given him an address: Second Avenue, corner of Twenty-Seventh Street. Under some kind of reflex hypnosis Pugin had driven off, then turned into a side street – and that was all he had managed to tell the police and the doctors. Seven bullet wounds had been found in his body – they'd fired straight through the back of his seat. Several thousand dollars Pugin was carrying with him were missing, as well as some file or other that he kept raving about until the moment of death.

'Except that the file,' Khanin said sadly, 'isn't missing. Here it is. He left it here, forgot it. Why don't you take a look? I'll just make a couple of calls in the meantime.'

Tatarsky picked up the loose-leaf binder. He remembered Pugin's mustachioed face, just as pasty and colourless as this cardboard, and his black-button eyes, like plastic studs. The folder evidently contained Pugin's own works – how many times had he hinted that he was more than just a passive observer when it came to judging what other people produced? 'He probably started back in New York,' Tatarsky thought to himself. While Khanin was discussing some rates or other on the phone, Tatarsky came across two genuine masterpieces. The first was for Calvin Klein:

An elegant, rather effeminate Hamlet (general stylisation – unisex) in black tights and a light blue tunic worn next to the skin, wanders slowly around a graveyard. Beside one of the graves he halts, bends down and picks up a pink skull out of the grass. Close-up: Hamlet knitting his brows slightly as he gazes at the skull. View from the rear: close-up of taut buttocks with the letters 'CK'. New camera angle: skull, hand, letters 'CK' on the blue tunic. Next frame: Hamlet tosses the skull into the air and kicks it. The skull soars upwards, then arcs back down and falls straight through the bronze wreath held by a bronze angel on one of the graves, just as though it were a basketball hoop. Slogan:

JUST BE. CALVIN KLEIN

The second slogan Tatarsky liked was intended for the Gap chain of shops in Moscow. The proposal was for a poster showing Anton Chekhov, first in a striped suit, and then in a striped jacket but with no trousers: the gap between his bare, skinny legs was emphasised in strong contrast, so that it resembled a Gothic hourglass. Then the outline of the gap between Chekhov's legs was repeated, but without Chekhov; now it really had become an hourglass, with almost all the sand already fallen through into the bottom half. The text was:

RUSSIA WAS ALWAYS NOTORIOUS FOR THE GAP BETWEEN CULTURE AND CIVILISATION. NOW THERE IS NO MORE CULTURE. NO MORE CIVILI-SATION. THE ONLY THING THAT REMAINS IS THE GAP. THE WAY THEY SEE YOU.

A few pages further on, Tatarsky came across his own text for Parliament. Suddenly it was clear to him that Pugin hadn't invented any of the other pieces either. By this stage his imagination had already built up the image of a masked giant of advertising thought, capable of punning fluently on Shakespeare or Russian history at will. But like some heavy metal from the bottom of the periodic table, this virtual Pugin existed in Tatarsky's consciousness for no more than a few seconds before he disintegrated.

Khanin said goodbye and hung up the phone. Tatarsky looked up and was amazed to see a bottle of tequila, two glasses and a saucer of lemon slices standing on the desk – Khanin had deftly set everything up while he was talking.

'One for the departed?' he suggested.

Tatarsky nodded. They clinked glasses and drank. Tatarsky squeezed a slice of lemon between his gums and began nervously composing a phrase to suit the occasion, but the telephone rang again.

'What's that? What's that?' Khanin said into the receiver. 'I don't know. This is a very serious matter. You go straight round to the Institute of Apiculture . . . Yes, yes, to the tower.'

He hung up and looked intently at Tatarsky.

'And now,' he said, removing the tequila from the table, 'let's get to grips with your latest works, if you have no objection. I presume you've understood that Dima was bringing them to me?'

Tatarsky nodded.

'Right, then. As far as Parliament is concerned I must admit, it's good. But once you've latched on to a theme like that, why do you hold back? Relax ! Let yourself go all the way! Put a Yeltsin on all four tanks with a glass in his hand.'

'That's an idea,' Tatarsky agreed, inspired, sensing he was sitting opposite a man of real understanding. 'But then we'd have to take out the parliament building, give each Yeltsin a rose and make it an advertisement for that whisky . . . What's it called – the one with the roses on the label . . .'

'Four Roses bourbon?' Khanin said, and chuckled. 'Why not? We could. Make a note of it somewhere for yourself.'

He pulled several sheets of paper held together by a paperclip towards himself, and Tatarsky immediately recognised the project that had cost him so much effort for Tampako, a company that produced juices but for some reason intended to sell shares – he'd given it to Pugin two weeks before. It wasn't a scenario but a concept, that is, a product of a somewhat paradoxical genre in which the author explains, as it were, to very rich people how they should earn their living and asks them to give him a little bit of money for doing it. The pages of the familiar text were covered with dense red scribblings.

'Aha,' said Khanin, glancing over the markings, 'here I see you've got problems. In the first place, they took serious offence at one of your pieces of advice.'

'Which one?'

'I'll read it to you,' said Khanin, leafing through the pages, 'where is it now . . . it was underlined in red . . . but almost all of this part is underlined . . . aha, here it is – triple underlining. Listen:

And so there exist two methods for advertising shares: the approach that shapes the investor's image of the issuing firm, and the approach that shapes the investor's image of the investor. In the language of the professional these approaches are called 'where to invest' and 'who to invest with' . . .

'No, they actually liked that bit . . . aha, here it is:

In our opinion, before the campaign begins it would make good sense to think about changing the name of the firm. The reason for this is that Russian TV carries a lot of advertising for Tampax sanitary products. This concept is so firmly positioned in the consumers' consciousness that displacing and replacing it would involve immense expenditure. The associative link Tampako–Tampax is exceptionally inappropriate for a firm that produces soft drinks. In our opinion, it is enough to change the penultimate vowel in the firm's name: 'Tampuko' or 'Tampeko'. This completely eliminates the negative association . . .'

Khanin looked up. 'You've learned a lot of good words, can't fault you there,' he said. 'But why don't you understand you just don't go making suggestions like that? Here they've poured their life's blood into this Tampako of theirs. For them it means . . . To keep it short, these people have totally identified themselves with their product, and you start telling them things like this. You might as well tell a mother: your son's a real freak, of course, but we'll give his face a couple of licks of paint and everything'll be just fine.'

'But the name really is appalling.'

'Just who are you trying to please, them or yourself?'

Khanin was right; and Tatarsky felt doubly stupid when he remembered how he had explained the very same idea to the guys in Draft Podium at the very beginning of his career.

'What about the concept in general?' he asked. 'There's a lot of other stuff in it.'

Khanin turned over another page. 'How can I put it? Here's

another bit they've underlined, at the end, where you go on about shares again . . . I'll read it:

Thus the answer to the question 'where to invest' is 'in America', and the answer to the question 'who to invest with' is 'with everyone who didn't invest in the various pyramid schemes, but waited until it was possible to invest in America'. This is the psychological crystallisation following the first stage of the campaign – note that the advertising should not promise to place the investors' funds in America, but it should arouse the feeling that it will happen . . .

'So why the hell did you underline that? Really smart that, is it? OK, what comes next . . .

The effect is achieved by the extensive use in the image sequence of stars and stripes, dollars and eagles. It is proposed that the main symbol of the campaign should be a sequoia tree, with hundred-dollar bills instead of leaves, which would evoke a subconscious association with the money tree in the story of Pinocchio . . .'

'So what's wrong with that?' asked Tatarsky.

'The sequoia is a conifer.'

Tatarsky said nothing for a few seconds while he explored a hole he had suddenly discovered in his tooth with the tip of his tongue . . . Then he said: 'Never mind that. We can roll up the hundred-dollar bills into tubes. You know, it could be even better because it could result in a positive psychological crystallisation in the minds of a signi–'

'Do you know what "schlemazl" means?' Khanin interrupted.

'No.'

'Me neither. They've written here in the margin that they don't want this "schlemazl" – that's you – to be let anywhere near their orders again. They don't want you.'

'Fair enough,' said Tatarsky. 'So they don't want me. And what if a month from now they change their name? And in two months they start doing what I suggested? Then what?'

'Then nothing,' said Khanin. 'You know that.'

'Yes, I know,' said Tatarsky with a sigh. 'And what about the other orders? There was one for West cigarettes in there.'

'Another wash-out,' said Khanin. 'You always used to do well with cigarettes, but now . . .'

66

He turned over a few more pages.

'What can I say . . . Image sequence . . . where is it now? . . . there it is:

Two naked men shot from behind, one tall and one short, arms round each other's hips, hitch-hiking on the highway. The short one has a pack of West in his hand, the tall one has his arm raised to stop a car – a light-blue Cadillac that's coming down the road. The hand of the short man holding the pack of cigarettes is set in the same line as the uplifted arm of the tall man, thereby creating another layer of meaning – 'choreographic': the camera seems to have frozen a single moment in a passionately emotional dance, filled with the anticipation of approaching freedom. Slogan: Go West.

'That's from a song by those Sex-Shop Dogs, the one they made from our anthem, right? That part is OK. But then you have this long paragraph about the heterosexual part of the target group. What did you write that for?'

'No, well, I . . . I just thought if the customer raised the point he would know we'd covered it . . .'

'The customer raised a point all right, but not that one. The customer's an old-time hood from Rostov who's been paid two million dollars in cigarettes by some Orthodox metropolitan. In the margin beside the word "heterosexual" he's written – the bandit, that is, not the metropolitan: "Wots he on abowt, queers?" And he turned the concept down. Pity – it's a masterpiece. Now if it had been the other way round – if the bandit was paying back the metropolitan – it would all have gone down a treat. But what can you do? This business of ours is a lottery.'

Tatarsky said nothing. Khanin rolled a cigarette between his fingers to soften it and lit up.

'A lottery,' he repeated with emphasis. 'Just recently you haven't been doing too well in the draw, and I know why.'

'Tell me.'

'Well, now,' said Khanin, 'it's a very subtle point. First you try to understand what people will like, and then you hand it to them in the form of a lie. But what people want is for you to hand them the same thing in the form of the truth.'

That was not at all what Tatarsky had been expecting.

'What's that? What do you mean by "in the form of the truth"?'

'You don't believe in what you do. Your heart isn't in it.'

'No, it isn't,' said Tatarsky. 'Of course it isn't. What do you expect? Do you want me to give my heart to Tampako? There's not a single whore on Pushkin Square would do that.'

'OK, OK, just drop the pose,' said Khanin, frowning.

'No, no,' said Tatarsky, calming down, 'don't get me wrong. We're all in the same frame nowadays; you just have to position yourself correctly, right?'

'Right.'

'So why do I say not a single whore would do it? Not because I'm disgusted. It's just that a whore always collects her money every time – whether she pleased the client or not – but I have to . . . You know what I mean. And the client only makes his mind up afterwards . . . There's no way any whore would work on those terms.'

'A whore might not,' Khanin interrupted, 'but we will, if we want to survive in this business. And we'll go even further than that.'

'I don't know,' said Tatarsky. 'I'm not absolutely convinced.'

'Oh, yes we will, Babe,' said Khanin, and looked straight into Tatarsky's eyes.

Tatarsky tensed. 'How do you know my name's not Vova, but Babe?'

'Pugin told me. And as far as positioning is concerned . . . Let's just say you've positioned yourself and I get where you're coming from. Will you come and work for me full-time?'

Tatarsky took another look at the poster with the three palm trees and the promise of never-ending metamorphoses.

'What as?' he asked.

'A creative.'

'Is that a writer?' Tatarsky asked. 'Translated into ordinary Russian?'

Khanin smiled gently.

'We don't need any fucking writers here,' he said. 'A creative, Babe, a creative.'

Out on the street, Tatarsky wandered slowly in the direction of the centre.

He wasn't feeling particularly overjoyed at finding himself employed so unexpectedly. One thing was really bothering him: he was sure he'd never told Pugin the story of his real name; he'd always just called himself Vladimir or Vova. Of course, there was just an infinitesimal chance that he'd blurted it out when they were drinking and then forgotten about it – they had got very drunk together a couple of times. Any other possible explanations drew so heavily on genetically transmitted fear of the KGB that Tatarsky dismissed them out of hand. Anyway, it wasn't important.

'This game has no name,' he whispered, and clenched his fists in the pockets of his jacket.

The uncompleted Soviet ziggurat rose up in his memory in such minute detail that he felt the forgotten tingling sensation of the fly-agaric run through his fingers several times. The mystic force had gone a bit over the top this time in presenting so many signs at once to his startled soul: first the poster with the palms and the familiar line of text, then the words 'tower' and 'lottery' that Khanin had used several times in a few minutes as though by chance, and finally the name 'Babe', which had alarmed him more than anything else.

'Perhaps I misheard,' thought Tatarsky. 'Perhaps it's just his pronunciation . . . But then I asked how he knew my name was Babe, and he said he knew from Pugin. No, I should never get drunk like that, never.'

After about forty minutes of slow, pensive walking he found himself beside the statue of Mayakovsky. He stopped and studied it closely for a little while. The bronze jacket in which Soviet power had invariably dressed the poet was back in fashion now – Tatarsky remembered that only recently he'd seen exactly the same style in a Kenzo advertisement.

After walking round the statue and admiring the firm, reliable backside of the Party's loudmouth, Tatarsky finally realised that depression had invaded his soul. There were two ways he could get rid of it – down a hundred grammes of vodka, or spend about a hundred dollars on buying something immediately (some time ago Tatarsky had realised with astonishment that the two actions evoked a similar state of light euphoria lasting for an hour to an hour and a half).

He didn't fancy the vodka in view of the newly surfaced memories of his drinking bouts with Pugin. Tatarsky glanced around. There were plenty of shops, but they were all very specialised. He had no real use for blinds, for instance. He began peering at the signboards on the far side of Tverskaya Street and suddenly started in amazement. This was too much: at an acute angle to him on the wall of a building on the Garden Ring he could make out a white signboard bearing the clearly distinguishable word 'ISHTAR'.

A couple of minutes later, slightly out of breath, he was already approaching the entrance. It was a tiny fly-by-night shop, newly converted from a sandwich bar, but already bearing the imprint of decline and imminent extinction: a poster in the window promised a fifty-per-cent sale.

Inside, in the cramped space doubled by the mirrors on the walls, there were several long rails with various types of jeans and a long shelf of shoes, mostly trainers. Tatarsky cast a weary glance over the splendour of leather and rubber. Ten years ago a new pair of trainers brought in from abroad by a distant relative used to mark the starting point of a new period in your life – the design on the sole was a simulacrum of the pattern on the palm of your hand, from which you could forecast the future for a year ahead. The happiness that could be extracted from such an acquisition was boundless. Nowadays, to earn the right to the same amount you had to buy at least a jeep, maybe even a house. Tatarsky didn't have that kind of money, and he didn't expect to have it at any time in the foreseeable future. True, he could buy a whole truckload of trainers, but they didn't gladden his heart in the same way any more. Tatarsky wrinkled up his forehead as he struggled to remember what this phenomenon was called in the professional jargon; and when he remembered, he took out his notebook and opened it at the letter 'R'. 'The inflation of happiness,' he jotted down hastily: 'having to pay more money for the same amount. Use in advertising real estate: Ladies and gentlemen! These walls offer you sure-fire protection against *cognitive dissonance*! You need never even know what it is.'

'What are you looking for?' the salesgirl asked. She definitely did not like the idea of this customer writing things down in a notebook – that sort of thing ended in unannounced visits from inspectors of one kind or another.

'I'd like some shoes,' Tatarsky replied with a polite smile. 'Something light, for summer.'

'Ordinary shoes? Trainers? Gym shoes?'

'Gym shoes' said Tatarsky. 'It's years since I've seen any gym shoes.'

The girl led him over to the shelf. 'There you are,' she said. 'Platform soles.'

Tatarsky picked up a thick-soled white gym shoe.

'What make is it?' he asked.

'No name,' said the girl. 'From England.'

'What d'you mean?' he asked in astonishment.

The girl turned the back of the gym shoe to face him, and there on the heel he saw a rubber badge with the words: 'NO NAME'.

'Do you have a forty-three?' Tatarsky asked.

He left the shop wearing his new gym shoes, his old shoes in a plastic bag. He was absolutely sure now that there was some meaning to the route he was following today and he was afraid of making a mistake by taking a wrong turning. He hesitated for a moment and then set off down Sadovaya Street.

About fifty metres further on he came across a tobacco kiosk, but when he stepped up to buy some cigarettes, Tatarsky was amazed to see a wide range of condoms looking more like the display in a chemist's shop. Standing out clearly among the Malaysian Kama-Sutra condoms with their bobbled shafts was a strange semi-transparent device of blue rubber covered with a multitude of thick knobs, looking very much like the head of the main demon from the film *Hellraiser*. The label underneath it said 're-usable'.

But Tatarsky's attention was caught by a neat black, yellow and red rectangle with a German eagle in a double black circle that looked like an official seal and the inscription 'Sico'. It looked so much like a small banner that Tatarsky bought two packs on the spot. On the back of the pack it said: 'In buying Sico condoms, you put your trust in traditional German quality control.'

71

'Clever,' thought Tatarsky. 'Very clever.'

He pondered the theme for several seconds, trying to invent a slogan. Eventually the phrase he was looking for lit up in his head.

'Sico. A Porsche in the world of condoms,' he whispered, and wrote down his invention. Then he put his notebook away and looked around. He was standing on the corner of Sadovo-Triumfalnaya Street and some other street that branched off to the right. There on the wall in front of his face was a poster with the words: 'The Path to Your Self' and a yellow arrow pointing round the corner. Tatarsky's heart skipped a beat, and then the vague realisation dawned that The Path to Your Self was a shop.

'Of course, what else?' Tatarsky muttered to himself.

He only found the shop after weaving his way for ages through nearby yards and passages – near the end of his journey he remembered that Gireiev had mentioned this shop to him, but he'd used the abbreviated form of its name, PYS. There were no large signboards anywhere to be seen, nothing but a small board with the handwritten word 'Open' in the doorway of an ordinary-looking two-storey building. Tatarsky realised, of course, that things hadn't been arranged like this through lack of foresight, but in order to induce a feeling of esoteric anticipation. Nonetheless, the method worked on him as well – as he climbed the stairs leading into the shop, he was aware of a sensation of subtle reverence.

Once inside the door he knew that instinct had led him to the right place. Hanging above the counter was a black tee shirt with a portrait of Che Guevara and the inscription: 'Rage Against the Machine'. On the piece of cardboard under the tee shirt it said: 'Bestseller of the month!' There was nothing surprising about that – Tatarsky knew very well (he had even written about it in one of his concepts) that in the area of radical youth culture nothing sells as well as well-packaged and politically correct rebellion against a world that is ruled by political correctness and in which everything is packaged to be sold.

'What sizes do you have?' he asked the sales assistant, a very pretty girl in a vaguely Babylonian-Assyrian style.

'There's only one left,' she answered. 'Just your size.'

He paid, put the tee shirt in his shoulder-bag and then froze in indecision at the counter.

'We've got a new lot of crystal balls, better buy one before they all go,' purred the girl, and she began sorting out a pile of children's bibs with inscriptions in runic characters.

'What are they for?' Tatarsky asked.

'For meditation.'

Tatarsky was just about to ask whether you were supposed to meditate on something through the crystal balls or something actually in them, when he suddenly noticed a small shelf on the wall – it had been hidden behind the tee shirt he had just bought. Slumbering on the shelf under a clearly visible layer of dust were two objects of an uncertain nature.

'Tell me,' he said, 'what are those things up there? Is that a flying saucer or something? What's that pattern on it?'

'That's a supreme practice frisbee,' said the girl, 'and what you call a pattern is a blue letter "hum".'

'But what's it for?' asked Tatarsky, a vague memory of something connected with mushrooms and Gireiev nudging briefly at the edge of his awareness. 'How is it different from an ordinary frisbee?'

The girl twisted her lips into a wry expression. 'When you throw a frisbee with a blue letter "hum", you're not simply throwing a plastic disc, but accumulating merit. Ten minutes throwing a frisbee with a blue letter "hum" generates the same amount of merit as three hours of samadhi meditation or one hour of vipassana meditation.'

'A-ha,' Tatarsky drawled uncertainly. 'But merit in whose eyes?'

'What do you mean, in whose eyes!' the girl said, raising her eyebrows. 'Are you buying or do you just want to talk?'

'I'm buying,' said Tatarsky. 'But I have to know what I'm buying. What's that to the right of the supreme practice?'

'That's a ouija board, a classic.'

'What's it for?'

The girl sighed. She was obviously tired of dealing with fools all day long. She took the ouija board down from the shelf and set it on the counter in front of Tatarsky.

'You stand it on a sheet of paper,' she said. 'Or you can attach it to a printer with these clips here. In that case you put the paper in through here and set the line print speed to 'slow'. It's easier if you load a roll. In this slot here you put a pen – best to buy a helium one, with a reservoir. You put your hands on it like this, see? Then you enter into contact with the spirit and just let your hands move however they want. The pen will write out the text that's received.'

'Listen,' said Tatarsky, 'please don't be angry, I really want to know – what spirit am I supposed to contact?'

'I'll tell you if you're buying.'

Tatarsky took out his wallet and counted out the money. For a piece of varnished plywood on three wheels the ouija board was refreshingly expensive – and this disproportion between price and object inspired a trust that could hardly have been generated by any explanation, no matter how profound.

'There you go,' he said, putting the banknotes on the counter. 'So what spirit do I get in contact with?'

'The answer to that question depends on your level of personal power,' said the girl, 'and especially on your belief in the existence of spirits. If you stop your internal dialogue using the method from Castaneda's second volume, you enter into contact with the spirit of the abstract. But if you're a Christian or a Satanist, you can contact a specific spirit . . . Which kinds are you interested in?'

Tatarsky shrugged.

The girl lifted up the crystal hanging on a narrow black leather strap round her neck and looked at Tatarsky through it for two or three seconds, gazing directly at the centre of his forehead.

'What kind of job are you in?' she asked. 'What do you do?'

'Advertising,' Tatarsky answered.

The girl slipped her hand under the counter and took out an ordinary exercise book with squared paper and spent some time leafing through pages covered with tables in which the columns were completely filled with fine handwriting.

'It would be best for you,' she said at last, 'to regard the text received as a free discharge of subconscious psychic energy facilitated by the motor skills of writing. A kind of spring-cleaning for an advertising man's personal Augean stables. That approach will be less offensive to the spirits.'

'I beg your pardon,' said Tatarsky, 'do you mean to tell me that the spirits will be offended when they find out I work in advertising?'

'Yes, I think so. So the best protection against their wrath would be to doubt their existence. When it comes down to it, everything in this world is a matter of interpretation, and a quasi-scientific description of a spiritualist seance is just as correct as any other. And then, any enlightened spirit will readily agree that he doesn't exist.'

'Interesting. But how will the spirits guess that I'm in advertising? Is it written on my forehead or something?'

'No,' said the girl. 'It's written in the adverts that came out of your forehead.'

Tatarsky was about to take offence at that, but after a moment's consideration he realised that he actually felt flattered.

'I'll tell you what,' he said, 'if I need a consultation on spiritual matters, I'll come to you. You don't mind, do you?'

'All things are in the hands of Allah,' the girl answered.

'I don't know about that,' said a young man with dilated pupils, swinging round from the huge crystal ball into which he had been gazing to face the girl. 'All things? What about Buddha-consciousness? The hands of Allah only exist in Buddha-consciousness. You won't argue with that, will you?'

The girl behind the counter smiled politely.

'Of course not,' she said. 'The hands of Allah only exist in Buddha-consciousness. The catch is that Buddha-consciousness still lies in the hands of Allah.'

'As Isikawa Takuboku wrote,' interrupted a gloomy-looking customer of a Mephistophelean appearance, who had approached the counter in the meantime, '"leave off, leave off this vain dispute" . . . I was told you had Swami Zhigalkin's brochure "Summer Thoughts of a Samsaric Being". Do you think you could have a look for it? It's probably up on that shelf, no, no, over there, to the left, under the tibial flute . . .'

CHAPTER 7

Homo Zapiens

On the table the ouija board looked like a tank on the central square of a small European town. The bottle of Johnny Walker standing beside it reminded Tatarsky of the town hall, and so in his mind the red wine he was drinking was fitted into the same pattern. Its vessel, a long narrow bottle, was like a Gothic cathedral occupied by the Communist Party committee, and the void within the bottle was reminiscent of the ideological exhaustion of communism, the senselessness of bloodshed and the general crisis of the Russian idea. Setting the mouth of the bottle to his lips, Tatarsky finished what was left of the wine and tossed the bottle into the waste-paper basket. 'The velvet revolution,' he thought.

Sitting at the table in the tee shirt with the inscription: 'Rage Against the Machine', he finished reading the manual for the ouija board. The helium pen he'd bought in a kiosk by the metro fitted into the slot without any effort and he secured it in place with the screw. It was suspended on a small spring that was supposed to press it against the paper. The paper – an entire pile of it – was already lying under the ouija board. He could begin.

He glanced around the room and was just about to place his hands on the board, when he rose nervously to his feet, walked across the room and back again and drew the blinds over the windows. After another moment's thought, he lit the candle standing on the table. Any further preparations would simply have been laughable. In actual fact, even the ones he had made were ridiculous.

He sat down at the table and set his hands on the ouija board. 'OK then,' he thought, 'so now what? Should I say something out loud or not?'

'I summon the spirit of Che Guevara. I summon the spirit of

Che Guevara,' he said, and immediately thought that he ought not just to summon the spirit; he ought to ask it a question. 'I'd like to know . . . mmm, let's say, something new about advertising, something that wasn't in Al Rice or comrade Ogilvy,' he said. 'I want to understand more than anybody else.'

At that very instant the ouija board began jerking epileptically beneath his spread palms and the pen set in the slot traced out a string of large capital letters at the top of the sheet of paper:

IDENTIALISM AS THE HIGHEST STAGE OF DUALISM

Tatarsky jerked his hands away and stared in fright at the words for several seconds. Then he put his hands back and the ouija board began moving again, but this time the letters produced by the pen were small and neat:

These thoughts were originally intended for the journal of the Cuban armed forces, Oliva Verde. But it would be foolish to insist on matters of such petty detail now that we know for certain that the entire plan of existence, in which journals are published and armed forces engage in action, is simply a sequence of moments of awareness, united solely by the fact that in each new moment the concept of the preceding moments is present. Although from time without beginning this sequence remains unbroken, awareness is never actually aware of itself. Therefore the condition of man in this life is lamentable.

That great champion of the liberation of humanity, Siddhartha Gautama, has indicated in many of his works that the principle reason for the lamentable condition of man in this life is first and foremost the very conception of man's existence, life and lamentable condition – that is to say, the dualism that imposes the division into subject and object of something that in actual fact has never existed and never will.

Tatarsky pulled out the sheet of paper covered in writing, set his hands on the ouija board and it trembled into motion again:

Siddhartha Gautama was able to convey this simple truth to many people because in his time their feelings were simple and strong, and their internal world was clear and unclouded. Hearing a single word could completely change a man's entire life and transport him instantly to the other shore, to a freedom unconstrained in any way. But since that time many centuries have passed. The words of the Buddha are now accessible to all, yet salvation comes to but few. There can be no doubt that this is the result of the cultural situation that the ancient texts of all religions called the 'dark age' to come.

Comrades in the struggle! This dark age has already begun. And its onset has been brought about primarily by the role that the so-called visual-psychic generators or type-two objects have come to play in the life of man.

In speaking of the fact that dualism was engendered by the arbitrary division of the world into subject and object, the Buddha was concerned with subject–object division of the first type. The major distinguishing feature of the dark age lies in the decisive influence exerted on the life of man by subject–object division of the second type, which in the time of the Buddha simply did not exist.

In order to explain what is meant by objects of the first and second types, let us take a simple example, a television set. This is simply a box with a glass wall, which we are free to watch or not watch. When an individual's gaze falls upon a dark screen, the movement of his or her eyes is controlled exclusively by internal nerve impulses or the psychological process taking place in his or her consciousness. For instance, an individual might notice that the screen is fly-spotted. Or he or she might decide that it would be a good idea to buy a television twice as big. Or think that it would be a good idea to stand it in a different corner. Until a television is switched on it is in no way different from the objects with which people had to deal in the Buddha's time, be it a stone, the dew on a blade of grass or an arrow with a divided head – in short, everything that the Buddha used to illustrate his talks.

But when a television is turned on, it is transformed from an object of the first type into an object of the second type. It becomes a phenomenon of an entirely different order. And although the person looking at the screen does not notice this customary transformation, it is truly immense. For the viewer the television disappears as a material object that possesses weight, size and other physical properties. Instead of this the viewer has the sensation of being present in a different space, a sensation familiar to all who are assembled there.

Tatarsky glanced around, as though expecting to find himself surrounded by this assembled company, but of course there was nothing to be seen. As he removed another sheet of paper covered in writing from under the board, he figured out roughly how long the paper would last, then set his palms back against the wooden surface.

Comrades in the struggle! The question is – who is actually present? Can we say that it is the viewer himself?

Let us repeat the question, since it is extremely important: is it possible to say that the television is being watched by the individual who is watching it?

We assert that it is not, for the following reason. When the individual viewed the television while it was switched off, the movement of his or her eyes and the flow of his or her attention were controlled by his own voluntary impulses, chaotic though they may have been. The dark screen with no image of any kind did not exert any influence over them, or if it did, it was only as a background.

When it is switched on, a television almost never transmits a static view from a single motionless camera, and therefore the image on it is not a background. Quite the contrary, this image changes at an extremely rapid rate. Every few seconds there is either a change of camera angle or a fade into close-up on some object, or a switch to a different camera – the image is constantly being modified by the cameraman and the producer who stands behind him. This changing of the image is known as technomodification.

We ask you to pay particularly close attention at this point, since our next thesis is rather difficult to grasp, although in essence it is extremely simple. In addition, the feeling might arise that we are dealing with something that is insignificant. But we make bold to assert that we are in fact dealing with the most real psychological phenomenon of the end of the second millennium.

The changes in the image produced by various technomodifications can be correlated with a virtual psychological process in which the observer is forced to switch his attention from one event to another and select the most interesting content from what is taking place – that is, to manage his own attention as the makers of the programme manage it. This psychological process creates its own virtual subject, which for the duration of the television programme exists in place of the individual, fitting into his or her consciousness like a hand into a rubber glove.

This is similar to the condition of possession by a spirit. The difference lies in the fact that in this case the spirit does not exist; all that does exist are the symptoms of possession. This is a virtual spirit, but from the moment the viewer entrusts the programme-makers with redi-

recting his or her attention at will from object to object, he or she effectively becomes this spirit, and the spirit, which does not actually exist, possesses this viewer and millions of others.

What is taking place could appropriately be called the experience of collective non-existence, since the virtual subject that replaces the viewer's actual consciousness is absolutely non-existent – it is merely an effect created by the collective efforts of editors, cameramen and producers. However, for the individual watching the television there is nothing more real than this virtual subject.

Furthermore, Lapsang Suchong of the Pu Er monastery believes that if a certain programme, for instance a football game, were to be watched simultaneously by more than four-fifths of the population of Earth, this virtual effect would become capable of displacing from the aggregate human consciousness the collective karmic vision of the human plane of existence, the consequences of which could be unpredictable (it is entirely possible that to the hell of molten metal, the hell of knife trees etc. there would be added a new hell, the hell of an eternal football championship). However, his calculations have yet to be verified, and in any case this is a matter for the future. Here we are interested not so much in the frightening prospects for tomorrow as in the no less frightening reality of today.

Let us draw our first conclusion. Corresponding to the object of the second type, that is, to a television that is switched on, we have a subject of the second type – that is, a virtual viewer, who manages his or her attention in exactly the same way as a programme production crew does. Feelings and thoughts, as well as the secretion of adrenalin and other hormones in the viewer's organism, are dictated by an external operator and determined by the calculations of another individual. And of course, the subject of the first type does not notice the moment when he is displaced by the subject of the second type, since following this displacement there is no longer anyone to notice it, as the subject of the second type is unreal.

But it is not merely unreal (this word is in effect applicable to everything in the human world). There are no words to describe the degree of its unreality. It is a heaping of one unreality upon another, a castle constructed of air, the foundations of which stand upon a profound abyss. The question might arise: why are we wallowing in these non-existences, attempting to gauge the degree of their unreality? However, this difference between subjects of the first and second types is of extreme importance.

Subject number one believes that reality is the material world. But subject number two believes that reality is the material world as it is shown on the television.

As a product of false subject–object division, subject number one is illusory. But at least there is an observer of the chaotic movement of his or her thoughts and moods – in metaphorical terms we can say that subject number one is constantly watching a television programme about himself or herself, gradually forgetting that he or she is an observer and identifying with the programme.

From this point of view subject number two is something absolutely improbable and indescribable. It is a television programme watching another television programme. Emotions and thoughts participate in this process, but the individual in whose consciousness they arise is entirely absent.

The rapid switching of a television from one channel to another, which is used to avoid watching the advertisements, is known as zapping. Bourgeois thought has investigated in considerable detail the psychological condition of the individual who engages in zapping, and the corresponding thought patterns, which are rapidly becoming the basic forms of the modern world. But the type of zapping that is considered by the researchers of this phenomenon corresponds only to switching between channels by the viewer.

The switching to and fro of the viewer that is controlled by the producer and cameraman (that is, the forcible induction of subject number two by means of technomodifications) is a different type of zapping, a coercive form, study of which is effectively prohibited in every country of the world except Bhutan, where television is forbidden. But coercive zapping, whereby the television is converted into a remote control for the viewer, is not simply one method among others of organising an image sequence; it is the very foundation of television broadcasting, the major means by which the advertising–informational field exerts its influence on consciousness. From this point on, therefore, we shall refer to the type-two subject as Homo Zapiens, or HZ.

Let us repeat this extremely important conclusion: in the same way as a viewer who does not wish to watch the advertisements switches between television channels, instantaneous and unpredictable technomodifications switch the actual viewer to and fro. Assuming the condition of Homo Zapiens, the viewer becomes a remotely controlled television programme. And he or she spends a significant part of his life in this condition.

Comrades in the struggle! The position of modern man is not merely lamentable; one might even say there is no condition, because man hardly exists. Nothing exists to which one could point and say: 'There, that is Homo Zapiens.' HZ is simply the residual luminescence of a soul fallen asleep; it is a film about the shooting of another film, shown on a television in an empty house.

At this point the question logically arises of why modern man has found himself in such a situation. Who is trying to replace the already deluded Homo Sapiens with a cubic metre of empty space in the condition of HZ?

The answer, of course, is clear: nobody. But let us not become fixated on the bitter absurdity of the situation. In order to understand it in greater depth, let us recall that the main reason for the existence of television is its advertising function, which is indissolubly linked with the circulation of money. We shall therefore have to turn our attention to that area of human thought which is known as economics.

Economics is the name of a pseudo-science that deals with the illusory relations between subjects of the first and second types as they are involved in the hallucinatory process of their imaginary enrichment.

This discipline regards each individual as a cell of an organism that the economists of the ancient world knew as Mammon. In the educational materials of the Front for Full and Final Liberation it is called simply ORANUS (which translates into Russian as 'moutharse'). This more accurately reflects its real nature and leaves less scope for mystical speculation. Each of these cells – that is, each individual, when regarded as an economic entity – possesses a kind of social membrane that allows money (which plays the role of blood and lymph in the organism of oranus) to pass into and out of the cell. From the point of view of economics, the function of each of these cells is to absorb as much money as possible through this membrane and to release as little as possible back through it.

But the imperative of oranus's existence as a whole requires its cellular structure to be bathed in a constantly increasing stream of money. Therefore oranus, in the process of its evolution (and it is located at a level of evolution close to that of a mollusc) develops a primitive nervous system, the so-called 'media'. This nervous system transmits throughout its virtual organism impulses that control the activity of the monadic cells.

These impulses are of three types, which are called oral, anal and displacing wow-impulses (from the commercial ejaculation 'wow!').

The oral wow-impulse induces a cell to ingest money in order to eliminate its suffering as a result of the conflict between its self-image and the image of the ideal 'super-self' created by advertising. Note that the point does not lie in the things that can be bought for money in order to embody this ideal 'self' – the point lies in the money itself. Certainly, many millionaires walk around in rags and drive cheap cars, but in order to be able to do that one has to be a millionaire. A poor man in the same circumstances would suffer inexpressible agonies as a result of cognitive dissonance, which is why many poor people will spend their last penny in an effort to dress well.

The anal wow-impulse induces the cell to eliminate money in order to experience pleasure from the coincidence of the above-mentioned images.

Since the two actions described (the ingestion of money and its elimination) contradict each other, the anal wow-impulse acts in a concealed form, and the individual genuinely believes that the pleasure is derived not from the act of spending money, but from the acquisition of a certain object. But of course it is quite obvious that as a physical object a watch that costs fifty thousand dollars cannot afford an individual any greater pleasure than a watch that costs fifty dollars – the whole point lies in the amount of money involved.

The oral and anal wow-impulses are so called by analogy with sphincteral functions, although it would be more accurate to compare them with inhaling and exhaling; the sensation that they induce is akin to psychological asphyxia, or, by contrast, hyperventilation. This oral–anal irritation achieves its greatest intensity at the gaming table in the casino or during speculation on the stock market, although the means of wow-stimulation may take any form.

The displacing impulse suppresses and displaces from an individual's consciousness all psychological processes that might hinder total identification with a cell of oranus. It arises when a psychological stimulus contains no oral–anal components. The displacing impulse is a jamming signal that blocks the transmission from an undesirable radio-station by generating intense interference. Its mode of action is admirably expressed in the sayings: 'Money talks, bullshit walks' and, 'If you're so clever, show me your money.' Without this lever of influence oranus would not be able to make individuals function as its cells. Under the influence of the displacing impulse, which blocks out all subtle psychological processes that are not directly related to the circulation of money, the world comes to be seen exclusively as the embodiment of oranus. This produces terrifying results. For instance, one broker from the London Stock Exchange has described his hallucinatory vision of the world, induced by the displacing wow-impulse as follows: 'The world is a place where business meets money.'

It is no exaggeration to say that this psychological condition is widespread. All the questions dealt with in modern economics, sociology and culturology are in effect the description of metabolic and somatic processes occurring in the organism of oranus.

By its nature oranus is a primitive virtual organism of a parasitic type. Its distinctive feature is that it does not attach itself to any single donor organism, but makes other organisms into its own cells. Each of its cells is a human being possessing unlimited potential and endowed by nature with the right to freedom. The paradox lies in the fact that oranus as an organism stands much lower on the evolutionary scale than any of its cells. It is incapable of abstract thought, or even of self-awareness. One might say that the famous eye in the triangle that is depicted on the one-dollar note actually sees nothing. It was simply daubed on the surface of the pyramid by some cartoonist and nothing more. Therefore, to avoid confusing the theorists of conspiracy, with their inclination to schizophrenia, it would be more correct to cover the said eye with a black blindfold.

Oranus has neither ears, nor nose, nor eyes, nor mind. And of course, it is far from being the embodiment of evil or the spawn of hell that many representatives of the religious business would have it be. In itself it wishes for nothing, since it is simply incapable of wishing in the abstract. It is an inane polyp, devoid of emotion or intention, which ingests and eliminates emptiness. Each of its cells is potentially capable of realising that it is not one of oranus's cells at all, in fact just the opposite: that oranus is merely one of the insignificant objects of its mind. It is in order to block this possibility that oranus requires the displacing impulse.

Previously oranus possessed only a vegetative nervous system, but the emergence of the mass media has allowed it to evolve, developing a central nervous system. In our times oranus's most important nerve ending, which reaches every individual, is the television. We have already mentioned that the consciousness of the television viewer is displaced by the consciousness of the virtual Homo Zapiens. Now let us consider the mode of action of the three wow-impulses.

In his or her normal state the human individual is theoretically capable of identifying the wow-impulses and resisting them. But Homo Zapiens in unconscious fusion with a television broadcast is no longer a personality, merely a condition. Subject number two is not capable of analysing events, in exactly the same way as an electromagnetic recording of a cock crowing is incapable of it. Even the illusion of critical assessment of what takes place on the screen is itself part of the induced psychological process.

After every few minutes of a television programme – that is, within the consciousness of subject number two – a sequence of advertising clips is shown, each of which is a complex and carefully constructed combination of anal, oral and displacing wow-impulses, which resonate in phase with various cultural strata of the psyche.

To employ a crude analogy with physical processes, the patient is first anaesthetised (subject number one is displaced by subject number two) and then follows a rapid and intensive session of hypnosis, each stage of which is fixed in the memory by means of a conditioned reflex mechanism.

At some stage subject number two switches off the television and once again becomes subject number one – that is, an ordinary individual. After that he no longer receives the three wow-impulses directly. But an effect is produced similar in nature to residual magnetisation: the mind begins to produce the same influences for itself. They arise spontaneously and act as a background against which all other thoughts appear. While the subject in the condition of HZ is subject to the three wow-impulses, on returning to a normal condition he or she is subjected to the action of the three wow-factors that are automatically generated by his or her mind.

The constant and regular assumption by an individual of the condition of HZ and exposure to the displacing wow-impulse lead to the development in consciousness of a specific filter that allows the ingestion of only that information which is saturated with oral–anal wow-content. The individual, therefore, is not even afforded the capability of inquiring after his or her own true nature.

But just what is this true nature?

By virtue of a number of circumstances that we have no space to deal with here, each individual can only answer that question for himself or herself. No matter how lamentable the condition of the ordinary individual might be, he or she still has the opportunity to find an answer. But subject number two has no such opportunity, since he or she does not exist. Despite this (or possibly, precisely because of it), the media system of oranus, which transmits the three wow-impulses through the informational field, confronts HZ with the question of self-identification.

Now we come to our most interesting and paradoxical conclusion. Since subject number two does not possess any inner nature, the only possible answer for it is to define itself via a combination of the material objects shown on the television, which are quite clearly neither it nor any part of it. This is reminiscent of the method of apophatic theology, in which God is defined through what He is not, only here we are dealing with apophatic anthropology.

For subject number two the only possible answer to the question 'What am I?' is: 'I am the individual who drives such-and-such a car, lives in such-and-such a house, wears such-and-such a type of clothes.' Identification of the self is only possible through the compilation of a list of goods consumed, and transformation is only possible by means of a change in the list. Therefore, most objects advertised are associated with a specific personality type, character trait, propensity or quality. The result is a completely convincing combination of these properties, propensities and features, which is capable of producing the impression of a real personality. The number of possible combinations is practically unlimited, as is the scope for choice. Advertising formulates this as follows: 'I am a calm and self-confident individual, therefore I buy red slippers.' The type-two subject, wishing to add to its collection the qualities of calmness and self-confidence, achieves this by remembering that it must buy red slippers, which is accomplished under the influence of the anal wow-factor. In the classic case the oral–anal stimulation forms a closed loop, as in the famous instance of a snake biting its own tail: you need a million dollars to buy a house in an expensive neighbourhood, you need the house to have somewhere to wear your red slippers, and you need red slippers to provide you with the calmness and self-confidence that will allow you to earn a million dollars, in order to buy the house in which you can wear the red slippers, thus acquiring the qualities of calmness and confidence.

When oral–anal stimulation forms a closed loop, we can say that the goal of advertising magic has been achieved: an illusory structure is created that has no centre, although all objects and qualities are related to each other via a fictional centre that is called 'identity'.

Identity is the type-two subject at the stage of development when it is capable of existing independently without constant activation by the three wow-impulses, under the influence only of the three residual wow-factors, generated independently by its own mind.

Identity is a false ego, which says everything there is to be said about it. In its analysis of the modern human situation, bourgeois thought regards the violent escape from identity back to one's own ego as a tremendous spiritual achievement. Perhaps that really is the case, since the ego is non-existent in relative terms, while identity is absolutely non-existent. The only difficulty with this is that it is impossible, since there is nowhere to escape from or to and nobody to escape. Despite that, however, we might allow that in this situation the slogans 'Back to the ego!' or 'Forward to the ego!' do acquire, if not actual meaning, then at least a certain aesthetic justification.

The superimposition of the three wow-impulses on the more subtle processes taking place in the human psyche is the source of all of the mediocre variety of modern culture. A special role is played in this by the displacing impulse. It is like the rumbling of a pneumatic drill, which drowns out all other sounds. All external stimuli apart from the wow-oral and wow-anal impulses are filtered out, and the individual loses interest in everything that has no oral or anal component. In this brief article we do not consider the sexual aspect of advertising, but let us note in passing that more and more frequently sex becomes attractive only because it symbolises the vital energy of youth that can be transformed into money. This can be confirmed by any competent psychoanalyst. In the final analysis the modern individual experiences a profound distrust of practically everything that is not connected with the ingestion or elimination of money.

Externally this is manifested in the fact that life becomes ever more boring, and people become ever more cold and calculating. In bourgeois science the new code of behaviour is usually explained by the attempt to maintain and conserve emotional energy, which is a response to the demands of the corporate economy and the modern lifestyle. In actual fact there is no less emotional content in human life, but the unremitting influence of the displacing wow-factor results in all of the individual's emotional energy being shunted into psychological processes related to oral and anal wow-content. Many bourgeois specialists instinctively sense the part played by the mass media in the paradigm shift that is taking place, but as comrade Allende junior used to say,

'They are searching for a black cat which has never existed in a dark room which will never exist.' Even when they go so far as to call television a prosthetic support for the wrinkled and withered 'self', or say that the media inflate a personality that has become unreal, they are still missing the point.

Only a personality that was real can become unreal. In order to become wrinkled and withered, this 'self' would have had to exist. In the preceding argument, and also in our previous writings (see The Russian Question and Cedera Luminosa) we have demonstrated the groundlessness of this approach.

Under the influence of the displacing wow-factor, the culture and art of the dark age are reduced exclusively to oral–anal content. The fundamental feature of this art may be succinctly defined as 'moutharsing'.

A black bag stuffed with hundred-dollar bills has already become the supremely important cultural symbol and a central element of the majority of films and books, for which the trajectory of its path through life provides the mainspring of the plot. In more precise terms, it is the presence in the work of art of this black bag that stimulates the audience's emotional interest in what is taking place on the screen or in the text. Note that in certain instances the bag of money is not directly present, in which case its function is fulfilled either by the participation of so-called 'stars', of whom it is known as a certain fact that they have such a bag at home, or by persistently touted information about the budget of the film and its takings at the box office. In the future, not a single work of art will be created simply for its own sake; the time is approaching when books and films will appear in which the dominant element of content will be a secret hymn of praise to Coca-Cola and an attack on Pepsi-Cola – or vice-versa.

The effect of the impact of oral–anal impulses is to encourage the development in the human individual of an internal auditor (a typical market-economy variant of the 'internal party committee'). He constantly assesses reality exclusively in terms of property and performs a punitive function by forcing consciousness to suffer intolerably as a result of cognitive dissonance. The oral wow-impulse corresponds to the internal auditor holding up the flag 'loser'. The anal wow-impulse corresponds to the flag 'winner'. The displacing wow-impulse corresponds to a condition in which the internal auditor simultaneously holds up the flags 'winner' and 'loser'. It is possible to identify several stable types of identity. These are:

a) the oral wow-type (the dominant pattern around which emotional and psychological life is organised is an obsessive yearning for money)

b) the anal wow-type (the dominant pattern is the pleasurable elimination of money or the manipulation of objects that are surrogates for it, also known as anal wow-exhibitionism)

c) the displaced wow-type (possible in combination with either of the first two types), in which the individual effectively becomes insensitive to all stimuli apart from oral–anal impulses.

The relative nature of this classification can be seen from the fact that one and the same identity may be anal in relation to those who stand lower in the wow-hierarchy and oral in relation to those who stand higher (of course, there is no 'identity in itself' – we are concerned here with a pure epiphenomenon). The linear wow-hierarchy that is formed by numerous ranked identities is known as a corporate string. It is a kind of social perpetuum mobile; its secret lies in the fact that any 'identity' is obliged constantly to validate itself against another that is located one step higher. In folklore this great principle is reflected in the colloquial phrase: 'keeping up with the Joneses'.

Individuals organised according to the principle of the corporate string are like fish threaded on a line. But in this case the fish are still alive. More than that – under the influence of the oral and anal wow-factors they crawl, as it were, along the corporate string in the direction that they think of as up. They are driven to do this by instinct or, if you will, by the urge to find the meaning of life. And from the point of view of economic metaphysics the meaning of life is the transformation of the oral identity into the anal.

The implications of the situation are not exhausted by the fact that the subject who is overcome by the influence of the three residual wow-factors is obliged to regard himself or herself as an identity. Coming into contact with another human being, he or she sees him or her as an identity too. The culture of the dark age has already correlated absolutely everything that can characterise a human being with its oral–anal system of coordinates and located it in a context of endless moutharsing.

The displaced wow-individual analyses everybody he or she meets as a video clip saturated with commercial information. The external appearance of the other person, his or her speech and behaviour, are immediately interpreted as a set of wow-symbols. A very rapid and uncontrollable process is initiated, consisting of a sequence of anal, oral and displacing impulses that flare up and fade away in consciousness, determining the relations people have with each other. *Homo homini lupus est*, as one inspired Latin saying has it. But man has long ceased being a wolf to man. Man is not even an image-maker to man, as some modern sociologists assume. It is all far more terrifying and much simpler than that. Man is *wow* to man – or if not to man, then to precisely another such wow, the result of which is that, projected on to the modern system of cultural coordinates the Latin saying becomes: 'Wow Wow Wow!'

This applies not only to people, but in general to everything that falls within the range of our attention. In assessing what we are looking at, we experience a weary sense of depression if we do not encounter the familiar stimuli. Our perception is subjected to a specific form of digitization – every phenomenon is disassociated into a linear combination of anal and oral vectors. Every image can be precisely expressed in terms of money. Even if it is emphatically non-commercial, the question immediately arises of how commercially valuable that type of non-commercialism is. Hence the feeling, familiar to us all, that in the end everything comes down to money.

And indeed, everything does come down to money, because money has long since been reduced to nothing but itself, and everything else proscribed. Surges of oral–anal activity become the only permitted psychological reaction. All other mental activity is blocked.

The type-two subject is absolutely mechanistic, because it is an echo of electromagnetic processes in the cathode-ray tube of a television. The only freedom that it possesses is the freedom to say 'Wow!' when it buys another thing, which as likely as not is a new television. This is precisely why oranus's controlling impulses are called wow-impulses, and the subconscious ideology of identialism is called 'wowerism'. As for the political regime corresponding to wowerism, it is sometimes known as telecracy or mediacracy, since it is a regime under which the object of choices (and also the subject, as we have demonstrated above) is a television programme. It should be remembered that the word 'democracy', which is used so frequently in the modern mass media, is by no means the same word 'democracy' as was so widespread in the nineteenth and early twentieth centuries. The two words are merely homonyms. The old word 'democracy' was derived from the Greek 'demos', while the new word is derived from the expression 'demo-version'.

And so, let us sum up.

Identialism is dualism at that stage of development when the major corporations are finalising the division of human consciousness which, being under the constant influence of oral, anal and displacing wow-impulses, begins independently to generate the three corresponding wow-factors. This results in the stable and permanent displacement of the personality and the appearance in its place of the so-called 'identity'. Identialism is dualism that possesses a triple distinction. It is dualism that is: a) dead; b) putrid; c) digitised.

Numerous different definitions of identity could be provided, but this would be a senseless exercise, because in any case it does not exist in reality. At the stage of identialism, the individual for whose freedom it was once possible to fight disappears completely from the field of view.

It follows, therefore, that the end of the world, which is the inevitable outcome of the wowerisation of consciousness, will present absolutely no danger of any kind – for the very subject of danger is disappearing. The end of the world will simply be a television programme. And this, comrades in the struggle, fills us all with inexpressible bliss.

Che Guevara
Mt Shumeru, eternity, summer.

'Sumer again. We're all Sumerians, then,' Tatarsky whispered quietly and looked up. The grey light of a new day was trembling beyond the blind at the window. To the left of the ouija board lay a heap of paper covered in writing, and the weary muscles of his forearms ached. The only thing he could remember from all that writing was the expression 'bourgeois thought'. Getting up from the table, he went across to the bed and threw himself on to it without getting undressed.

'Just what is bourgeois thought?' he wondered. 'God only knows. About money, I suppose. What else?'

CHAPTER 8

A Safe Haven

The lift that was elevating Tatarsky towards his new job contained only a single solitary graffito, but even that was enough to make it clear at a glance that the heart of the advertising business beat somewhere close at hand. The graffito was a variation on a classic theme, the advertisement for Jim Beam whisky in which a simple basic hamburger evolved into a complex, multi-tiered sandwich, then the sandwich became an even more intricate baguette, and finally the baguette turned back into the basic hamburger, which all went to show that everything returns to its origins. Traced out on the wall in gigantic three-dimensional letters casting a long drawn shadow were the words: FUCK YOU.

Written below it in small letters was the original Jim Beam slogan: 'You always get back to the basics.'

Tatarsky was simply delighted at the way the entire evolutionary sequence implied in the inscriptions had simply been omitted – he could sense the laconic hand of a master at work. What was more, despite the risqué nature of the subject, there wasn't even the slightest trace of Freudianism in the text.

It was quite possible that the unknown master was one of his two colleagues who also worked for Khanin. They were called Seryozha and Malyuta, and they were almost complete opposites. Seryozha, a short man with light hair, wore gold-rimmed spectacles and strove with all his might to resemble a Western copywriter, but since he didn't know what a Western copywriter actually looked like and relied on nothing but his own strange ideas about the matter, the impression he actually produced was of something touchingly Russian and very nearly extinct.

Malyuta, a robust slob in a dirty denim suit, was Tatarsky's comrade in misfortune – he had also suffered from his romantically-minded parents' love for exotic names – in this case the name borne by Ivan the Terrible's most infamous lieutenant – but that didn't make them close. When he began talking to Tatarsky about his favourite theme, geopolitics, Tatarsky said that in his opinion it consisted mostly of an irresolvable conflict between the right hemisphere and the left that certain people suffer with from birth. After that Malyuta began behaving towards him in an unfriendly fashion.

Malyuta was a frightening individual in general. He was a rabid anti-Semite, not because he had any reason to dislike Jews, but because he tried as hard as he could to maintain the image of a patriot, logically assuming there was nothing else a man called Malyuta could do with his life. All the descriptions of the world Malyuta encountered in the analytical tabloids were in agreement that anti-Semitism was an indispensable element of the patriotic image. The result was that, following long efforts to mould his own image, Malyuta had come to resemble most of all a villain from Bin Laden's gang in a stupid low-budget action movie, which started Tatarsky wondering whether these low-budget action movies were quite so stupid after all, if they were capable of transforming reality after their own image.

When they were introduced, Tatarsky and Khanin's other two employees exchanged folders of their work; it was a bit like the mutual positioning of dogs sniffing each other's ass the first time they meet. Leafing through the works in Malyuta's folder, Tatarsky several times found himself shuddering in horror. The very same future he had playfully described in his concept for Sprite (the folk-costume image of the pseudo-Slavonic aesthetic, visible ever more clearly through the dark, swirling smoke of a military coup) was present in full-blown form in these sheets typed with carbon paper. Tatarsky was particularly badly shaken by the scenario for a Harley-Davidson clip:

A street in a small Russian town. In the foreground a rather blurred, out-of-focus motorcycle, looming over the viewer. In the distance is a church; the bell is ringing. The service has only just finished and people are walking down along the street. Among the passers-by are two young men wearing red Russian shirts outside their trousers – they could be

93

cadets from military college on holiday. Close-up: each of them is carrying a sunflower in his hands. Close-up: a mouth spitting out a husk. Close-up: foreground – the handlebars and petrol tank of the motorcycle, behind it – our heroes, gazing obsessively at the motorcycle. Close-up: fingers breaking seeds out of a sunflower. Close-up: the two heroes exchange glances; one says to the other:

'Sergeant in our platoon was called Harley. A real bull of a man. But he took to the drink.'

'Why'd he do that?'

'You know. No one gives a Russian a chance these days.'

Next frame – a Hassidic Jew of massive proportions comes out of the door of a house wearing a black leather jacket and a black wide-brimmed hat. Beside him our two heroes appear skinny and puny – they involuntarily take a step backwards. The Jew gets on to the motorcycle, starts it up with a roar, and a few seconds later has disappeared from view – all that's left is a blue haze of petrol smoke. Our two heroes exchange glances again. The one who recalled the sergeant spits out a husk and says with a sigh:

'Just how long can the Davidsons keep riding the Harleys? Russia, awake!'

(Or: 'World history. Harley-Davidson'. A possible softer version of the slogan: 'The Harley motorcycle. Not to say Davidson's.')

At first Tatarsky decided it must be a parody, and only after reading Malyuta's other texts did he realise that for Malyuta sunflowers and sunflower-seed husks were positive aesthetic characteristics. Having been convinced by the analytical tabloids that sunflower seeds were inseparably fused with the image of a patriot, Malyuta had cultivated his love of them as dedicatedly and resolutely as he cultivated his anti-Semitism.

The second copywriter, Seryozha, would leaf for hours at a time through Western magazines, translating advertising slogans with a dictionary, on the assumption that what worked for a vacuum cleaner in one hemisphere might well do the job for a wall-clock ticking away in the other. In his good English he would spend hours interrogating his cocaine dealer, a Pakistani by the name of Ali, about the cultural codes and passwords to which Western advertising made reference. Ali had lived for a long time in Los Angeles and even if he couldn't provide explanations for the most obscure elements of obscurity, he could at least lie convincingly about what he didn't understand. Perhaps it was Seryozha's intimate familiarity with advertising theory and Western culture in general that made him think so highly of the first job Tatarsky based on the secret wow-technology imparted by *commendante* Che during the seance. It was an advert for a tourist firm organising tours to Acapulco. The slogan was:

WOW! ACAPULYPSE NOW!

'Right on!' Seryozha said curtly, and shook Tatarsky by the hand.

Tatarsky in turn was quite genuinely delighted by one of Seryozha's early works, which the author himself regarded as a failure:

No, you're not a sailor any more ... Your friends will reproach you for your indifference. But you will only smile in reply – you never really were a sailor anyway. All your life you've simply been heading for this safe haven.

SAFE HAVEN. THE PENSION FUND

Malyuta never touched Western magazines – he only ever read the tabloids, or *The Twilight of the Gods*, always with a bookmark in one and the same place. But soon Tatarsky was astonished to notice that for all their serious differences in intellectual orientation and personal qualities, Seryozha and Malyuta were both sunk equally deeply in the bottomless pit of moutharsing. It was evident in numerous details and traits of behaviour. For instance, when they spoke to Tatarsky about a certain common acquaintance of theirs, both of them in turn described him as follows:

'You know,' said Seryozha, 'in psychological terms he's something like a novice broker who earns six hundred dollars a month, but is counting on reaching fifteen hundred by the end of the year ...'

'And then,' added Malyuta, raising a finger, 'when he takes his dame out to Pizza Hut and spends forty dollars on the two of them he thinks it's a big deal.'

Immediately following this phrase Malyuta was overwhelmed by the influence of the anal wow-factor: he took out his expensive mobile phone, twirled it between his fingers and made an entirely unnecessary call.

Apart from all that, Seryozha and Malyuta actually turned out a remarkably similar product – Tatarsky realised this when he discovered two works devoted to the same item in their folders.

Two or three weeks before Tatarsky joined the staff, Khanin's office had submitted a big order to a client. Some shady customers, who urgently needed to sell a large lot of fake runners, had ordered an advert from Khanin for Nike – that was the brand their canvas slippers were disguised to look like. The intention was to off-load the goods at the markets around Moscow, but the lot was so large that the shady characters, having mumbled a few incantations over their calculators, had decided to shell out for a television advert in order to accelerate their turnover. And the kind of ad they wanted had to be heavy stuff – 'the kind,' as one of them said, 'that'll do their heads in straight off'. Khanin submitted two versions, Seryozha's and Malyuta's. Seryozha, who read at least ten textbooks on advertising written in English while he was working on the job, produced the following text:

The project employs an American cultural reference familiar to the Russian consumer from the mass media – that is, the mass suicide of members of the occult group Heaven's Gate from San Diego, which was intended to allow them to make the transition to their subtle bodies so that they could travel to a comet. All those who killed themselves were lying on simple two-level bunk-beds; the video sequence was shot strictly in black and white. The faces of the deceased were covered with simple black cloth, and on their feet they were wearing black Nike runners with a white symbol, the so-called 'swoosh'. In aesthetic terms the proposed video is based on an Internet clip devoted to the event – the picture on the television screen duplicates the screen of a computer monitor, in the centre of which well-known frames from a CNN report are repeated in sequence. At the end, when the motionless soles of the runners with the inscription 'Nike' have been displayed for long enough, the shot shifts to the end-board of a bed with a sheet of Whatman paper glued to it, on which a 'swoosh' looking like a comet has been drawn with a black felt-tip pen:

The camera moves lower, and we see the slogan, written in the same felt-tip pen:

JUST DO IT.

While Malyuta was working on his scenario he didn't read anything at all except the gutter tabloids and so-called patriotic newspapers with their scatalogically eschatalogical positioning of events; but he obviously must have watched a lot of films. His version went like this:

A street in a small Vietnamese village lost deep in the jungle. In the foreground a typical third-world country Nike workshop – we recognise it from the sign: NIKE sweatshop No. 1567903. All around there are tall tropical trees, a section of railway line suspended on the village fence rings like a bell. Standing in the doorway of the workshop is a Vietnamese with a Kalashnikov automatic rifle, wearing khaki trousers and a black shirt, which automatically bring to mind the film The Deer Hunter. *Close-up: hands on an automatic rifle. The camera enters the door and we see two rows of work-tables with workers who are chained in place sitting at them. The scene brings to mind the galley scene from the film* Ben Hur. *All of the workers are wearing incredibly old, torn and tattered American military uniforms. They are the last American prisoners of war. On the table in front of them there are Nike runners in various stages of completion. All of the prisoners of war have curly black beards and hooked noses. (This last phrase was written in between the lines in pencil – evidently the inspiration had struck Malyuta after the text had been printed.) The prisoners of war are dissatisfied with something – at first they murmur quietly, then they start banging on the tables with the half-glued runners. There are shouts of:* 'We demand a meeting with the American consul!' *and,* 'We demand a visit from a UN commissioner!' *Suddenly a burst of automatic rounds is fired into the ceiling, and the noise instantly ceases. The Vietnamese in the black shirt is standing in the doorway, with a smoking automatic in his hands. The eyes of everyone in the room are fixed on him. The Vietnamese strokes his automatic rifle, then jabs his finger in the direc-*

97

tion of the nearest table with half-finished runners and says in broken English: 'Just do it!'

Voice-over: 'Nike. Good 2, Evil 0.'

Once when he caught Khanin alone in his office, Tatarsky asked: 'Tell me, this work Malyuta produces – does it ever get accepted?'

'It does,' said Khanin, putting aside the book he was reading. 'Of course it does. The runners may be American, but they have to be sold to the Russian mentality. So it all suits very well. We edit it a bit, of course, so as not to fall foul of the law.'

'And you say the advertisers like it?'

'The advertisers we have here have to have it explained to them what they like and what they don't. And anyway, why does any advertiser give us an ad?'

Tatarsky shrugged.

'No, go on, tell me.'

'To sell product.'

'That's in America – to sell product.'

'Then so he can feel like a big-shot.'

'That was three years ago,' Khanin said in a didactic tone. 'Things are different now. Nowadays the client wants to show the big guys who keep a careful eye on what's happening on screen and in real life that he can simply flush a million dollars down the tubes; and for that, the worse his advert is, the better. The viewer is left with the feeling that the client and the producers are absolute idiots, but then' – Khanin raised one finger and his eyes twinkled wisely – 'the signal indicating how much money it costs reaches the viewer's brain. The final conclusion about the client is as follows – he may be a total cretin, but his business is doing so well he can afford to put out any old crap over and over again. And that's the best kind of advertising there can possibly be. A man like that will get credit anywhere, no sweat.'

'Complicated,' said Tatarsky.

'Sure it is. There's more to it than reading your Al Rice.'

'And where can you gather such profound insight into life?' asked Tatarsky.

'From life itself,' Khanin said with feeling.

Tatarsky looked at the book lying on the desk in front of him. It looked exactly like a Soviet-era secret edition of Dale Carnegie for Central Committee members – there was a three-digit copy number on the cover and below that a typed title: *Virtual Business and Communications*. There were several bookmarks set in the book: on one of them Tatarsky read the words: 'Suggest. schizo-blocks'.

'Is that something to do with computers?' he asked.

Khanin picked up the book and hid it away in the drawer of his desk.

'No,' he replied unwillingly. 'It actually is about virtual business.'

'And what's that?'

'To cut it short,' said Khanin, 'it's business in which the basic goods traded are space and time.'

'How's that?'

'It's just like things are here in Russia. Look around: the country hasn't produced anything for ages. Have you done a single advertising project for a product produced here?'

'I can't recall one,' Tatarsky replied. 'Hang on, though, there was one – for Kalashnikov. But you could call that an image ad.'

'There, you see,' said Khanin. 'What's the most important feature of the Russian economic miracle? Its most important feature is that the economy just keeps on sinking deeper and deeper into the shit, while business keeps on growing stronger and expanding into the international arena. Now try this: what do the people you see all around you trade in?'

'What?'

'Things that are absolutely non-material. Air time and advertising space – in the newspapers or out on the street. But time in itself can't be air time, just as space in itself can't be advertising space. The first person who managed to unite time and space via the fourth dimension was the physicist Einstein. He had this theory of relativity – maybe you've heard of it. Soviet power did it as well, only via a paradox – you know that. They lined up the guys in the camps, gave them shovels and told them to dig a trench from the fence as far as lunchtime. But

now it's very easily done – one minute of prime air time costs the same as a two-column colour ad in a major magazine.'

'Then that means the fourth dimension is money?' asked Tatarsky.

Khanin nodded.

'Not only that,' he said, 'from the point of view of monetarist phenomenology, it is the substance from which the world is constructed. There was an American philosopher called Robert Pirsig who believed that the world consists of moral values; but that was just the way things could seem in the sixties – you know, the Beatles, LSD, all that stuff. A lot more has become clear since then. Have you heard about the cosmonauts' strike?'

'I think I heard something,' Tatarsky answered, vaguely recalling some newspaper article.

'Our cosmonauts get twenty to thirty thousand dollars a flight. The Americans get two hundred or three hundred thousand. So our guys said: "We're not going to fly at thirty grand; we want to fly at three hundred grand too." What does that mean? It means they're not really flying towards the twinkling points of light of those unknown stars, but towards absolutely specific sums of hard currency. Such is the nature of the cosmos. And the non-linear nature of time and space is expressed in the fact that we and the Americans burn equal amounts of fuel and fly equal numbers of kilometres in order to arrive at absolutely different amounts of money. That is one of the fundamental secrets of the Universe . . .'

Khanin suddenly broke off and began to light a cigarette, clearly winding up the conversation. 'Now go and get some work done,' he said.

'Can I read the book some time?' Tatarsky asked, nodding towards the desk where Khanin had hidden his secret text. 'For my general development?'

'All in good time,' said Khanin, giving him a sweet smile.

Even without any secret handbooks Tatarsky was already beginning to find his bearings in the commercial relations of the age of virtual business. As he was quick to realise from observing the behaviour of his colleagues at work, the basis of these relations was so-called 'black PR', or as Khanin pronounced it in full: 'black public relations'. The first time Tatarsky heard the words the bard of the Literary Institute was resurrected briefly in his soul, intoning in sombre tones: 'Black public relations, uniting all nations . . .' But there wasn't actually any real romantic feeling behind this abbreviation, and it was entirely devoid of the baggage of negative connotations ascribed to it by those who use the phrase 'black PR' to mean an attack mounted via the mass media.

It was actually quite the opposite – advertising, like other forms of human activity in the vast, cold expanses of Russia, was inextricably intertwined with the 'black cash flow', which in practical terms meant two things. Firstly, journalists were quite willing to deceive their newspapers and magazines by extracting black cash from anyone who more or less naturally fell within their field of attention – and it wasn't just restaurant-owners who wanted to be compared with Maxim's who had to pay, but writers who wanted to be compared with Marquez, which meant that the boundary between literary and restaurant criticism grew ever finer and more arbitrary. Secondly, copywriters took pleasure in deceiving their agencies by finding a client through them and then concluding an unwritten deal with him behind their bosses' backs. After he'd taken a good look around, Tatarsky took a cautious first step on to this fruitful ground, where he met with immediate success: he managed to sell his slightly modified project for Finlandia vodka (the new slogan was: 'Reincarnation Now!').

Usually he dealt with lowly cogs in the PR machinery, but this time he was summoned to the owner of the firm that intended to take on the dealership for Finlandia, who was a dour and serious-minded youth. Having read several times through the two pages Tatarsky had brought, he chuckled, thought for a moment, rang his secretary and asked her to prepare the paperwork. Half an hour later a stunned Tatarsky emerged on to the street, carrying in his inside pocket an envelope containing two and a half thousand dollars and a contract for the full and unconditional transfer of all rights to the young man's company.

For those changed times this was an absolutely fantastic haul.

But a couple of months later Tatarsky accidentally discovered an incredibly insulting little detail: it turned out Finlandia's future distributor hadn't paid up because he'd decided to use his text in his advertising, but because he was afraid Tatarsky might sell it to Absolut or Smirnoff dealers. Tatarsky even started to write a sonnet dedicated to this event, but after a couple of minutes discarded it as non-functional. In general, it was hard to believe that not so very long ago he had been wont to spend so much time searching for meaningless rhymes that had long since been abandoned by the poetry of the market democracies. It seemed simply inconceivable that only a few short years ago life had been so gentle and undemanding that he could waste entire kilowatts of mental energy in dead-end circuits of his brain that never paid back the investment.

Tatarsky suspected that black PR was a more widespread and significant phenomenon than just a means of survival for certain protein-based life-forms in the era of the mass media; but he couldn't connect up his heterogeneous suspicions concerning the true nature of the phenomenon to form a clear and unified understanding. There was something missing.

'Public relations are people's relations with each other,' he jotted down in confused fashion in his notebook.

People want to earn money in order to gain freedom, or at least a breathing space from their interminable suffering. And we copywriters manipulate reality in front of people's eyes so that freedom comes to be symbolised by an iron, or a sanitary towel with wings, or lemonade. That's what they pay us for. We pawn this stuff off on them from the screen, and then they pawn it off on each other, and on us who write the stuff, and it's like radioactive contamination, when it makes no difference any longer who exploded the bomb. Everyone tries to show everyone else that they've already achieved freedom, and as a result, while we pretend to socialise and be friendly, all we really do is keep pawning each other off with all sorts of jackets, mobile phones and cars. It's a closed circle. And this closed circle is called black PR.

Tatarsky became so absorbed in his thoughts on the nature of this phenomenon that he wasn't in the least surprised when one day Khanin stopped him in the corridor, grabbed hold of one of his buttons and said: 'I see you know all there is to know about black PR.'

'Almost,' Tatarsky answered automatically, because he'd just been thinking about the topic. 'There's just some central element that's still missing.'

'I'll tell you what it is. What's missing is the understanding that black public relations only exist in theory. What happens in real life is grey PR.'

'That's interesting,' said Tatarsky enthusiastically, 'very interesting! Quite astounding! But what does it mean in practical terms?'

'In practical terms it means you have to shell out.'

Tatarsky started. The fog of thoughts clouding his mind was dispersed in an instant to be replaced by a terrifying clarity.

'How d'you mean?' he asked feebly.

Khanin took him by the arm and led him along the corridor.

'Did you take delivery of two grand from Finlandia?' he asked.

'Yes,' Tatarsky replied uncertainly.

Khanin bent the middle and fourth fingers of his hand over slightly – far enough to suggest that he was about to shift to the hand-gestures characteristic of New Russian thugs, but not too far, so the situation still seemed to be peaceful.

'Now remember this,' he said quietly. 'As long as you work here, you work to me. There's no other way to figure it and make sense. So the figures say one grand of greenbacks is mine. Or were you thinking of setting up on your own?'

'I, I . . . I'd be delighted . . .' Tatarsky stammered in a state of shock. 'That is, of course I don't want to . . . That is, I do. I wanted to split it; I just didn't know how to bring up the subject.'

'No need to be shy about it. Someone might get the wrong idea. You know what? Why don't you come round to my place this evening. We can have a drink and a talk. And you can drop in the mazuma while you're at it.'

Khanin lived in a large, newly refurbished flat, in which Tatarsky was astonished by the patterned oak doors with gold locks – what astonished him about them was the fact that the wood had already cracked and the gaps in the panels had been filled in a slapdash fashion with mastic. Khanin was already drunk when he greeted his guest. He was in an excellent mood – when Tatarsky held out the envelope to him from the doorway, Khanin knitted his brows and waved it aside, as though offended at such a brusque businesslike entrance, but at the extreme extent of the gesture he lifted the envelope out of Tatarsky's fingers and immediately tucked it away somewhere.

'Let's go,' he said, 'Liza's cooked something.'

Liza proved to be a tall woman with a face red from some kind of cosmetic scrubbing. She fed Tatarsky stuffed cabbage leaves, which he had hated ever since he was a small child. In order to overcome his revulsion he drank a lot of vodka, and by the time the dessert arrived he had almost reached Khanin's state of intoxication, which meant socialising went a lot smoother.

'What's that you have up there?' Tatarsky asked, nodding in the direction of the wall.

There was a reproduction of a Stalinist poster hanging at the spot he indicated: ponderous red banners with yellow tassels and the blue-looking Moscow university building visible in the gaps between them. The poster was obviously twenty years or thereabouts older than Tatarsky, but the print was absolutely fresh.

'That? A young guy who used to work for us before you did that on the computer,' answered Khanin. 'You see, there used to be a hammer and sickle there, and a star, but he took them out and put in Coca-Cola and Coke instead.'

'Yes, I see,' Tatarsky said, amazed. 'But you can't see it at first – they're exactly the same yellow colour.'

'If you look closely you'll see it. I used to have the poster over my desk, but the other guys started getting awkward about it. Malyuta took offence for the flag and Seryozha took offence for Coca-Cola. In the end I had to bring it home.'

'Malyuta took offence?' Tatarsky asked in surprise 'Have you seen what he put up over his own desk yesterday?'

'Not yet.'

'"Every pogrom has its programme, every brand has its bend".'

'So what?'

Tatarsky suddenly realised that Khanin really didn't see anything strange in such sentiments. And what was more, he suddenly stopped seeing anything strange in them himself.

'I didn't understand what it meant: "Every brand has its bend".'

'Bend. That's the way we translate the expression "brand essence". That's to say, the concentrated expression of a comprehensive image policy. For instance, the Marlboro bend or essence is a country of real men. The Parliament essence is jazz, and so on. You mean you didn't know that?'

'No, of course I knew that. What d'you take me for? It's just a very odd kind of translation.'

'What's to be done about it?' said Khanin. 'This is Asia.'

Tatarsky got up from the table. 'Where's your toilet,' he asked.

'First door after the kitchen.'

When he stepped into the toilet, Tatarsky's gaze was confronted by a photograph of a diamond necklace with the text: 'De Beers. Diamonds are for ever', hanging on the wall facing the door. This rather threw him off balance and for several seconds he couldn't recall why he was there. When he remembered, he tore off a sheet of toilet paper and wrote on it:

1) *Brand essence (bend). Include in all concepts in place of 'psychological crystallisation'.*

2) *Parliament with tanks on the bridge. Instead of 'the smoke of the Motherland' – 'All that jazz'.*

Tucking the piece of paper into his breast pocket and flushing the toilet conspiratorially, he went back to the kitchen and walked right up to the Coca-Cola red banners.

'It's quite incredible,' he said. 'Looks like it said "Coke" on this flag from the very beginning.'

'So what did you expect? What's so surprising about that? D'you know what the Spanish for "advertising" is?' Khanin hiccupped: '"Propaganda." So you and me are ideological workers, if you hadn't realised it yet. Propagandists and agitators. I used to work in ideology, as it happens. At Komsomol Central Committee level. All my friends are bankers now; I'm the only one .... I tell you, I didn't have to reconstruct myself at all. It used to be: "The individual is nothing, the collective is everything," and now it's: "Image is nothing, thirst is everything." Agitprop's immortal. It's only the words that change.'

Tatarsky felt an uneasy presentiment.

'Listen,' he said, 'you didn't happen to speak at party personnel meetings outside Moscow, did you?'

'Yes, I did,' said Khanin. 'Why?'

'In Firsanovka?'

'Yes, in Firsanovka.'

'So that's it,' said Tatarsky, gulping down his vodka. 'All the time I had this feeling your face was familiar, but I couldn't remember where I'd seen it. Only you didn't have a beard then.'

'You mean you used to go to Firsanovka too?' Khanin asked in delighted surprise.

'Only once,' Tatarsky answered. 'You came out on the platform with such a hangover I thought you were going to puke the moment you opened your mouth . . .'

'Hey, take it easy in front of the wife . . . Although you're right: the main reason we went out there was to drink. Golden days!'

'And so what happened? You came out with this great speech,' Tatarsky continued. 'I was studying at the Literary Institute at the time, and it really upset me. I felt jealous, because I realised I would never learn to manipulate words like that. No sense to it whatsoever, it just blew me away; all at once everything was absolutely clear. That's to say, what the speaker – you – was trying to say wasn't clear, because he didn't really want to say anything, but everything in life was clear. I suppose that's what those party personnel meetings were held for. I sat down to write a sonnet that evening, but I just got drunk instead.'

'What was I speaking about, d'you remember?' Khanin asked. He obviously found reminiscing pleasant.

'Something or other to do with the twenty-seventh Party congress and its significance.'

Khanin cleared his throat: 'I think there is no need to explain to you Komsomol activists,' he said in a loud, well-trained voice, 'why the decision of our Party's twenty-seventh congress are regarded as not merely significant, but epoch-making. Nonetheless, the methodological distinction between these two concepts occasions misunderstanding even among propagandists and agitators. After all, the propagandists and agitators are the builders of our tomorrow, and they should not be unclear in any way about the plan for the future that they have to build . . .'

He hiccupped loudly and lost the thread of his speech.

'That's it, that's it,' said Tatarsky. 'I recognise you now all right. The most amazing thing is that you actually did spend an entire hour explaining the methodological difference between "significant" and "epoch-making", and I understood every single sentence perfectly. But if I tried to understand any two sentences together, it was like running my head against a brick wall . . . There was just no way. And there was no way I could repeat it in my own words. But then, on the other hand . . . What's "Just do it" supposed to mean? And what's the methodological difference between "Just do it" and "Just be"?'

'Exactly what I'm getting at,' said Khanin, pouring the vodka. '''S exactly the same.'

'What are you men doing drinking away like that?' put in Liza, speaking for the first time. 'You might at least propose a toast.'

'OK, let's have a toast,' said Khanin, and he hiccupped again. 'Only, you know, one that's not only significant, but epoch-making as well. Komsomol member to party member, you follow?'

Tatarsky held on to the table as he rose to his feet. He looked at the poster and thought for a second before raising his glass and speaking:

'Comrades! Let us drown the Russian bourgeoisie in a flood of images!'

CHAPTER 9

The Babylonian Stamp

On arriving home, Tatarsky felt the kind of energy rush he hadn't experienced in ages. Khanin's metamorphosis had positioned the entire recent past in such a strange perspective it simply had to be followed by something miraculous. Pondering on what he might amuse himself with, Tatarsky strode restively around the flat several times until he remembered the acid tab he had bought in the Poor Folk bar. It was still lying in the drawer of the desk – in all that time he'd not had any reason to swallow it, and anyway he'd been afraid.

He went over to the desk, took the lilac-coloured stamp out of the drawer and looked at it carefully. The face with the pointed beard smirked up at him; the stranger was wearing an odd kind of hat, something between a helmet and a dunce's cap with a very narrow brim. 'Wears a pointed cap,' thought Tatarsky; 'probably a jester, then. That means it'll be fun.' Without giving it any more thought, he tossed the tab into his mouth, ground it up between his teeth and swallowed down the small ball of soft fibres. Then he lay down on the divan and waited.

He was soon bored just lying there. He got up, lit a cigarette and walked around the flat again. Reaching the closet, he remembered that since his adventure in the forest outside Moscow he hadn't taken another look into the 'Tikhamat-2' folder. It was a classic case of displacement: not once had he recalled that he wanted to finish reading the materials in the file, although, on the other hand, he didn't really seem to have forgotten it either. It had been exactly the same story with the acid tab, as though both of these items had been reserved for that special occasion which, in the course of normal life, never arrives. Tatarsky took down the folder from the top shelf and went back into the room. There were a lot of photographs inside, glued to the pages. One of them fell out as soon as he opened the folder, and he picked it up from the floor.

The photo showed a fragment of a bas-relief – a section of sky with large stars carved into it. In the lower part of the photograph there were two upraised arms, cut off by the edge of the shot. These were genuine stars of heaven – ancient, immense and alive. Stars like that had long ago ceased to shine for the living and continued to exist only for stone heroes in antediluvian sculptures. But then, thought Tatarsky, the stars themselves can hardly have changed since then – it's people who've changed. Each star consisted of a central circle and pointed rays with bundles of sinuous parallel lines set between them.

Tatarsky noticed there were almost invisible little red and green veins twinkling around the lines, as though he was watching a badly adjusted computer monitor. The shiny surface of the photograph took on a brilliant rainbow gleam and its glimmering began to occupy more of his attention than the actual image. 'It's started,' thought Tatarsky. 'Now that's really quick . . .'

Finding the page the photograph had come unstuck from, he ran his tongue across the dried-up spot of casein glue and set it back in its place. Then he carefully turned over the page and smoothed it down with the palm of his hand, so the photograph would stick properly. Glancing at the next photo, he almost dropped the folder on the floor.

The photograph showed the same face as on the lilac tab-stamp. It was shown from a different angle, in profile, but there was absolutely no doubt about it.

It was a complete photograph of the same bas-relief. Tatarsky recognised the fragment with the stars – they were small now and hard to pick out, and the arms uplifted towards them turned to belong to the tiny figure of a man standing on the roof of a house, frozen in a pose of absolute terror.

The central figure in the bas-relief, whose face Tatarsky had recognised, was several times larger than the figure on the roof and all the other figures around it. It was a man wearing a pointed iron cap with a mysterious, half-drunk smile playing about his lips. His face seemed strangely, even absurdly out of place in the ancient image – it looked so natural Tatarsky could easily have believed the bas-relief had not been made three thousand years ago in Nineveh, but some time late last year in Yerevan or Calcutta. Instead of the spade-shaped beard with symmetrical curls an ancient Sumerian was supposed to wear, the man was wearing a sparse goatee, and he looked like a cross between Cardinal Richelieu and Lenin.

Tatarsky hastily turned over the page and found the text relating to the photograph.

Enkidu (Enki fecit) is a fisherman-god, the servant of the god Enki (Lord of the Earth). He is the god of the Great Lottery and protector of ponds and canals; there are also examples of spells invoking Enkidu against various ailments of the digestive tract. He was made from clay, like Adam in the Old Testament story – the clay tablets with the questions for the Lottery were believed to be the flesh of Enkidu, and the ritual drink prepared in his temple was his blood . . .

It was hard to read the text – the sense wasn't getting through to him, and the letters were shimmering and blinking in all the colours of the rainbow. Tatarsky began studying the image of the deity in detail. Enkidu was draped in a mantle covered with oval plaques and in his hands he held bundles of strings that radiated out like fans towards the ground, so that he reminded Tatarsky of Gulliver with an army of Lilliputians trying to restrain him by cables attached to his arms. None of the pools and canals Enkidu was supposed to be concerned with were to be seen anywhere – he was walking through a burning city, where the houses came up to his waist. Under his feet lay prostrate figures with their arms extended in identical gestures – looking at them, Tatarsky noted the quite definite kinship between Sumerian art and socialist realism. The most interesting detail of the image were the strings radiating from Enkidu's hands. Each string ended in a large wheel, in the centre of which was a triangle containing the crudely traced image of an eye. There were human bodies threaded on the strings – like the fish Tatarsky used to dry in his childhood, hanging them out in the yard on a length of fishing line.

On the next page there was an enlarged fragment of the bas-relief showing the little human figures on one of the strings. Tatarsky was even slightly nauseated. With quite repulsive realism, the bas-relief showed the cable entering each human figure at the mouth and exiting from its backside. Some of the people's arms were flung out to the sides, others were pressing their hands to their heads, and large-headed birds hung in the spaces between them. Tatarsky carried on reading:

According to tradition Endu, wife of the god Enki (another account regards her as his female hypostasis, which seems unlikely; she can also be identified with the figure of Ishtar) was once sitting on the bank of a canal and telling the rosary of rainbow-coloured beads her husband had given her. The sun was shining very brightly and Endu was overcome by sleep. She dropped her rosary, which fell into the water, where the beads scattered and sank. After this the rainbow-coloured beads decided that they were people and settled throughout the pond. They built towns and had their own kings and gods. Then Enki took a lump of clay and moulded it into the form of a fisherman. He breathed life into it and called it Enkidu. He gave him a spindle of golden thread, and told him to go down into the water and gather up all the beads. Since the name 'Enkidu' contains Enki's own name, it possesses special power and the beads are obliged to submit to the will of the god and string themselves on to the golden thread. Some researchers believe that Enkidu gathers up the souls of the deceased and transports them on his threads to the kingdom of the dead; numerous images have been preserved in which merchants and officials are shown appealing to Enkidu for help. These prayers contain a repeated plea to 'raise the strong higher on the thread of gold' and to 'endow with the earthly enlility' (see 'Enlil'). There are also eschatological motifs to be found in the myth of Enkidu – as soon as Enkidu gathers everyone living on earth on to his thread life will cease, because they will once again become beads on the necklace of the great goddess. This event, due to happen at some point in the future, is identified with the end of the world.

The ancient legend contains one motif for which it is difficult to provide an explanation: several versions describe in detail exactly how the bead-people crawl up along Enkidu's threads. They don't use their hands for this – their hands serve to cover their eyes and ears or to beat off the white birds that attempt to tear them from the threads. The bead-people ascend the string by first swallowing it and then grasping it alternately with their mouths and anuses. It is not clear how such Pantagruelesque details come to be found in the myth of Enkidu – possibly they are echoes of another myth that has been lost.

The wheels in which Enkidu's threads end are also worth some consideration. They bear the likeness of an eye inscribed in a triangle. Here we have the intersection of the real with the mythical: the wheels of ancient Sumerian war chariots actually were secured by a triangular bronze plate attached to the wheel externally, and the form drawn on the plate, which is similar to the outline of an eye, symbolises the spindle on which the golden thread was wound. The wheel is a symbol of movement; thus we have the self-propelling spindle of the god Enki (cf. for instance Ariadne's thread or the many-eyed wheels in the vision of the prophet Ezekiel). The power of the name 'Enki' is such that although originally there was only one such spindle, it might have come to seem to people that their numbers were beyond count.

Tatarsky noticed a glimmering in the semi-darkness of the room. Thinking it must be the reflection of some light in the street, he stood up and looked out of the window, but there was nothing of any interest going on outside. He caught sight of his own orange divan reflected in the glass and was amazed to observe that, seen in mirror inversion, the tattered couch he had so often felt like throwing out on to the dump and burning was the finest part of an unfamiliar and quite amazingly beautiful interior. Returning to his seat, he glimpsed the glimmering light again out of the corner of his eye. He looked round, but the light shifted too, as though its source was a spot on his iris. 'OK,' Tatarsky thought happily, 'so now we're into the glitches.' The focus of his attention shifted to the spot and rested there for only the briefest of moments, but that was enough for his mind to record an event that began gradually unfolding as it surfaced in his memory, like a photograph in a bath of developing fluid.

It was summer, and he was standing on a city street lined with identical small houses. Towering up above the city was something between a conical factory chimney and a television tower – it was hard to tell what it was, because mounted on the summit of the chimney-tower was a blinding white torch, blazing so brilliantly that the haze of hot air obscured the outline. He could see its lower section was like a stepped pyramid, but higher up, in the white radiance, it was impossible to make out any details. Tatarsky thought the construction was probably something like the gas flares they have at oil refineries, except that the flame was so bright. There were people standing motionless at the open windows of the houses and on the street – they were gazing upwards at the white fire. Tatarsky turned his eyes in the same direction, and immediately felt himself jerked upwards. He could feel the fire drawing him towards itself and he knew that if he didn't turn his eyes away the flame would drag him upwards and consume him completely. Somehow he knew a lot about this fire. He knew many had already entered it ahead of him and were drawing him after them. He knew there were many who could only enter it after him, and they were pressing at his back. Tatarsky forced himself to close his eyes. When he opened them, he saw the tower had moved.

Now he could see it wasn't a tower – it was an immense human figure, towering up over the town. What he had taken for a pyramid now looked like the folds of a garment resembling a cloak or a mantle. The source of the light was the conical helmet on the figure's head. Tatarsky could clearly see the face, with some kind of gleaming battering ram in the place of a beard. It was turned towards him, and he realised he could only see the face and the helmet instead of the flame, because the flame was looking at him, and in reality there was nothing human about it. The gaze directed towards Tatarsky expressed anticipation, but before he had time to think about what he actually wanted to say or ask, or whether he really wanted to say or ask anything at all, the figure gave him its answer and turned its gaze away. The same intolerably bright radiance appeared where the face had been and Tatarsky lowered his eyes.

He noticed two people beside him, an elderly man in a shirt with an anchor embroidered on it and a boy in a black tee-shirt: they were holding hands and gazing upwards, and he had a feeling they had almost completely melted and merged with the bright fire, and their bodies, the street around them and the entire city were no more than shadows. Just a moment before the picture faded, Tatarsky guessed the bright fire he'd seen wasn't burning high in the sky, but down below, as though he'd glimpsed a reflection of the sun in a puddle and forgotten he wasn't looking at the actual position of the sun. Where the sun actually was, and what it was, he didn't have time to find out, but he did manage to understand something else, something very strange: it wasn't the sun that was reflected in the puddle, but the other way round; everything and everybody else – the street, the houses, the other people and he himself – were all reflected in the sun, which was entirely uninterested in the whole business, because it wasn't even aware of it.

This idea about the sun and the puddle filled Tatarsky with such a feeling of happiness that he laughed out loud in his joy and gratitude. All the problems of life, all those things that had seemed so unsolvable and terrifying, simply ceased to exist – for an instant the world was transformed in the same way as his divan had been transformed when it was reflected in the window pane.

When Tatarsky came round he was sitting on the divan, holding between his fingers the page that he still hadn't turned. There was an incomprehensible word pulsating in his ears, something like 'sirrukh' or 'sirruf'. It was the answer the figure had given him.

'Sirrukh, sirruf,' he repeated. 'I don't understand.'

The happiness he had been feeling only a moment before was replaced by fright. He suddenly felt it must be unlawful to learn anything like that, because he couldn't see how you could live with the knowledge. 'And I'm the only one who knows it,' he thought nervously; 'how can I be allowed to know it and still stay here and keep on walking around in this world? What if I tell someone? But then, who is there to permit it or forbid it, if I'm the only one who knows? Just a second, though – what can I actually tell anyone anyway?'

Tatarsky started thinking about it: there really was nothing in particular he could tell anyone. What was the point of telling a drunken Khanin it was the puddle that was reflected in the sun, and not the sun that was reflected in the puddle? Of course, he could tell him, but then . . . Tatarsky scratched the back of his head. He remembered this was the second revelation of this kind in his life: after gorging himself on fly-agarics with Gireiev, he'd understood something of equal importance. But then he'd completely forgotten it. All that remained in his memory were the words that were supposed to convey the truth: 'There is no death, because the threads disappear but the sphere remains.'

'Oh, Lord,' he muttered, 'how difficult it is to bring anything at all back here . . .'

'That's exactly right,' said a quiet voice. 'Any insight of true breadth and profundity will inevitably be reduced to words. And the words will inevitably be reduced to themselves.'

Tatarsky thought the voice sounded familiar. 'Who's there?' he asked, looking round the room.

'Sirruf has arrived,' the voice replied.

'What's that, a name?'

'This game has no name,' the voice replied. 'It's more of an official position.'

Tatarsky remembered where it was he'd heard the voice – on the military building site in the woods outside Moscow. This time he could see the speaker, or rather, he was able to imagine him instantly and without the slightest effort. At first he thought it was the likeness of a dog sitting there in front of him – something like a greyhound, but with powerful paws with claws and a long vertical neck. The beast had an elongated head with conical ears and a very pleasant-looking, if slightly cunning, little face crowned by a coquettish mane of fur. There seemed to be a pair of wings pressed against its sides. After a short while Tatarsky realised the beast was so large and so strange that the word 'dragon' would suit him best, especially since he was covered in shimmering rainbow scales (but then, just at that moment almost every object in the room was shimmering with every hue of the rainbow). Despite its distinctly reptilian features, the being radiated good-will so powerfully that Tatarsky wasn't at all frightened.

'Yes, everything is reduced to words,' repeated the Sirruf. 'As far as I am aware, the most profound revelation ever to visit a human being under the influence of drugs was occasioned by a critical dose of ether. The recipient summoned up the strength to write it down, even though it cost a supreme effort. What he wrote was: 'The universe is permeated by a smell of oil.' You've got a long way to go before you reach depths like that. Well, anyway, that's all beside the point. Why don't you tell me where you got the stamp from?'

Tatarsky remembered the collector from the Poor Folk bar and his album. He was about to reply, but the Sirruf interrupted him:

'Grisha the stamp-collector. I thought as much. How many of them did he have?'

Tatarsky remembered the page of the album and the three lilac-coloured rectangles in the plastic pocket.

'I see,' said the Sirruf. 'So there are two more.'

After that he disappeared, and Tatarsky returned to his normal state. He understood now what happens to a person who has the *delirium tremens* he'd read so much about in the classics of nineteenth-century Russian literature. He had no control at all over his hallucinations, and he simply couldn't tell which way he would be tossed by the next thought. He began to feel afraid. He got up and walked quickly into the bathroom, put his head under a stream of water and held it there until the cold became painful. He dried his hair on a towel, went back into the room and took another look at its reflection in the window pane. The familiar interior appeared to him now like a Gothic stage set for some menacing event due to occur at any moment, and the divan appeared like some sacrificial altar for large animals.

'Why on earth did I have to go and swallow that garbage?' he thought in anguish.

'Absolutely no reason whatsoever,' said the Sirruf, resurfacing in some obscure dimension of his consciousness. 'It really isn't good for man to go taking drugs. Especially psychedelics.'

'Yes, I know that myself,' Tatarsky replied quietly. 'Now I do.'

'Man has a world in which he lives,' the Sirruf said didactically. 'Man is man because he can see nothing except that world. But when you take an overdose of LSD or dine on panther fly-agarics, you're stepping way out of line – and you're taking a grave risk. If you only realised how many invisible eyes are watching you at that moment you would never do it; and if you were to see even just a few of those who are watching you, you'd die of fright. By this act you declare that being human is not enough for you and you want to become someone else. But in the first place, in order to cease being human, you have to die. Do you want to die?'

'No,' said Tatarsky, earnestly pressing his hand to his heart.

'And who is it you want to be?'

'I don't know,' Tatarsky said, crushed.

'You see what I mean? Just one more tab from happy Holland might not have meant too much, but what you swallowed was something quite different. It's a numbered issue, an official service document, by eating which you shift across into a different realm where there are absolutely no idle pleasures or amusements. And which you're not supposed to go wandering about in without an official commission. And you don't have any commission. Do you?'

'No,' agreed Tatarsky.

'We've settled things with Grisha. He's a sick man, a collector; and he came by the pass by accident . . . But what did you eat it for?'

'I wanted to feel the pulse of life,' Tatarsky said with a sob.

'The pulse of life? Very well, feel it,' said the Sirruf.

When Tatarsky came to his senses, the only thing in the world he wanted was that the experience he'd just been through and had no words to describe, merely a feeling of black horror, should never happen to him again. For that he was prepared to give absolutely anything.

'Again, perhaps?' asked the Sirruf.

'No,' said Tatarsky, 'please, don't. I'll never, never eat that garbage again. I promise.'

'You can promise the local policeman. If you live till morning, that is.'

'What d'you mean ?'

'Just what I say. Do you at least realise that was a pass for five people? And you're here alone. Or are there really five of you?'

When Tatarsky recovered his senses again he felt he really didn't have much chance of surviving the night. There had just been five of him, and every one of them had felt so bad that Tatarsky had instantly realised what a blessing it was to exist in the singular, and he was astonished how people could be so blind as not to appreciate their good fortune.

'Please,' he said, 'please, don't do that to me again.'

'I'm not doing anything to you,' replied the Sirruf. 'You're doing it all yourself.'

'Can I explain?' Tatarsky asked piteously. 'I realise I've made a mistake. I realise it's not right to look at the Tower of Babel. But I didn't . . .'

'What has the Tower of Babel got to do with it?' the Sirruf interrupted.

'I've just seen it.'

'You can't see the Tower of Babel, you can only ascend it,' replied the Sirruf. 'I tell you that as its guardian. And what you saw was the complete opposite. One could call it the Carthaginian Pit. The so-called *tofet*.'

'What's a tofet?'

'It's a place of sacrificial cremation. There were pits of the kind in Tyre, Sidon, Carthage and so forth, and they really did burn people in them. That, by the way, is why Carthage was destroyed. These pits were also known as Gehenna – after a certain ancient valley where the whole business started. I might add that the Bible calls it the "abomination of the Ammonites" – but you haven't read the Bible anyway, you only search through it for new slogans.'

'I don't understand.'

'Very well. You can regard the tofet as an ordinary television.'

'I still don't understand. Do you mean I was inside a television?'

'In a certain sense. You saw the technological space in which your world is being consumed by fire. Something like a garbage incinerator.'

Once again Tatarsky glimpsed the figure holding the glittering strings on the periphery of his field of vision. The vision lasted for only a fraction of a second.

'But isn't he the god Enkidu?' he asked. 'I was just reading about him. I even know what those strings are he has in his hands. When the beads from the great goddess's necklace decided they were people and they settled right across the reservoir . . .'

'In the first place, he isn't a god, quite the opposite. Enkidu is one of his less common names, but he is better known as Baal. Or Baloo. In Carthage they tried to sacrifice to him by burning their children, but there was no point, because he makes no allowances and simply cremates everyone in turn. In the second place, the beads didn't decide they were people, it was people who decided they were beads. That's why the entity you call Enkidu gathers up those beads and cremates them, so that some day people will realise they aren't beads at all. Do you follow?'

'No. What are the beads, then?'

The Sirruf said nothing for a moment.

'How can I explain it to you? The beads are what that Che Guevara of yours calls "identity".'

'But where did these beads come from?'

'They didn't come from anywhere. They don't actually exist.'

'What is it that burns then?' Tatarsky asked doubtfully.

'Nothing.'

'I don't understand. If there's fire, then there must be something burning. Some kind of substance.'

'Have you ever read Dostoievsky?'

'I can't stand him, to be honest.'

'A pity. In one of his novels there was an old man called Zosima who was horrified by intimations of *the material fire*. It's not clear quite why he was so afraid. The material fire is your world. The fire in which you burn has to be maintained. And you are one of the service personnel.'

'Service personnel?'

'You are a copywriter, aren't you? That means you are one of those who force people to gaze into the consuming fire.'

'The consuming fire? But what is it that's consumed?'

'Not what, but who. Man believes that he is the consumer,

but in reality the fire of consumption consumes him. What he receives in return are certain modest joys. It's like the safe sex that you all indulge in ceaselessly, even when you are alone. Environmentally friendly garbage incineration. But you won't understand it anyway.'

'But who's the garbage, who is it?' Tatarsky asked. 'Is it man?'

'Man by nature is almost as great and beautiful as Sirruf,' the Sirruf replied. 'But he is not aware of it. The garbage is this unawareness. It is the identity that has no existence in reality. In this life man attends at the incineration of the garbage of his identity . . .'

'Why should man gaze into this fire if his life is burning in it?'

'You have no idea of what to do with these lives anyway; and whichever way you might turn your eyes, you are still gazing into the flames in which your life is consumed. There is mercy in the fact that in place of crematoria you have televisions and supermarkets; but the truth is that their function is the same. And in any case, the fire is merely a metaphor. You saw it because you ate a pass to the garbage incineration plant. All most people see in front of them is a television screen . . .'

And with that he disappeared.

'Hey there,' Tatarsky called.

There was no reply. Tatarsky waited for another minute before he realised he'd been left alone with his own mind, ready to wander off in any direction at all. He had to occupy it with something quickly.

'Phone,' he whispered. 'Who? Gireiev! He knows what to do.'

For a long time no one answered. Eventually, on the fifteenth or twentieth ring, Gireiev's morose voice responded.

'Hello.'

'Andrey? Hello. This is Tatarsky.'

'Do you know what time it is?'

'Listen,' Tatarsky said hastily, 'I'm in trouble. I've done too much acid. Someone in the know tells me it was five doses. Anyway, to cut it short, I'm coming apart at all the seams. What can I do?'

'What can you do? I don't know what you can do. In cases like that I recite a mantra.'

'Can you give me one?'

'How can I give you one? It has to be conferred.'

'Aren't there any you can just give me without any conferring?'

Gireiev thought. 'Right, just hang on a minute,' he said, and put the receiver down on the table.

For several minutes Tatarsky tried to make sense of the distant sounds borne to him along the wires on an electric wind. At first he could hear fragments of conversation; then an irritated woman's voice broke in for a long time; then everything was drowned out by the abrupt and demanding sound of a child crying.

'Write this down,' Gireiev said at last. 'Om melafefon bva kha sha. I'll give you it letter by letter: o, em . . .'

'I've got it,' said Tatarsky. 'What does it mean?'

'That's not important. Just concentrate on the sound, OK? Have you got any vodka?'

'I think I had two bottles.'

'You can drink them both. It goes well with this mantra. In an hour it'll be all over. I'll call you tomorrow.'

'Thanks. Listen, who's that crying there?'

'My son,' Gireiev answered.

'You have a son? I didn't know. What's his name?'

'Namhai,' Gireiev replied in a disgruntled voice. 'I'll call tomorrow.'

Tatarsky put down the receiver and dashed into the kitchen, rapidly whispering to himself the incantation he'd just been given. He took out a bottle of Absolut and drank it all in three glassfuls, followed it up with some cold tea and then went into the bathroom – he was afraid to go back into the room. He sat on the edge of the bath, fixed his eyes on the door and began to whisper:

'Om melafefon bva kha sha, om melafefon bva kha sha . . .'

The phrase was so difficult to pronounce, his mind simply couldn't cope with any other thoughts. Several minutes went by and a warm wave of drunkenness spread throughout his body. Tatarsky had almost relaxed when suddenly he noticed the familiar glimmering on the periphery of his field of vision. He clenched his fists and began whispering the mantra more quickly, but it was already too late to halt the new glitch.

Something like a firework display erupted at the spot where the bathroom door had just been, and when the red and yellow blaze died down a little, he saw a burning bush in front of him. Its branches were enveloped in bright flame, as though it had been doused in blazing petrol, but the broad dark-green leaves were not consumed in the fire. No sooner had Tatarsky studied the bush in detail than a clenched fist was extended towards him from out of its heart. Tatarsky swayed and almost fell backwards into the bath. The fist unclenched and on the palm extended in front of his face Tatarsky saw a small, wet, pickled cucumber covered in green pimples.

When the bush disappeared, Tatarsky could no longer recall whether he had taken the cucumber or not, but there was a distinctly salty taste in his mouth. Perhaps it was blood from a bitten lip.

'Oh no, Gireiev, this mantra of yours isn't doing the business,' Tatarsky whispered, and went into the kitchen.

After drinking more vodka (he had to force it down), he went back into the room and turned on the television. The room was filled with solemn music; the blue spot on the screen expanded and transformed itself into an image. They were broadcasting some concert or other.

'Lord, hear Thou my plea,' sang a man with a powdered face, wearing a bow tie and a shot silk waistcoat under black tails. As he sang he rolled his goggling eyes and sawed at the air with his open hand in a strange manner, as though he was being borne away on a current of celestial ether.

Tatarsky clicked on the remote and the man in the bow tie disappeared. 'Maybe I should pray?' he thought. 'It might do some good . . .' He remembered the man from the bas-relief with his arms upraised to the starry sky.

He went out into the centre of the room and knelt down with some difficulty, then crossed his arms on his chest and raised his eyes to the ceiling.

'Lord, hear Thou my plea,' he said quietly. 'I have sinned greatly against Thee. I live a bad life, a wrong one. But in my soul there are no abominable desires, cross my heart. I'll never eat any of that junk again. I . . . I only want to be happy, and I just can't manage it. Perhaps it's what I deserve. I can't do anything else except write bad slogans. But for Thee, oh Lord, I'll write a good one – honest I will. You know, they do position Thee quite wrongly. They haven't got a clue. Take that latest clip, where they're collecting money for that church. There's this old woman standing there with a box, and first someone driving an old jalopy puts in a rouble and then someone driving a Mercedes drops in a hundred bucks. The idea's clear enough, but in terms of positioning it's way off beam. The guy in the Mercedes wouldn't wait in the queue of jalopies. A blind horse could see it. And the target group we need is all those guys in their Mercedes, because in terms of yield one Mercedes is worth a thousand jalopies. That's not the way to do it. Here . . .'

Managing somehow to scramble upright, Tatarsky struggled over to the desk, picked up a pen and began writing in a jerky, spiderish scrawl:

Poster (theme for a clip). A room in a very expensive hotel. Carrara marble table. A laptop computer flashes out a message: 'Transaction confirmed'. Near the computer we see a rolled-up hundred-dollar bill and a hotel-room Bible in three languages. Slogan:

THE SHINING WORD
FOR YOUR SHINING WORLD!

Variant: another setting – a private jet airplane, a stock exchange, a Manhattan penthouse, a Côte d'Azur estate, etc. Instead of the Bible we see the Saviour Himself approaching the camera in the rays of His glory. Slogan:

A FIRST-CLASS LORD
FOR YOUR HAPPY LOT!

Tatarsky dropped the pen and raised his red, tear-stained eyes to the ceiling. 'Dost Thou like it, Lord?' he asked quietly.

CHAPTER 10

Wee Vova

God's love for man is manifest in a great principle that defies adequate expression in words: 'and yet it can be done'. The phrase 'and yet it can be done' means an immense number of things, including, for instance, that the principle itself, despite being absolutely impossible to express, can yet be expressed and manifested. Even more than that, it can be expressed an infinite number of times, and each time in a completely new way – which is why poetry exists. Such is the love of God. And what is man's response to it?

Tatarsky woke in a cold sweat, unable to understand what the pitiless onslaught of the daylight was punishing him for. He could vaguely recall shouting out in his sleep and apparently trying to justify himself to someone – in other words he'd had an alcoholic nightmare. Now his hangover was so fundamental and profound that there was no point in seeking salvation by simply pouring a shot of vodka down his throat. He couldn't even think about it, because the very thought of alcohol triggered spasms of retching; but to his great good fortune, that irrational and mystical manifestation of the divine love that spreads its trembling wings over Russia had already embraced his suffering soul.

He could yet take a hair of the dog that bit him. There was a special method for it, known as a 'locomotive'. It had been perfected over generations of alcoholics and handed down to Tatarsky by a certain individual from the esoteric circles of St Petersburg the morning after a monstrous drinking session. 'In essence the method is Gurdjieffian,' the man had explained. 'It belongs to what he called "the path of the cunning man". You have to regard yourself as a machine. This machine has receptors, nerve endings and a central control centre that is declaring quite unambiguously that any attempt to consume alcohol will instantly result in vomiting. What does the cunning man do? He deceives the machine's receptors. From a practical point of view it goes like this: you fill your mouth with lemonade. Then you pour a glass of vodka and raise it to your mouth. Then you swallow the lemonade, and while the receptors are reporting to the supreme control centre that you're drinking lemonade, you quickly swallow the vodka. Your body simply doesn't have time to react, because its mind's fairly sluggish. But there is one subtle point involved. If you swallow Coca-Cola before the vodka instead of lemonade, there's a fifty per cent chance you'll puke anyway; and if you swallow Pepsi-Cola, you're absolutely certain to puke.'

'What a concept that would make,' Tatarsky pondered dourly as he entered the kitchen. There was still a little vodka in one of the bottles. He poured it into a glass and then turned towards the fridge. He was frightened by the thought that there might not be anything in it except Pepsi-Cola, which he usually bought out of faithfulness to the ideals of his own generation, but fortunately, standing there on the bottom shelf was a can of Seven-Up some visitor or other had brought together with the vodka.

'Seven-Up,' Tatarsky whispered, licking his desiccated lips. 'The Uncola . . .'

The operation was a success. He went back into the room and over to the desk, where he discovered several sheets of paper covered in crooked lettering. Apparently the previous evening's flood-tide of religious feeling had cast up some debris on the paper shoreline.

The first text was printed in very neat and tidy capital letters:

'ETERNAL LIFE' COCKTAIL
MAN, DESIRE NOUGHT FOR THYSELF.
WHEN PEOPLE WHO SUFFER COME TO YOU
IN MULTITUDES GIVE OF THYSELF WITHOUT
REMAINDER

YOU SAY YOU'RE NOT READY?
TOMORROW WE BELIEVE YOU WILL BE!
BUT IN THE MEANTIME – *BOMBAY SAPPHIRE* GIN
WITH TONIC, JUICE OR YOUR FAVOURITE MIXER

The second text must have been delivered from the great advertising agency in the sky when Tatarsky had already reached an extreme stage of drunkenness – it took him several minutes just to decipher his own scrawl. The slogan had evidently been written when his prayerful ecstasy had passed its peak and his consciousness had finally reverted to a mode of pragmatic rationalism:

DO IT YOURSELF, MOTHERFUCKER
REEBOK

The phone rang. 'Khanin,' Tatarsky thought in fright as he picked up the receiver. But it was Gireiev.

'Babe? How're you doing?'

'So-so,' Tatarsky replied.

'Sorry about yesterday. You phoned so late, and my wife went on the warpath. Did you get by OK?'

'More or less.'

'Know what I wanted to tell you? You might find it interesting from a professional point of view. This lama's arrived in town – Urgan Djambon Tulku the Seventh, from the Gelugpa sect – and he gave an entire lecture about advertising. I've got it on cassette; you can have a listen to it. There was loads of all sorts of stuff, but the central idea was very interesting. From the Buddhist point of view the meaning of advertising is extremely simple. It attempts to convince us that consuming the product advertised will result in a high and auspicious reincarnation – and not even after death, but immediately following the act of consumption. Like, chew Orbit sugar-free and straightaway you're an *asura*. Chew Dirol, and you're a god with snow-white teeth.'

'I don't understand a word you're saying,' said Tatarsky, wincing at his gradually dissipating spasms of nausea.

'Well, to keep it simple, what he was trying to say was that the main purpose of advertising is to show people other people who've managed to find happiness in the possession of material objects. But in reality people suffering from that delusion don't exist anywhere except in the ads.'

'Why?' asked Tatarsky, struggling to keep up with the ebbs and flows of his friend's thought.

'Because it's never the things that are advertised, it's human happiness. The people they show are always equally happy, only the happiness comes from buying different things in different cases. So people don't go to a shop to buy things, they go there looking for this happiness; but the shops don't sell it. Then the lama criticised the theory of someone called Che Guevara. He said Che Guevara wasn't a proper Buddhist and therefore wasn't a proper authority for a Buddhist; and he hadn't actually given the world anything except a burst of machine-gun fire and his famous trademark. But then, the world hadn't give him anything else either . . .'

'Listen,' said Tatarsky, 'finish up, will you? I can't take anything in anyway – my head hurts. Why don't you just tell me what that mantra was you gave me?'

'It's not a mantra,' replied Gireev. 'It's a sentence in Hebrew from a textbook. My wife's studying it.'

'Your wife?' Tatarsky echoed in surprise, wiping the beads of cold sweat from his forehead. 'But of course. If you have a son, then you have a wife. What's she studying Hebrew for?'

'She wants to get out of here. Not long ago she had this terrible vision. No glitches, mind, just while she was meditating. Anyway, there's this rock and this naked girl lying on it and the girl is Russia. So stooping over her there's this . . . You can't make out the face, but he seems to be wearing an army coat with epaulettes, or some kind of cloak. And he's giving her . . .'

'Don't pile it on,' said Tatarsky. 'I'll be sick. I'll call you back later, OK?'

'OK,' agreed Gireiev. ·

'Hang on. Why'd you give me that sentence and not a mantra?'

'What's the difference? In that state it doesn't matter what you recite. The main thing is to keep your mind occupied and drink as much vodka as possible. Who's going to give you a mantra without conferring it properly anyway?'

'So what does the phrase mean?'

'Let me have a look. Where is it now . . . Aha, here it is. 'Od melafefon bva kha sha.' It means "Please give me another cucumber". What a gas, eh? A natural born mantra. Of course, it starts with "od", not "om", I changed that. And if you put "hum" at the end as well . . .'

'OK, OK,' said Tatarsky. 'Cheers. I'm going out for some beer.'

It was a clear, fresh morning; its cool purity seemed to conceal some incomprehensible reproach. Tatarsky emerged from the entrance-way of his house and stopped, absorbed in thought. It would take him ten minutes to walk as far as the round-the-clock shop he normally went to for hangover remedies (the local winos called it 'the round-the-bend place') and the same amount of time to get back. Close by, just a couple of minutes away, were the kiosks in one of which he had formerly worked. Since then he hadn't gone anywhere near them, but he had no time right now to worry about any vague, ill-defined fears. Struggling against his own reluctance to carry on living, Tatarsky set off towards the kiosks.

Several of them were already open, and there was a newspaper stand beside them. Tatarsky bought three cans of Tuborg and an analytical tabloid – it was one he used to look through for the sake of the advertising spreads, which aroused his professional interest even in a severely hung-over state. He drank the first can while he leafed through the tabloid. His attention was caught by an advertisement for Aeroflot showing a married couple climbing up a gangway set against a palm tree laden with paradisaical fruit. 'What idiots,' Tatarsky thought. 'Who advertises themselves like that? Someone needs to fly to Novosibirsk, and they promise him he'll end up in heaven. But maybe he's not due in heaven just yet; maybe he's got business in Novosibirsk . . . Might as well invent an "Icarus" airbus . . .' The next page was taken up by a colourful advertisement for an American restaurant on Uprising Square – a photograph of the entrance with a jolly neon sign blazing above it:

BEVERLY KILLS
A CHUCK NORRIS ENTERPRISE

Tatarsky folded up the newspaper, laid it flat on a dirty crate standing between the kiosks, sat down on it and opened up the second can.

He felt better almost immediately. In order not to look at the world around him, Tatarsky fixed his gaze on the can. There was a large picture on it under the yellow word 'Tuborg': a fat man in braces wiping the sweat from his forehead with a white handkerchief. Above the man's head was a searing expanse of blue, and he was standing on a narrow track that led away beyond the horizon; in short, the picture was so heavily loaded with symbolism that Tatarsky couldn't understand how the thin aluminium of the can could support it. He automatically began composing a slogan.

'Something like this,' he thought: 'Life is a solitary journey beneath a scorching sun. The road we walk along leads to nowhere; and no one knows where death lies in wait. Remembering this, everything in the world seems empty and meaningless. And then – enlightenment. Tuborg. Prepare yourself. Variant: Think final.'

Part of the slogan could be written in Latin – Tatarsky still had the taste for that going back to his first job. For instance, 'Halt, wayfarer' – something-something *viator*. Tatarsky couldn't remember precisely; he'd have to look it up in his *Inspired Latin Sayings*. He rummaged in his pockets to find a pen to note down his creation. There wasn't one. Tatarsky decided to ask a passer-by for one and he looked up. Standing there right in front of him was Hussein.

Hussein was smiling with the corners of his mouth, his hands were thrust into the pockets of his broad velvet trousers, and his gleaming oily eyes were quite expressionless – he was just surfacing from a recent fix. He'd hardly changed at all, except for maybe putting on a little weight. There was a short astrakhan hat on his head.

The can of beer slipped from Tatarsky's fingers and a symbolic yellow stream traced out a dark spot on the asphalt. The feelings that flitted through his heart in the space of a second were a perfect match for the concept he'd just invented for Tuborg – except for the fact that no enlightenment ensued.

'Come on,' said Hussein, beckoning with his finger.

For one second Tatarsky hesitated, wondering whether to make a dash for it, but he decided it would be wiser not to. As far as he could recall, Hussein's reflex response was to regard any fast-moving object larger than a dog and smaller than a car as a target. Of course, in the time that had elapsed the influence of morphine and Sufi music could have wrought serious change in the world of his spirit, but Tatarsky wasn't seriously tempted to test this possibility in practice.

The trailer in which Hussein lived had hardly changed either, except that now there were thick curtains at the windows, and a green satellite dish perched on the roof. Hussein opened the door and prodded Tatarsky gently in the back.

Inside it was half dark. A huge television was switched on, and on its screen three figures were frozen beneath the spreading branches of a tree. The image was trembling slightly – the TV was connected to a VCR set on 'pause'. Opposite the television was a bench and sitting on it, leaning back against the wall, was a man who hadn't shaved for a long time, wearing a crumpled club jacket with gold buttons. He gave off a mild stink. His right leg was chained to his hand with handcuffs that passed under the bench, so that his body was held in a semi-recumbent position hard to describe, reminding Tatarsky of the wow-anal position of the business-class passenger from the Korean Air ad (except that in the Korean Air ad the body was twisted so that the handcuffs were hidden). At the sight of Hussein the man twitched. Hussein took a mobile phone out of his pocket and waved it at the man chained to the bench, who shook his head, and Tatarsky noticed that his mouth was gagged with a strip of flesh-coloured sticky tape, on which someone had drawn a smile in red marker.

'Pain in the ass,' mumbled Hussein.

He picked up the remote control from the table and pressed a button. The figures on the television stirred sluggishly into life – the VCR was working on slow play-back. Tatarsky recognised an unforgettably politically correct sequence from a Russian film set in Chechnya – *Prisoner of the Caucasus*, he thought it was called – a Russian commando in a crumpled uniform gazing uncertainly about him, two militants in national costume with blazing eyes holding him by the arms, and a third, wearing the same kind of astrakhan hat as Hussein, raising a long museum-piece of a sabre to his throat. Several close-ups followed each other in sequence on the screen – the commando's eyes, the blade set against the tight-stretched skin (Tatarsky thought it must be a deliberate reference to Buñuel's *Un Chien Andalou*, included for the benefit of the jury at Cannes) and then the killer pulling the sabre sharply back towards himself. Immediately the screen showed the start of the scene again: once again the killer raised his sabre to the throat of his victim. The sequence had been set in a loop. Only now did Tatarsky realise he was watching something like an advertising video being shown at an exhibition stand. Not even something like one – it actually was a promotional video: information technology had influenced Hussein too, and now he was using an image sequence to position himself in the consciousness of a client. The client was evidently very familiar with the clip and what Hussein was trying to position – he closed his eyes and his head slumped on to his chest.

'Come on, watch it, watch it,' said Hussein, grabbing him by the hair and turning his face towards the screen. 'You jolly bastard. I'll teach you how to smile . . .'

The unfortunate victim moaned quietly, but because of the broad beaming smile painted on his face, Tatarsky felt nothing but irrational dislike for him.

Hussein let go of him, straightened his astrakhan hat and turned towards Tatarsky: 'All he has to do is make just one phone call, but he doesn't want to. Just makes things hard on himself and everyone else. These people . . . How're you doing? On a bad trip, I see?'

'No,' said Tatarsky, 'it's a hangover.'

'Then I'll pour you a drink,' said Hussein.

He went over to the safe and took out a bottle of Hennessy and a pair of none-too-clean tooth-glasses.

'A welcome to my guest,' he said as to he poured the cognac.

Tatarsky clinked glasses with him and drank.

'What are you up to nowadays?' asked Hussein.

'Working.'

'Where would that be?'

He had to say something, and something that meant Hussein couldn't claim compensation for his withdrawal from the business. Tatarsky didn't have any money right now. His eyes came to rest on the television screen, where death was advancing yet again. 'They'll kill me like that,' he thought, 'and no one will even put flowers on my grave . . .'

'So where is it then?' Hussein asked again.

'In the flower business,' Tatarsky blurted out. 'With the Azerbaidjanis.'

'With the Azerbaidjanis?' Hussein repeated doubtfully. 'What Azerbaidjanis?'

'With Rafik,' Tatarsky replied, inspired, 'and Eldar. We charter a plane, fly in flowers and fly out . . . Well, you know what. I don't charter the plane, of course. I'm just the gopher.'

'Yeah? So why couldn't you just explain what was going on? Why'd you just drop off the keys?'

'I was hitting the sauce,' Tatarsky answered.

Hussein thought it over. 'I don't know,' he said. 'Flowers are good business. I wouldn't have said anything, if you'd told me man to man. But now . . . I'll have to have a word with this Rafik of yours.'

'He's in Baku right now,' said Tatarsky. 'Eldar too.'

The pager on his belt bleeped.

'Who's that?' asked Hussein.

Tatarsky glanced at the screen and saw Khanin's number.

'Just a friend of mine. He's got nothing to do . . .'

Hussein held out his hand without speaking, and Tatarsky submissively placed his pager in it. Hussein took out his phone, dialled the number and gave Tatarsky a glance filled with meaning. At the other end of the line someone picked up the receiver.

"Allo,' said Hussein, 'who am I talking to? Khanin? How do you do, Khanin. I'm calling from the Caucasian Friendly Society. My name's Hussein. Sorry to bother you, but we have your friend Vova here. He has a bit of a problem – he owes us money. Doesn't know where to get it from. So he asked me to call you and see if you could help out. You're in the flower business with him, aren't you?'

He winked at Tatarsky and then listened without speaking for a minute or two.

'What?' he asked, frowning. 'Just tell me if you're in the flower business with him or not. What's that mean –

metaphorical flowers? What rose of the Persians? Which Ariosto? Who? What? Give me your friend then . . . Right then, I'm listening . . .'

Tatarsky realised from Hussein's expression that someone at the other end of the line had said something unthinkable.

'I don't care who you are,' Hussein replied after a long pause. 'Send anyone you like . . . Yes . . . Send an entire regiment of your arsehole troops on tanks. Only you'd better warn them they're not going to find some wounded boy-scout from the White House in here, get it? What? You'll come yourself? Come on then . . . Write down the address . . .'

Hussein put down his phone and looked inquiringly at Tatarsky.

'I told you it would be best not to,' said Tatarsky.

Hussein chuckled.

'Worried about me? I appreciate that. But there's no need.'

He took two grenades out of the safe, half-straightened the whiskers on the detonators and put a grenade in each pocket. Tatarsky pretended to be looking the other way.

Half an hour later the legendary Mercedes-600 with dark-tinted glass drew up a few metres away from the trailer, and Tatarsky set his eye to the gap in the curtains at the window. Two men got out of the car – the first was Khanin, his suit looking crumpled and untidy, and the second was someone Tatarsky didn't know.

All the wow-indicators suggested he was a representative of the so-called middle class – a typical red-necked, red-faced hitman from some gang down in the Southern Port. He was wearing a black leather jacket, a heavy gold chain and track-suit trousers; but judging from the car, he represented that rare instance when a private gets himself promoted to the rank of general. He exchanged a couple of words with Khanin and came towards the door. Khanin stayed where he was.

The door opened. The stranger lumbered into the wagon and looked first at Hussein, then at Tatarsky, then at the man chained to the bench. An expression of astonishment appeared on his face. For a second he stood there motionless, as though he couldn't believe his eyes, then he took a step towards the prisoner, grabbed him by the hair and smashed his face twice against his knee. The prisoner tried to protect himself with his free hand, but he was too late.

'So that's where you got to, you bastard!' the newcomer yelled, squatting down, his face turning more scarlet than ever. 'We've been looking for you all over town for two weeks now. Wanted to hide, did you? Keeping out of sight, were you, you fucking merchant?'

Tatarsky and Hussein exchanged glances.

'Hey now, don't get carried away,' Hussein said uncertainly. 'He's a merchant, OK, but he's my merchant.'

'What?' the stranger asked, letting go of the bloody head. 'Yours? He was my merchant when you were still herding cows in the mountains.'

'I didn't herd cows in the mountains, I herded bulls,' Hussein replied and nodded at the TV screen. 'And bulls like you don't bother me any more than they did. I'll soon set a ring through your nose, better believe it.'

'What did you say?' the stranger asked with a frown, unbuttoning his jacket, where there was an interesting bulge under the left flap. 'What ring?'

'This one,' said Hussein, taking a grenade out of his pocket. The sight of the straightened whiskers had an instant calming effect on the stranger.

'This bastard owes me money,' he said with emphasis.

'Me too,' said Hussein, putting away the grenade.

'He owes me first.'

'No. He owes me first.'

'All right,' said the stranger. 'We'll meet tomorrow to discuss it. Ten o'clock in the evening. Where?'

'Just come back here.'

'You're on,' said the stranger and jabbed his finger in Tatarsky's direction. 'I take the young guy. He's one of mine.'

Tatarsky looked inquiringly at Hussein, who smiled affectionately.

'I've no more claims on you. Your friend here's in the firing line now. Call round some time, as a friend. Bring some flowers. Some roses. I like them.'

Hussein followed the two of them out on to the street, lit a cigarette and leaned back against the wall of the trailer.

134

Tatarsky took two steps and then turned back.'

'I forgot my beer,' he said.

'Go and get it,' Hussein answered.

Tatarsky went back into the wagon and took the last can of Tuborg from the table. The man chained to the bench moaned and raised his free hand. Tatarsky noticed the small rectangle of coloured paper in it. He took it and hastily shoved it into his pocket. The prisoner gave out a quiet groan an octave higher, dialled an invisible phone with his finger and pressed his open hand to his heart. Tatarsky nodded and went out. Hussein was still smoking on the porch and didn't seem to have noticed anything. The stranger and Khanin were already in the car. As soon as Tatarsky got into the front seat, it moved off.

'Let me introduce you,' said Khanin. 'Babe Tatarsky, one of our best specialists. And this' – Khanin nodded in the direction of the stranger who was driving the car out on to the road – 'is Wee Vova, almost your namesake. Also known as the Nietzschean.'

'Ah, that's all a load of crap,' Wee Vova mumbled, blinking rapidly. 'That was a long time ago.'

'This man,' Khanin continued, 'performs an extremely important economic function. You might call him the key link in the liberal model in countries with a low annual average temperature. D'you understand at least a bit about the market economy?'

'About that much,' Tatarsky replied, bringing his thumb and forefinger together until there was just a millimetre gap left between them.

'Then you must know that in an absolutely free market by definition there must be services provided by the limiters of absolute freedom. Wee Vova here happens to be one of those limiters. In other words, he's our protection . . .'

When the car braked at a traffic light, Wee Vova raised his small expressionless eyes to look at Tatarsky. It was hard to see why he should be called 'wee' – he was a man of ample dimensions and advanced years. His face had the vague meat-dumpling contours of the typical bandit physiognomy, but it didn't inspire any particular revulsion.

He looked Tatarsky over and said: 'So, to cut it short, tell me, you into the Russian idea?'

Tatarsky started and his eyes gaped wide.

'No,' he said. 'I've never thought about that theme.'

'All the better,' Khanin interrupted. 'A fresh approach, as they say.'

'A fresh approach to what?' Tatarsky asked, turning to face him.

'You've got a commission to develop a concept,' answered Khanin.

'Who from?'

Khanin nodded in the direction of Wee Vova.

'Here, take this pen and this notepad,' he said, 'listen carefully to what he has to say and make notes. You can use them to write it up later.'

'No listening needed,' Wee Vova blurted out. 'It's obvious enough. Tell me, Babe, when you're abroad, d'you feel humiliated?'

'I've never been abroad,' Tatarsky confessed.

'And good for you. 'Cause if you do go you will. I tell you straight – over there they don't reckon we're people at all, like we're all shit and animals. Of course, like when you're in some Hilton or other and you rent the entire floor, they'll all stand in line to suck your cock. But if you're out at some buffet or socialising, they talk to you like you're some kind of monkey. Why d'you wear such a big cross, they say, are you some kind of theologian? I'd show them some fucking theology if they was in Moscow . . .'

'But why do they treat us like that?' Khanin interrupted. 'What d'you think?'

'The way I reckon it,' said Wee Vova, 'it's all because we're living on their handouts. We watch their films, ride their wheels, even eat their fodder. And we don't produce nothing, if you think about it, 'cept for mazuma . . . Which is still only their dollars, whichever way you look at it, which makes it a mystery how come we can be producing 'em. But then somehow we must be producing 'em – no one'd give us 'em for free. I ain't no economist, but I got a gut feeling something's rotten here, somehow something somewhere don't add up.'

Wee Vova fell silent and started thinking hard. Khanin was about to make some remark, but Wee Vova suddenly erupted: 'But they think we're some kind of cultural scumbags. Like some kind of nig-nogs out in Africa, get it? Like we was animals with money. Pigs, maybe, or bulls. But what we are, is Russia! Makes you frightened to think of it! A great country!'

'That's right,' said Khanin.

'It's just that we've lost our roots for the time being 'cause of all this crap that's going down. You know yourself what life's like now. No time for a fart. But that don't mean we've forgot where we come from, like some half-baked golly-wogs . . .'

'Let's try to keep feelings out of it,' said Khanin. 'Just explain to the boy here what you want him to do. Keep it simple, without the trimmings.'

'OK, listen up and I'll lay it out for you just like counting on my fingers,' said Wee Vova. 'Our national business is expanding into the international market. Out there there's all kinds of mazuma doing the rounds – Chechen, American, Columbian – you get the picture. And if you look at them like mazuma, then they're all the same; but in actual fact behind every kind of mazuma there's a national idea. We used to have Orthodoxy, Autocracy and Nationality. Then came this communism stuff. Now that's all over, and there's no idea left at all 'cept for mazuma. But there's no way you can have nothing but mazuma behind mazuma, right? 'Cause then there's just no way to understand why some mazuma's up front and some's in behind, right?'

'Spot on,' said Khanin. 'Listen and learn, Babe.'

'And when our Russian dollars are doing the rounds somewhere down in the Caribbean,' Wee Vova continued, 'you can't even really figure why they're Russian dollars and not anyone else's. We don't have no national i-den-ti-ty . . .'

Wee Vova articulated the final word syllable by syllable.

'You dig it? The Chechens have one, but we don't. That's why they look at us like we're shit. There's got to be some nice, simple Russian idea, so's we can lay it out clear and simple for any bastard from any of their Harvards: one-two, tick-

137

ety-boo, and screw all that staring. And we've got to know for ourselves where we come from.'

'You tell him what the job is,' said Khanin, and he winked at Tatarsky in the driving mirror. 'He's my senior creative. A minute of his time costs more than the two of us earn in a week.'

'The job's simple,' said Wee Vova. 'Write me a Russian idea about five pages long. And a short version one page long. And lay it out like real life, without any fancy gibberish, so's I can splat any of those imported arseholes with it – bankers, whores, whoever. So's they won't think all we've done in Russia is heist the money and put up a steel door. So's they can feel the same kind of spirit like in '45 at Stalingrad, you get me?'

'But where would I get . . .' Tatarsky began, but Khanin interrupted him:

'That's your business, sweetheart. You've got one day, it's a rush job. After that I'll be needing you for other work. And just bear in mind we've given this commission to another guy as well as you. So try your best.'

'Who, if it's not a secret?' Tatarsky asked.

'Sasha Blo. Ever heard of him?'

Tatarsky said nothing. Khanin made a sign to Wee Vova and the car stopped. Handing Tatarsky a hundred-rouble bill, Khanin said: 'That's for your taxi. Go home and work. And no more drinking today.'

Out on the pavement Tatarsky waited for the car to leave before taking out the business card from the prisoner of the Caucasus. It looked strange – in the centre there was a picture of a sequoia, covered with leaf-like dollar bills, and all the rest of the space was taken up by stars, stripes and eagles. All of this Roman magnificence was crowned by the following text in curly gold lettering:

TAMPOKO
OPEN JOINT STOCK COMPANY
SOFT DRINKS AND JUICES
Shares Placement Manager:
Mikhail Nepoiman

'Aha,' muttered Tatarsky. 'I see we're old acquaintances.'

He tucked the card in his pocket, turned towards the stream of cars and raised his hand. A taxi stopped almost immediately.

The taxi-driver was a fat-faced bumpkin with an expression of intense resentment on his face. The thought flashed through Tatarsky's mind that he was like a condom filled so full of water you barely needed to touch it with something sharp for it to soak anyone nearby in a one-off disposable waterfall.

'Tell me,' Tatarsky asked on a sudden impulse, 'you wouldn't happen to know what the Russian idea is, would you?'

'Ha,' said the driver, as if he been expecting this very question. 'I'll tell you about that. I'm half Mordvinian. So when I was serving in the army, the first year, on training, there was this sergeant there called Harley. Used to say, "I hate Mords and nig-nogs," and he'd send me off to scrub the shit-house with a toothbrush. Two months the bastard took the piss out of me. Then all of a sudden these three Mordvin brothers arrived for their training, and all of them weightlifters, can you imagine that? "So who is it round here doesn't like Mordvinians?" they said.'

The driver laughed happily and the car swerved across the road, almost skipping out into the opposite lane.

'What's that got to do with the Russian idea?' Tatarsky asked, hunched down in his seat in fear.

'I'll tell you what. That Harley got such a belting he spent two weeks on his back with a medical battalion. That's what. They worked him over another five times until he was fit for nothing but demobbing. But they didn't just work him over ...'

'Can you stop there, please,' Tatarsky said, not wanting to hear any more.

'I can't stop here,' said the driver, 'I've got to find a place to turn. I tell you, if only they'd just beaten him ... But, oh no!'

Tatarsky gave in, and as the car took him home the driver shared the fate of the chauvinist sergeant in a degree of detail that destroyed even the slightest possibility of sympathy – after all, sympathy is always based on a brief instant of identification, and in this case that was impossible – neither heart nor mind would dare risk it. In fact, it was just a typical army story.

When Tatarsky got out of the car, the driver said to him: 'As for that idea of yours, I'll tell you straight: fuck only knows. All I want is the chance to earn enough to keep me in petrol and booze. Yeltsin-Schmeltsin – what do I care, so long as they don't go smashing my face against a table?'

Perhaps it was these words that made Tatarsky remember the handcuffed manager who'd dialled the telephone number in the empty air. Inside the entrance-way of his house, he stopped. He'd only just realised what the case really required. He took the card out of his pocket and wrote on its reverse:

THERE'S ALWAYS SOMEBODY WHO CARES!
PUT YOUR TRUST IN *TAMPOKO* SHARES!

'So it's a conifer, is it?' he thought.

CHAPTER 11

The Institute of Apiculture

It happens so often: you step outside on a summer's morning and come face to face with this immense, beautiful world hastening on its way to some unknown destination and filled with mysterious promise, and the blue sky is awash with happiness, and suddenly your heart is pierced by a feeling, compressed into a single split second, that there life is in front of you and you can follow it on down the road without a backwards glance, gamble on yourself and win, go coursing across life's seas on a white speedboat and hurtling along her roads in a white Mercedes; and your fists tighten and clench of their own accord, and the muscles on your temples stand out in knots, and you promise yourself that you will rip mountains of money out of this hostile void with your bare teeth and you'll brush aside anybody you have to, and nobody will ever dare to use that American word 'loser' about you.

That is how the oral wow-factor manifests itself in our hearts. But as Tatarsky wandered towards the underground with a folder under his arm, he was indifferent to its insistent demands. He felt exactly like a 'loser' – that is, not only a complete idiot, but a war criminal as well, not to mention a failed link in the biological evolution of humanity.

Yesterday's attempt to compose the Russian idea had ended in the first total and absolute failure of Tatarsky's career. At first the task hadn't seemed very complicated, but once he'd sat down to it he'd been horrified to realise there wasn't a single idea in his head, not a thing. Not even the ouija board was any help when he turned to it in his despair after the hands of the clock had crept past midnight. Che Guevara did respond, but in reply to a question about the Russian idea he produced a rather strange passage:

Fellow compatriots! It would be more correct to talk of the oral–anal wow-effect, since these influences fuse into a single impulse and it is precisely this complex of emotions, this conglomerate of the two, that is regarded as defining the socially valuable aspects of human existence. Note that advertising occasionally prefers a quasi-Jungian approach to a quasi-Freudian one: it sometimes happens that the acquisition of a material object is not the expression of a naked act of monetarist copulation, but of the search for a magical quality capable of relegating oral–anal stimulation to the background. For instance, a blue-green toothbrush somehow guarantees the safety of an attempt to clamber from an upper balcony to a lower one, a refrigerator protects you from being crushed to death amidst the fragments of a grand piano that has fallen off the roof, and a jar of kiwi fruit in syrup saves you from an aeroplane crash – but this is an approach that most of the professionals regard as outmoded. Amen.

The only thing in all this that reminded Tatarsky of the Russian idea was the use of Yeltsin's favourite phrase: 'Fellow compatriots', which had always seemed to Tatarsky akin to the address 'Fellow prisoners' with which the institutionalised mobsters used to begin their written missives to the labour camps, their so-called 'daubs'. But despite this similarity, Wee Vova would hardly have been satisfied by the brief extract produced. Tatarsky's attempts to establish contact with some other spirit more competent in the question concerned came to nothing. True, an appeal to the spirit of Dostoievsky, in whom Tatarsky had placed especially high hopes, did evoke certain interesting side-effects, with the ouija board trembling and leaping into the air, as though it was being pulled in all directions at once by several equally strong presences, but the crooked scribbles left on the paper were useless to Tatarsky, although, of course, he could console himself with the thought that the idea he was seeking was so transcendent that this was the only way it could be expressed on paper. However that might be, Tatarsky hadn't got the job done.

There was no way in the world he could show Khanin the sheet of paper in his folder with the fragment about the toothbrush and kiwi fruit, but he had to show him something, and Tatarsky's mind retreated into self-flagellation, rewriting all the brand names with the word 'laser' in them and savouring them as he applied them to himself; 'Loser-Jet' and 'Loser-Max' lashed sweetly at his very soul, allowing him just for a moment to forget his impending disgrace.

As he drew closer to the metro, however, Tatarsky was distracted from his thoughts somewhat. Something strange was going on there. A cordon of about twenty military police with automatic rifles were talking to each other on their walkie-talkies, pulling heroic and mysterious faces. In the centre of the cordoned-off area a small crane was loading the burnt-out remains of a limousine on to the platform of a truck. Several men in civilian clothes were walking round the skeleton of the car, carefully examining the asphalt, gathering up bits of something from it and putting them into plastic bags like rubbish bags. Tatarsky had a good view of all this from higher up the street, but once he came down to the same level as the station, the impenetrable crowd concealed what was happening from view. Tatarsky jostled briefly at the sweaty backs of his fellow citizens, then sighed and went on his way.

Khanin was out of sorts. With his forehead propped in the palm of his hand, he was tracing some kind of cabbalistic symbols in the ashtray with a cigarette-butt. Tatarsky sat on the edge of the chair at the other side of the desk, pressing the folder to his chest and stuttering his rambling excuses.

'I've written it, of course. As best I could, that is. But I think I've made a balls of it, and it's not something you should give to Wee Vova. The problem is, the theme is so . . . It turns out it's not such a simple theme at all . . . Maybe I can think up a slogan, or add something to the brand essence of the Russian idea, or expand somehow on what Sasha Blo writes, but I'm still not ready to write a concept. I'm not just being modest, I'm just being objective. In general . . .'

'Forget it,' Khanin interrupted.

'Why, what's happened?'

'Wee Vova's been taken out.'

'How?' Tatarsky slumped back on his chair.

'Dead easy,' said Khanin. 'Yesterday he had a shoot-out with the Chechens. Right beside your house it was, as it happens. He arrived on two sets of wheels with his fighters, everything fair and up front. He thought it would all be done right. But those bastards dug a trench on the hill opposite during the night, and as soon as he turned up they blasted him with a pair of "bumble-bee" flame-throwers. They're fearsome fucking things: produce a volumetric explosion with a temperature of two thousand degrees. Wee's car was armour-plated, but armour's only good against normal people, not these abortions . . .'

Khanin gestured in disgust.

'Wee never stood a chance,' he added quietly. 'And they picked off the rest of his fighters, the ones who survived the explosion, with a machine-gun when they jumped out of the cars. I don't know how you can do business with people like that. That's if they are people . We-ell.'

Instead of a sense of grief befitting the moment, to his shame Tatarsky felt a relief bordering on euphoria.

'Yeah,' he said, 'now I understand. I saw one of those cars today. Last time he was in a different one, so I didn't even think about anything being wrong. They've blown another guy away, I thought – every day someone or other gets it . . . But now I see – it all fits in. But what does it mean for us, in a practical sense?'

'Leave,' said Khanin. 'Indefinite leave. There's one hell of a big question to be answered. Hamlet's question. I already had two calls since the morning.'

'The police?'

'Yeah. And then from the Caucasian Friendly Society. The bastards could smell a trader had been cut free. Like sharks. Straight for the scent of blood. So the question of the moment is very specific. Our swarthy wops can offer real protection, but all the filth want to do is line their pockets. You'd have to lick their boots till they shone to get them to a shoot-out. But either of them could blow you away. And especially the filth, as it happens. They came on to me real heavy today . . . "We know you've got diamonds," they said. What kind of diamonds have I got? Tell me that. What diamonds have I got?'

'I don't know,' Tatarsky replied, remembering the photograph of the diamond necklace with the promise of eternity that he'd seen in the toilet at Khanin's place.

'OK. Don't you bother your head about it. Just carry on living, loving, working . . . Oh, and by the way, there's someone waiting for you in the next room.'

Morkovin looked just as he had the last time they'd met, only now there were more grey hairs in his parting, and his eyes were sadder and wiser. He was wearing a severe dark suit and a striped tie with a matching handkerchief in his breast pocket. When he saw Tatarsky, he got up from the table with a broad smile and opened his arms to embrace him.

'Oho!' he said, slapping Tatarsky on the back, 'what a face, Babe. Been on the sauce long?'

'I'm just pulling out of a deep one,' Tatarsky answered guiltily. 'They gave me this job to do here; there was just no other way.'

'Is that what you were talking about on the phone?'

'When?'

'Don't remember, huh? I thought not. You were in a real state – said you were writing a concept for God and the ancient serpent was giving you a real tough time about it . . . Asked me to find you a new job, said you were real world-weary . . .'

'That's enough,' said Tatarsky, raising an open palm towards him. 'No need to pile it on. I'm up to my ears in shit as it is.'

'So you do need a job, then?'

'And how! We've got the filth clutching at one leg and the Chechens grabbing at the other. Everybody's being given leave.'

'Let's go then. It just so happens I've got some beer in the car.'

Morkovin had arrived in a tiny blue BMW like a torpedo on wheels. Tatarsky felt strange sitting in it – his body assumed a semi-recumbent position, his knees were raised to his chest and the bottom of the car itself hurtled along so low over the road-surface his stomach muscles involuntarily contracted every time it bounced over another hole in the road.

'Aren't you afraid of riding in a car like this?' Tatarsky asked. 'What if somewhat leaves a crowbar sticking out of a manhole? Or there's one of those iron bars sticking up out of the road . . .'

Morkovin chuckled. 'I know what you're trying to say,' he said. 'But I've been used to that feeling at work for so long now . . .'

The car braked at a crossroads. A red jeep with six powerful headlamps on its roof halted to the right of them. Tatarsky stole a glance at the driver, a man with a low forehead and massive eye-ridges, with almost every inch of his skin sprouting thick wool. One of his hands was stroking the steering wheel and the other held a plastic bottle of Pepsi. Tatarsky suddenly realised Morkovin's car was way cooler, and he had one of his very rare experiences of the anal wow-factor at work. The feeling, it must be confessed, was enthralling. Sticking his elbow out of the window, he took a swig of beer and looked at the driver of the jeep pretty much the same way as the sailors on the bow of an aircraft carrier look down on a pygmy paddling over his raft to trade in rotten bananas. The driver caught Tatarsky's glance and for a while they stared each other in the eye. Tatarsky could sense the man in the jeep took this long exchange of glances as an invitation to fight – when Morkovin's car eventually moved off there was fury bubbling in the shallow depths of his eyes. Tatarsky realised he'd seen this face somewhere before. 'Probably a film actor,' he thought.

Morkovin moved out into a free lane and started going faster.

'Listen, where are we going?' Tatarsky asked.

'Our organisation.'

'What organisation's that?'

'You'll see. I don't want to spoil the impression.'

A few minutes later the car braked to a halt at some gates in a set of tall railings. The railings looked impressive: the bars were like Cyclopean cast-iron spears with gilded tips. Morkovin showed a policeman in a little hut some card or other and the gates slowly swung open. Behind them was a huge Stalinist-style building from the forties, looking like something between a stepped Mexican pyramid and a squat skyscraper constructed with the low Soviet sky in mind. The upper part of the façade was covered in moulded decorations – lowered banners, swords, stars and some kind of lances with jagged edges; it was all redolent of ancient wars and the forgotten smell of gunpowder and glory. Screwing up his eyes, Tatarsky read the moulded inscription up under the very roof: 'To the heroes' eternal glory!'

'Eternal glory's a bit over the top for them,' he thought gloomily. 'They'd be happy enough with a pension.'

Tatarsky had often walked past this building; a very, very long time ago someone had told him it was a secret institute where they developed new types of weapons. It seemed as though that must have been somewhere near the truth, because hanging by the gates like some hoary greeting from antiquity was a board bearing the crest of the Soviet Union and an inscription in gold: 'The Institute of Apiculture'. Underneath it Tatarsky just had time to make out an inconspicuous plaque bearing the words 'Interbank Committee for Information Technology'.

The parking lot was packed with cars and Morkovin barely managed to squeeze in between an immense white Lincoln and a silver Mazda racer.

'I want to introduce you to my bosses,' Morkovin said as he locked the car. 'Just act natural. But don't go saying too much.'

'What exactly does "too much" mean? Who says what's too much?'

Morkovin cast him a sideways glance: 'What you just said is a good example. It's definitely too much.'

After walking across the yard they went into a side entrance and found themselves in a marble hallway with an unnaturally high ceiling where several security men in black uniforms were sitting. They looked far more serious than the ordinary cops, and not just because of the Czech Scorpion automatics hanging at their shoulders. The cops just weren't in the same league – for Tatarsky their blue uniform, which once used to radiate the oppressive power of the state from every button and badge, had long ago become an object of disdainful incomprehension – such a totally empty symbol only emphasised the absurdity of these people constantly stopping cars on the roads and demanding money. But the bodyguards' black uniform was a real mind-blower: the designer (Morkovin said it was Yudashkin) had brilliantly combined the aesthetic of the SS *Sonderkomande*, motifs from anti-utopian films about the totalitarian society of the future and nostalgic gay fashion themes from the Freddie Mercury period. The padded shoulders, the deep décollage on the chest and the Rabelaisian codpiece blended together in a heady cocktail that made you want to steer clear of anybody wearing such a uniform. The message was crystal clear even to a total cretin.

In the lift Morkovin took out a small key, inserted it into a hole on the control panel and pressed the top button.

'And another thing,' he said, turning to face the mirror and smoothing down his hair: 'don't worry about looking stupid. In fact, be careful not to seem too smart.'

'Why?'

'Because if you do, a certain question will arise: if you're so smart, how come you're looking for a job instead of hiring people yourself?'

'Logical,' said Tatarsky.

'And pile on the cynicism.'

'That's easy enough.'

The doors of the lift opened to reveal a corridor carpeted in a grey runner with yellow stars. Tatarsky remembered from a photograph that the sidewalk on some boulevard in Los Angeles looked like that. The corridor ended in a black door with no nameplate, with a small TV camera set above it. Morkovin walked to the middle of the corridor, took his phone out of his pocket and entered a number. Two or three minutes passed in silence. Morkovin waited patiently. Finally someone at the other end of the line answered.

'Cheers,' said Morkovin. 'It's me. Yes, I've brought him. Here he is.'

Morkovin turned and beckoned Tatarsky towards him from where he'd been standing timidly by the doors of the lift. Tatarsky walked up to him and raised his eyes dog-like to the camera lens. The person talking to Morkovin must have said something funny, because Morkovin suddenly giggled and shook Tatarsky by the shoulder.

'That's OK,' he said, 'we'll soon take off the rough edges.'

A lock clicked open and Morkovin pushed Tatarsky forward. The door immediately closed behind them. They were in an entrance-hall where an antique bronze mirror with a handle hung on the wall below a golden Venetian carnival mask of astounding beauty. 'I've seen them before somewhere,' Tatarsky thought, 'a mask and a mirror. Or have I? My mind's been on the blink all day today . . .' Below the mask there was a desk and sitting behind the desk was a secretary of cold avian beauty.

'Hello, Alla,' said Morkovin.

The secretary flapped her hand at him and pressed a button on her desk. There was the sound of a discreet buzzer and the tall sound-proofed door at the other end of the hall opened.

For a moment Tatarsky thought the spacious office with blinds drawn over the windows was empty. At least there was no on sitting at the immense desk with the gleaming metal supports. Above the desk, at the spot where a portrait of the leader would have hung in Soviet times, there was a picture in a heavy round frame. The coloured rectangle set at the centre of a white field was hard to make out from the door, but Tatarsky recognised it from its colours – he had one just like it on his baseball shirt. It was a standard label with the American flag and the words: 'Made in the USA. One size fits all'. Mounted on another wall was an uncompromising installation consisting of a line of fifteen tin cans with a portrait of Andy Warhol on a typical salt-pork label.

Tatarsky lowered his gaze. The floor was covered with a genuine Persian carpet with an incredibly beautiful design that looked like the patterns he'd seen some time in his childhood in an ancient edition of *The Thousand and One Nights*. Following the lines of the design, Tatarsky's eyes slid along a capricious spiral to the centre of the carpet, where they encountered the occupant of the office.

He was a man still young, a stocky, overweight individual with the remnants of a head of red hair combed backwards and a rather pleasant face, and he was lying on the carpet in a totally relaxed posture. He was hard to spot because the hue of his clothes blended almost perfectly into the carpet. He was wearing a 'pleb's orgasm' jacket – neither business uniform nor pyjamas, but something quite excessively carnivalesque, the kind of outfit in which particularly calculating business-men attire themselves when they want to make their partners feel things are going so well for them they don't have to bother about business at all. A bright-coloured retro tie with a lecherous monkey perched on a palm tree spilled out of his jacket and ran across the carpet like a startling pink tongue.

However, it wasn't the young man's outfit that astonished Tatarsky, but something else: he knew his face. In fact he knew it very well, although he'd never met him. He'd seen that face in a hundred short television news reports and ad-vertising clips, usually playing some secondary part; but who the man was he had no idea. The last time it had happened was the evening before, when Tatarsky had been distractedly watching TV as he tried to think about the Russian idea. The office's owner had appeared in an advertisement for some tablets or other – he was dressed in a white doctor's coat and a cap with a red cross, and a blonde beard and moustache had been glued on to his broad face, making him appear like a good-natured young Trotsky. Sitting in a kitchen surrounded by a family in the grip of an incomprehensible euphoria, he had said in a didactic tone: 'All these adverts can easily leave you feeling all at sea. And often they're not even honest. It's not so bad if you make a mistake buying a saucepan or a washing powder, but when it comes to medicines, you're tak-ing risks with your health. So who will you believe – the heartless advertising or your own family doctor? Of course! The answer's obvious! Nobody but your own family doctor, who recommends that you take Sunrise pills!'

'So that's it,' thought Tatarsky, 'he's our family doctor.'

In the meantime the family doctor had raised one hand in a gesture of greeting, and Tatarsky noticed he was holding a short plastic straw.

'Join the club,' he said in a dull voice.

'We're old members,' Morkovin replied.

Morkovin's response was evidently the usual one in this place, because the owner of the office nodded his head indul-gently.

Morkovin took two straws from the table, handed one to Tatarsky and then lay down on the carpet. Tatarsky followed his example. Once seated on the carpet he looked inquiringly at the owner of the office, who smiled sweetly in reply. Tatarsky noticed he had a watch on his wrist with a bracelet made of unusual links of different sizes. The winding knob was decorated with a small diamond, and there were three diamond spirals set round the face of the watch. Tatarsky recalled an editorial about expensive watches he'd read in some radical youth magazine and he gulped respectfully. The owner of the office noticed his gaze and looked at his watch.

'You like it?' he asked.

'Of course,' said Tatarsky. 'A Piaget Possession, if I'm not mistaken? I think it costs seventy thousand?'

'Piaget Possession?' The young man glanced at the dial. 'Yes, so it is. I don't know how much it cost.'

Morkovin gave Tatarsky a sideways glance.

'There's nothing that identifies someone as belonging to the lower classes of society so clearly as knowing all about expensive watches and cars, Babe,' he said.

Tatarsky blushed and lowered his eyes.

The section of carpet immediately in front of his face was covered in a pattern depicting fantastic flowers with long petals of various colours. Tatarsky noticed that the nap of the carpet was thickly covered with minute white pellets like pollen, as though with frost. He glanced across at Morkovin. Morkovin stuck his small tube into one nostril, closed the other nostril with one finger and ran the free end of the tube across the petal of a fantastical violet daisy. Tatarsky finally got the idea.

For several minutes the silence in the room was broken only by the sound of intense snorting. Eventually the owner of the office raised himself up on one elbow. 'Well?' he asked, looking at Tatarsky.

Tatarsky tore himself away from the pale-purple rose that he was absorbed in processing. His resentment had completely evaporated.

'Excellent,' he said. 'Simply excellent!'

He found talking easy and pleasurable; he might have felt a certain constraint when he entered this huge office, but now it had disappeared without trace. The cocaine was the real thing, and hardly cut at all – except perhaps for the very slightest aftertaste of aspirin.

'One thing I don't understand, though,' Tatarsky continued, 'is why all this fancy technology? It's all very elegant, but isn't it a bit unusual!'

Morkovin and the owner of the office exchanged glances.

'Didn't you see the sign on our premises?' the owner asked: 'The Institute of Apiculture?'

'Yes,' said Tatarsky.

'Well then. Here we are, making like bees.'

All three of them laughed, and they laughed for a long time, even when the reason for laughing had been forgotten.

Finally the fit of merriment passed. The owner of the office looked around as though trying to recall what he was there for, and evidently remembered. 'OK,' he said, 'let's get down to business. Morky, you wait with Alla. I'll have a word with the man.'

Morkovin hurriedly sniffed a couple of paradisaical cornflowers, stood up and left the room. The owner of the office got to his feet, stretched, walked round the desk and sat down in the armchair.

'Have a seat,' he said.

Tatarsky sat in the armchair facing the desk. It was very soft, and so low that he fell into it like falling into a snowdrift. When he looked up, Tatarsky was struck dumb. The table towered over him like a tank over a trench, and the resemblance was quite clearly not accidental. The twin supports decorated with plates of embossed nickel looked exactly like broad caterpillar tracks, and the picture in the round frame hanging on the wall was now exactly behind the head of the office's owner, so it looked like a trapdoor from which he had just emerged – the resemblance was further reinforced by the fact that only his head and shoulders could be seen above the desk. He savoured the effect for a few seconds, then he rose, leaned out across the desk and offered Tatarsky his hand:

'Leonid Azadovsky.'

'Vladimir Tatarsky,' said Tatarsky, rising slightly as he squeezed the plump, limp hand.

'You're no Vladimir; you're called Babylen,' said Azadovsky.

'I know all about it. And I'm not Leonid. My old man was a wanker too. Know what he called me? Legion. He probably didn't even know what the word means. It used to make me miserable too, at first. Then I found out there was something about me in the Bible, so I felt better about it. OK then . . .'

Azadovsky rustled the papers scattered around on his desk.

'Now what have we here . . . Aha. I've had a look at your work, and I liked it. Good stuff. We need people like you. Only in a few places . . . I don't completely believe it. here, for instance; you write about the "collective unconscious". Do you actually know what that is?'

Tatarsky shuffled his fingers as he tried to find the words.

'At the unconscious collective level,' he answered.

'Aren't you afraid someone might turn up who knows exactly what it is?'

Tatarsky twitched his nose. 'No, Mr Azadovsky,' he said, 'I'm not afraid of that; and the reason I'm not is that for a long time now everyone who knows what the "collective unconscious" is has been selling cigarettes outside the metro. One way or another, I mean. I used to sell cigarettes outside the metro myself. I went into advertising because I was sick of it.'

Azadovsky said nothing for a few seconds while he thought over what he'd just heard. Then he chuckled.

'Is there anything at all you believe in?' he asked.

'No,' said Tatarsky.

'Well, that's good,' said Azadovsky, taking another look into the papers, this time at some form with columns and sections. 'OK . . . Political views – what's this we have here? It says "upper left" in English. I don't get it. What a fucking pain – soon every form and document we have'll be written in English. So what are your political views?'

'Left of right centrists,' Tatarsky replied.

'And more specifically?'

'More specifically . . . Let's just say I like it when life has big tits, but I'm not in the slightest bit excited by the so-called Kantian tit-in-itself, no matter how much milk there might be splashing about in it. That's what makes me different from selfless idealists like Gaidar . . .'

The phone rang and Azadovksy held up his hand to stop

the conversation. He picked up the receiver and listened for a few minutes, his face gradually hardening into a grimace of loathing.

'So keep looking,' he barked, dropped the receiver on to its cradle and turned towards Tatarsky. 'What was that about Gaidar? Only keep it short, they'll be ringing again any minute.'

'To cut it short,' said Tatarsky, 'I couldn't give a toss for any Kantian tit-in-itself with all its categorical imperatives. On the tit market the only tit that gives me a buzz is the Feuerbachian tit-for-us. That's the way I see the situation.'

'That's what I think too,' Azadovksy said in all seriousness. 'Even if it's not so big, so long as it's Feuerbachian . . .'

The phone rang again. Azadovsky picked up the receiver and listened for a while, and his face blossomed into a broad smile.

'Now that's what I wanted to hear! And the control shot? Great! Good going!'

The news was obviously very good: Azadovsky stood up, rubbed his hands together, walked jauntily over to a cupboard set in the wall, took out a large cage in which something started dashing about furiously, and carried it over to the desk. The cage was old, with traces of rust, and it looked like the skeleton of a lampshade.

'What's that?' asked Tatarsky.

'Rostropovich,' replied Azadovsky.

He opened the little door, and a small white hamster emerged from the cage on to the desk. Casting a glance at Tatarsky from its little red eyes, it buried its face in its paws and began rubbing its nose. Azadovsky sighed sweetly, took something like a toolbag out of the desk, opened it and set out a bottle of Japanese glue, a pair of tweezers and a small tin on the desktop.

'Hold him,' he ordered. 'Don't be afraid, he won't bite.'

'How should I hold him?' Tatarsky asked, rising from his armchair.

'Take hold of his paws and pull them apart. Like a little Jesus. Aha, that's right.'

Tatarsky noticed there were several small discs of metal with toothed edges on the hamster's chest, looking like watch cog-wheels. When he looked closer he saw they were tiny medals made with remarkable skill – he even thought he could see tiny precious stones gleaming in them, accentuating the similarity to parts of a watch. He didn't recognise a single one of the medals – they clearly belonged to a different era, and they reminded him of the dress uniform regalia of a general from the times of Catherine the Great.

'Who gave him those?' he asked.

'Who could give them to him, if not me?' Azadovsky chanted, extracting a short little ribbon of blue watered silk from the tin. 'Hold him tighter.'

He squeezed a drop of glue out on to a sheet of paper and deftly ran the ribbon across it before applying it to the hamster's belly.

'Oh,' said Tatarsky, 'I think he's . . .'

'He's shit himself,' Azadovsky confirmed, dipping a diamond snowflake clasped in the pincers into the glue. 'He's so happy. Hup . . .'

Tossing the tweezers down on the desk, he leaned down over the hamster and blew hard several times on his chest.

'Dries instantly,' he announced. 'You can let him go.'

The hamster began running fussily around the table – he would run up to the edge, lower his nose over it as though he was trying to make out the floor far below, twitch it rapidly and then set off for the opposite edge, where the same procedure was repeated.

'What did he get the medal for?' Tatarsky asked.

'I'm in a good mood. Why, are you jealous?'

Azadovsky caught the hamster, tossed it back into the cage, locked the door and carried it back to the cupboard.

'Why does he have such a strange name?'

'You know what, Babylen,' said Azadovsky, sitting back down in his chair, 'Rostropovich could ask you the same thing.'

Tatarsky remembered he'd been advised not to say too much or ask too many questions. Azadovsky put the medals and accessories away in the desk, crumpled up the sheet of paper stained with glue and tossed it into the waste bin.

'To cut it short, we're taking you on for a trial period of three months,' he said. 'We have our own advertising department now, but we don't produce so much ourselves; we're more into coordinating the work of several of the major agencies. Sort of like we don't play, but we keep score. So for the time being you'll be in the internal reviews department on the third floor from the next entrance. We'll keep an eye on you and think things over, and if you suit, we'll move you on to something with more responsibility. Have you seen how many floors we have here?'

'Yes, I have,' said Tatarsky.

'All right then. The potential for growth is unlimited. Any questions?'

Tatarsky decided to ask the question that had been tormenting him since the moment they met.

'Tell me, Mr Azadovsky, yesterday I saw this clip about these pills – wasn't it you playing the doctor?'

'Yes, it was,' Azadovsky said drily. 'Is there some law against that?'

He looked away from Tatarsky, picked up the phone and opened his notebook. Tatarsky realised that the audience was over. Shifting uncertainly from one foot to the other, he glanced at the carpet.

'D'you think I could . . .'

He didn't need to finish. Azadovsky smiled, pulled a straw out of the vase and tossed it on to the desk.

'Shit-stupid question,' he said, and began dialling a number.

CHAPTER 12

A Cloud in Pants

The pivotal element of the office environment was the piercing voice of the western Ukrainian cook that emanated from the small canteen almost all day long. All the other elements of aural reality were strung on it like beads on a thread: telephones ringing, voices, the fax squeaking and the printer humming. The material objects and people occupying the room all condensed around this primary reality – or at least at was the way things had seemed to Tatarsky for quite a w months now.

'So there I am yesterday driving down Pokrovka,' a cigarette critic who'd just dashed in was telling the secretary in a high, thin tenor, 'and I brake at the crossroads there for this queue. Beside me there's this Chaika, and out of it gets this real heavy-looking Chechen, and he looks around like he's just shit on everyone from a great height. He stands there, you know, like really getting into it; then suddenly up pulls this real gen-u-ine Cadillac, and out gets this girl in tattered jeans and runners and dashes over to a kiosk to get some Pepsi-Cola. You can just imagine what's going on with the Chechen! Imagine having to swallow that!'

'Wow!' replied the secretary, without looking up from her computer keyboard.

There were talking behind Tatarsky too, and very loudly. One of his subordinates, a late-middle-aged editor and old Communist Party publication type, was hauling someone over the coals on the speaker-phone in a rumbling bass voice. Tatarsky could tell the editor's deafening volume and implacable heartiness were intended for his ears. This only irritated him, and his sympathy was captured by the thin, sad voice replying from the speaker-phone.

'I corrected one but not the other,' the voice said quietly.

'That's how it happened.'

'Well, well,' growled the editor. 'So what on earth do you think about when you're working? You're handling two pieces – one called "Prisoner of Conscience" and the other called "Eunuchs of the Harem", right?'

'Right.'

'You put headings on the clipboard to change the font, and then on page thirty-five you find "Prisoner of the Harem", right?'

'Right.'

'Then shouldn't it be obvious enough that on page seventy-four you're going to have "Eunuchs of Conscience"? Or are you just a total tosser?'

'I'm a total tosser,' agreed the sad voice.

'You're both fucking tossers,' thought Tatarsky. He'd been feeling depressed since the morning – probably because of the constant rain. He'd been sitting by the window and staring at the roofs of the cars as they ploughed through the streams of murky water. Old Ladas and Moskviches built back in Soviet times stood rusting along the edge of the pavement like garbage the river of time had tossed up on to its muddy shore. The river of time itself consisted for the most part of bright-coloured foreign cars with water spurting up in fountains from under their tyres.

Lying on the desk in front of Tatarsky was a pack of Gold Yava cigarettes, the new version of the old Soviet favourite, set in a cardboard display frame, and a heap of papers.

'Just take a Mercedes, even,' he thought feebly. 'A great car, no denying that. But somehow the way life's arranged round here all you can do with it is ride from one heap of shit to another . . .'

He leaned his head against the glass and looked down at the car park, where he could see the white roof of the second-hand Mercedes he'd bought a month earlier that was already starting to give him trouble. 'Second-hand,' he thought. 'A good name for a prosthesis shop . . .'

He sighed and mentally switched round the 'c' and the 'd' to make 'Merdeces'.

'But it doesn't really matter,' his train of thought ploughed on wearily, 'because if you keep riding around in these heaps long enough, you turn into such a shit yourself that nothing around you leaves any kind of mark on you. Of course, you don't turn into a shit just because you buy a Mercedes-600. It's the other way round: the reason you can afford to buy a Mercedes-600 is that you turn into a shit . . .'

He looked out of the window again and jotted down: 'Merde-SS. In the sense of the occult group or movement.'

It was time he got back to work. Or rather, it was time he started work. He had to write an internal review on the Gold Yava advertising campaign, then on the Camay soap and Gucci male fragrances scenarios. The Yava job was a real pain because Tatarsky hadn't been able to work out whether or not they were expecting a positive review from him, so he wasn't sure which way he should direct his thoughts So he decided to start with the scenarios. There were six pages of the soap text, filled with close-set writing. Opening it at the last page with a gesture of squeamish disgust, Tatarsky read the final paragraph: 'It's getting dark. The heroine is falling asleep and she dreams of waves of bright, gleaming hair greedily drinking in a blue liquid pouring down on them from the sky, full of proteins, vitamin B-5 and infinite happiness.'

He frowned, picked up the red pencil from his desk and wrote in above the text: 'Too literary. How many times do I have to tell you: we don't need writers here, we need creatives. Infinite happiness can't be conveyed by means of an image sequence. Scrap it!'

The scenario for Gucci was much shorter:

Opening shot – the door of a country lavatory. Flies buzzing. The door slowly opens and we see a skinny man with a horseshoe moustache who looks as though he has a hangover squatting over the hole. Caption on-screen: 'Literary critic Pavel Bisinsky'. The man looks up towards the camera, and as though continuing a conversation that's been going on for a long time, says: 'The argument over whether Russia is a part of Europe is a very old one. In principle a real professional has no difficulty in telling what Pushkin thought on this matter at any period of his life, within a few months either way. For instance, in a letter of 1833 to Prince Vyazemsky he wrote . . .'

At this point there is a loud cracking sound, the boards beneath the man break and he plunges into the cesspit. We hear a loud splash. The camera closes in on the pit, rising higher at the same time (camera movement modelled on the aerial shot of the Titanic*) and shows us the surface of the dark sludge from above. The literary critic's head emerges at the surface, he looks upwards and continues where he was interrupted by his sudden tumble.*

'Perhaps the origins of the debate should be sought in the division of the church. Krylov had a point when he said to Chaadaev: "Sometimes you look around and it seems as though you don't live in Europe, but in some kind of . . ."'

Something jerks the critic violently downwards, and he sinks to the bottom with a gurgling sound. There is silence, broken only by the buzzing of the flies. Voice-over:

GUCCI FOR MEN
BE A EUROPEAN: SMELL BETTER.

Tatarsky took up his blue pencil. 'Very good,' he wrote in under the text. 'Approved. But replace the flies with Michael Jackson/Sex-Shop Dogs, change the critic for a new Russian and Pushkin, Krylov and Chaadaev for another new Russian. Cover the walls of the lavatory with pink silk. Rewrite the monologue so the speaker is recalling a fight in a restaurant on the Côte d'Azur. It's time to have done with literary history and think about our real clientele.'

The scenario had inspired Tatarsky and he decided finally to settle accounts with Yava. He picked up the item to be reviewed and looked it over closely once again. It was a pack of cigarettes with an empty cardboard box of the same dimensions glued to it. There was a bird's-eye view of New York on the cardboard, with a pack of Gold Yava swooping over it like a missile warhead. The caption under the picture was: 'Counter-Strike'. Tatarsky pulled over a clean sheet of paper and hesitated for a while over which pencil to choose, the red or the blue. He laid them side by side, closed his eyes, waved his hand around above them and jabbed downwards with his forefinger. He hit the blue one.

We must certainly acknowledge that the use in advertising of the idea and the symbolism of the counter-strike is a fortunate choice. It suits the mood of the broad masses of the lumpen intelligentsia, who are the pri-

mary consumers of these cigarettes. For a long time already the mass media have been agitating for some healthy national 'response' in opposition to the violent domination of American pop culture and Neanderthal liberalism. The problem is to locate the basis of this response. In an internal review not intended for outsiders' eyes, we can state that it simply doesn't exist. The authors of this advertising concept attempt to plug this semantic breach with a pack of Gold Yava, which will undoubtedly trigger a highly positive crystallisation in the potential consumer. It will take the form of the consumer unconsciously believing that every cigarette he smokes brings the planetary triumph of the Russian idea a little closer . . .

After a moment's hesitation Tatarsky changed the first letter of 'idea' to a capital.

On the other hand, we have to take into account the overall impact of all the symbolism that is incorporated in the brand essence. In this connection it would seem that the combination of the slogan 'Counter-Strike' with the logo of British–American Tobacco Co., the company that produces these cigarettes now, could induce a kind of mental short-circuit in one section of the target group. The question that quite logically arises is whether the pack is descending on New York or actually being launched from there. If the latter is the case (and this would appear to be the more logical assumption, since the pack is shown with its lid upwards) it is not clear why this is a 'counter-strike'.

Outside the window the bells in the tower of a small church nearby began chiming rapidly. Tatarsky listened thoughtfully for several seconds and then wrote:

The consumer might be led to conclude that Western propaganda is superior in a general sense, and that it is impossible for an introverted society to compete with an extroverted one in the provision of images.

Re-reading the last sentence, Tatarsky saw that it stank of the Slavophilic complex. He crossed it out and rounded off the theme decisively:

However, only the least materially well-off section of the target group is capable of drawing such analytical conclusions, and therefore this slip is unlikely to have any adverse effect on sales. The project should be approved.

The phone on his desk rang and Tatarsky picked up the receiver: 'Hello.'

'Tatarsky! On the boss's carpet at the double,' said Morkovin.

Tatarsky told the secretary to type up what he'd written and went downstairs. It was still raining. He pulled his collar up and dashed across the yard to the other wing of the building. The rain was heavy and he was almost soaked through before he'd run as far as the entrance to the marble hall. 'Surely they could have built an internal connection,' he thought irritably. 'It's the same building, after all. Now I'll make a mess of the entire carpet.' But the sight of the guards with their sub-machine guns had a calming effect on him. One of the guards with a Scorpion on his shoulder was waiting for him by the lift, toying with a key on a chain.

Morkovin was sitting in Azadovsky's reception room. When he saw that Tatarsky was soaked, he gave a laugh of satisfaction. 'Nostrils flaring are they? Forget it. Leonid's away; there won't be any bee-keeping today.'

Tatarsky sensed something was missing in the reception room. He looked around and saw the round mirror and golden mask had disappeared from the wall.

'Where's he gone then?'

'Baghdad.'

'What for?'

'The ruins of Babylon are near there. He got some kind of idea into his head about climbing that tower they still have there. Showed me a photo. Real heavy stuff.'

Tatarsky gave no sign of being affected in any way by what he'd just heard. Trying to make his movements look normal, he picked up the cigarettes lying on the desk and lit one.

'What makes him so interested in that?' he asked.

'Says his soul's thirsting for the heights. Why've you gone so pale?'

'I haven't had a cigarette for two days,' said Tatarsky. 'I was trying to give up.'

'Buy a nicotine patch.'

Tatarsky was already back in control of himself.

'Listen,' he said, 'yesterday I saw Azadovsky in another two clips. I see him every time I turn on the TV. One day he's dancing in the corps de ballet, the next he's reading the weather forecast. What does it all mean? Why's he on so often? Does he just like being filmed?'

'Yeah,' said Morkovin, 'it's a weakness of his. My advice to you is not to stick your nose into that for the time being. Some time maybe you'll find out all about it. OK?'

'OK.'

'Let's get down to business. What's the latest on our Kalash-nikov scenario? Their brand manager was just on the phone.'

'Nothing new. It's still the same: two old guys shoot down Batman over the Moskvoretsky market. Batman falls on to this kebab brazier and flaps his webbed wing in the dust; then he's hidden by this group of old women in sarafans dancing and singing folk songs.'

'But why two old guys?'

'One has a short-barrel version and the other has a stan-dard. They wanted the whole range.'

Morkovin thought for a moment.

'Probably a father and son would do better than just two old guys. Give the father the standard and the son the short barrel. And let's have not just Batman, but Spawn and Night-man and the whole fucking gang. The budget's huge; we have to cover it.'

'Thinking logically,' Tatarsky said, 'the son should have the standard and the father should have the sawn-off.'

Morkovin thought again for a moment.

'That's right,' he agreed. 'Good thinking. Only we won't have the mother with a holster, that would be overkill. OK, that wasn't what I called you over for. I've got some good news.'

He paused tantalisingly.

'What news is that?' Tatarsky asked with feeble enthusiasm.

'The first section has finally checked you out. So you're being promoted – Azadovsky told me to put you in the pic-ture. So I'll do that right now.'

The canteen was empty and quiet. The television hanging on a pole in the corner was showing a news broadcast with the sound turned off. Morkovin nodded for Tatarsky to sit at the table by the television, then went over to the counter and returned with two glasses and a bottle of Smirnoff Citrus Twist.

'Let's have a drink. You're soaked; you could catch a cold.'

He sat down at the table, then shook the bottle with some special kind of movement and gazed for a long time at the small bubbles that appeared in the liquid.

'Well, would you believe it!' he said in astonishment. 'I can understand it in some kiosk out on the street . . . But even in here it's fake. I can tell for sure it's homebrew out of Poland . . . Just look at it fizz! So that's what an upgrade can do . . .'

Tatarsky realised that the final phrase referred not to the vodka, but the television, and he switched his gaze from the opaque bubbly vodka to the screen, where a ruddy-faced, chortling Yeltsin was sawing rapidly at the air with a hand missing two fingers.

'Upgrade?' queried Tatarsky. 'Is that some kind of cardiac stimulator?'

'Who on earth spreads all of those rumours?' said Morkovin, shaking his head. 'What for? They've just stepped up the frequency to six hundred megahertz, that's all. But we're taking a serious risk.'

'You've lost me again,' said Tatarsky.

'It used to take two days to render a report like this; but now we do it in a single night, which means we can program more gestures and facial expressions.'

'But what is it we render?'

'We render him,' said Morkovin with a nod in the direction of the television. 'And all the rest of them. 3-D.'

'3-D?'

'Three-dimensional modelling, if you want the precise term. The guys call it "fiddly-dee".'

Tatarsky gaped at his friend, trying to work out whether he was joking or serious. His friend withstood his gaze in silence.

'What the hell is all this you're telling me?'

'I'm telling you what Azadovsky told me to tell you. I'm putting you in the picture.'

Tatarsky looked at the screen. Now it was showing the rostrum in the Duma, occupied by a dour-looking orator who seemed to have just surfaced from the agitated and murky millpond of folk fury. Suddenly Tatarsky had the impression that the Duma deputy really wasn't alive: his body was completely motionless; only his lips and occasionally his eyebrows moved at all.

'Him as well,' said Morkovin. 'Only his rendering's coarser; there's too many of them. He's episodic. That's a dummy.'

'What?'

'Oh, that's what we call the Duma 3-Ds. Dynamic video bas-relief – the appearance is rendered always at the same angle. It's the same technology, but it cuts the work down by two orders of magnitude. There's two types – stiffs and semi-stiffs. See the way he moves his hands and head? That means he's a stiff. And that one over there, sleeping across his newspaper – he's a semi-stiff. They're much smaller – you can squeeze one of them on to a hard disk. Yes, by the way, our legislature department recently won a prize. Azadovsky was watching the news from the State Duma, and all the semi-stiffs were saying how television's whorish and calculating, all that kind of stuff. Naturally, Azadovsky took offence – he heard the word "calculating" and thought that they were trying to poke their noses into our business. So he decided to get to the bottom of this. He even got as far as picking up the phone and he was already dialling the number when he remembered there was nothing to get to the bottom of! We must be doing a good job if we manage to impress ourselves.'

'You mean they're all . . .?'

'Every last one of them.'

'Oh come off it,' Tatarsky said uncertainly. 'What about all the people who see them every day?'

'Where?'

'On TV . . . Oh, right . . . Well, I mean . . . After all, there are people who meet them every day.'

'Have you seen those people?'

'Of course.'

'Where?'

Tatarsky thought about it. 'On TV,' he said.

'You get my point, then?'

'I'm beginning to,' Tatarsky replied.

'Speaking strictly theoretically, you could meet someone

165

who tells you he's seen them himself or even knows them. There's a special service for that called The People's Will. More than a hundred of them, former state security agents, and all Azadovsky's men. That's their job: to go around telling people they've just seen our leaders. One at his three-storey dacha, one with an under-age whore, one in a yellow Lamborghini on the Rubliovskoe Highway. But The People's Will mostly works the beer halls and railway stations, and you don't hang around those places.'

'Are you telling me the truth?' Tatarsky asked.

'The truth, cross my heart.'

'But it's such a massive scam.'

'Aagh, no,' Morkovin said with a grimace, 'please, not that. By his very nature every politician is just a television broadcast. Even if we do sit a live human being in front of the camera, his speeches are going to be written by a team of speechwriters, his jackets are going to be chosen by a group of stylists, and his decisions are going to be taken by the Interbank Committee. And what if he suddenly has a stroke – are we supposed to set up the whole shebang all over again?'

'OK, let's say you're right,' said Tatarsky. 'But how is it possible on such a huge scale?'

'Are you interested in the technology? I can give you the general outline. First you need a source figure – a wax model or a human being. You use it to model the corporeal cloud. D'you know what a corporeal cloud is?'

'Isn't it some kind of astral thing?'

'No. Some blockheads or other have been feeding you a load of nonsense. A corporeal cloud is the same thing as a digital cloud-form. Just a cloud of points in space. You define it either with a probe or with a laser scanner. Then the points are linked up – you impose a digital grid on them and close up the cracks. That involves a whole bundle of procedures – stitching, clean-up, and so on.'

'But what do they stitch it up with?'

'Numbers. They stitch up numbers with other numbers. I don't understand it all by a long way – I studied the humanities, you know that. Anyway, when we've stitched everything up and cleaned it all up, we end up with a model. There are two types – one's called polygonal, and the other's called NURBS patch. A polygonal model consists of triangles, and a NURBS – that is 'non-union rational bi-spline' – consists of curves. That's the advanced technology for serious 3-Ds. The Duma dummies are all polygonals – it's less hassle and it keeps the faces more folksy. So when the model's ready, you put a skeleton inside it, and that's digital too. It's like a set of sticks on ball-joints – on the monitor it actually looks like a skeleton, but without the ribs – and you animate the skeleton like they do for a cartoon film: move an arm this way, move a leg that way. Only we don't actually do it by hand any more. We have special people who work as skeletons.'

'Work as skeletons?'

Morkovin glanced at his watch. 'They're shooting right now in studio number 3. Let's go take a look. It'll take me all day to try to explain things to you.'

Several minutes later Tatarsky timidly followed Morkovin into a space that resembled the studio of a conceptual artist who has received a large grant for working with plywood. It was a hall two storeys high filled with numerous plywood constructions of various shapes and indefinite function – there were staircases leading into nowhere, incomplete rostrums, plywood surfaces sloping down to the floor at various angles, and even a long plywood limousine. Tatarsky didn't see any cameras or studio lights, but there were large numbers of mysterious electrical boxes looking like musical equipment heaped up by the wall, and sitting beside them on chairs were four men who seemed to be engineers. Standing on the floor beside them were a half-empty bottle of vodka and a large number of beer cans. One of the engineers, wearing earphones, was staring into a monitor. They waved in friendly greeting to Morkovin, but no one took his attention off his work.

'Hey, Arkasha,' the man in the earphones called out. 'Don't laugh now, but we'll have to go again.'

'What?' said a hoarse voice somewhere in the centre of the hall.

Turning towards the voice, Tatarsky saw a strange device: a plywood slope like the ones you see in children's playgrounds, only higher. The sloping surface broke off above a hammock supported on wooden poles, and an aluminium stepladder led up to its summit. A heavy, elderly man with the face of a veteran policeman was sitting on the floor beside the hammock. He was wearing tracksuit trousers and a tee shirt with an inscription in English: 'Sick my duck'. Tatarsky thought the inscription too sentimental and not quite grammatically correct.

'You heard, Arkasha. Let's go for it again.'

'How many more times?' Arkasha mumbled. 'I'm getting dizzy.'

'Try another shot to loosen you up. So far it's still kind of tight. I mean it; take one.'

'The last glass hasn't hit me yet,' Arkasha replied, getting up off the floor and wandering over to the engineers. Tatarsky noticed there were black plastic discs attached to his wrists, elbows, knees and ankles; and there were more of them on his body – Tatarsky counted fourteen in all.

'Who's that?' he asked in a whisper.

'That's Arkady Korzhakov. No, don't go getting any ideas. Not Yeltsin's old bodyguard. He's just got the same name. Works as Yeltsin's skeleton. Same weight, same dimensions; and he's an actor, too. Used to do Shakespeare at the Young People's Theatre.'

'But what does he do?'

'You'll see in a moment. Like some beer?'

Tatarsky nodded. Morkovin brought over two cans of Tuborg. It gave Tatarsky a strange feeling to see the familiar figure in the white shirt on the can – Tuborg man was still wiping the sweat from his forehead in the same old way, afraid of continuing his final journey.

Arkasha downed a glass of vodka and went back to the slope. He scrambled up the slope and stood motionless at the top of the plywood structure.

'Shall I start?' he asked.

'Hang on,' said the man in the earphones, 'we'll just recalibrate.'

Arkasha squatted down on his haunches and took hold of the edge of the plywood surface with his hand, so that he resembled a huge fat pigeon.

'What are those washers he's got on him?' asked Tatarsky.

'Those are sensors,' replied Morkovin. 'Motion-capture technology. He wears them at the points where the skeleton has its ball-joints. When Arkasha moves, we record their trajectory. Then we filter it a little bit, superimpose it on the model and the machine works it all out. It's a new system, called Star Trak. The hottest thing on the market right now. No wires, thirty-two sensors, works anywhere you like, but the price – you can imagine . . .'

The man in the earphones turned away from the monitor.

'Ready,' he said. 'Right I'll run through it from the top. First you hug him, then you invite him to walk down, then you stumble. Only when you lower your arm, make it grander, more majestic. And fall flat, full length. Got it?'

'Got it,' Arkasha mumbled, and rose carefully to his feet. He was swaying slightly.

'Let's go.'

Arkasha turned to his left, opened his arms wide and slowly brought them together in empty space. Tatarsky was amazed at the way his movements were instantly filled with stately grandeur and majestic pomp. At first it put Tatarsky in mind of of Stanislavsky's system, but then he realised Arkasha was simply having difficulty balancing on such a tiny spot high above the floor and was struggling not to fall. When he opened his arms again, Arkasha gestured expansively for his invisible companion to descend the slope, took a step towards it, swayed on the edge of the plywood precipice and went tumbling clumsily downwards. As he fell he somersaulted twice, and if his heavy frame had not landed in the hammock there would certainly have been broken bones. Having fallen into the hammock, Arkasha carried on lying there, with his arms wrapped round his head. The engineers crowded round the monitor and began arguing about something in quiet voices.

'What's it going to be?' Tatarsky asked.

Without saying a word, Morkovin held out a photograph. Tatarsky saw some kind of hall in the Kremlin with malachite columns and a wide, sweeping marble staircase with a red-carpet-runnner.

'Listen, why do we show him pissed if he's only virtual?'

'Improves the ratings.'

'This improves his ratings?'

'Not his rating. What kind of rating can an electromagnetic wave have? The channel's ratings. Never tried to figure out why it's forty thousand a minute during prime time news?'

'I just did. How long has he been . . . like this?'

'Since that time he danced in Rostov during the election campaign. When he fell off the stage. We had to get him coded double quick. Remember that by-pass operation he had? There were no end of problems. By the time they finished digitising him, he stank so bad that everyone was working in respirators.

'But how do they do the face?' Tatarsky asked. The movement and the expression?'

'Same thing. Only it's an optical system, not a magnetic one. "Adaptive optics". And for the hands we have the "Cyber Glove" system. Slice two fingers off one of them – and Boris is your uncle.'

'Hey, guys,' said one of the engineers, 'keep it down a bit, can you? Arkasha's got another jump to do. Let him rest up.'

'What?' said Arkasha, sitting up in the hammock. 'You lost your marbles, have you?'

'Let's go,' said Morkovin.

The next space Morkovin took Tatarsky into was called the 'Virtual Studio'. Despite the name, inside there were genuine cameras and studio lights that gave off a pleasant warmth. The studio was a large room with green walls and floor. They were filming several people got up in fashionable rural outfits. They were standing round an empty space and nodding thoughtfully, while one of them rolled a ripe ear of wheat between his hands. Morkovin explained that they were prosperous farmers, who were cheaper to shoot on film than to animate.

'We tell them more or less which way to look,' he said, 'and when to ask questions. Then we can match them up with anyone we like. Have you seen *Starship Troopers*? Where the starship troopers fight the bugs?'

'Yeah.'

'It's the same thing. Only instead of the troopers we have farmers or small businessmen, inside of the automatics we have bread and salt, and instead of the bug we have Zyuganov or Lebed. Then we match them up, paste in the Cathedral of Christ the Saviour or the Baikonur launch-pad in the background, copy it to Betacam and put it out on air . . . Let's go take a look at the control room as well.'

The control room, located behind a door with the coy inscription 'Engine Room', failed to make any particular impression on Tatarsky. The two guards with automatic rifles standing by the door made an impression all right, but the actual premises seemed uninteresting. They consisted of a small room with squeaky parquet flooring and dusty wallpaper with green gladioli that could clearly remember Soviet times very well. There was no furniture in the room, but hanging on one wall was a colour photograph of Yuri Gagarin holding a dove in his hands, and the wall opposite was covered with metal shelving holding numerous identical blue boxes, on which the only decoration was the Silicon Graphics logo, looking like a snowflake. In appearance the boxes were not much different from the device Tatarsky had seen once in Draft Podium. There were no interesting lamps or indicators on these boxes – any old run-of-the-mill transformer might have looked just the same – but Morkovin behaved with extreme solemnity.

'Azadovsky said you like life to have big tits,' he said. 'Well, this is the biggest of the lot. And if it doesn't excite you yet, that's just because you're not used to it yet.'

'What is it?'

'A 100/400 render-server. Silicon Graphics turns them out specially for this kind of work – high end. In American terms it's already outdated, of course, but it does the job for us. All of Europe runs on these, anyway. It can render up to one hundred primary and four hundred secondary politicians.'

'A massive computer,' Tatarsky said without enthusiasm.

'It's not even a computer. It's a stand with twenty-four computers controlled from a single keyboard. Four 1,5-gigahertz processors in every one. Each block calculates the frames in turn and the entire system works a bit like an aviation cannon with revolving barrels. The Americans took big bucks off us for this baby! But what can you do? When everything was just starting up, we didn't have anything like it. Now, you know yourself, we never will have. The Americans, by the way, are our biggest problem. They keep cutting us back like we were some kind of jerks.'

'How d'you mean?'

'The processor frequency. First they cut us back by two hundred megahertz for Chechnya. It was really for the pipeline – you realise that, anyway. Then because we stole those loans. And so on, for any old reason at all. Of course, we push things to the limit at night, but they watch TV in the embassy like everyone else. As soon we step up the frequency they pick it up and send round an inspector. It's plain shameful. A great country like this stuck on four hundred megahertz – and not even our own.'

Morkovin went over to the stand, pulled out a slim blue box and lifted up its lid to expose a liquid-crystal monitor. Below it was a keyboard with a track-ball.

'Is that the keyboard it's controlled from?' Tatarsky asked.

'Of course not,' said Morkovin with a dismissive wave of his hand. 'You need clearance to be able to get into the system. All the terminals are upstairs. This is just a check monitor. I want to see what we're rendering at the moment.'

He prodded at the keys and a window with a progress indicator appeared at the bottom of the screen. It also had several incomprehensible messages in English in it: *memory used 5184 M, time elapsed 23:11:12*, and something else in very fine script. Then the pathway selected appeared in large letters: *C:/oligarchs/berezka/excesses /field_disgr/slalom.prg.*

'I see,' said Morkovin. 'It's Berezovsky in Switzerland.'

Small squares containing fragments of an image began covering the screen, as though someone was assembling a jigsaw. After a few seconds Tatarsky recognised the familiar face with a few black holes in it still not rendered – he was absolutely astounded by the insane joy shining in the already computed right eye.

'He's off skiing, the bastard,' said Morkovin, 'and you and me are stuck in here breathing dust.'

'Why's the folder called "excesses"? What's so excessive about skiing?'

'Instead of those sticks with flags on them the storyboard has him skiing round naked ballerinas,' Morkovin replied. 'Some of them have blue ribbons and some of them have red ones. We filmed the girls out on the slope. They were delighted to get a free trip to Switzerland. Two of them are still doing the rounds over there.'

He turned off the control monitor, closed it and pushed the unit back into place. Tatarsky was suddenly struck by an alarming thought. 'Listen,' he said, 'you say the Americans are doing the same?'

'Sure. And it started a lot earlier. Reagan was animated all his second term. As for Bush – d'you remember that time he stood beside a helicopter and the hair he'd combed across his bald patch kept lifting up and waving in the air? A real masterpiece. I don't reckon there's ever been anything in computer graphics to compare with it. America . . .'

'But is it true their copywriters work on our politics?'

'That's a load of lies. They can't even come up with anything any good for themselves. Resolution, numbers of pixels, special effects – no problem. But it's a country with no soul. All their political creatives are pure shit. They have two candidates for president and only one team of scriptwriters. It's just full of guys who've been given the push by Madison Avenue, because the money's bad in politics. I've been looking through their election campaign material for ages now, and it's dreadful. If one of them talks about a bridge to the past, then a couple of days later the other one's bound to start talking about a bridge to the future. For Bob Dole all they did was rewrite the Nike slogan from "just do it" to "just don't do it". And the best they can come up with is a blow job in the Oral Office . . . Nah, our scriptwriters are ten times as good. Just look what rounded characters they write. Yeltsin, Zyuganov, Lebed. As good as Chekhov. *The Three Sisters*. Anyone who says Russia has no brands of its own should have the words rammed down their throat. With the talent we have here, we've no need to feel ashamed in front of anyone. Look at that, for instance, you see?'

173

He nodded at the photograph of Gagarin. Tatarsky took a closer look at it and realised it wasn't Gagarin at all, but General Lebed in dress uniform, and it wasn't a dove in his hands but a white rabbit with its ears pressed back. The photograph was so similar to its prototype that it produced a kind of *trompe l'oeil* effect: for a moment the rabbit in Lebed's hands actually seemed to be an indecently obese pigeon.

'A young miner did that,' said Morkovin. 'It's for the cover of our *Playboy*. The slogan to go with it is: "Russia will be glossy and sassy". For the hungry regions it's spot on, a bull's eye – instant association with "sausage". The young guy probably only used to eat every other day, and now he's one of the top creatives. He still tends to focus on food a lot, though . . .'

'Hang on,' said Tatarsky, 'I've got a good idea. Let me just write it down.'

He took his notebook out of his pocket and wrote:

Silicon Graphics/big tits – new concept for the Russian market. Instead of a snowflake the outline of an immense tit that looks like its been filled out with a silicon implant (casually drawn with a pen, for 'graphics'). In the animation (the clip) an organic silicon worm crawls out of the nipple and curves itself into a $ sign (model on Species-II). Think about it.

'A rush of sweaty inspiration?' Morkovin asked. 'I feel envious. OK, the excursion's over. Let's go to the canteen.'

The canteen was still empty. The television was playing away with no sound, and their two glasses and unfinished bottle of Smirnoff Citrus Twist were still standing on the table below it. Morkovin filled the glasses, clinked his own glass against Tatarsky's without saying a word and drank up. The excursion had left Tatarsky feeling vaguely uneasy.

'Listen,' he said, 'there's one thing I don't understand. OK, so copywriters write all their texts for them; but who's responsible for what's in the texts? Where do we get the subjects from? And how do we decide which way national policy's going to move tomorrow?'

'Big business,' Morkovin answered shortly. 'You've heard of the oligarchs?'

'Uhuh. You mean, they get together and sort out things? Or do they send in their concepts in written form?'

Morkovin put his thumb over the opening of the bottle, shook it and began gazing at the bubbles – he obviously found something fascinating in the sight. Tatarsky said nothing as he waited for an answer.

'How can they all get together anywhere,' Morkovin replied at long last, 'when all of them are made on the next floor up? You've just seen Berezovsky for yourself.'

'Uhuh,' Tatarsky responded thoughtfully. 'Yes, of course. Then who writes the scripts for the oligarchs?'

'Copywriters. All exactly the same, just one floor higher.'

'Uhuh. And how do we decide what the oligarchs are going to decide?'

'Depends on the political situation. "Decide" is only a word, really. In actual fact we don't have too much choice about it. We're hemmed in tight by the iron law of necessity. For both sets of them. And for you and me too.'

'So you mean there aren't any oligarchs, either? But what about that board downstairs: the Interbank Committee . . .?'

'That's just to stop the filth from trying to foist their protection on us. We're the Interbank Committee all right, only all the banks are intercommittee banks. And we're the committee. That's the way it is.'

'I get you,' said Tatarsky. 'I think I get you, anyway . . . That is, hang on there . . . That means this lot determine that lot, and that lot . . . That lot determine this lot. But then how . . . Hang on . . . Then what's holding the whole lot up?'

He broke off in a howl of pain: Morkovin had pinched him on the wrist as hard as he could – so hard he'd even torn off a small patch of skin.

'Don't you ever,' he said, leaning over the table and staring darkly into Tatarsky's eyes, 'not ever, think about that. Not ever, get it?'

'But how?' Tatarsky asked, sensing that the pain had thrown him back from the edge of a deep, dark abyss. 'How can I not think about it?'

'There's this technique,' said Morkovin. 'Like when you realise that any moment now you're going to think that thought all the way through, you pinch yourself or you prick yourself with something sharp. In your arm or your leg – it doesn't matter where. Wherever there are plenty of nerve endings. The way a swimmer pricks his calf when he gets cramp. In order not to drown. And then gradually you build up something like a callus around the thought and it's no real problem to you to avoid it. Like, you can feel it's there, only you never think it. And gradually you get used to it. The eighth floor's supported by the seventh floor, the seventh floor's supported by the eighth floor; and everywhere, at any specific point and any specific moment, things are stable. Then, when the work comes piling in, and you do a line of coke, you'll spend the whole day on the run fencing concrete problems. You won't have time left for the abstract ones.'

Tatarsky drained the rest of the vodka in a single gulp and pinched his own thigh several times. Morkovin gave a sad laugh.

'Take Azadovsky,' he said, 'why d'you think he winds everyone up and comes on heavy like that? Because it never even enters his head that there's something strange in all of this. People like that are only born once in a hundred years. He's got a real sense of life on an international scale . . .'

'All right,' said Tatarsky, pinching his leg again. 'But surely someone has to control the economy, not just wind people up and come on heavy? The economy's complicated. Doesn't it take some kind of principles to regulate it?'

'The principle's very simple,' said Morkovin. 'Monetarism. To keep everything in the economy normal, all we have to do is to control the gross stock of money we have. And everything else automatically falls into place. So we mustn't interfere in anything.'

'And how do we control this gross stock?'

'So as to make is as big as possible.'

'And that's it?'

'Of course. If the gross stock of money we have is as big as possible, that means everything's hunky-dory.'

'Yes,' said Tatarsky, 'that's logical. But still someone has to run everything, surely?'

'You want to understand everything far too quickly,' Morkovin said with a frown. 'I told you, just wait a while. That, my friend, is a great problem – trying to understand just who's running things. For the time being let me just say the world isn't run by a "who", it's run by a "what". By certain factors and impulses it's too soon for you to be learning about. Although in fact, Babe, there's no way you could not know about them. That's the paradox of it all . . .'

Morkovin fell silent and began thinking about something. Tatarsky lit a cigarette – he didn't feel like talking any more. Meanwhile a new client had appeared in the canteen, one that Tatarsky recognised immediately: it was the well-known TV political analyst Farsuk Seiful-Farseikin. In real life he looked a bit older than he did on the screen. He was obviously just back from a broadcast: his face was covered with large beads of sweat, and the famous pince-nez was set crooked on his nose. Tatarsky expected Farseikin to dash over to the counter for vodka, but he came over to their table.

'Mind if I turn on the sound?' he asked, nodded towards the television. 'My son made this clip. I haven't seen it yet.'

Tatarsky looked up. Something strangely familiar was happening on the screen: there was a choir of rather dubious-looking sailors standing in a clearing in a birch forest (Tatarsky recognised Azadovsky right away – he was standing in the middle of the group, the only one with a medal gleaming on his chest). With their arms round each other's shoulders, the sailors were swaying from side to side and gently singing in support of a yellow-haired soloist who looked like the poet Esenin raised to the power of three. At first Tatarsky thought the soloist must be standing on the stump of a gigantic birch tree, but from the ideally cylindrical form of the stump and the small yellow lemons drawn on it, he realised it was a soft drinks can magnified many times over and painted to resemble either a birch tree or a zebra. The slick image-sequencing testified that this was a very expensive clip.

'Bom-bom-bom,' the swaying sailors rumbled dully. The soloist stretched out his hands from his heart towards the camera and sang in a clear tenor:

My motherland gives me
For getting it right
My fill of her fizzy,
Her birch-bright Sprite!

Tatarsky crushed his cigarette into the ashtray with a sharp movement.

'Motherfuckers,' he said.

'Who?' asked Morkovin.

'If only I knew . . . So tell me then, what area do they want to move me into?'

'Senior creative in the *kompromat* department; and you'll be on standby when we have a rush on. So now we'll be standing, shoulder to shoulder, just like those sailors . . . Forgive me, brother, for dragging you into in all this. Life's much simpler for the punters, who don't know anything about it. They even think there are different TV channels and different TV companies . . . But then, that's what makes them punters.'

CHAPTER 13

The Islamic Factor

It happens so often: you're riding along in your white Mercedes and you go past a bus stop. You see the people who've been standing there, waiting in frustration for their bus for God knows how long, and suddenly you notice one of them gazing at you with a dull kind of expression that just might be envy. For a second you really start to believe that this machine stolen from some anonymous German burgher, that still hasn't been fully cleared through the customs in fraternal Belorussia but already has a suspicious knocking in the engine, is the prize that witnesses to your full and total victory over life. A warm shiver runs up and down your spine, you proudly turn your face away from the people standing at the bus stop, and in your very heart of hearts you know that all your trials were not in vain: you've really made it.

Such is the action of the anal wow-factor in our hearts; but somehow Tatarsky failed to experience its sweet titillation. Perhaps the difficulty lay in some specific after-the-rain apathy of the punters standing at their bus stops, or perhaps Tatarsky was simply too nervous: there was a review of his work coming up, and Azadovsky himself was due to attend. Or perhaps the reason lay in the increasingly frequent breakdowns of the social radar locating unit in his mind.

'If we regard events purely from the point of view of image animation,' he thought, glancing round at his neighbours in the traffic jam, 'then we have all our concepts inverted. For the celestial Silicon that renders this entire world, a battered old Lada is a much more complicated job than a new BMW that's been blasted with gales for three years in aerodynamic tunnels. The whole thing comes down to creatives and scenario writers. But what bad bastard could have written this scenario? And who's the viewer who sits and stuffs his face while he watches this screen? Most important of all, could it all really only be happening so that some heavenly agency can rake in something like money from something like advertising? Certainly looks like it. It's a well-known fact that everything in the world is based on similitudes.'

The traffic jam finally began to ease. Tatarsky lowered the window. His mood was completely spoiled; he needed live human warmth. He pulled out of the stream of cars and braked at the bus stop. The broken glass panel in the side of the shelter had been patched over with a board carrying an advertisement for some TV channel showing an allegorical representation of the four mortal sins holding remote controls. An old woman was sitting motionless on the bench under the shelter with a basket on her knees, and sitting beside her was a curly-headed man of about forty, clutching a bottle of beer. He was dressed in a shabby, padded military coat. Noting that the man still seemed to possess a fair amount of vital energy, Tatarsky stuck out his elbow.

'Excuse me, soldier,' he said, 'can you tell me where the Men's Shirts shop is around here?'

The man looked up at him. He must have understood Tatarsky's real motivation, because his eyes were immediately flooded with an ice-cold fury. The brief exchange of glances was most informative – Tatarsky realised that the man realised, and the man realised Tatarsky realised he'd been realised.

'Afghanistan was way heavier,' said the man.

'I beg your pardon, what did you say?'

'What I said was', the man replied, shifting his grip to the neck of the bottle, 'that Afghanistan was way heavier. And don't you even try to beg my pardon.'

Something told Tatarsky the man was not approaching his car in order to tell him the way to the shop, and he flattened the accelerator against the floor. His instinct had not deceived him – a second later something struck hard against the rear windsow and it shattered into a spider's web of cracks, with white foam trickling down over them. Driven by his adrenalin rush, Tatarsky accelerated sharply. 'What a fucker,' he thought, glancing round. 'And they want to build a market economy with people like that.'

After he parked in the yard of the Interbank Committee, a red Range-Rover pulled up beside him – the latest model, with a set of fantastical spotlights perched on its roof and its door decorated with a cheerful drawing of the sun rising over the prairie and the head of an Indian chief clad in a feather headdress. 'I wonder who drives those?' Tatarsky thought, and lingered at the door of his car for a moment.

A fat, squat man wearing an emphatically bourgeois striped suit clambered out of the Range-Rover and turned round, and Tatarsky was amazed to recognise Sasha Blo – fatter than ever, even balder, but still with that same old grimace of tormented failure to understand what was really going on.

'Sasha,' said Tatarsky, 'is that you?'

'Ah, Babe,' said Sasha Blo. 'You're here too? In the dirt department?'

'How d'you know?'

'Elementary, my dear Watson. That's where everybody starts out. Till they get their hand in. There aren't all that many creatives on the books. Everyone knows everyone else. So if I haven't seen you before and now you're parking at this entrance, it means you're in *kompromat*. And you've only been there a couple of weeks at most.'

'It's been a month already,' Tatarsky answered. 'So what're you doing now?'

'Me? I'm head of the Russian Idea department. Drop in if you have any ideas.'

'I'm not much good to you,' Tatarsky answered. 'I tried thinking about it, but it was a flop. You should try driving around the suburbs and asking the guys on the street.'

Sasha Blo frowned in dissatisfaction.

'I tried that at the beginning,' he said. 'You pour the vodka, look into their eyes, and then it's always the same answer: "Bugger off and crash your fucking Mercedes." Can't think of anything cooler than a Mercedes . . . And it's all so destructive . . .'

'That's right,' sighed Tatarsky and looked at the rear window of his car. Sasha Blo followed his glance.

'Is it yours?'

'Yes it is,' Tatarsky said with pride.

'I see,' said Sasha Blo, locking the door of his Range-Rover; 'forty minutes of embarrassment gets you to work. Well, don't let it get you down. Everything's still ahead of you.'

He nodded and ran off jauntily towards the door, flapping a fat, greasy attache case as he went. Tatarsky gazed after him for a long moment, then looked at the rear window of his car again and took out his notebook. 'The worst thing of all', he wrote on the last page, 'is that people base their intercourse with each other on senselessly distracting chatter, into which they cold-bloodedly, cunningly and inhumanly introduce their anal impulse in the hope that it will become someone else's oral impulse. If this happens, the winner shudders orgiastically and for a few seconds experiences the so-called "pulse of life".'

Azadovsky and Morkovin had been sitting in the viewing hall since early morning. Outside the entrance several people were walking backwards and forwards, sarcastically discussing Yeltsin's latest binge. Tatarsky decided they must be copywriters from the political department practising corporate non-action. They were called in one by one; on average they spent about ten minutes with the bosses. Tatarsky realised that the problems discussed were of state significance – he heard Yeltsin's voice emanate from the hall at maximum volume several times. The first time he burbled:

'What do we want so many pilots for? We only need one pilot, but ready for anything! The moment I saw my grandson playing with Play Station I knew straightaway what we need . . .'

The second time they were obviously playing back a section from an address to the nation, because Yeltsin's voice was solemn and measured: 'For the first time in many decades the population of Russia now has the chance to choose between the heart and the head. Vote with your heart!'

One project was wound up – that was obvious from the face of the tall man with a moustache and prematurely grey hair who emerged from the hall clutching a crimson looseleaf folder with the inscription 'Tsar'. Then music began playing in the hall – at first a balalaika jangled for a long time, then

Tatarsky heard Azadovsky shouting: 'Bugger it! We'll take him off the air. Next.'

Tatarsky was the last in the queue. The dimly lit hall where Azadovsky was waiting looked luxurious but somewhat archaic, as though it had been decorated and furnished back in the forties. For some reason Tatarsky bent down when he entered. He trotted across to the first row and perched on the edge of the chair to the left of Azadovsky, who was ejecting streams of smoke into the beam of the video-projector. Azadovsky shook his hand without looking at him – he was obviously in a bad mood. Tatarsky knew what the problem was: Morkovin had explained it to him the day before.

'They've dropped us to three hundred megahertz,' he said gloomily. 'For Kosovo. Remember how under the communists there were shortages of butter? Now it's machine time. There's something fatal about this country. Now Azadovsky's watching all the drafts himself. Nothing's allowed on the main render-server without written permission, so give it your best shot.'

It was the first time Tatarsky had seen what a draft – that is a rough sketch before it's been rendered in full – actually looked like. If he hadn't written the scenario himself, he would never have guessed that the green outline divided by lines of fine yellow dots was a table with a game of Monopoly set up on it. The playing pieces were identical small red arrows, and the dice were two blue blobs, but the game had been modelled honestly – in the lower section of the screen pairs of numbers from one to six flickered on and off, produced by the random number generator. The players themselves didn't exist yet, though their moves corresponded to the points scored. Their places were occupied by skeletons of graduated lines with little circles as ball-joints. Tatarsky could only see their faces, constructed of coarse polygons – Salaman Raduev's beard was like a rusty brick attached to the lower section of his face and a round bullet scar on his temple looked like a red button. Berezovsky was recognisable from the blue triangles of his shaved cheeks. As was only to be expected, Berezovsky was winning.

'Yes,' he said, 'in Mother Russia, Monopoly's a bit dicey. You buy a couple of streets, and then it turns out there are people living on them.'

Raduev laughed: 'Not just in Russia. It's like that every-where. And I'll tell you something else, Boris: not only do peo-ple live there; often they actually think the streets are theirs.'

Berezovsky tossed the dice. Once again he got two sixes.

'That's not quite how it is,' he said. 'Nowadays people find out what they think from the television. So if you want to buy up a couple of streets and still sleep well, first you have to buy a TV tower.'

There was a squeak, and an animated insert appeared in the corner of the table: a military walkie-talkie with a long aerial. Raduev lifted it to his head-joint, said something curt in Chechen and put it back.

'I'm selling off my TV announcer,' he said, and flicked a playing piece into the centre of the table with his finger. 'I don't like television.'

'I'm buying,' Berezovsky responded quickly. 'But why don't you like it?'

'I don't like it because piss comes into contact with skin too often when you watch it,' said Raduev, shaking the dice in the green arrows of his fingers. 'Every time I turn on the televi-sion, there's piss coming into contact with skin and causing irritation.'

'You must be talking about those commercials for Pampers, are you? But it's not your skin, Salaman.'

'Exactly,' said Raduev irritably, 'so why do they come into contact in my head? Haven't they got anywhere else?'

The upper section of Berezovsky's face was covered by a rectangle with a pair of eyes rendered in detail. They squinted in concern at Raduev and blinked a few times, then the rec-tangle disappeared.

'Anyway, just whose piss is it?' Raduev asked as if the idea had only just entered his head.

'Drop it, Salaman,' Berezovsky said in a reconciliatory tone. 'Why don't you take your move?'

'Wait, Boris; I want to know whose piss and skin it is com-ing into contact in my head when I watch your television.'

'Why is it my television?'

'If a pipe runs across my squares, then I'm responsible for the pipe. You said that yourself. Right? So if all the TV anchormen are on your squares, you're responsible for TV. So you tell me whose piss it is splashing about in my head when I watch it!'

Berezovsky scratched his chin. 'It's your piss, Salaman,' he said decisively.

'How come?'

'Who else's can it be? Think it out for yourself. In Chechnya they call you "the man with a bullet in his head" for your pluck. I don't think anyone who decided to pour piss all over you while you're watching TV would live very long.'

'You think right.'

'So, Salaman, that means it's your piss.'

'So how does it get inside my head when I'm watching TV? Does it rise up from my bladder?'

Berezovsky reached out for the dice, but Raduev put his hand over them. 'Explain,' he demanded. 'Then we'll carry on playing.'

An animation rectangle appeared on Berezovsky's forehead, containing a deep wrinkle. 'All right,' he said,' I'll try to explain.'

'Go on.'

'When Allah created this world,' Berezovsky began, casting a quick glance upwards, 'he first thought it; and then he created objects. All the holy books tell us that in the beginning was the word. What does that mean in legal terms? In legal terms it means that in the first place Allah created concepts. Coarse objects are the lot of human beings, but instead of them Allah' – he glanced upwards quickly once again – 'has ideas. And so Salman, when you watch advertisements for Pampers on television, what you have in your head is not wet human piss, but the concept of piss. The idea of piss comes into contact with the concept of skin. You understand?'

'More or less,' said Raduev thoughtfully. 'But I didn't understand everything. The idea of piss and the concept of skin come into contact inside my head, right?'

'Right.'

'And instead of things, Allah has ideas. Right?'

'Right,' said Berezovsky, and frowned. An animation patch

appeared on his blue-shaven cheeks, showing his jaw muscles clenched tightly.

'That means what happens inside my head is Allah's piss coming into contact with Allah's skin, blessed be his name? Right?'

'You probably could put it like that,' said Berezovsky, and the insert with the wrinkle appeared again on his forehead (Tatarsky had indicated this point in the scenario with the words: 'Berezovsky senses the conversation is taking a wrong turning.')

Raduev stroked the rusty brick of his beard.

'Al-Halladj spoke truly,' he said, 'in saying that the greatest wonder of all is a man who sees nothing wonderful around him. But tell me, why does it happen so often? I remember one time when piss came into contact with skin seventeen times in one hour.'

'That was probably to settle up with Gallup Media,' Berezovsky replied condescendingly. 'The customer must've been a tough guy. So they had to account for his money before his protection could account for them. But what of it? If we sell the time, we show the material.'

Raduev's skeleton swayed towards the table. 'Hang on, hang on. Are you telling me that piss comes into contact with skin every time they give you money?'

'Well, yes.'

Raduev's skeleton was suddenly covered with a crudely drawn torso dressed in a Jordanian military uniform. He put his hand down behind the back of his chair, pulled out a Kalashnikov and pointed it at his companion's face.

'What's wrong, Salaman?' Berezovsky asked quietly, automatically raising his hands.

'What's wrong? I'll tell you. There's a man who gets paid for splashing piss on the skin of Allah, and this man is still alive. That's what's wrong.'

The insert with the Jordanian uniform disappeared, the thin lines of the skeleton returned to the screen and the Kalashnikov was transformed into a wavering line of dots. The upper section of Berezovsky's head, at which this line was pointed, was concealed by an animation patch with a

Socratean brow covered with large beads of sweat among sparse hair.

'Easy, now, Salaman, easy,' said Berezovsky. 'Two men with bullets in their heads at one table would be too much. Don't get excited.'

'What d'you mean, don't get excited? You're going to wash away every drop of piss you've spilled on Allah with a bucket of your blood, I'm telling you.'

Furiously working thought was reflected in Berezovsky's screwed-up eyes. That was what it said in the scenario – 'furiously working thought' – and Tatarsky couldn't even begin to imagine what kind of technology could have allowed the animators to achieve such literal accuracy.

'Listen,' said Berezovsky, 'I'll start getting worried if you keep this up. Of course my head isn't armour-plated, that's obvious. But then neither is yours, as you know very well. And my protection are all over the place . . . Aha . . . That's what they told you on your radio?'

Raduev laughed. 'They wrote in *Forbes* magazine that you grasp everything instantly. Looks like they were right.'

'You subscribe to *Forbes*?'

'Why not? Chechnya's part of Europe now. We should know our clientele.'

'If you're so fucking cultured,' Berezovsky said irritably, 'then why can't we talk like two fucking Europeans? Without all this barbarism?'

'Go on then.'

'You said I would wash away every drop of piss with a bucket of my blood, right?'

'Right,' Raduev agreed with dignity. 'And I'll say it again.'

'But you can't wash away piss with blood. It's not Tide, you know.'

(Tatarsky had the idea that the phrase 'You can't wash away piss with blood' would make a wonderful slogan for an all-Russian campaign for Tide, but it was too dark for him to note it down.)

'That's true,' Raduev agreed.

'And then, you agree that nothing in the world happens against Allah's will?'

'Yes.'

'Right then, let's go further. Surely you don't think that I could . . . I could . . . well, that I could do what I've done if it was against the will of Allah?'

'No.'

'Then let's go further,' Berezovsky continued confidently. 'Try looking at things this way: I'm simply an instrument in the hands of Allah, and what Allah does and why are beyond understanding. And then, if it wasn't Allah's will, I wouldn't have gathered all the TV towers and anchormen in my three squares. Right?'

'Right.'

'Can we stop here?'

Raduev stuck the barrel of the gun against Berezovsky's forehead. 'No,' he said. 'We'll go a bit further than you suggest. I'll tell you what the old folks say in my village. They say that according to Allah's original idea this world should be like a sweet raspberry that melts in your mouth, but people like you with their avarice have turned it into piss coming into contact with skin. Perhaps it is Allah's wish that people like you should come into the world; but Allah is merciful, and so it is his will too that people like you who stop life tasting like a sweet raspberry should be blown away. After talking to you for five minutes life tastes like piss that's eaten away all my brains, get it? And in fucking Europe they pay compensation for things like that, get it? Haven't you ever heard of deprived adulthood?'

Berezovsky sighed. 'I see you prepared thoroughly for our talk. All right, then. What kind of compensation?

'I don't know. You'd have to something pleasing to God.'

'For instance?'

'I don't know,' Raduev repeated. 'Build a mosque; but it would have to be a very big mosque. Big enough to pray away the sin I've committed by sitting at the same table with a man who has splashed piss on the skin of the Inexpressible.'

'I'm with you,' said Berezovsky, lowering his hands slightly. 'And to be precise, just how big?'

'I think the first contribution would be ten million.'

'Isn't that a lot?'

'I don't know if it's a lot or not,' said Raduev, stroking his beard pensively, 'because we can only comprehend the notions of "a lot" and "a little" in comparative terms. But perhaps you noticed a herd of goats when you arrived at my headquarters?'

'I noticed them. What's the connection?'

'Until that twenty million arrives in my account in the Islamic bank, seventeen times every hour they'll duck you in a barrel of goat's piss, and it'll come into contact with your skin, and cause irritation, and you'll have plenty of time to think about whether it's a lot or a little – seventeen times an hour.'

'Hey-hey-hey,' said Berezovsky, lowering his hands. 'What's that? Just a moment ago it was ten million.'

'You forgot about the dandruff.'

'Listen Salaman, my dear, that's not the way business is done.'

'Do you want to pay another ten for the smell of sweat?' Raduev asked, shaking his automatic. 'Do you?'

'No, Salaman,' Berezovsky said wearily. 'I don't want to pay for the smell of sweat. Tell me, by the way, who is it filming us with that hidden camera?'

'What camera?'

'What's that briefcase over there on the window sill?' Berezovsky jabbed his finger towards the screen.

'Ah, spawn of Satan,' Raduev muttered and raised his automatic.

A white zigzag ran cross the screen, everything went dark, and the the lights came on in the hall.

Azadovsky exchanged glances with Morkovin.

'Well, what do you think?' Tatarsky asked timidly.

'Tell me, where do you work?' Azadovsky asked disdainfully. 'In Berezovsky's PR department or in my dirt squad?'

'In the dirt squad,' Tatarsky replied.

'What were you asked for? A scenario of negotiations between Raduev and Berezovsky, with Berezovsky giving the Chechen terrorists twenty million dollars. And what's this you've written? He's not giving them money! You've got him building a mosque! A fucking good job it's not the Cathedral of Christ the Saviour. If we didn't produce Berezovsky ourselves, I might imagine you were being paid by him. And who's this Raduev of yours? Some kind of professor of theology? He reads magazines even I've never heard of.'

'But there has to be some development of the plot, some logic . . .'

'I don't want logic, I want dirt. And this isn't dirt, it's just plain shit. Understand?'

'Yes,' replied Tatarsky, lowering his eyes.

Azadovsky softened slightly.

'But in general,' he stated, 'there is a certain healthy core to it. The first plus is that it makes you hate television. You want to watch it and hate it, watch it and hate it.. The second plus is that game of Monopoly. Was that your own idea?'

'Yes,' Tatarsky said, more brightly.

'That works. Terrorist and oligarch dividing up the people's wealth at the gaming table . . . The punters'll go raging mad at that.'

'But isn't it a bit too . . .' Morkovin put in, but Azadovsky interrupted him.

'No. The most important thing is to keep brains occupied and feelings involved. So this move with the Monopoly is OK. It'll improve the news rating by five per cent at least. That means it'll increase the value of one minute at prime time . . .'

Azadovsky took his calculator out of his pocket and began to press tiny buttons.

' . . . by nine thousand,' he said when he'd finished. 'So what does that mean for an hour? Multiply by seventeen. Not bad. We'll do it. To cut it short, let them play Monopoly and you tell the producer to inter-cut it with shots of queues for the savings bank, miners, old women, hungry children, wounded soldiers – the works. Only take out that stuff about TV anchormen, or else we'll have to create a stink over it. Better give them a new piece for their Monopoly – a TV drilling tower. And have Berezovsky say he wants to build these towers everywhere so they can pump out oil and pump in advertising at the same time. And do a montage of the Ostankino TV tower with a rock drill. How d'you like it?'

'Brilliant,' Tatarsky readily agreed.

'How about you?' Azadovsky asked Morkovin.

'I'm for it one hundred per cent.'

'Yeah, right! I could replace the lot you all on my own. Right, listen to the doctor's orders. Morkovin, you give him that new guy who writes about food for reinforcements. We'll leave Raduev basically the way he is, only give him a fez instead of that cap of his; I'm sick of it already. That means we get in a poke at Turkey as well. And then I've been meaning to ask for ages about his dark glasses. Why's he always wearing them? Are we saving time on rendering the eyes or something?'

'That's right,' said Morkovin. 'Raduev's always in the news, and dark glasses cut down the time by twenty per cent. We get rid of all the expressions.'

Azadovsky's face darkened somewhat.

'God grant, we'll get this business with the frequency sorted out. But give Berezovsky a boost, OK?'

'OK.'

'And do it now, urgent material.'

'We'll do it,' answered Morkovin. 'As soon as the viewing's over we'll go back to my office.'

'What have we got next?'

'Ads for televisions. A new type.'

Tatarsky rose halfway out of his chair, but Morkovin put out a hand to stop him.

'Get on with it,' Azadovsky said with a wave of his hand. 'There's still twenty minutes to go.'

The lights went out again. A small, pretty Japanese woman in a kimono appeared on the screen. She was smiling. She bowed and then spoke with a distinct accent:

'You will now be addressed by Yohohori-san. Yohohori-san is the oldest employee at Panasonic, which is why he has been given this honour. He suffers from a speech impediment due to war wounds, so please, dear viewers, forgive him this shortcoming.'

The young woman moved aside. A thickset Japanese man appeared, holding a sword in a black scabbard. At his side there was a black streamlined television looking like an eye ripped from the head of some huge monster – the comparison occurred to Tatarsky because the background was scarlet.

'Panasonic presents a revolutionary invention in the world of television,' said the Japanese. 'The first television in the world with voice control in all languages of the planet, including Russian. Panasword V-2!

The Japanese stared into the viewer's eyes with an intense hatred and suddenly pulled his sword from its scabbard.

'Sword forged in Japan!' he yelled, setting the cutting edge up against the camera lens. 'Sword that will slit the throat of the putrefied world! Long live the Emperor!'

Some people in white medical coats fluttered across the screen – Mr Yohohori was ushered off somewhere, a pale-faced girl in a kimono began bowing in apology and across all this disgrace appeared the Panasonic logo. A low voice-over commented with satisfaction: 'Panasodding!'

Tatarsky heard a telephone trill.

'Hello,' said Azadovsky's voice in the darkness. 'What? I'm on my way.'

He stood up, blocking out part of the screen.

'Ogh,' he said, 'seems like Rostropovich'll get another medal today. They're about to call me from America. I sent them a fax yesterday telling them democracy was in danger and asking them to raise the frequency two hundred mega-hertz. They finally seem to have twigged we're all in the same business.'

Tatarsky suddenly had the impression that Azadovsky's shadow on the screen wasn't real, but just an element of a video recording, a black silhouette like the ones you get in pirate copies of films shot from the cinema screen. For Tatarsky these black shadows on their way out of the cinema, known to the owners of underground video libraries as 'runners', served as a special kind of quality indicator: the influence of the displacing wow-factor drove more people out of a good film than a bad one, so he usually asked for the 'films with runners' to be kept for him; but now he felt almost afraid at the thought that if a man who'd just been sitting beside you could turn out to be a runner, it could mean you were just an-other runner yourself. The feeling was complex, profound and new, but Tatarsky had no time to analyse it: humming a vague tango, Azadovsky wandered over to the edge of the screen and disappeared.

The next video began in a more traditional manner. A

family – father, mother, daughter with a pussy cat and granny with a half-knitted stocking – were sitting round a fire in a hearth set in a strange mirror-surface wall. As they gazed into the flames blazing behind the grate, they made rapid, almost caricatured movements: the granny knitted, the mother gnawed on the edge of a piece of pizza, the daughter stroked the pussy cat and the father sipped beer. The camera moved around them and passed in through the mirror-wall. From the other side the wall was transparent: when the camera completed its movement, the family was overlaid by the flames in the hearth and bars of the grate. An organ rumbled threateningly; the camera pulled back and the transparent wall was transformed into the flat screen of a television with stereo speakers at each side and the coy inscription 'Tofetissimo' on its black body. The image on television showed flames in which four black figures were jerking in rapid movements behind metal bars. The organ fell silent and an insidious announcer's voice took over:

'Did you think there was a vacuum behind the absolutely flat Black Trinitron's screen? No! there's a flame blazing there that will warm your heart! The Sony Tofetissimo. It's a Sin.'

Tatarsky didn't understand very much of what he'd seen; he just thought that the coefficient of involvement could be greatly improved if the slogan was replaced by another reference to those Sex-Shop Dogs or what-d'you-call-them: Go Fumes.

'What was that?' he asked, when the lights came on. 'It wasn't much like an advertisement.'

Morkovin smiled smugly.

'It's not; that's the whole point,' he said. 'In scientific terms, it's a new advertising technology reflecting the reaction of market mechanisms to the increasing human revulsion at market mechanisms. To cut it short, the viewer is supposed gradually to develop the idea that somewhere in the world – say, in sunny California – there is a final oasis of freedom unconstrained by the thought of money, where they make advertisements like this one. It's profoundly anti-market in form, so it promises to be highly market-effective in content.'

He looked to make sure there was no one else in the hall and began talking in a whisper.

'And now down to business. I don't think this place is bugged, but talk quietly just in case. Well done, that went just great. Here's your share.'

Three envelopes appeared in his hand – one fat and yellow and two rather slimmer.

'Hide these quick. This is twenty from Berezovsky, ten from Raduev and another two from the Chechens. Theirs is the thickest because it's in small bills. They took up a collection round the hill villages.'

Tatarsky swallowed hard, took the envelopes and quickly stuffed them into the inside pockets of his jacket. 'Do you think Azadovsky could have twigged?' he whispered.

Morkovin shook his head.

'Listen,' whispered Tatarsky, glancing round again, 'how is this possible? I can understand about the hill villages, but Berezovsky doesn't exist, and neither does Raduev. That is, they do exist, but they're only a combination of ones and zeroes, ones and zeroes. How can they send us money?'

Morkovin shrugged.

'I don't really understand it myself,' he answered in a whisper. 'Maybe it's some interested parties or other. Maybe some gangs are involved and they're re-defining their image. Probably if you work it all out it all comes back down to us. Only why bother to work it all out? Where else are you going to earn thirty grand a throw? Nowhere. So don't worry about it. Nobody really understands a single thing about the way this world works.'

The projectionist stuck his head into the hall. 'Hey, are you guys going to stay there much longer?'

'We're discussing the clips,' Morkovin whispered.

Tatarsky cleared his throat.

'If I've grasped the difference correctly,' he said in an unnaturally loud voice, 'then an ordinary advertisement and what we've seen are like straight pop-music and the alternative music scene?'

'Precisely,' Morkovin replied just as loudly, rising to his feet and glancing at his watch. 'But just what exactly is alternative music – and what is pop? How would you define it?'

'I don't know,' Tatarsky answered. 'From the feel, I suppose.'

They walked past the projectionist loitering in the doorway and went towards the lifts.

'There is a precise definition,' said Morkovin didactically. 'Alternative music is music the commercial essence of which consists in its extreme anti-commercial ethos. Its anti-pop quality, so to speak. Which means that, in order to get this quality right, an alternative musician must first of all be a really shrewd merchant, and those are rare in the music business. There are plenty of them, of course, but they're not performers, they're managers . . . OK, relax. Have you got the text with you?'

Tatarsky nodded.

'Let's go to my office. I'll give you a co-author, just like Azadovsky ordered. And I'll stick the co-author three grand so he won't spoil the scenario.'

Tatarsky had never gone up to the seventh floor where Morkovin worked. The corridor they entered on leaving the lift looked dull and reminded him of an old Soviet-period office building – the floor was covered with scuffed and dirty wooden parquet and the doors were upholstered with black imitation leather. On each door, though, there was an elegant metal plaque with a code consisting of numbers and letters. There were only three letters – 'A', 'O' and 'D', but they occurred in various combinations. Morkovin stopped beside a door with a plaque marked '1 – A-D' and entered a code in the digital lock.

Morkovin's office was imposingly large and impressively furnished. The desk alone had obviously cost several times as much as Tatarsky's Mercedes. This masterpiece of the furniture-maker's art was almost empty – there was a file containing papers and two telephones without number pads, one red and one white. There was also a strange device: a small metal box with a glass panel in its top. Hanging above the desk was a picture that Tatarsky took at first for a cross between a socialist realist landscape and a piece of Zen calligraphy. It showed a bushy corner of a shady garden depicted with photographic precision, but daubed carelessly across the bushes was a giant hieroglyph covered with identical green circles.

'What's that?'

'The president out walking,' said Morkovin. 'Azadovsky

presented it to me to create an air of responsible authority. Look, you see, the skeleton's wearing a tie. And some kind of badge as well – it's right on top of a flower, so you have to look closely. But that's just something the artist dreamed up.'

Turning away from the picture, Tatarsky noticed they weren't alone in the office. At the far end of the spacious room there was a stand with three flat monitors and ergonomic keyboards, with their leads disappearing into a wall covered with cork. A guy with a ponytail was sitting at one of the monitors and grazing his mouse with lazy movements on a small grey mat. His ears were pierced by at least ten small earrings, and there were two more passing through his left nostril. Remembering Morkovin's advice to prick himself with something sharp whenever he began thinking about the lack of any general order of things in the Universe, Tatarsky decided this wasn't a case of excessive enthusiasm for piercing; it was the result of close proximity to the technological epicentre of events – the guy with the ponytail simply never bothered to remove his pins.

Morkovin sat at the desk, picked up the receiver of the white phone and issued a brief instruction.

'Your co-author'll be here in a minute,' he said to Tatarsky. 'You haven't been here before, have you? These terminals are linked into the main render-server. And this man here is our head designer, Semyon Velin. You realise what a responsibility that is?'

Tatarsky deferentially approached the guy at the computer and glanced at the screen, which showed a trembling grid of finely spaced blue lines. The lines were linked up in the form of two extended hands, the palms held close together with the middle fingers touching. They were slowly revolving around an invisible vertical axis. In some elusive fashion the picture reminded Tatarsky of a shot from a low-budget science-fiction movie of the eighties. The guy with the ponytail moved his mouse across the mat, stuck the arrow of the cursor into a menu that appeared at the top of the screen and the angle between the palms of the hands changed.

'Didn't I say we should program in the golden section straightaway?' he said, turning to face Morkovin.

'What are you talking about?'

'The angle. We should have made it the same as in the Egyptian pyramids. It'll give the viewer this unconscious feeling of harmony, peace and happiness.'

'Why are you wasting time messing about with that old rubbish?' Morkovin asked. '"Our Home Russia" has no chance.'

'"Our Home Russia" be buggered,' Velin replied. 'They had a good slogan – "The Roof of Your House". We can make this roof out of fingers. The target group will instantly be reminded of bandits' finger-talk and the works. The message will be clear: we provide protection. We're bound to come back round to it anyway.'

'OK,' said Morkovin, 'put in your golden section. Let the punters relax. Only don't mention it in the documentation.'

'Why not?'

'Because,' said Morkovin, 'you and I know what the golden section is. But the accounts department' – he jerked his head upwards – 'might not approve the budget. They'll think if it's gold it must be expensive. They're economising on "Our Home Russia" now.'

'I get you,' said Velin. 'Then I'll just put in the angle. Call to get them to open the root directory.'

Morkovin pulled over the red phone.

'Hello? This is Morkovin from the anal-displacement department. Open the root directory for terminal five. We're doing some cosmetic repairs. All right . . .'

'That's done,' said Morkovin. 'Just a moment, Alla, Semyon wants to ask you something.'

Velin grabbed the receiver. 'Alla, hi! Could you check the hair density for Chernomyrdin? What? No, that's the whole point, I need it for the poster. OK, I'm writing – thirty-two hpi, colour Ray-Ban black. Have you given me access? OK, then that's the lot.'

'Listen,' Tatarsky asked quietly, when Velin was back at his terminal, 'what's that – hpi?'

'Hairs per inch,' Morkovin answered. 'Like dots per inch with those laser printers.'

'And what does that mean – "the anal displacement department"?'

'That's what our department is called.'

'Why such a strange name?'

'Well it's the general theory of elections,' Morkovin said with a frown. 'To cut it short, there should always be three wow-candidates: oral, anal and displacing. Only don't go asking me what that means, you don't have security clearance yet. And anyway I don't remember. All I can say is that in normal countries they get by with the oral and anal wow-candidates, because the displacement has been completed; but things are only just getting started here and we need the displacing candidate as well. We give him about fifteen per cent of the votes in the first round. I think I can write you a clearance if you're that interested.'

'Thanks,' said Tatarsky, 'forget it.'

'Dead right. Why the fuck should you strain your brains on your salary. The less you know, the easier you breathe.'

'Exactly,' said Tatarsky, noting to himself that if Davidoff started making ultra-lights there couldn't possibly be a better slogan.

Morkovin opened his file and took up a pencil. Out of a sense of delicacy Tatarsky moved away to the wall and began studying the sheets of paper and pictures pinned to it. At first his attention was caught by a photograph of Antonio Banderas in the Hollywood masterpice *Stepan Banderas*. Banderas, romantically unshaven, holding a giant balalaika case, was standing on the outskirts of some abstract Ukrainian village and gazing sadly at a burned-out Russian tank in a sunflower chaparral (from the first glance at the crowd of droopy-mustachioed villagers in their cockerel-embroidered ponchos, who were squinting at the reddish-yellow sun, it was obvious that the film had been shot in Mexico). The poster wasn't genuine – it was a collage. Some anonymous joker had matched up Banderas' torso in dark leather with a heavy-assed pair of girl's legs in dark-brown tights. There was a slogan under the image:

SAN PELEGRINO TIGHTS
FASHIONED TO RESIST ANY STRAIN

Sellotaped directly on to the poster was a fax on the letterhead of Young and Rubicam. The text was short:

Sergei! Essence correction for three brands:
Chubais – green stuff in the bank / green stuff in the jar
Yavlinsky – think different / think doomsday ('Apple' doesn't object)
Yeltsin – stability in a coma / democracy in a coffin

Hi there,
Wee Kolya.

'It's a weak idea for Chubais,' said Tatarsky, turning towards Morkovin, 'and where are the communists?'

'They write them in the oral displacement department,' Morkovin answered. 'And thank God for that. I wouldn't take them for twice my salary.'

'Do they pay more over there?'

'The same. But they have some guys who are willing to slave away for free. You'll meet one of them in a moment, by the way.'

Hanging beside Banderas was a greetings card produced on a colour printer, showing a golden double-headed eagle clutching a Kalashnikov in one taloned foot and a pack of Marlboro in the other. There was an inscription in gold below the eagle's feet:

SANTA BARBARA FOR EVER!
THE RUSSIAN IDEA DEPARTMENT
CONGRATULATES OUR COLLEAGUES
ON ST VARVARA'S DAY

To the right of the greetings card there was another advertising poster: Yeltsin leaning over a chessboard on which no figures had been moved. He was looking at it sideways on (the setting seemed to emphasise his role as the supreme arbiter). The king and the rook on the white side had been replaced by small bottles labelled 'Ordinary Whisky' and 'Black Label'. Next to the chessboard there stood a small model of a seashore villa looking more like a fortress. The text was:

BLACK LABEL: THE TIME TO CASTLE

Tatarsky reached for his notebook – an idea for another poster had suddenly occurred to him.

He wrote down: 'A view from inside a car. The president's sullen face with the window behind it. Outside in the street – poor old women, street urchins, bandaged soldiers, etc. Inscription in large letters at the top of the poster: "How low can we go?" In tiny print at the very bottom: "As low as 2.9 per cent intro. Visa Next."'

There was a knock at the door. Tatarsky turned round and froze. So many meetings with old acquaintances in the same day seemed rather unlikely – into the office came Malyuta, the anti-Semite copywriter he'd worked with in Khanin's agency. He was dressed in a Turkish-made Russian folk shirt with a soldier's belt supporting an entire array of office equipment: a mobile phone, a pager, a Zippo lighter in a leather case and an awl in a narrow black scabbard.

'Malyuta! What are you doing here?'

Malyuta, however, gave no sign of being surprised.

'I write the image menu for the whole cabal,' he replied. 'Russian style. Have you ever heard of *pelmeni* with *kapusta*? Or *kvass* with *khrenok*? Those are my hits. And I work in the oral displacement department on half-pay. Are you in dirt?'

Tatarsky didn't answer.

'You know each other?' Morkovin asked with curiosity. 'Yes, of course, you worked together at Khanin's place. So you shouldn't have any problems working together.'

'I prefer working alone,' Malyuta said drily. 'What d'you want done?'

'Azadovsky wants you to finish up a project. With Berezovsky and Raduev. Don't touch Raduev, but you need to boost Berezovsky up a bit. I'll call you this evening and give you a few instructions. Will you do it?'

'Berezovsky?' Malyuta asked. 'And how. When d'you need it?'

'Yesterday, as always.'

'Where's the draft?'

Morkovin looked at Tatarsky, who shrugged and handed Malyuta the file with the printout of the scenario.

'Don't you want to talk with the author?' Morkovin asked. 'So he can put you in the picture?'

'I'll figure it out for myself from the text. It'll be ready to-morrow at ten.'

'OK, you know best.'

When Malyuta left the room, Morkovin said: 'He doesn't like you much.'

'Nor I him,' said Tatarsky. 'We had an argument once about geopolitics. Listen, who's going to change that bit about the television-drilling towers?'

'Damn, I forgot, A good job you reminded me – I'll explain it to him this evening. And you'd better make peace with him. You know how bad our frequency problem is right now, but Azadovsky's still allowed him one 3-D general. To liven up the news. He's a guy with a future. No one can tell how the market will shift tomorrow. Maybe he'll be head of depart-ment instead of me, and then . . .'

Morkovin didn't finish his train of thought. The door swung open and Azadovsky burst into the room. Behind him came two of the guards with Scorpions on their shoulders. Azadovsky's face was white with fury and he was clenching and unclenching his fists with such force that Tatarsky was reminded of the talons of the eagle from the greetings card. Tatarsky had never seen him like this.

'Who edited Lebed the last time?'

'Semyon Velin, as usual,' Morkovin replied in fright. 'Why, what's happened?'

Azadovsky turned towards the young guy with the ponytail. 'You?' he asked. 'Did you do this?'

'What?' asked Velin.

'Did you change Lebed's cigarettes? From Camel to Gitanes?'

'Yes I did,' said Velin. 'What of it? I just thought it would be better stylistically. After we rendered him together with Alain Delon.'

'Take him away,' Azadovsky commanded.

'Wait, wait,' said Velin, thrusting his hands out in front of him in fear. 'I'll explain everything . . .' But the guards were already dragging him out into the corridor.

Azadovsky turned to face Morkovin and stared intensely at him for several seconds.

'I knew nothing about it,' said Morkovin, 'I swear.'

'Then who is supposed to know about it? Me? D'you know where I just got a call from? J. R. Reynolds Tobacco – who paid us for Lebed's Camels two years in advance. You know what they said? They're going to get their congressman to drop us fifty megahertz; and they'll drop us another fifty if Lebed goes on air next time with Gitanes again. I don't know how much this asshole was raking in from black PR, but we stand to lose a lot, an awful fucking lot. Do we want to ride into the twenty-first fucking century on a hundred mega-hertz? When's the next broadcast with Lebed?'

'Tomorrow. An interview on the Russian Idea. It's all rendered already.'

'Have you watched the material?'

Morkovin clutched his head in his hands. 'I have,' he replied. 'Oh, God . . . That's right. He's got Gitanes. I noticed it, but I thought it must have been approved upstairs. You know I don't decide these things. I couldn't imagine.'

'Where are his cigarettes? On the table?'

'If only! He waves the pack around all through the interview.'

'Can we undo?'

'Not the whole thing.'

'Change the design on the pack then?'

'Not that either. Gitanes are a different size; and the pack's in shot all the time.'

'So what are we going to do?'

Azadovsky's gaze came to rest on Tatarsky, as though he'd only just noticed him there. Tatarsky cleared his throat.

'Perhaps,' he said timidly, we could put in a patch with a pack of Camel on the table? That's quite simple.'

'And then what? Have him waving one pack around in the air and the other one lying in front of him? You're raving.'

'And we put the arm in plaster,' Tatarsky went on, giving way to a sudden wave of inspiration. 'So we get rid of the pack.'

'In plaster?' Azadovsky repeated thoughtfully. 'But what'll we say?'

'An assassination attempt,' said Tatarsky.

'You mean they shot him in the arm?'

'No,' said Tatarsky, 'they tried to blow him up in his car.'

'And he's not going to say anything about the attempt to kill him in the interview?' Morkovin asked.

Azadovsky thought for a moment. 'That's actually OK. Imperturbable –' he waved his fist in the air – 'never even said a word. A real soldier. We'll put the attack out in the news. And we won't just patch in a pack of Camel on the table, we'll patch in a whole block. Let the bastards choke on that.'

'What'll we say in the news?'

'As little as possible. Clues pointing to Chechens, the Islamic factor, investigations proceeding and so forth. What car does Lebed's legend say he drives? An old Mercedes? Get a film crew sent out into the country straightaway, find an old Mercedes, blow it up and film it. It's got to be on the air by ten. Say the general left immediately to get on with his work and he's keeping up with his schedule. Yes, and have them find a fez at the site of the crime, like the one Raduev's going to have. Is the idea clear?'

'Brilliant,' said Morkovin. 'It really is brilliant.'

Azadovsky gave a crooked smile that was more like a nervous twitch.

'But where'll we get an old Mercedes?' asked Morkovin. 'All ours are new.'

'There's someone here who drives one,' said Azadovsky. 'I've seen it in the parking lot.'

Morkovin looked up at Tatarsky.

'But . . . But . . .' Tatarsky mumbled, but Morkovin just shook his head.

'No,' he said, 'forget it. Give me the keys.'

Tatarsky took his car keys out of his pocket and submissively placed them in Morkovin's open hand.

'The seat-covers are new,' he said piteously; 'maybe I could take them off?'

'Are you fucking crazy?' Azadovsky exploded. 'D'you want them to drop us to fifty megahertz so we have to dismiss the government and disband the Duma again? Bloody seat-covers! Use your head!'

The telephone rang in his pocket .

"Allo,' he said, raising it to his ear. 'What? I'll tell you what to do with him. There's a camera crew going out into the country straightaway – to film a bombed car. Take that arse-hole, put him in the driver's seat and blow him up. Make sure there's blood and scraps of flesh, and you film it all. It'll be a lesson for the rest of them, with their black PR . . . What? You tell him there isn't anything in the world more important than what's about to happen to him. He shouldn't let himself be distracted by minor details. And he shouldn't think he can tell me anything I don't already know.'

Azadovsky folded up his phone and tossed it into his pocket, sighed several times and clutched at his heart.

'It hurts,' he complained. 'Do you bastards really want me to have a heart attack at thirty? Seems to me I'm the only one in this committee who's not on the take. Everybody back to work on the double. I'm going to phone the States. We might just get away with it.'

When Azadovsky left the room, Morkovin looked mean-ingfully into Tatarsky's eyes, tugged a small tin box out of his pocket and tipped out a pile of white powder on the desk.

'Right,' he said, 'be my guest.'

When the procedure was completed, Morkovin moistened his finger, picked up the white grains left on the table and licked them off with his tongue.

'You were asking', he said, 'how things could be this way, what everything's based on, who it's all controlled by. I tell you, all you need to think about here is to cover your own ass and get your job done. There's no time left for any other thoughts. And by the way, there's something you'd better do: put the money into your pockets and flush the envelopes down the john. Straightaway. Just in case. The toilet's down the corridor on the left . . .'

Tatarsky locked himself in the cubicle and distributed the wads of banknotes around his pockets – he'd never seen such a load of money at one time before. He tore the envelopes into small pieces and threw the scraps into the toilet bowl. A folded note fell out of one of the envelopes – Tatarsky caught it in mid-air and read it:

Hi, guys! Thanks a lot for sometimes allowing me to live a parallel

life. Without that the real one would be so disgusting!
Good luck in business,
    B. Berezovsky.

The text was printed on a laser printer, and the signature was a facsimile. 'Morkovin playing the joker again,' thought Tatarsky. 'Or maybe it's not Morkovin . . .'

He crossed himself, pinched his thigh really hard and flushed the toilet.

CHAPTER 14

Critical Times

They were shooting from the bridge, the way they do these things in Moscow. The old T-80s only fired at long intervals, as though the sponsors, short of money for shells, were afraid it would all be over too quickly and so they wouldn't make the international news. There was apparently some unwritten minimal requirement for reports from Russia: there had to be at least three or maybe four tanks, a hundred dead and something else as well – Tatarsky couldn't remember what exactly. This time an exception must have been made because of the picturesque visual quality of the events: although there were only two tanks, the quayside was packed with television crews with their optical bazookas blasting out megatons of somnolent human attention along the river Moscow at the tanks, the bronze Peter the Great and the window behind which Tatarsky was concealed.

The cannon of one of the tanks standing on the bridge roared and the same instant Tatarsky was struck by an interesting idea: he could offer the people in the Bridge image-service the silhouette of a tank as a promising logo to replace that incomprehensible eagle of theirs. In a split second – less time than it took for the shell to reach its target – Tatarsky's conscious mind had weighed up the possibilities ('the image of the tank symbolises the aggressive power of the group and at the same time introduces a traditional Russian note into the context of cosmopolitical finance') and immediately the idea was rejected. 'They'd piss themselves,' Tatarsky decided. 'Pity, though.'

A shell caught Peter the Great in the head, but it didn't explode, passing straight on through and continuing its flight roughly in the direction of Gorky Park. A tall plume of steam shot up into the air. Tatarsky remembered that the head of the monument contained a small restaurant complete with full services and facilities, and he decided the blank must have severed a pipe in the heating system. He heard the TV crews yelling in delight. The swirling plume made Peter look like some monster knight out of Steven King. Remembering how the rotting brains of the monster in *The Talisman* had dribbled down over its shoulders, Tatarsky thought the resemblance would be complete if the next shell severed a sewage pipe.

Peter's head was defended by the Defence of Sebastopol committee. They said in the news that didn't mean the city, but the hotel, which was being fought over by two mafia groups, the Chechens and the Solntsevo mob. They also said the Solntsevo mob had hired stuntmen from Mosfilm and set up this strange shoot-out in order to attract TV coverage and generally inflame anti-Caucasian feeling (if the abundance of pyrotechnics and special effects was anything to go by, it had to be true). The simple-minded Chechens, who weren't too well versed in the protocol of PR campaigns, hadn't figured out what was going on, and they'd hired the two tanks somewhere outside Moscow.

So far the stuntmen were returning fire and giving as good as they got – there was a puff of smoke in the hole beside Peter's ragged eye and a grenade exploded on the bridge. A tank fired in reply. The blank struck Peter's head, sending fragments of bronze showering downwards. For some reason every new hit made the emperor even more goggle-eyed.

Of all the participants in the drama the only one Tatarsky felt any sympathy for was the bronze idol dying slowly before the glass eyes of the TV cameras; and he didn't feel that very strongly – he hadn't finished his work, and had to conserve the energy of his emotional centre. Tatarsky lowered the blinds, cutting himself off completely from what was going on, sat at his computer and re-read the quotation written in felt-tip pen on the wallpaper over the monitor:

In order to influence the imagination of the Russian customer and win his confidence (for the most part customers for advertising in Russia are representatives of the old KGB, GRU and party nomenklatura), an advertising concept should borrow as far as possible

from the hypothetical semi-secret or entirely secret techiques devel-
oped by the Western special services for the programming of con-
sciousness, which are imbued with a quite breathtaking cynicism
and inhumanity. Fortunately, it is not too difficul to improvise on
this theme – one need only recall Oscar Wilde's words about life im-
itating art.

'The Final Positioning'
'Sure,' said Tatarsky, 'that's not too difficult.'

He tensed as though he was about to leap into cold water,
frowned, took a deep breath and held the air in his lungs
while he counted to three, then launched his fingers at the
keyboard:

We can sum up the preceding by saying that in the foreseeable longer
term television is likely to remain the primary channel for the implan-
tation of the customer's schizo-units in the consciousness of the Russian
public. In view of this, we regard as extremely dangerous a tendency
that has emerged in recent times among the so-called middle class – the
most promising stratum of viewers from the point of view of the social
effectiveness of teleschizomanipulation. We are referring to total absti-
nence or the conscious limitation of the amount of television watched in
order to save nervous energy for work. Even professional television
writers are doing it, because it is an accepted maxim of post-Freudian-
ism that in the information age it is not sexuality that should be subli-
mated, so much as the energy that is squandered on the pointless daily
viewing of television.

In order to nip this tendency in the bud, for this concept it is pro-
posed to employ a method developed jointly by MI5 and the US Central
Intelligence Agency for neutralising the remnants of an intellectually in-
dependent national intelligentsia in Third World Countries. (We have
proceeded from the initial assumption that the middle class in Russia is
formed directly from the intelligentsia, which has ceased thinking na-
tionally and begun thinking about where it can get money.)

The method is extremely simple. Since every television channel's
programming contains a fairly high level of synapse-disrupting mater-
ial per unit of time . . .

There was a boom outside the window, and shrapnel
drummed across the roof. Tatarsky drew his head down into

his shoulders. Having re-read what he'd written, he deleted 'synapse-disrupting' and replaced it with 'neuro-destructive'.

. . . the goal of schizosuggestology will be achieved simply as a result of holding the individual to be neutralised in front of a television screen for a long enough period of time. It is suggested that in order to achieve this result one can take advantage of a typical feature of a member of the intelligentsia – sexual frustration.

Internal ratings and data from secret surveys indicate that the biggest draw for the member of the intelligentsia is the erotic night-time channels. But the effect achieved would be maximised if instead of a certain set of television broadcasts the television receiver itself were to achieve the status of an erotic stimulus in the consciousness of the subject being processed. Bearing in mind the patriarchal nature of Russian society and the determinative role played by the male section of the population in the formation of public opinion, it would seem most expedient to develop the subconscious associative link: 'television–female sexual organ'. This association should be evoked by the television itself regardless of its make or the nature of the material being transmitted in order to achieve optimal results from schizomanipulation.

The cheapest and technically simplest means of achieving this goal is the massive oversaturation of air time with television adverts for women's panty-liners. They should be constantly doused with blue liquid (activating the associations: 'blue screen, waves in the ether, etc.'), while the clips themselves should be constructed in such a way that the panty-liner seems to crawl on to the screen itself, implanting the required association in the most direct manner possible.

Tatarsky heard a light ringing sound behind him and he swung round. To the accompaniment of a strange-sounding, somehow northern music, a golden woman's torso of quite exceptional, inexpressible beauty appeared on the television screen, rotating slowly. 'Ishtar,' Tatarsky guessed; 'who else could it be?' The face of the statue was concealed from sight behind the edge of the screen, but the camera was slowly rising and the face would come into sight in just a moment. But an instant before it became visible, the camera moved in so close to the statue that there was nothing left on the screen but a golden shimmering. Tatarsky clicked on the remote, but the image on the television didn't change – the television itself changed instead. It began distending around the edges, transforming itself into the likeness of an immense vagina, with a powerful wind whistling shrilly as the air was sucked right into its black centre.

'I'm asleep,' Tatarsky mumbled into his pillow. 'I'm asleep ...'

He carefully turned over on to his other side, but the shrill sound didn't disappear. Raising himself up on one elbow, he cast a gloomy eye over the thousand-dollar prostitute snoring gently beside him: in the dim light it was quite impossible to tell she wasn't Claudia Schiffer. He reached out for the mobile phone lying on the bedside locker and croaked into it: 'Allo.'

'What's this, been hitting the sauce again?' Morkovin roared merrily. 'Have you forgotten we're going to a barbecue? Get yourself down here quick, I'm already waiting for you. Azadovsky doesn't like to be kept waiting.'

'On my way,' said Tatarsky. 'I'll just grab a shower.'

The autumn highway was deserted and sad, and the sadness was only emphasised by the fact that the trees along its edges were still green and looked just as though it was still summer; but it was clear that summer had passed by without fulfilling a single one of its promises. The air was filled with a vague presentiment of winter, snowfalls and catastrophe – for a long time Tatarsky was unable to understand the source of this feeling, until he looked at the hoardings installed at the side of the road. Every half-kilometre the car rushed past a Tampax advertisement, a huge sheet of plywood showing a pair of white roller skates lying on virginal white snow. That explained the presentiment of winter all right, but the source of the all-pervading sense of alarm still remained unclear. Tatarsky decided that he and Morkovin must have driven into one of those psychological waves of depression that had been drifting across Moscow and its surroundings ever since the beginning of the crisis. The nature of these waves remained mysterious, but Tatarksy had no doubt whatever that they existed, so he was rather offended when Morkovin laughed at him for mentioning them.

'As far the snow goes you were spot on,' he said; 'but as far as these wave things are concerned . . . Take a closer look at the hoardings. Don't you notice anything?'

Morkovin slowed down at the next hoarding and Tatarsky suddenly noticed a large graffito written in blood-red spray paint above the skates and the snow: 'Arrest Yeltsin's gang!'

'Right!' he said ecstatically. 'There was the same kind of thing on all the others! On the last one there was a hammer and sickle, on the one before that there was a swastika, and before that, something about wops and nig-nogs . . . Incredible. Your mind just filters it out – you don't even notice. And the colour, what a colour! Who dreamed it all up?'

'You'll laugh when you hear,' answered Morkovin, picking up speed. 'It was Malyuta. Of course, we rewrote almost all the texts – they were much too frightening – but we didn't change the idea. As you're so fond of saying, an associative field is formed: 'days of crisis – blood could flow – Tampax – your shield against excesses'. Figure it out: nowadays there are only two brands selling the same volumes they used to in Moscow, Tampax and Parliament Lights.'

'Fantastic,' said Tatarsky, and clicked his tongue. 'It just begs for the slogan: 'Tampax ultra-safe. The reds shall not pass!' Or personalise it: not the reds, but Zyuganov – and according to Castaneda, menstruation is a crack between the worlds. If you want to stay on the right side of the crack . . . No, like this: Tampax. The right side of the crack . . .'

'Yes,' said Morkovin thoughtfully, 'we should pass these ideas on to the oral department.'

'We could bring up the theme of the white movement as well. Imagine it: an officer in a beige service jacket on a hillside in the Crimea, something out of Nabokov . . . They'd sell five times as many.'

'What does that matter?' said Morkovin. 'Sales are just a side effect. It's not Tampax we're promoting; it's alarm and uncertainty.'

'What for?'

'We have a crisis on our hands, don't we?'

'Oh, right,' said Tatarsky, 'of course. Listen, about the crisis – I still don't understand how Semyon Velin managed to delete the entire government. It was all triple protected.'

'Semyon wasn't just a designer,' replied Morkovin. 'He was a programmer. D'you know the scale he was working on? They found thirty-seven million in greenbacks in his accounts afterwards. He even switched Zyuganov's jacket from Pierre Cardin to St Lauren. Even now nobody can figure out how he managed to break into the oral directory from our terminal. And as for what he did with neckties and shirts . . . Azadovsky was sick for two whole days after he read the report.'

'Impressive.'

'Sure it was. Our Semyon had a roving eye, but he knew what he was getting into. So he decided he needed some insurance. He wrote a program that would delete the entire directory at the end of the month if he didn't cancel it personally, and he planted it in Kirienko's file. After that the program infected the entire government. We have anti-virus protection, of course, but Semyon thought up this fucking program that wrote itself on to the ends of sectors and assembled itself at the end of the month, so there was no way it could be picked up from the control sums. Just don't ask me what all that means – I don't understand it myself – I just happened to overhear someone talking about it. To cut it short, when they were taking him out of town in your Mercedes, he tried to tell Azadovsky about it, but he wouldn't even talk to him. Then everything defaulted. Azadovsky was tearing his hair out.'

'So will there be a new government soon?' Tatarsky asked. 'I'm already tired of doing nothing.'

'Soon, very soon. Yeltsin's ready – tomorrow we'll discharge him from the Central Kremlin Hospital. We had him digitised again in London. From the wax figure in Madame Tussaud's – they've got it in the store room. It's the third time we've had to restore him – you wouldn't believe the amount of hassle he's given everyone – and we're finishing off the NURBS for all the others. Only the govenment's turning out really leftist; I mean, it's got communists in it. It's those schemers in the oral department. But that doesn't really bother me much – it'll only make things easier for us. And for the people too: one identity for the lot and ration cards for butter. Only so far Sasha Blo's still holding us back with the Russian Idea.'

'Hold hard there,' Tatarsky said, suddenly cautious; 'don't frighten me like that. Who's going to be next? After Yeltsin?'

'What d'you mean, who? Whoever they vote for. We have honest elections here, like in America.'

'And what in hell's name do we need them for?'

'We don't need them in anybody's name. But if we didn't have them they'd never have sold us the render-server. They've got some kind of amendment to the law on trade – in short, everything has to be the way it is there. Total lunacy, of course, the whole thing . . .'

'Why should they care what we do? What do they want from us?'

'It's because elections are expensive,' Morkovin said gloomily. 'They want to finally destroy our economy. At least, that's one of the theories . . . Anyway, we're moving in the wrong direction. We shouldn't be digitising these deadheads; we need to make new politicians, normal young guys. Develop them from the ground up through focus-groups – the ideology and the public face together.'

'Why don't you suggest it to Azadovsky?'

'You try suggesting anything to him . . . OK, we've arrived.'

There was an earth road adorned on both sides with Stop signs branching off from the road they were on. Morkovin turned on to it, slowed down and drove on through the forest. The road soon led them to a pair of tall gates in a brick wall. Morkovin sounded his horn twice, the gates opened and the car rolled into a huge yard the size of a football pitch.

Azadovsky's dacha created a strange impression. Most of all it resembled the Cathedral of St Basil the Holy Fool, doubled in size and overgrown with a multitude of domestic accretions. The corkscrew attics and garrets were decorated with little balconies with balustrades of short fat columns, and all the windows above the second floor were hidden completely behind shutters. There were several Rottweilers strolling around the yard and a ribbon of blue-grey smoke was rising from the chimney of one of the extensions (evidently they were stoking up the bath-house). Azadovksy himself, surrounded by a small entourage including Sasha Blo and Malyuta, was standing on the steps leading up into the house. He was wearing a Tyrolean hat with a feather, which suited him very well and even lent his plump face a kind of bandit nobility.

'We were just waiting for you,' he said when Tatarsky and Morkovin walked up. 'We're going out among the people. To drink beer at the station.'

Tatarsky felt an urgent desire to say something his boss would like.

'Just like Haroun el-Raschid and his viziers, eh?'

Azadovsky stared at him in amazement.

'He used to change his clothes and walk around Baghdad,' Tatarsky explained, already regretting he'd started the conversation. 'And see how the people lived. And find out how his rating was doing.'

'Around Baghdad?' Azadovsky asked suspiciously. 'Who was this Haroun guy?'

'He was the Caliph. A long time ago, about five hundred years.'

'I get it. You wouldn't do too much strolling around Baghdad these days. It's just like here, only you have to take three jeeps full of bodyguards. Right, is everyone here? Wagons roll!'

Tatarsky got into the last car, Sasha Blo's red Range-Rover. Sasha was already slightly drunk and obviously feeling elated.

'I keep meaning to congratulate you,' he said. 'That material of yours about Berezovsky and Raduev – it's the best *kompromat* there's been all autumn. Really. Especially the place where they plan to pierce the mystical body of Russia with their television-drilltowers at the major sacred points. And those inscriptions on the Monopoly money: 'In God we Monopolise!' And putting that Jewish prayer cap on Raduev – that must have taken some thinking up . . .'

'OK, OK,' said Tatarsky, thinking gloomily to himself: 'That jerk Malyuta was asked not to touch Raduev. Now the mazuma goes back. And I'll be lucky if they didn't have the meter running on it.'

'Why don't you tell me when your department's going to throw up a decent idea?' he asked. 'What stage is the project at?'

214

'It's all supposed to be strictly secret. But without getting specific, the idea's coming on, and it'll make everyone sick as parrots. We just have to think through the role of Attila and polish up the stylistic side – so we have something like an on-going counterpoint between the pipe organ and the balalaika.'

'Attila? The one who burnt Rome? What's he got to do with it?'

'Attila means "the man from Itil". In Russian, a Volga man. Itil is the ancient name for the Volga. D'you get my drift?'

'Not really.'

'We're the third Rome – which, typically enough, happens to lie on the Volga. So there's no need to go off on any campaigning. Hence our total historical self-sufficiency and profound national dignity.'

Tatarsky sized up the idea. 'Yeah,' he said, 'that's neat.'

Glancing out of the window, he caught sight of a gigantic concrete structure above the edge of the trees, a crooked spiral rising upwards, crowned with a small grey tower. He screwed up his eyes and then opened them again – the concrete monolith hadn't disappeared, only shifted backwards a little. Tatarsky nudged Sasha Blo so hard in the ribs that the car swerved across the road.

'You crazy, or what?' asked Sasha.

'Look quick, over there,' said Tatarsky. 'D'you see it, that concrete tower?'

'What of it?'

'D'you know what it is?'

Sasha looked out of the window.

'Oh, that. Azadovksy was just telling us about it. They started building an Air Defence station here. Early warning or some such thing. They got as far as building the foundations and the walls and then, you know, there was no one left to warn. Azadovsky has this plan to privatise the whole thing and finish building it, only not for a radar station – for his new house. I don't know. Speaking for myself, I can't stand concrete walls. What's got you so wound up?'

'Nothing,' said Tatarsky. 'It just looks very strange. What's this station we're going to called?'

'Rastorguevo.'

'Rastorguevo,' Tatarsky repeated. 'In that case, everything's clear.'

'And here it is. We're headed for that building over there. This is the dirtiest beer-hall anywhere near Moscow. Leonid likes to drink beer here at weekends. So's he can really appreciate what he's achieved in life.'

The beer-hall, located in the basement of a brick building with peeling paint not far from the railway platform, really was quite exceptionally dirty and foul-smelling. The people squeezed in at the tables with their quarter-litres of vodka matched the institution perfectly. The only ones who didn't fit in were two bandits in tracksuits standing behind a table at the entrance. Tatarsky was amazed to see Azadovsky actually greet some of the customers – he obviously really was a regular here. Sasha Blo swept up two glass mugs of pale beer in one hand, took Tatarsky by the arm with the other and dragged him off to a distant table.

'Listen,' he said. 'There's something I want to talk to you about. Two of my brothers have moved up here from Yerevan and decided to set up business. To cut it short, they've opened an exclusive funeral parlour with top-class service. They just figured out how much mazuma there is stuck between banks up here. They're all beginning to beat it out of each other now, so a real market niche has opened up.'

'That's for sure,' said Tatarsky, glancing at the bandits by the entrance, who were drinking Czech beer out of bottles they'd brought with them. He couldn't figure out what they were doing in a place like this – although their motives could have been the same as Azadovsky's.

'Just for friendship's sake,' Sasha Blo rattled on, 'write me a decent slogan for them, something that'll actually get to the target group. When they get on their feet they'll pay you back.'

'Why not, for old times' sake?' Tatarsky answered. 'So what's our brand essence?'

'I told you – high-class death.'

'What's the firm called?'

'The family name. The Brothers Debirsian Funeral Parlour. Will you think about it?'

216

'I'll do it,' said Tatarsky. 'No problem.'

'By the way,' Sasha went on, 'you'll laugh when I tell you, but they've already had one of our acquaintances as a client. His wife paid for a top-rate funeral before she slung her hook and split.'

'Who's that?'

'Remember Khanin from the Privy Councillor agency? Someone took him out.'

'That's terrible. I didn't hear about it. Who did it?'

'Some say the Chechens, and some say the filth. Something to do with diamonds. To cut it short, a murky business. Where are you off to?'

'The toilet,' Tatarsky answered.

The washroom was even dirtier than the rest of the beer-hall. Glancing at the wall covered in patches of geological damp that rose up from the urinal, Tatarsky noticed a triangular piece of plaster that was remarkably similar in shape to the diamond necklace in the photograph hanging in Khanin's toilet. At the first glimpse of this formation the feeling of pity for his former boss that filled Tatarsky's heart was alchemically transformed into the slogan ordered by Sasha Blo.

When he emerged from the toilet he stopped, astounded at the view that suddenly confronted him. There must have been a double door in the corridor before, but it had been broken out and its frame, daubed with black paint, was protruding from the walls and ceiling. With its slightly rounded outline the opening looked like the frame around a television screen – so much like it, in fact, that for a moment Tatarsky thought he was watching the country's biggest TV set. Azadovsky and his company were outside his field of view, but he could see the two bandits by the nearest table and the new customer who had appeared beside them. He was a tall, thin old man wearing a brown raincoat, a beret and powerful spectacles with earpieces that were too short. Through the lenses his eyes appeared disproportionately large and child-ishly honest. Tatarsky could have sworn he'd seen him some-where before. The old man had already gathered around himself a few listeners, who looked like homeless tramps.

'You guys,' he was saying in a thin voice full of astonishment, 'you'll never believe it! There I was picking up half a litre in the vegetable shop at the Kursk station, you know. I'm queuing up to pay, and guess who comes into the shop? Chubais! Fuck me . . . He was wearing this shabby grey coat and a red mohair cap, and not a bodyguard in sight. There was just a bit of a bulge in his right pocket, as though he had his rod in there. He went into the pickles section and took a big three-litre jar of Bulgarian tomatoes – you know, the green ones, with some green stuff in the jar? And he stuck it in his string bag. I'm standing there gawping at him with my mouth wide open, and he noticed, gave me a wink and hopped out the door. I went across to the window, and there was this car with a light on the roof, winking at me just like he did. He hops in and drives off. Bugger me, eh, the things that happen . . .'

Tatarsky cleared his throat and the old man looked in his direction.

'The People's Will,' Tatarsky said and winked, unable to restrain himself.

He pronounced the words very quietly, but the old man heard. He tugged on one of the bandits' sleeves and nodded in the direction of the gap in the wall. The bandits put down their half-finished bottles of beer on the table in synchronised motion and advanced on Tatarsky, smiling slightly. One of them put his hand in his pocket, and Tatarsky realised they were quite possibly going to kill him.

The adrenalin that flooded through his body lent his movements incredible lightness. He turned, shot out of the beer-hall and set off across the yard at a run. When he reached the very middle of it he heard several loud cracks behind him and something hummed by him very close. Tatarsky doubled his speed. He only allowed himself to glance around close to the corner of a tall log-built house that he could hide behind – the bandits had stopped shooting, because Azadovsky's security guards had come running up with automatics in their hands.

Tatarsky slumped against the wall, took out his cigarettes with fingers that refused to bend and lit up. 'That's the way it happens,' he thought, 'just like that. Simple, out of the blue.'

By the next time he screwed up the nerve to glance round the corner his cigarette had almost burnt away. Azadovsky and his company were getting into their cars; both the bandits, their faces beaten to pulp, were sitting on the back seat of a jeep with the bodyguards, and the old man in the brown raincoat was heatedly arguing his case to an indifferent bodyguard. At last Tatarsky remembered where he'd seen the old man before – he was the philosophy lecturer from the Literary Institute. He didn't really recognise his face – the man had aged a lot – so much as the intonation of astonishment with which he once used to read his lectures. 'The object's got a pretty strong character,' he used to say, throwing back his head to look up at the ceiling of the auditorium; 'it demands disclosure of the subject: that's the way it is! And then, if it's lucky, merging may take place . . .'

Tatarsky realised that merging had finally taken place. 'That happens too,' he thought and, taking out his notebook, jotted down the slogan he'd invented in the beer-hall:

DIAMONDS ARE NOT FOR EVER!
THE BROTHERS DEBIRSIAN FUNERAL PARLOUR

'They'll probably fire me,' he thought, when the cavalcade of cars disappeared round a bend. 'Where now? God only knows where. To Gireiev. He lives somewhere just around here.'

Gireiev's house proved surprisingly easy to find – Tatarsky recognised it from the garden with its forest of unbelievably tall dill umbrellas, looking more like small trees than large weeds. Tatarsky knocked several times on the gate and Gireiev appeared on the verandah. He was wearing trousers of an indefinite colour, baggy at the knees, and a tee shirt with a large letter 'A' in the centre of a rainbow-coloured circle.

'Come on in,' he said, 'the gate's open.'

Gireiev had been drinking for a few days, drinking away a fairly large sum of money, which was now coming to an end. This was the deduction that could be drawn from the fact that there were empty bottles from expensive brands of whisky and brandy standing along the wall, while the bottles standing closer to the centre of the room were from various kinds of vodka bootlegged from the Caucasus, the kinds that had romantic and passionate names and were sold around the railway stations. In the time that had elapsed since Tatarsky's last visit the kitchen had hardly changed at all, except for becoming even dirtier, and images of rather frightening Tibetan deities had appeared on the walls. There was one other innovation: a small television glimmering in the corner.

When he sat down at the table, Tatarsky noticed the television was standing upside down. The screen was showing the animated titles from some programme – a fly was buzzing around an eye with long lashes thickly larded with mascara. The name of the programme appeared – *Tomorrow* – at which very moment the fly landed on the pupil and stuck fast, and the lashes began to wrap themselves around it like a Venus fly-trap. The anchor man appeared, dressed in the uniform of a jail guard – Tatarsky guessed that must be the insulted response of a copywriter from the seventh floor to the recent declaration by a copywriter from the eighth floor that television in Russia is one of the state power structures. Because the anchor man was inverted, he looked very much like a bat hanging from an invisible perch. Tatarsky was not particularly surprised to recognise him as Azadovsky. His hair was dyed jet-black and he had a narrow shoelace moustache under his nose. He grinned like a halfwit and spoke:

'Very soon now in the city of Murmansk the nuclear jet-powered cruiser *The Idiot* will slide down the slipway. Its keel was laid to mark the hundred and fiftieth anniversary of the birth of Fedor Mikhailovich Dostoievsky. It is not clear as yet whether the government will be able to find the money needed to lay the keel of another ship of the same kind, the *Crime and Punishment*. Book news!' – Azadovsky produced a book with a cover depicting the holy trinity of a grenade-thrower, a chainsaw and a naked woman – 'Good needs hard fists. That's something we've known for a long time, but there was still something missing! Now here is the book we've been waiting for all these years – good with hard fists and a big dick: *The Adventures of Svyatoslav the Roughneck*. Economic news: in the State Duma today the make-up was announced of the new minimum annual consumer goods basket. It includes twenty kilogrammes of pasta, a centner of potatoes, six kilogrammes of pork, a padded coat, a pair of shoes, a fur cap with earflaps and a Sony Black Trinitron television. Reports from Chechnya . . .'

Gireiev turned off the sound.

'Did you come to watch the television, then?' he asked.

'Course not. It's just strange – what's it doing upside down?'

'That's a long story.'

'Like the one with the cucumbers, is it? Has to be properly conferred?'

'No, not that,' Gireiev said with a shrug. 'It's open information, but it's part of the practice of true dharma, so if you ask someone to tell you about it, you take on the karmic obligation to adopt the practice yourself. And I don't think you will.'

'Maybe I will. Try me.'

Gireiev sighed and glanced at the tall umbrellas swaying outside the window.

'There are three Buddhist ways of watching television. In essential terms, they're all the same way, but at different stages of training they appear different. First you watch television with the sound turned off. About half an hour a day, your favourite programmes. When you get the idea they're saying something important and interesting on the television, you become aware of the thought at the moment it arises and so neutralise it. At first you're bound to give way and turn on the sound, but gradually you'll get used to it. The main thing is not to allow a feeling of guilt to develop when you can't restrain yourself. It's like that for everybody at first, even for lamas. Then you start to watch the television with the sound switched on but the picture off. And finally you start watching the television completely switched off. That's actually the main technique and the first two are only preparatory. You watch all the news programmes, but you don't turn the television on. It's very important to keep your back straight while you do this, and it's best to fold your hands across your belly, right hand underneath, left hand on top – that's for men; for women it's the other way round – and you mustn't be distracted even for a second. If you watch the television like that for ten years at least an hour a day, you can come to understand the nature of television. And of everything else as well.'

'So then why do you turn it upside down?'

'That's the fourth Buddhist method. It's used when you really do need to watch the television after all. For instance, if you want to know the dollar exchange rate, but you don't know exactly when or how they're going to announce it – whether they'll read it out loud or show one of the boards outside the bureaux de change.'

'But why turn it upside down?'

'That's another long story.'

'Try.'

Gireiev ran his palm across his forehead and sighed again. He seemed to be searching for the right words.

'Have you ever wondered where that heavy, piercing hate in the anchormen's eyes comes from?' he eventually asked.

'Come off it,' said Tatarsky. 'They don't even look at the camera; it just seems like they do. There's a special monitor right under the camera lens that shows the text they're reading out and special symbols for intonation and facial expression. I think there are only six of them; let me just try to remember . . . irony, sadness, doubt, improvisation, anger and joke. So nobody's radiating any kind of hate – not their own or even any official kind. That much I know for certain.'

'I'm not saying they radiate anything. It's just that, when they read their text, there are several million people staring straight into their eyes, and as a rule they're very angry and dissatisfied with life. Just think about what kind of cumulative effect it generates when so many deceived consciousnesses come together in a single second at the same point. D'you know what resonance is?'

'More or less.'

'Well then: if a battalion of soldiers marches across a bridge in step, then the bridge can easily collapse – there have been cases – and so when a column crosses a bridge, the soldiers are ordered to march out of step. When so many people stare into this box and see the same thing, can you imagine what kind of resonance that sets up in the noosphere?'

'Where?' Tatarsky asked, but at that moment the mobile phone in his pocket rang and he raised a hand to halt the conversation. He could hear loud music and indistinct voices in the earpiece.

'Babe!' Morkovin's voice cut through the music. 'Where are you? Are you alive?'

'I'm alive,' replied Tatarsky. 'I'm in Rastorguevo.'

'Listen,' Morkovin went on merrily, 'we've given those fucking tossers a good working over, and now we'll probably send them off to jail, give them ten years. After the interrogation Azadovsky was laughing like mad! Said you'd released all his stress. Next time you'll get a medal together with Rostropovich. Shall I send some wheels round for you?'

No, they're not going to fire me, Tatarsky thought, feeling a pleasant warm glow spreading through his body. Definitely not. Or do me in me either.

'Thanks,' he said. 'I think I'll go home. My nerves are shot.'

'Yeah? I can understand that,' Morkovin agreed. 'Away with you then, get yourself fixed up. But I've got to be going – the bugle's sounding loud and clear. Only don't be late tomorrow – we have a very important occasion. We're going to Ostankino TV headquarters. You'll see Azadovsky's collection there, by the way – the Spanish section. Cheers for now.'

Tatarsky hid the phone in his pocket and looked around the room with unseeing eyes. 'So they take me me for a hamster, then,' he said pensively.

'What?'

'Nothing. What was that you were saying?'

'To keep it short,' Gireiev continued, 'all the so-called magic of television is nothing but psychoresonance due to the fact that so many people watch it at the same time. Any professional knows that if you do watch television–'

'I can tell you, professionals never do watch it,' Tatarsky interrupted, examining a patch he'd only just noticed on his friend's trouser-leg.

'–if you do watch television, you have to look at a point somewhere in the corner of the screen, but never under any circumstances into the eyes of the announcer, or else you'll start to develop gastritis or schizophrenia. But the safest thing is to turn it upside down the way I do. That's the same thing as not marching in step; and in general, if you're interested, there's a fifth Buddhist method for watching television, the highest and the most secret one of all . . .'

It often happens: you're talking with someone, and you kind

of like what he's saying, and there seems to be some truth in it. Then suddenly you notice he's wearing an old tee shirt, his slippers are darned, his trousers are patched at the knee and the furniture in his room is worn and cheap. You look a bit closer and all around you you see signs of humiliating poverty you didn't notice before, and you realise everything your interlocutor has done and thought in his life has failed to lead him to that single victory that you wanted so badly on that distant May morning when you gritted your teeth and promised yourself you wouldn't lose, even though it still wasn't really very clear just who you were playing with and what the game was. And although it hasn't become the slightest bit clearer since then, you immediately lose interest in what he's saying. You want to say goodbye to him in some pleasant fashion, get away as quickly as possible and finally get down to business.

That is how the displacing wow-factor operates in our hearts; but when Tatarsky was struck by its imperceptible blow, he gave no sign that he'd lost interest in the conversation with Gireiev, because an idea had struck him. He waited until Gireiev stopped speaking; then he stretched, yawned and asked as though it was a casual question: 'By the way, have you got any of those fly-agarics left?'

'Yes,' said Gireiev, 'but I won't take any with you. I'm sorry, but you know, after what happened the last time . . .'

'But will you give me some?'

'Why not? Only don't eat them here, please.'

Gireiev got up from the table, opened the crooked cupboard hanging on the wall and took out a bundle wrapped in newspaper.

'This is a good dose. Where are you going to take them – in Moscow?'

'No,' said Tatarsky; 'in the town I always get a bad trip. I'll go into the forest. Since I'm already out in the countryside.'

'You're right. Hang on, I'll give you some vodka. Softens the effect. They can bugger up your brains if you take them neat. Don't worry, don't worry, I've got some Absolut.'

Gireiev picked up an empty Hennessy bottle from the floor, twisted out the cork and began carefully pouring in vodka from a litre bottle of Absolut he'd taken from the same cupboard the mushrooms had been in.

'Listen, you've got something to do with television,' he said; 'there was a good joke going round about you. Have you heard the one about the blow job with singing in the dark?'

'No.'

'Well, this guy comes to a brothel. He looks at the price-list and sees the most expensive service: a blow job with singing in the dark for fifteen hundred bucks; and he thinks, That's strange. What could that be? And he buys a ticket. When his turn comes, he finds himself in a dark room and everything seems to go as promised – someone sucks his dick while singing. Afterwards he goes outside and thinks, But that's impossible! So he goes to a department store and buys a flashlight. Then he borrows another fifteen hundred and goes back to the brothel. To cut it short, everything happens all over again. And just as he's about to come, he whips out the flashlight and turns it on; and he sees that he's standing in a giant round room. There's a stool by the wall, and on top of the stool there's a giant glass eye.'

Gireiev stopped.

'So what's next?' Tatarsky asked.

'That's it. Some people just don't get it. I mean the joke. A blow job in the dark is something that everyone gets.'

'Ah . . . Now I do get it . . . What d'you think – is that the same eye that's on the dollar bill?'

'I never thought about it,' Gireiev answered.

'Frankly, this kind of humour's too glum for me. You have to believe in something.'

Gireiev shrugged. 'Hope dies last,' he said. 'What's that you're writing down? The joke?'

'No,' said Tatarsky, 'an idea for work.' *Idea for a poster*, he jotted down in his notebook:

A dirty room covered in cobwebs. On the table a still for moonshine, by the table an alcoholic dressed in rags , who is pouring his product from a large Absolut bottle into a small Hennessy bottle. Slogan:

ABSOLUT HENNESSY

Offer to Absolut and Hennessy distributors first, and if they don't take it, to Finlandia, Smirnoff and Johnny Walker.

'There you go,' said Gireiev, holding out the bundle and the bottle to Tatarsky. 'Only let's agree between ourselves that when you eat them, you don't come back here. I still haven't forgotten that time in autumn.'

'I promise,' said Tatarsky. 'By the way, where's that unfinished radar tower around here? I saw it from the car when we were driving here.'

'It's quite near. You go across the field and then the road through the forest starts. When you see a wire fence, just follow it. It's about three kilometres. Why, do you want to go wandering around it?'

Tatarsky nodded. 'I'm not so sure about that,' said Gireiev. 'It's not so bad when you're clean, but if you're on the mushrooms . . . The old men say it's a bad place; but then, where can you find a good place around Moscow?'

In the doorway Tatarsky turned back and hugged Gireiev round the shoulders. 'You know, Andriusha,' he said, 'I don't want this to sound sentimental, but thank you very, very much!'

'What for?' asked Gireiev.

'For sometimes allowing me to live a parallel life. Without that the real one would be so disgusting!'

'Thank you,' Gireiev replied, 'thank you.' He was obviously touched.

'Good luck in business,' Tatarsky said, and left.

The fly-agarics kicked in when he'd already been walking along the wire-netting fence for half an hour. First came the familiar symptoms: the pleasant trembling and itching in the fingers. Then looming up out of the bushes came the pillar with the notice: 'Campfires forbidden!' that he'd once taken for Hussein. As was only to be expected, in the daylight there was no noticeable resemblance. Even so, Tatarsky felt a certain nostalgia as he recalled the story of Semurg the king of the birds.

'Semurg, Sirruf,' said a familiar voice in his head: 'what difference does it make? Just different dialects. So you've been guzzling garbage again?'

'Now it's started,' thought Tatarsky; 'the beastie's here.'

But the Sirruf gave no further indication of its presence all the way to the tower. The gates that Tatarsky had climbed over were open. There was no one to be seen on the construction site; the trailers were locked and the telephone that used to hang on the sentry's mushroom shelter had disappeared.

Tatarsky climbed to the summit of the structure without any adventures. In the lift-tower everything was still the same as it had been: empty bottles and a table in the centre of the room.

'Well,' he asked out loud, 'where's the goddess here?'

There was no reply, nothing but the sound of the autumn forest rustling in the wind somewhere below. Tatarsky leaned against the wall, closed his eyes and began to listen. For some reason he decided it was willows that were whispering in the wind, and he recalled a line from a play he'd heard on the radio: 'It's the sisters of sorrow, who live in the willows.' And immediately he could hear snatches of women's voices in the quiet murmuring of the trees, sounding like a dim echo of words spoken to him long, long ago that had lost their way among the cul-de-sacs of memory.

'But do they know,' the quiet voices whispered, 'that this famous world of theirs consists of nothing but the condensation of darkness – neither breathing in, nor breathing out; neither right, nor left; neither fifth, nor tenth? Do they know that their extensive fame is known to no one?'

'Everything is the precise opposite of what they think,' the quiet voices whispered; 'there is no truth or falsehood; there is one infinitely clear, pure and simple thought in which the spirit of man swirls like a drop of ink that has fallen into a glass of water. When man ceases to swirl in this simple purity, absolutely nothing happens and life turns out to be merely the rustling of curtains in the window of a long-ruined tower, and every thread in those curtains thinks that the great goddess is with it. And the goddess truly is with it.'

'Once, my love, all of us were free – why did you have to create this terrible, ugly world?'

'Was it I who created it?' whispered Tatarsky.

No one replied. Tatarsky opened his eyes and looked out

through the doorway. Above the horizontal of the forest hung a cloud shaped like a heavenly mountain – it was so large that the infinite height of the sky, forgotten already in childhood, was suddenly visible again. On one of the slopes of the cloud there was a narrow conical projection, like a tower seen through mist. Something trembled inside Tatarsky – he recalled that once the ephemeral celestial substance of which these white mountains and this tower consisted had also been within him. And then – long, long ago, probably even before he was born – it had cost no effort at all for him to become such a cloud and float up to the very summit of the tower. But life had squeezed this strange substance out of his soul and there was only just enough of it left to allow him to recall it for a second and instantly lose the recollection.

Tatarsky noticed that the floor under the table was covered with a panel made from boards nailed together. Peering through a gap between them, he saw the blackness of a dark multi-storey abyss. 'Of course,' he recalled, 'it's the lift-shaft; and this is the engine room, just like the room with that render-server. Only there aren't any automatic rifles.' He sat at the table and gingerly placed his feet on the boards. At first he felt a bit afraid that the boards under his feet would break and that he and they would go tumbling down together into the deep shaft with the stratified garbage of the years lying at its bottom. But the boards were thick and secure.

The chamber had obviously been visited by someone, most likely the local tramps. There were freshly trampled cigarette butts on the floor, and on the table there was a fragment of newspaper with the television programmes for the week. Tatarsky read the title of the final programme before the jagged line of the torn edge: *0:00 – The Golden Room*

'What kind of programme's that?' he thought. 'Must be something new.' He rested his chin on his folded hands and gazed at the photograph of the woman running along the sand, which was still hanging in the same place. The daylight exposed the blisters and blots the damp had produced on the paper. One of the blots lay directly over the face of the goddess, and in the daylight it appeared warped, pock-marked and old.

Tatarsky drank the remainder of the vodka and closed his eyes.

The brief dream he saw was very strange. He was walking along a sandy beach towards a golden statue gleaming in the sun – it was still a long way off, but he could see it was a female torso without a head or hands. Slowly trudging along beside Tatarsky was the Sirruf, with Gireiev sitting on its back. The Sirruf was sad and looked like an ass exhausted by heavy work, and the wings folded on its back looked like an old felt saddle.

'You write slogans,' Gireiev said, 'but do you know the most important slogan of all? The base slogan, you could call it?'

'No,' said Tatarsky, screwing up his eyes against the golden radiance.

'I'll tell you it. You've heard the expression "Day of Judgement"?'

'Of course.'

'Well, there's nothing really frightening about that judgement. Except that it's already begun, and what happens to all of us is no more than a phase in a court experiment, a re-enactment of the crime. Think about it: surely it's no problem for God to create this entire world out of nothing, with its eternity and infinity, for just a few seconds in order to test a single soul standing before him?'

'Andrei,' Tatarsky answered, squinting at the darned slippers in the string stirrups, 'just leave it out, will you? I get enough shit at work. At least you could lay off.'

CHAPTER 15

The Golden Room

When they removed Tatarsky's blindfold, he was chilled to the bone. His bare feet were suffering particularly badly from the cold stone floor. Opening his eyes, he saw he was standing in the doorway of a spacious chamber similar to the foyer of a cinema where, as far as he could judge, there was something like a buffet supper taking place. One strange thing he noticed immediately: there wasn't a single window in the walls faced with yellow stone, but one of the walls reflected like a mirror, which meant that in the light of the bright halogen lamps the hall appeared substantially larger than it actually was. The people gathered in the hall were conversing quietly and studying sheets of paper with typewritten texts hung round the walls. Despite the fact that Tatarsky was standing in the doorway completely naked, the assembled company paid no particular attention to him, except perhaps for two or three who cast an indifferent glance in his direction. Tatarsky had seen virtually everyone in the hall many times on television, but there was no one he knew personally apart from Farsuk Seiful-Farseikin, who was standing by the wall with a wineglass in his hand. He also spotted Azadovsky's secretary Alla, engaged in conversation with two elderly playboys – her loose washed-out blonde hair made her look like a slightly debauched Medusa. Tatarsky thought that somewhere in the crowd he caught a glimpse of Morkovin's check jacket, but he lost sight of him immediately.

'I'm coming, I'm coming,' Tatarsky heard Azadovsky's voice say, and then he appeared out of a passage leading to some inner chamber. 'So you're here? Why're you standing in the doorway? Come on in; we won't eat you.'

Tatarsky stepped towards him. Azadovsky smelled

slightly of wine; in the halogen lighting his face looked tired.

'Where are we?' asked Tatarsky.

'About a hundred metres underground, near the Ostankino pond. I'm sorry about the blindfold and all the rest – that's just the way things are supposed to be before the ritual. Traditions, fuck 'em. You scared?'

Tatarsky nodded, and Azadovksy laughed contentedly. 'Don't let it bother you,' he said. 'It's a load of old cobblers. Have a wander around in the meantime, take a look at the new collection. It's been hung for two days now. I've got to have a word with a couple of people.'

He summoned his secretary with a snap of his fingers. 'Alla here can tell you about it. This is Babe Tatarsky. You know each other? Show him everything in the place, OK?'

Tatarsky was left in the company of the secretary.

'Where shall we start the viewing from?' she asked with a smile.

'Let's start from here,' said Tatarsky. 'But where's the collection?'

'There it is,' said the secretary, nodding towards the wall. 'It's the Spanish collection. Who do you like best of the great Spanish artists?'

'That would be . . .' Tatarsky said, straining to recall an appropriate name, '. . . Velasquez.'

'I'm crazy about the old darling too,' said the secretary, glancing at him with a cold green eye. 'I would call him the Cervantes of the brush.'

She took a precise grip on Tatarsky's elbow and, with her tall hip pressing against his naked thigh, she led him towards the nearest sheet of paper on the wall. Tatarsky saw that it held a couple of paragraphs of text and a blue seal. The secretary leaned shortsightedly towards the paper in order to read the fine print.

'Yes, this is the very canvas. A relatively little known pink version of the portrait of the Infanta. What you can see is a notarised certificate issued by Oppenheim and Radler to certify that the picture really was acquired for seventeen million dollars from a private collection.'

Tatarsky decided not to show that he was surprised by anything. Anyway, he didn't really know for certain whether he was surprised by anything or not.

'And this one?' he asked, indicating the next sheet of paper with a text and seal.

'Oh,' said Alla, 'that's the pride of our collection. It's a Goya – the Maja with a fan in the garden. Acquired from a certain small museum in Castile. Once again Oppenheim and Radler certify the price – eight and a half million. Astonishing.'

'Yes,' said Tatarsky, 'it is. But I must admit I find sculpture much more interesting than painting.'

'I should think so,' said the secretary. 'That must be because you're used to working in three dimensions, I suppose?'

Tatarsky gave an inquiring glance.

'Well, three-dimensional graphics. With those stiffs . . .'

'Ah,' said Tatarsky, 'that's what you're talking about. Yes, I'm used to working with them, and living with them.'

'Well here's a sculpture,' said the secretary, and she dragged Tatarsky over to a new sheet of paper on which the text was a little larger than on the others. 'It's a Picasso. Ceramic figurine of a woman running. Not much like Picasso, you might say. You'd be right, but that's because it's the post-cubist period. Almost thirteen million dollars – can you imagine it?'

'And where's the actual statue?'

'I don't actually know,' said the secretary with a shrug. 'Probably in some warehouse somewhere. But if you want to see what it looks like, the catalogue's over there on that little table.'

'What difference does it make where the statue is?'

Tatarsky swung round. Azadovksy had come up behind him unnoticed.

'Maybe none at all,' said Tatarsky. 'To tell the truth, it's the first time I've come across this kind of a collection.'

'It's the cutting edge in design,' said the secretary. 'Monetaristic minimalism. They say it was invented here in Russia.'

'Take a walk,' Azadovsky said to her, and turned to Tatarsky. 'D'you like it?'

'It's interesting. But I don't really understand it.'

'Then I'll explain,' said Azadovsky. 'This bastard Spanish collection cost something like two hundred million dollars, and another hundred thousand went on the art historians – which picture would suit, which picture wouldn't fit in, which order to hang them in, and so forth. Everything mentioned on the invoices has been bought. But if we brought all those paintings and statues here – and there are tapestries and suits of armour as well – there'd be no space left in here to move. You'd choke to death on the dust alone. And afterwards . . . Well let's be honest, after you've seen these pictures once – maybe twice – what're you going to see that's new?'

'Nothing.'

'That's right. So why keep them in your own place? Anyway, I reckon this Picasso's a complete and utter plonker.'

'I couldn't entirely agree with you there,' said Tatarsky, swallowing. 'Or rather, I could, but only starting from the post-cubist period.'

'I can see you're a brainbox,' said Azadovsky. 'But I don't get it. What's the damn point, anyway? In a week's time it'll be the French collection. Just think: you figure one lot out, then a week later they cart it away and hang up another lot – so you're supposed to figure that lot out as well? What's the point?'

Tatarsky couldn't think of a good answer.

'I tell you, there isn't one,' Azadovsky insisted. 'OK, let's go. It's time to get started. We'll come back here afterwards. For some champagne.'

He turned and set off towards the mirror wall. Tatarsky followed him. When he reached the wall, Azadovsky pushed against it with his hand and the vertical row of mirror blocks casting an electrical reflection on him swung silently around their axis. Through the opening created a corridor built of rough-hewn stone came into view.

'Go on in,' said Azadovsky. 'Only keep your head down: the ceiling's low in here.'

Tatarsky entered the corridor and the damp immediately made him feel even more cold. When will they let me get dressed? he thought. The corridor was long, but Tatarsky couldn't see where it was leading: it was dark. Occasionally he felt a sharp stone under his foot and winced with the pain. At last there was a glimmer of light up ahead.

They emerged into a small room lined with wooden boards that reminded Tatarsky of a changing room for a gym. In actual fact, it was a changing room, as the lockers by the wall and the two jackets hanging on a coat-stand made clear. Tatarsky thought one of them belonged to Sasha Blo, but he couldn't be absolutely certain – Sasha had too many different jackets. There was a second exit from the changing room, a dark wooden door with a golden plaque engraved with a jagged line, looking like the teeth of a saw. Tatarsky still remembered from school that that was how the Egyptian hieroglyph for 'quickly' looked. He'd only remembered it then because of a funny story connected with it: the ancient Egyptians, so their teacher had explained, used to build their ziggurats very slowly, and so in the inscriptions of the greatest and most powerful Pharaohs the short jagged line meaning 'quickly' had become very long and even took up several lines, meaning 'very, very quickly'.

Hanging beside the washbasin, looking like decrees from some unknown authority, there were three sheets of paper with typed texts and seals (Tatarsky guessed they were not decrees at all, but more likely part of the Spanish collection), and one of the walls was covered with shelves with numbered pigeon-holes containing bronze mirrors and golden masks exactly like the ones in Azadovsky's reception room.

'What's that?' Azadovsky asked. 'Did you want to ask something?'

'What are these sheets of paper on the walls?' Tatarsky asked. 'More of the Spanish collection?'

Instead of replying Azadovsky took out his mobile phone and pressed its one and only button.

'Alla,' he said, 'some questions here for you.' He handed the telephone to Tatarsky.

'Yes?' said Alla's voice in the handset.

'Ask her what we've got in the bath-house changing room,' said Azadovsky, pulling off his vest. 'I keep forgetting all the time.'

'Hello,' said Tatarsky, embarrassed, 'this is Tatarsky again.

234

Tell me, this exhibition in the changing room, what is it?'

'Those are absolutely unique exhibits,' said the secretary. 'I'm not allowed to talk about them over the phone.'

Tatarsky covered the mouthpiece with his hand. 'She says it's not for discussion on the phone.'

'Tell her I give my permission.'

'He says he gives his permission,' Tatarsky echoed.

'Very well,' sighed the secretary. 'Number one: fragments of the gates of Ishtar from Babylon – lions and sirrufs. Official place of keeping, the Pergamon museum in Berlin. Certified by a group of independent experts. Number two: lions, bas-relief of moulded brick and enamel. Street of Processions, Babylon. Official place of keeping, the British Museum. Certified by a group of independent experts. Number three: Fukem-Al, a dignitary from Mari. Official place of keeping, the Louvre ...'

'Fukem-Al?' Tatarsky repeated, and remembered he'd seen a photograph of this statue in the Louvre. It was thousands of years old, and it was a portrait of a cunning-looking little man carved in brilliant white stone – with a beard and dressed in strange, fluffy, skirtlike culottes.

'I really like that one,' said Azadovsky, lowering his trousers. 'No doubt he woke up every morning and said: "Ah, fukem al ..." And so he was all alone all his life, exactly like me.'

He opened a locker and took out two unusual-looking skirts made either of feathers or fluffed-up wool. He tossed one over to Tatarsky and pulled the other up over his red Calvin Klein underpants, which immediately made him look like an overfed ostrich.

'Let's have the phone,' he said. 'What are you waiting for? Get changed. Then pick up a set of this junk here and go on through. You can take any pair you like, just as long as the muzzle's the right size.'

Azadovsky took a mask and a mirror from one of the pigeon-holes and clanged them against each other, then raised the mask and looked at Tatarsky through the eye-slits. The small golden face of an unearthly beauty, which might have appeared out of a crowd of maskers at a Venetian carnival, was so out of keeping with his barrel-shaped torso covered in ginger hair that Tatarsky suddenly felt afraid. Pleased with the effect he'd produced, Azadovsky laughed, opened the door and disappeared in a beam of golden light.

Tatarsky began getting changed. The skirt Azadovsky had given him was made out of strips of long-haired sheepskin stitched together and glued to nylon Adidas shorts. Squeezing himself into it somehow or other (if Tatarsky hadn't seen the statue of Fukem-Al, he would never have believed the ancient inhabitants of Mesopotamia actually wore anything of the kind), he put on the mask, immediately pressing it firmly over his face, and picked up the mirror. There could be no doubt that the gold and bronze were genuine – it was obvious from the weight alone. Breathing out as though he was about to plunge into cold water, he pushed open the door marked with the jagged line.

The room he entered blinded him with the golden gleam of its walls and floor, lit by bright studio lights. The sheet-metal cladding of the walls rose up to form a smoothly tapering cone, as though the room were an empty church dome gilded on the inside. Directly opposite the door stood an altar – a cubic gold pediment on which there lay a massive crystal eye with an enamel iris and a bright reflective pupil. In front of the altar there was a gold chalice standing on the floor, and towering up on each side of it were two stone sirrufs, covered in the remnants of gilt and painted designs. Hanging above the eye was a slab of black basalt, which appeared to be very ancient. Chiselled into its very centre was the Egyptian hieroglyph for 'quick', which was surrounded by complicated figures – Tatarsky could make out a strange dog with five legs and a woman in a tall tiara reclining on some kind of couch and holding a chalice in her hands. Along the edges of the slab there were images of four terrible-looking beasts, and between the dog and the woman there was a plant growing up out of the ground, resembling a Venus fly-trap, except that for some reason its root was divided into three long branches, each of which was marked with an unintelligible symbol. Also carved into the slab were a large eye and a large ear, and all the rest of the space was taken up by dense columns of cuneiform text.

Azadovsky, dressed in his gold mask, skirt and red flip-flops, was sitting on a folding stool near the altar. His mirror was lying on his knee. Tatarsky didn't notice anybody else in the room.

'Right on!' said Azadovsky, giving the thumbs-up sign. 'You look just great. Having doubts, are you? Just don't turn sour on us, OK; don't you go thinking we're nothing but a set of fuckheads. Personally I couldn't give a toss for all this, but if you want to be in our business, you can't get by without it. To cut it short, I'll fill in the basic picture for you, and if you want more detail, you can ask our head honcho; he'll be here in a minute. The important thing is, you just take everything as it comes; be cool. Ever go to pioneer camp?'

'Sure,' Tatarsky replied.

'Did you have that business with the Day of Neptune? When everybody got dunked in the water?'

'Yeah.'

'Well, you just figure like this is another Day of Neptune. Tradition. The story goes that once there was this ancient goddess. Not that I mean to say she really existed – there was just this legend, see. And the storyline says the gods were mortal as well and carried their deaths around inside them, just like ordinary folks. So when her time was up, this goddess had to die too; and naturally enough, she didn't fancy the idea. So then she separated into her own death and the part of her that didn't want to die. See there, on the picture?' – Azadovsky jabbed his finger in the direction of the bas-relief – 'That dog there's her death. And the dame in the fancy headgear – that's her. To cut it short – from here on in you just listen and don't interrupt, 'cause I'm not too hot on this stuff myself – when they split apart, this war immediately started between them, and neither of them could stay on top for long. The final battle in the war took place right above the Ostankino pond – that is, where we are right now, only not underground, but way high up in the air. That's why they reckon it's a sacred spot. For a long time no one could win the battle, but then the dog began to overpower the goddess. Then the other gods got frightened for themselves, so they interfered and made them make peace. It's all written down right here. This is like the

237

text of a peace treaty witnessed in the four corners of the earth by these bulls and . . .'

'Gryphons,' Tatarsky prompted him.

'Yeah. And the eye and the ear mean that everyone saw it and everyone heard it. To cut it short, the treaty gave them both a drubbing. It took away the goddess's body and reduced her to a pure concept. She became gold – not just the metal, though: in a metaphorical sense. You follow me?'

'Not too well.'

'Not surprising,' sighed Azadovsky. 'Anyway, to cut it short, she became the thing that all people desire, but not just a heap of gold, say, that's lying around somewhere, but all gold in general. Sort of like – the idea.'

'Now I'm with you.'

'And her death became this lame dog with five legs who had to sleep for ever in this distant country in the north. You've probably guessed which one. There he is on the right, see him? Got a leg instead of a prick. Wouldn't want to run into him in the back yard.'

'And what's this dog called?' Tatarsky asked.

'A good question. To tell the truth, I don't know. But why d'you ask?'

'I read something similar. In a collection of university articles.'

'What exactly?'

'It's a long story,' answered Tatarsky. 'I don't remember it all.'

'What was the article about, though? Our firm?'

Tatarsky guessed his boss was joking.

'No,' he said, 'about Russian swear words. It said swear words only became obscenities under Christianity, but before that they had an entirely different meaning and they signified incredibly ancient pagan gods. One of these gods was the lame dog Phukkup with five legs. In the ancient chronicles he was indicated by a large letter 'P' with two commas. Tradition says he sleeps somewhere among the snow, and while he sleeps, life goes along more or less OK; but when he wakes up, he attacks. When that happens, the land won't yield crops, you get Yeltsin for president, and all that kind of stuff. Of course, they didn't actually know anything about Yeltsin, but overall it's pretty similar.'

'And who is it this Phukkup attacks in this article?' Azadovsky asked.

'Not anyone or anything special – just everything in general. That's probably why the other gods interfered. I asked what the dog was called specially – I thought maybe it was some kind of transcultural archetype. So what do they call the goddess?'

'They don't call her anything,' broke in a voice behind them, and Tatarsky swung round.

Farsuk Seiful-Farseikin was standing in the doorway. He was wearing a long black cloak with a hood framing his gleaming golden mask, and Tatarsky only recognised him from his voice.

'They don't call her anything,' Seiful-Farseikin repeated, entering the room. 'Once a long time ago they used to call her Ishtar, but her name has changed many times since then. You know the brand No Name, don't you? And the story's the same with the lame dog. But you were right about all the rest.'

'You talk to him, will you, Farsuk?' said Azadovksy. 'He knows everything anyway, without us telling him.'

'What do you know, I wonder?' Farseikin asked.

'Just a few bits and pieces,' answered Tatarsky. 'For instance, that jagged sign in the centre of the slab. I know what it means.'

'And what does it mean?'

'"Quick" in ancient Egyptian.'

Farseikin laughed. 'Yes,' he said, 'that's certainly original. New members usually think it's M&M chocolate. Actually it's a symbol that indicates a certain very ancient and rather obscure dictum. All the ancient languages in which it existed have been dead for ages, and even translating it into Russian is difficult – there aren't any appropriate glosses. But English has an exact equivalent in Marshall MacLuhan's phrase: "The medium is the message." That's why we decode the symbol as two 'M's joined together. And we're not the only ones, of course – altars like this are supplied with all render-servers.'

'You mean the slab isn't genuine?'

'Why not? It's absolutely genuine,' answered Farseikin. 'Three-thousand-year-old basalt. You can touch it. Of course,

I'm not sure this drawing always meant what it means now.'

'What's that Venus fly-trap plant between the goddess and the dog?'

'It's not a Venus fly-trap; it's the Tree of Life. It's also the symbol of the great goddess, because one of her forms is a tree with three roots that blossoms in our souls. This tree also has a name, but that is only learned at the very highest stages of initiation in our society. At your stage you can only know the names of its three roots – that is, the root names.'

'What are these names?'

Farseikin solemnly pronounced three strange long words that had absolutely no meaning for Tatarsky. He could only note that they contained many sibilants.

'Can they be translated?'

'It's the same problem of there being no appropriate glosses. The root names can only be rendered very approximately as "oral", "anal" and "displacing".'

'Uhuh,' said Tatarsky. 'I see. And what society's that? What do its members do?'

'As if you really don't know. How long have you been working for us now? All that is what its members do.'

'What's it called?'

'Once long ago it was called the Chaldean Guild,' Farseikin replied. 'But it was called that by people who weren't members and had only heard about it. We ourselves call it the Society of Gardeners, because our task is to cultivate the sacred tree that gives life to the great goddess.'

'Has this society existed for a long time?'

'For a very, very long time. They say it was active in Atlantis, but for the sake of simplicity we regard it as coming to us from Babylon via Egypt.'

Tatarsky adjusted the mask that had slipped from his face. 'I see,' he said. 'So did it build the Tower of Babel?'

'No. Definitely not. We're not a construction firm. We're simply servants of the great goddess. To use your terminology, we watch to make sure that Phukkup doesn't awaken and attack; you understood that part right. I think you understand that here in Russia we bear a special responsibility. The dog sleeps here.'

'But where exactly?'

'All around us,' replied Farseikin. 'When they say he sleeps among the snow, that's a metaphor; but the fact that several times this century he has almost awoken isn't.'

'So why do they keep cutting back our frequency?'

Farseikin spread his hands and shrugged. 'Human frivolity,' he said, going over to the altar and picking up the golden chalice. 'Immediate advantage, a short-sighted view of the situation; but they'll never actually cut us off, don't worry about that. They watch that very closely. And now, if you have no objections, let us proceed with the ritual.'

He moved close to Tatarsky and put his hand on his shoulder. 'Kneel down and remove your mask.'

Tatarsky obediently went down on his knees and removed the mask from his face. Farseikin dipped a finger into the chalice and traced a wet zigzag on Tatarsky's forehead.

'Thou art the medium, and thou art the message,' he said, and Tatarsky realised that the line on his forehead was a double 'M'.

'What liquid is that?' he asked.

'Dog's blood. I trust I don't need to explain the symbolism?'

'No,' said Tatarsky, rising from the floor. 'I'm not an idiot; I've read a thing or two. What next?'

'Now you must look into the sacred eye.'

For some reason Tatarsky shuddered at this, and Azadovsky noticed it.

'Don't be scared,' he put in. 'Through this eye the goddess recognises her husband; and since she already has a husband, it's a pure formality. You take a look at yourself in the eye, it's clear you're not the god Marduk, and we calmly get on with business.'

'What god Marduk?'

'Well, maybe not Marduk, then,' said Azadovsky, taking out a pack of cigarettes and a lighter; 'it doesn't matter. I didn't mean anything in particular. Farsuk, you explain to him; you've got it all taped. Meanwhile I'll take a trip to Marlboro country.'

'It's another mythologeme,' said Farseikin. 'The great goddess had a husband, also a god, the most important of all the gods, to whom she fed a love potion, and he fell asleep in the shrine on the summit of his ziggurat. Since he was a god, his dreaming was so powerful that . . . In general, it's all a bit confused, but all of our world, including all of us, and even the goddess, are apparently his dream. And since he can't be found, she has a symbolic earthly husband, whom she chooses herself.'

Tatarsky cast a glance in the direction of Azadovsky, who nodded and released a neat smoke ring through the mouth-hole of his mask.

'You guessed,' said Farseikin. 'At the moment it's him. For Leonid, it's naturally a rather tense moment when someone else looks into the sacred eye, but so far it's been all right. Go on.'

Tatarsky went up to the eye on the stand and knelt down in front of it. The blue enamel iris was separated from the pupil by a fine gold border; the pupil itself was dark and reflected like a mirror. In it Tatarsky could see his own distorted face, Farseikin's crooked figure and Azadovsky's bloated knee.

'Turn the light this way,' Farseikin said to someone. 'He won't be able to see like that, and he has to remember for the rest of his life.'

A bright beam of light fell on the pupil, and Tatarsky could no longer see his own reflection, which was replaced by a blurred golden glimmering, as though he had just spent several minutes watching the rising sun, then closed his eyes and seen its imprint lost and wandering through his nerve endings. 'Just what was it I was supposed to see?' he wondered.

Behind him there was a rapid scuffle, something metallic clanged heavily against the floor and he heard a hoarse gasp. Tatarsky instantly leapt to his feet, sprang back from the altar and swung round.

The scene that met his eyes was so unreal that it failed to frighten him, and he decided it must be part of the ritual. Sasha Blo and Malyuta, wearing fluffy white skirts, with golden masks dangling at their chests, were strangling Azadovsky with yellow nylon skipping ropes, trying to keep themselves as far away from him as possible, while Azadovsky, his sheep's eyes staring out of his head, was pulling the thin nylon rope with both hands towards himself with all his might. Alas, it was an unequal struggle: blood appeared on his lacerated palms, staining the yellow string red, and he fell first to his knees and then on to his belly, covering his fallen mask with his chest. Tatarsky caught the moment when the expression of dumbfounded astonishment disappeared from the eyes gazing at him and was not replaced by any other. It was only then he realised that if this was part of the ritual, it was an entirely unexpected part for Azadovsky.

'What is this? What's happening?'

'Take it easy,' said Farseikin. 'Nothing's happening any more. It's already happened.'

'But why?' asked Tatarsky.

Farseikin shrugged. 'The great goddess had grown weary of her mismatch.'

'How do you know?'

'At the sacred divination in Atlanta the oracle foretold that in our country Ishtar would have a new husband. We'd been having problems with Azadovsky for ages, but it took us a long time to figure out who the new husband could be. All that was said about him was that he was a man with the name of a town. We thought and thought about it, we searched, and then suddenly they brought in your file from the first section. Everything adds up: you're the one.'

'Me???'

Instead of replying, Farseikin gave a sign to Sasha Blo and Malyuta. They went over to Azadovsky's body, took hold of his legs and dragged him out of the altar room into the changing room.

'Me?' Tatarsky repeated. 'But why me?'

'I don't know. Ask yourself that one. For some reason the goddess didn't choose me. How fine it would have sounded: "He who has abandoned his name" . . .'

'Abandoned his name?'

'I come from a Volga German background; but when I was due to graduate from university, an order came in from state TV for a nig-nog to be their Washington correspondent. I was the Komsomol secretary, which meant I was first in line for America. So they changed my name for me in the Lyubyanka.

243

Anyway, that's not important. It's you that's been chosen.'

'And would you have accepted?'

'Why not? It certainly sounds impressive: husband of the great goddess! It's a purely ritual post, no responsibilities at all, but the opportunities are absolutely immense. No limits at all, you could say. Of course, it all depends on how imaginative you are. Every morning the deceased here had his cleaning-lady scatter cocaine across his carpet from a bucket; and he built himself a bunch of dachas, bought a load of pictures . . . And that was all he could think of. As I said: a mismatch.'

'And can I refuse?'

'I think not,' said Farseikin.

Tatarsky glanced through the open door, behind which there was something strange going on. Malyuta and Sasha Blo were packing Azadovsky into a container in the form of a large green sphere. His body, hunched over in an unnatural fashion, was already in the container, but one hairy leg with a red flip-flop still protruded from the container's small door and stubbornly refused to fit inside.

'What's the sphere for?'

'The corridors here are long and narrow,' answered Farseikin. 'Carrying him would be the devil's own job; and when you roll it outside, nobody takes the slightest notice. Semyon Velin thought it up before he died. What a designer he was . . . And we lost him because of this idiot as well. I wish Semyon could see all this!'

'But why is it green?'

'I don't know. What difference does it make? Don't go looking for symbolic significance in everything, Babe – you might regret it when you find it.'

There was a quiet crunching sound in the changing room and Tatarsky winced.

'Will they strangle me some time too?' he asked.

Farseikin shrugged: 'As you've seen, the consorts of the great goddess are sometimes changed, but that goes with the job. If you don't get too full of yourself, you could easily reach old age. Even retire. The main thing is, if you have any doubts about anything, you just come to me; and follow my advice. The first thing I'd advise you to do is get rid of that cocaine-polluted carpet. There are rumours going round town. That's something we can do without.'

'I'll get rid of the carpet; but how do we explain to all the others about me moving into his office?'

'No need to explain anything to them. They understand all right, or they wouldn't be working for us.'

Malyuta put his head out of the changing room. He was already changed. He glanced at Tatarsky for a moment then looked away and held out Azadovsky's mobile phone to Farseikin.

'Shall we roll it out?' he asked briskly.

'No,' said Farseikin. 'Roll it in. Why d'you ask such stupid questions?'

Tatarsky waited until the metallic rumbling in the long burrow of the corridor had died away and asked in a low voice: 'Farsuk Karlovich, will you tell me something, in confidence?'

'What?'

'Who actually controls all of this?'

'My advice to you is not to stick your nose in,' said Farseikin. 'That way you'll stay a living god for longer; and to be honest about it, I don't know. Even after all the years I've been in the business.'

He went over to the wall beside the altar, unlocked a small concealed door, bent down and went in through the opening. A light came on beyond the door and Tatarsky saw a large machine that looked like an open black book flanked by two vertical cylinders of frosted glass. The flat black surface facing Tatarsky bore the word 'Compuware' in white and some unfamiliar symbol, and standing in front of the machine was a seat rather like a dentist's chair with straps and latches.

'What's that?' Tatarsky asked.

'A 3-D scanner.'

'What's it for?'

'We're going to scan in your image.'

'Do I have to go through with it?'

'Absolutely. According to the ritual, you only become the husband of the great goddess after you've been digitised – converted, as they say, into a sequence of visual images.'

'And then I'll be inserted into all the clips and broadcasts? Like Azadovsky?'

'That's your main sacramental function. The goddess really doesn't have a body, but there is something that takes the place of her body. Her corporeal nature consists of the totality of all the images used in advertising; and since she manifests herself via a sequence of images, in order to become godlike, you have to be transformed. Then it will be possible for you to enter into mystical union. In effect, your 3-D model will be her husband, and you'll be . . . a regent, I suppose. Come over here.'

Tatarsky shifted his feet nervously and Farseikin laughed: 'Don't be afraid. It doesn't hurt to be scanned. It's like a photocopier, only they don't close the lid . . . At least, not yet they don't . . . OK, OK, I'm only joking. Let's get on with it; they're waiting for us upstairs. It's a celebration – your coming-out party, so to speak. You can relax in a circle of close friends.'

Tatarsky took a last look at the basalt slab with the dog and the goddess before plunging decisively through the doorway beyond which Farseikin was waiting for him. The walls and ceiling of the small room were painted white and it was almost empty – apart from the scanner it contained a desk with a control panel on it and several cardboard boxes that had once held electronic goods standing over by the wall.

'Farsuk Karlovich, have you heard of the bird Semurg?' Tatarsky asked as he sat in the armchair and set his forearms on the armrests.

'No. What kind of a bird is it?'

'There was an oriental poem,' said Tatarsky; 'I haven't read it myself, only heard about it. About how thirty birds flew off to search for their king Semurg and then, after all kinds of different tests and trials, at the very end they learned that the word "Semurg" means "thirty birds".'

'So?' Farseikin asked, pushing a black plug into a socket.

'Well,' said Tatarsky, 'I just thought, maybe the entire Generation "P", that is the one that chose Pepsi – you chose Pepsi when you were young as well, didn't you?'

'What other choice was there?' Farseikin muttered, clicking switches on the control panel.

'Yes, well . . . I had this rather frightening thought: that dog with five legs – maybe it's all of us together? And now we're all on the attack, sort of.'

Farseikin was clearly too absorbed in his manipulations to take in what Tatarsky had said.

'Right,' he said, 'now hold dead still and don't blink. Ready?'

Tatarsky gave a deep sigh.

'Ready,' he said.

The machine began to hum and whirr and the frosted white lamps at each side of it lit up with a blinding brilliance. The structure that looked like an open book began slowly rotating around its axis, a ray of white light struck Tatarsky in the eyes and he was blinded for several seconds.'

'I bow before the living god,' Farseikin said solemnly.

When Tatarsky opened his eyes, Farseikin was kneeling in front of the armchair with his head bowed, holding out to him a small black object. It was Azadovsky's phone. Tatarsky took it gingerly and examined it: the phone looked like an ordinary small Phillips, except that it had only one button, in the form of a golden eye. Tatarsky wanted to ask if Alla knew what was happening, but he had no chance: Farseikin bowed, rose to his feet, walked backwards to the exit and tactfully closed the door behind him.

Tatarsky was left alone. He got up from the chair, walked over to the door and listened. He couldn't hear anything: Farseikin must already be in the changing room. Tatarsky moved across into the farthest corner of the room and cautiously pressed the button on the phone.

'Hello,' he said quietly into the handset. 'Hello!'

'I bow before the living god,' Alla's voice replied. 'What are your instructions for today, boss?'

'None yet,' Tatarsky replied, amazed to sense that he could play his new part without the slightest effort. 'Although, you know what, Alla, there will be a few after all. Firstly, have the carpet in the office taken up – I'm fed up with it. Secondly, make sure that from today on there's nothing but Coca-Cola in the buffet, no Pepsi. Thirdly, Malyuta doesn't work for us any more . . . because he's about as much use to us as a fifth leg to a dog. All he does is spoil other people's scenarios, and then the mazuma has to go back . . . And you, Alla my love, remember: if I say something, you don't ask "why?", you just jot it down. You follow? That's all right then.'

When the conversation was over, Tatarsky tried to hook the phone on to his belt, but his Fukem-Al sheepskin skirt was too thick. He thought for a few moments about where he could stick it, and then recalled that he'd forgotten to say something, and pressed the golden eye again.

'And one more thing,' he said; 'I completely forgot: take care of Rostropovich.'

CHAPTER 16

Tuborg Man

Babylen Tatarsky's 3-D double appeared on screen times
without number, but Tatarsky himself only liked to rewatch a
few of the tapes. The first was a press conference given by officers of the State Security Forces who had been ordered to
eliminate the well-known businessman and political figure
Boris Berezovsky: Tatarsky, wearing a black mask covering
his entire face, is sitting at the extreme left of a table crowded
with microphones. The second tape was the funeral of the TV
commentator Farsuk Seiful-Farseikin, who was strangled
with a yellow skipping rope in strange circumstances in the
entrance-way of his own house: Tatarsky, wearing dark
glasses and a black armband, is seen kissing the inconsolable
widow and tossing a green billiard ball on to the coffin half-
covered in earth. The event shown in the next report is rather
harder to understand: it's live footage from a hidden camera
of the unloading of an American Hercules C-130 military
transport plane following a night landing on Red Square. The
cargo being carried out of the plane consists of a large number
of cardboard boxes bearing the inscription 'electronic equipment' and an unusual-looking logo – the casually traced outline of a human mammary gland of a size that can only be
achieved by the installation of a silicone implant. Tatarsky,
wearing the uniform of a crack commando, is standing there
stock-still. His next appearance is one familiar to everybody,
as Charles I in the monumental ad for the shampoo Head and
Shoulders. Far less well known is another clip filmed on Red
Square, an advert for Coca-Cola that was shown several times
on St Petersburg TV, showing a congress of radical funda-
mentalists from all of the world's major confessions. Dressed
completely in black, Tatarsky plays an evangelist from Albu-
querque, New Mexico. Stamping in fury on a can of Pepsi-

Cola he raises his arm to point to the Kremlin wall and intones a verse from Psalm 14:

> There were they in great fear;
> for God is in the generation of the righteous.

Many still remember his appearance in the clip for Adidas (slogan: 'Three More White Lines'), but for some reason Tatarsky didn't keep it in his collection. It didn't even include the famous ad for the Moscow chain of Gap stores, in which Tatarsky appeared together with his deputy Morkovin, Morkovin wearing a denim jacket embroidered with gold in the shop window and Tatarsky wearing a padded army uniform hurling a brick at the reinforced glass and yelling: 'Afghanistan was heavier' (slogan: 'Enjoy the Gap'). But his very favourite video clip, the one – as his secretary Alla used to say in a whisper – that would bring tears to his eyes, was never shown on television even once.

It is a commercial for Tuborg beer with the slogan: 'Sta, viator!' (and the variants: 'Prepare Yourself' and 'Think Final' for the regional TV networks) in which the famous picture of the solitary wanderer is animated. There were rumours that a version of this clip was made in which there were thirty Tatarskys walking along the road one after the other, but there doesn't seem to be any way to determine whether or not that's true. The only thing we know for sure is that the existing clip is very short and simple.

Tatarsky, wearing a white shirt open at the chest, is walking along a dusty track under a sun standing at its zenith. Suddenly he is struck by some kind of thought. He halts, leans against a wooden fence and wipes the sweat from his face with a handkerchief. A few seconds go by, and the hero seems to grow calmer. Turning his back to the camera, he stuffs the handkerchief into his pocket and slowly walks on towards the bright-blue horizon, where a few wispy clouds hang high in the sky.

–1998

THE
VISITOR'S GUIDE TO
NORTH WALES
and SNOWDONIA

MPC

British Library Cataloguing in
Publication Data:
Macdonald, Colin
   The visitor's guide to North
   Wales. - 2nd ed.
   1. North Wales - Visitor's guides
   I. Title
   914.29'104858

1st Edition   1982
2nd Edition (fully revised and
redesigned)   1989

Published by:
Moorland Publishing Co Ltd,
Moor Farm Road,
Airfield Estate,
Ashbourne,
Derbyshire DE6 1HD
England

ISBN 0 86190 293 9 (paperback)
ISBN 0 86190 292 0 (hardback)

Published in the USA by:
Hunter Publishing Inc,
300 Raritan Centre Parkway,
CN 94, Edison, NJ 08818

ISBN 1 55650 118 8 (USA)

Cover photograph: *Conwy Castle and
Telford's suspension Bridge* (International Photobank, Peter Baker)

Illustrations have been supplied by:
C. Barnes: p 136; J. P. Walker: p 159.
All other photographs are by the author
and from the MPC Picture Collection.

Colour and black & white
origination by:
Scantrans, Singapore
Printed in the UK by:
Richard Clay Ltd, Bungay, Suffolk

CONTENTS

Key to Symbols Used on Maps and in Text Margin

 Recommended walk

 Parkland

 Archaeological site

 Nature reserve/Animal interest

 Birdlife

 Garden

 Watersports

 Steam railway

 Church/ecclesiastical site

 Building of interest

 Castle/Fortification

 Museum/Art gallery

 Beautiful view/Scenery, Natural phenomenon

 Other place of interest

 Industrial Archaeology

Note on the maps

The maps drawn for each chapter, while comprehensive, are not designed to be used as route maps, but rather to locate the main towns, villages and places of interest. For exploration, visitors are recommended to use the 1:50,000 (approximately 1¼in to the mile) Ordnance Survey 'Landranger' maps. The sheets covering the areas included in this book are shown on page 7. For greater detail the Ordnance Survey 'Outdoor Leisure' maps, which cover the area in four sheets at 1:25,000 (2½in to one mile) are recommended. The area is also covered by the OS Tourist Map T10 *Snowdonia and Anglesey* at 1in to 1 mile.

INDEX TO 1:50 000 MAPS OF GREAT BRITAIN

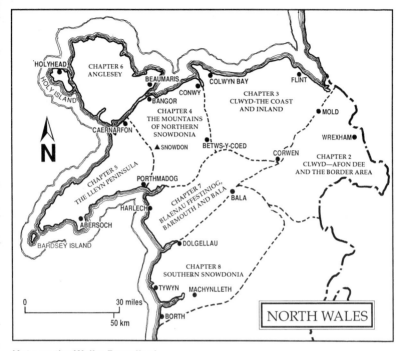

Note on the Walks Described

The walks in this book are not intended to be a field-by-field guide, but recommendations for the best routes. Many have been chosen so that they avoid the popular and crowded areas, while many are more interesting or give better views than the better-known routes. Walkers must be equipped according the the severity of the terrain: a lakeside stroll or woodland walk requires only stout shoes and weather protection. High level mountain walks need proper boots and clothing, map and compass and the ability to use them correctly

Mountain Recue

Telepone 999 and ask for Mountain Resue

For the walks in the text the distance and estimated time is given, together with the information below:

H	High level route for fine weather
M	Medium level route
L	Low level route, often recommended when the weather is poor
*	Well signposted and easily followed
**	Easy to follow with the aid of a map
***	Requires careful map reading
****	Recommended for experienced hill walkers only
†	Of least interest
††	
†††	
††††	Of most interest

INTRODUCTION

Arriving in North Wales for the first time most visitors will be agreeably surprised by the change of scenery. From the border counties of England the hills rise gradually from the plains, getting more rugged and grander the further one journeys west. The border counties are green and luxuriant, the western counties craggy and steep and although the mountains are not as high as their counterparts in other countries they are nevertheless quite impressive.

Many visitors will come solely to walk and climb in these hills, while many more will come for the glorious beaches that almost surround the region. Few parts of Great Britain are so accessible and can offer so much variety to the visitor; the combination of sea and mountains make it irresistable for many. One can be bathing on one of the many fine beaches and within the hour be heading for the summit of a mountain, though a change of dress would be recommended.

The larger coastal resorts offer excellent facilities for the tourist, good hotels, camping and caravan sites plus a range of activities for all ages. There has in recent years been an increase in visitor facilities besides the more traditional entertainments. You can go down a slate mine, make your own pottery, travel on a miniature railway, visit any number of museums, enjoy indoor watersports or

9

go round a gaol. There is something for everyone. There is no need to be bored in North Wales.

Many first time visitors to the region will naturally head for the better known areas. However, a little in depth investigation will uncover a vast amount of history, places and detail that can only enhance your visit. The Welsh are naturally warm hearted and honest but they do expect these feelings to be reciprocated. The Welsh language should cause the visitor no problems as all who do speak Welsh also speak English. Road signs are now mainly in the Welsh form which in most cases is very similar to the earlier anglicised spelling. Welsh names are used where possible throughout this book, while the Ordnance Survey has been used as the mediator if any doubt has arisen.

For the purposes of this book North Wales is taken to be the northern counties of Clwyd and Gwynedd. Clwyd is that part of the north-east along the estuary of the Dee and adjoining the English counties of Cheshire and Shropshire; to the west it has the Afon Conwy as its boundary. It has more than 50 per cent of the population of the whole of the area and certainly most of the industry around Wrexham and along Deeside. It also contains the larger coastal resorts of Rhyl, Colwyn Bay and Llandudno. It too has its fair share of hills, castles and beauty spots. Close to the major cities of Liverpool and Manchester it is popular with day trippers.

To the west and bordering the Irish Sea is the county of Gwynedd, with its beautiful coastline, its rugged mountains and quieter resorts. The two counties are as different as chalk and cheese. The shared county boundary is almost like crossing another border, for Gwynedd has a far greater proportion of Welsh speakers and one always feels closer to Wales in Gwynedd. Gwynedd also has the Snowdonia National Park as its heartland, with much of the finest scenery and the highest mountains in Wales.

The island of Anglesey, or Ynys Mon, separated by the narrow straits from the north-west coast, gives this varied county a further dimension. Gwynedd is considered by many to be the heart of Wales, epitomising every aspect of the country and its culture.

Snowdonia is the name that for centuries has been given by travellers to the mountains in the old county of Caernarfonshire. In 1951 these, along with the ranges of mountains to the south and the

Sunset over Llynau Mymbyr and the Snowdon range

east were designated a National Park and the name Snowdonia was adopted as the official title of the park. As a park it extends from Conwy in the north to Aberdyfi in the south and from Bala in the east to Tremadog in the west, roughly 50 miles long and 35 miles wide though this does vary. Besides the mountains there are a multitude of lakes and 22 miles of coast are included with some of the finest beaches in Wales.

The National Park has fourteen peaks over 3,000ft with many more falling only a few feet short. The area is scantily populated by comparison with the adjacent counties and is almost purely Welsh speaking, it could be said that the sheep outnumber the people and even the sheepdogs only respond to commands given in Welsh.

Unlike National Parks in other parts of the world, Snowdonia and the other parks in Great Britain are all working areas. The people own the land, they work it and in most cases live on it. The balance between access for the visitor to any area within the park is generally with the goodwill of the landlord and care must always be taken to leave the area as you found it, so take nothing but memories and photographs.

You will find many beautiful areas in North Wales. If you enjoy peace and tranquility you can easily escape from the hustle and bustle of modern life. There are quiet little valleys, beaches and villages. The area is so compact it is not difficult to enjoy a varied holiday without travelling too far.

The area considered in this book has been divided into sub areas and each has a separate chapter. There are suggestions for places to visit, things to do and walks to enjoy. These are unlikely to be the only attractions available and a little individual exploration will uncover a wealth of hidden pleasures.

There are few, if any, properties (either National Trust or privately owned) that are open all year round. As many are open only on summer weekdays, it is always sensible to check visiting hours beforehand with the local Tourist Information Centres.

Some walks are suggested, and while most are fairly easy and can be tackled by the average person, many — particularly within Snowdonia — are more arduous and should not be attempted without due preparation. As the weather can change quickly, extra clothing and waterproofs should always be taken on a long walk. A map, too, adds so much to the enjoyment. A 1:50,000 Ordnance Survey map of the area will be invaluable. Many small areas and forests have their own nature trails or forest trails; individual leaflets are generally available at nearby information offices or shops.

Throughout this guide are suggestions for visits and walks, and at the end of the book is useful information for visitors. Every effort has been made to ensure the accuracy of the information and, though lack of space precludes much that may be of interest, it is hoped that visitors will use it as a basis for an enjoyable holiday.

1

NORTH WALES:
A BACKGROUND

Wales is made up geologically of ancient hard rocks 200 million or more years old. Parts of Snowdonia and Anglesey consist, however, of much that is 650 million years old, some of the oldest rocks to be found anywhere in the world. The names of these extremely early geological epochs, such as the Cambrian, Ordovician and Silurian periods, as used by earth scientists throughout the world, are taken from the names of the early tribes that lived in Wales.

These rocks are hardwearing and resistant to erosion, and where they have been upthrust have resisted wear to leave us the mountains that are such a feature of the landscapes, though these are mere stumps of their predecessors. These hard volcanic rocks form the bulk of the western areas, while Clwyd and the lower hills in eastern areas are made up of softer sedimentary rocks, limestones and sandstones which stretch out towards England. These hills are more rounded, less craggy and gentler on the eye.

Formed by huge upthrusts that wrinkled the earth's surface many millions of years ago and worn low by huge sheets of ice that covered the area in subsequent years the hard igneous rocks of Snowdonia have survived to form the mountains we enjoy today. The evidence of this wearing is everywhere: the moraines high up in the cwms, the drumlins which the glaciers deposited and on the

Rhinogs the huge glacial erratics — the rocks left high and dry when the ice receded. It was this wearing by ice and by water that cut the deep valleys throughout the area.

Minerals were formed in pockets in the rock: coal, iron ore and lead in the east and copper in the mountains of Snowdonia and all were exploited by man. Layers of mud became compacted and hardened by intense pressure and heat to form slate in bands up to 40ft thick, which was later to be mined and quarried throughout the area. It is probable that when man first came to the area he knew little of this wealth below the surface, but later he left hardly a hill untouched by his scratchings in search of something to sell or exchange or make into something useful.

Man's first forays were probably to the coastlands where he could survive on a diet of fish supplemented by the occasional wild ox or reindeer he could catch. His camps were temporary and we know little of his lifestyle; some caves he occupied close to Prestatyn which have been excavated, suggest that he was itinerant and show evidence that he may have been around just after the last Ice Age, approximately 18,000 years ago.

The first real evidence of man's industry in North Wales are the stone axe 'factories' as at Craig Llywd above Penmaenmawr and Mynydd Rhiw on the Lleyn Peninsula. Examples of stone axes from here have been found throughout Great Britain, but whether they were traded, exchanged or bartered we will never know. They were certainly valued, perhaps they were the first souvenirs taken home by palaeolithic visitors to the country.

The land was mainly forests of pine and birch and what scant evidence is available from the stone age periods shows that early man favoured coastal sites, river banks or lakeside locations. Stone tools are occasionally found on these low lying areas.

Later visitors brought more advanced tools and domestic farm animals but it was not until the Bronze Age that any great impact was felt in the area. It was during this period that many of the surviving standing stones, hut circles and burial chambers were erected.

From around 1800BC to 500BC the Bronze Age people worked and traded in the area. However, they were gradually overrun by, or became intermingled with, a group of settlers from Europe bringing with them the techniques of iron working. These immigrants were followed, in about 300BC, by the first Celts who arrived from Gaul and settled mainly in the western areas of the country. Besides bringing agricultural skills they are noteworthy for the many hillforts they built in Wales, Tre'r Ceiri on Yr Eifl being a fine example.

It is likely that the roots of Welsh culture and probably the language lay with this pre-Roman group of settlers, though it is difficult to pin down with complete certainty. Celtic undoubtedly formed the basis of the language used in many western areas of Britain and France around that time. There is a similarity with Gaelic in Scotland and Ireland and the Breton language in France.

The coming of the Romans in AD43 further pushed the Celts to the peninsulas and western areas of Britain, cutting them off even further from mainland influences. By AD78 the Romans had conquered North Wales, though whether they ever subjugated the natives is doubtful. They built several forts as at *Deva* (Chester), used as the base for sorties into the hostile country. *Segontium* (Caernarfon) was the major base within Gwynedd with many smaller camps throughout the county. Many of the present roads follow the lines of early Roman roads. It is likely that the Roman influence was small and much of the activity was to maintain a presence and trade with the natives. There is evidence that during their occupation the Romans mined gold and copper and other minerals, particularly lead, in the eastern areas of Wales.

In the fourth century AD the Romans returned home to save their falling Empire and left the Celts to return to their former primitive life. They have, however, left some signs of their presence and though their forts were small they are fairly plentiful.

The next major influence came in the fifth and sixth centuries with the arrival of the first Christians from the Continent and Ireland. These priests and monks came to form the backbone of the Celtic Church and established many of the early churches, such as at St Asaph and Bangor. There was a post-Roman Christian movement and by the sixth century AD Celts had been converted from paganism to this new religion. The word was spread by itinerant saints who travelled the country creating religious settlements and building churches. The inclusion of 'Llan' coupled with the saint's name usually indicates such a place, such as Llanbadrig, The Church of Patrick, or Llandudno, The Church of St Tudno. Wales by the seventh century was fully converted and a major religious influence on the rest of the British Isles. There are many sites associated with those early wandering saints as at St Seriols Well close to Penmon Priory on Anglesey and St Beuno's Well (Ffynnon Beuno) at Clynnog on the Lleyn Peninsula.

The Norman invasion of England in 1066 was followed by the gradual conquest of Wales, though the principality of Gwynedd in the north formed an almost impregnable bastion of high hills and mountains. It was Edward I in the thirteenth century who systematically built a ring of steel in the form of castles at Flint, Rhuddan, Conwy, Beaumaris, Caernarfon and Harlech, all of which could be supplied by sea and all were virtually impregnable on the landward side. Edward strengthened some of the Welsh princes' castles at Criccieth and Dolwyddelan and was not only able to control the coastlands but also the very heartland of the country. It was Edward who anglicised the organisation of the country and named his eldest son the first Prince of Wales.

The native Welsh princes from then on fought a spasmodic rearguard action culminating with the abortive Owain Glyndwr revolt in the fifteenth century. There is a cave above Beddgelert on the slopes of Moel Hebog romantically associated with Glyndwr, which is said to be his hideaway during his escape. This was the last serious attempt to overthrow the English crown and subsequent to this the Welsh influence was purely cultural, with the language playing a major unifying role throughout the country.

The seventeenth century saw the industrial revolution arrive in North Wales with the mining of coal and iron around Wrexham, the mining of lead ore in the limestone hills in the north-east and copper in the mountains of Snowdonia. As you travel around you will see the great heaps of waste from some long dead mining operation, and there are few hillsides untouched by man's eager searches for profit.

Gwynedd is particularly rich in industrial archaeology, everywhere are the massive tips of the slate quarries and mines. North Wales is said to have roofed the world, providing much of the slate for the tremendous building projects during the industrial revolution.

The Eagle Tower, Caernarfon Castle, one of the castles built by Edward I to subdue the Welsh

The quarries are everywhere in the mountains, often on a huge scale, the mines have vast inner chambers where men worked in treacherous conditions for a pittance. The scale of these burrowings are often difficult to believe, particularly now all is quiet and little evidence remains of those who worked them.

Wild goats, although rare, may still be seen in Snowdonia

Ports developed around the coast specifically to handle the products from these enterprises, and were served by tramways and railways direct from mine to quay. For instance on the Ffestiniog-Porthmadog route, populations grew around both ends of the line and gradually the communities took shape. They are the villages and townships which exist today, but though the streets and houses are the same, economic conditions have changed. The mines and ports are closed, alternative work has had to be found or created, and while in most cases this has been successful, conditions can still be hard in the hills. The communities are still there, though depleted, vacant houses have been sold as weekend cottages as tourism has become a major industry. The old railways have been revived to carry tourists, the old mines are now museums, the ports

*One of the many elegant stone bridges found in North Wales, this one over the
Afon Croesor, with Cnicht — 'the Welsh Matterhorn' — in the background*

cater for yachtsmen and fishermen, old crafts have been re-discovered and marketed, the hills are now being walked for leisure instead of necessity. The whole country has seen greater changes during the last 100 years than at any time during its previous history.

Today's visitor should take plenty of time to explore, and those who look deeper than the surface will find a wealth of interesting places to be discovered and so will enjoy their visit even more.

The Language

It is known with some certainty that the Celts who populated Britain from Europe in the fourth century BC brought not only their iron working skills but also their language. Those who arrived in Wales spoke Brythonic or a British language similar to that spoken in Brittany and Cornwall.

Pressures of the Roman invasion forced the Celtic people into the western areas of Britain where they became further isolated and the language began to develop on its own. In later centuries the subsequent invasion of the island by the Anglo-Saxons from Europe pushed the Celts into the extremes of the country, into Wales, Scotland and Cornwall.

During each occupation the developing language borrowed words freely from the invasion force and for much of the time they lived in peace. The language continued to adopt words from other invaders, Norman French through medieval English and right up to modern English. Other languages developed in a similar fashion.

Welsh was the main spoken language in the principality until the seventeenth century. The English influence, however, was spreading, as wealthy traders found it more convenient to be bilingual. English was also becoming used more widely for state purposes and as a public medium.

The church continued to use Welsh and through recent centuries has been the saviour of the language. Bishop Morgan had translated the Bible into Welsh in 1588 and this alone had ensured the survival of the language more than any other single act.

Nowadays many Welsh people are bilingual, particularly in western areas of the country like Gwynedd, less so in the border counties and on the northern coastlands where English is their first language. The Welsh language is taught to all pupils in school and

Most signposts are now both in Welsh and English

thankfully recent years have seen a swing to using the Welsh form on road signs and maps. There is now a widespread interest in the language and culture and though only a small proportion of the whole country is Welsh speaking, there is a revival in the customs and traditions of the country and much is being done to ensure the survival of the language.

The visitor to Wales will see place names that are different and will hear people speak in a very different language. This can be baffling to the non-Welsh speaker, while finding your way around can be a daunting task particularly if you have to ask your way.

Many place names are descriptive of the physical feature of the area, eg Moelwyn Mawr means the big bare hill. Others are named after the local church; hence the predominance of the names preceded by *Llan*, church of, as in Llanbadrig which means the church of Patrick. It can add interest and enjoyment to any holiday to try to solve the mystery of the language and find out where you are. A few words that may be useful are given overleaf; most are found in place names.

Aber — river mouth
Adwy — gap, pass
Afon — river
Allt — wooded hill or cliff
Aran — high place, mountain

Bach — small, corner
Bala — joining of lake to river
Banc — bank, hill
Bedd — grave
Bont — bridge
Bron — breast of hill or slope
Bryn — hill
Bwlch — pass or col
Bychan — small

Cadair — seat, strong-hold
Cae — field
Caer — fort
Capel — chapel
Carn — cairn
Carreg — stone
Carrog — stream
Cefn — ridge
Celli — grove
Clogwyn — cliff, precipice
Clwyd — gate
Coed — trees
Craig — rock
Crib — ridge
Croes — cross, crossroads

Din, Dinas — fort
Dre — homestead

Drws — door, pass
Du, Ddu — black
Dwy — two
Dyffryn — valley

Eglwys — church
Erw — acre
Esgair — long ridge

Fach — small
Fawr — large, great, extensive
Fechan — small
Ffair — fair
Fford — road
Ffraw — rapid
Ffrith — meadow
Foel — bare hill
Fychan — small

Garth — hill
Glan — brink, edge
Glas — blue, green
Glyder — sheltered valley
Glyn — valley
Gwydd — trees
Gwyddfa — wild place
Gwynt — wind

Hafod — summer home
Hen — old
Hendre — winter home
Hyll — ugly

Isaf — lower

Llain — stretch of land
Llan — church or enclosed space
Llanerch — clearing glade
Llech — stone slab
Llety — small house
Llyn — lake

Maen — stone
Maes — field
Mam — mother
Mawr — great, extensive
Melin — mill
Merch (plural Merchedd) — woman
Moel — bare or rounded mountain
Morfa — coastal marsh
Mynydd — mountain

Nant — brook, valley
Neuadd — hall
Newydd — new
Nos — night

Ogof — cave

Penrhyn — headland
Pant — hollow ground
Parc — field

Penmaen — rocky headland
Pennant — head of valley
Pentre — village, hamlet
Pig — summit
Pistyll — cataract
Plas — hall
Pont — bridge
Porth — harbour, bay

Rhos — moorland
Rhyd — ford

Saeth — arrow
Sarn — causeway

Tal — front
Tan — below
Traeth — beach
Tyn — small farm
Tywyn — shore

Uchaf — upper

Wen — white

Y — the
Yr — the
Ynys — island
Ysbyty — hospital
Ystryd — street

2

CLWYD
— AFON DEE AND THE
BORDER AREA

Approaching the county of Clwyd across the plains of Shropshire or Cheshire, the hills can be seen ahead for many miles. They sit dark and sombre along the horizon. Then almost immediately you cross the border you are amongst them, either climbing steeply or winding along deep valleys. The contrast between the landscapes of England and Wales is sometimes surprising.

The Clwydian hills, stretching from the northern coast down to Llangollen and with the Berwyns to the south, form a natural boundary which in years gone by must have been formidable for travellers and invaders. They are in general comfortable hills, pleasing to the eye and pleasant, on a fine day, to stroll amongst.

The Afon Dee, one of the major rivers of Wales, bisects these great ranges and winds through Llangollen, round far to the east of Wrexham and through the old city of Chester, *Deva* to the Romans, finally emerging to the sea at Flint to form the northern seaboard. There are few visitors to North Wales who will not cross it somewhere on their journey.

The eastern foothills which follow the curve of the Dee are composed mainly of coal measures with an underlying bed of limestone that comes to the surface occasionally as the scarp edges south of Maeshafn and on the Eglwyseg Mountains above Llangollen. It was probably the limestone deposits and the minerals

PLACES TO VISIT IN AND NEAR WREXHAM

Erddig Hall
1 mile south of Wrexham off
A438.
Late seventeenth- and early
eighteenth-century mansion,
features include outbuildings,
domestic offices and portraits of
staff. Original furniture in main
rooms. Large gardens and
parkland with Visitor Centre.
National Trust Property.

St Giles Church
Wrexham
Fine wrought iron gates dating
from 1720. Decorated steeple,
some interesting contents within
church. Grave of Elihu Yale,
benefactor of Yale University.

**Wrexham-Maelor Library and
Art Centre**
Rhosddu Road, Wrexham
Has visiting exhibitions from
England and Wales.

Bersham Industrial Centre
2 miles south-west of Wrexham.
Industrial archaeology museum
relating to iron and coal. Leaflet
available.

Milestone Visitor Centre
Bwlchgwyn, on A525 Wrexham-
Ruthin Road.
Geological Museum of Wales,
housing relics of distant and
recent past. Folk displays and
trails.

in these hills, particularly lead ores, which brought the first industry to the area. It is known that the Romans mined lead here using local labour, but it was not until the sixteenth and seventeenth centuries, when lead became such an important commodity, that the industry really developed. The most important use for lead was the lining of the roofs of houses and churches. During the heyday of the lead industry money was invested heavily in mining in these limestone hills. The mines stretch from Halkyn Mountain near Prestatyn in the north to Minera west of Wrexham. Massive beam engines were brought up from Cornwall to pump the mines clear of water, but it is only the overgrown square stone remains of the engine houses and their chimneys with the surrounding waste tips which survive as reminders of a once-thriving industry.

Iron ore mined in the hills and coal fields surrounding Wrexham led to the establishment in the eighteenth century of a thriving

Horse-powered mine winding engine at the Bersham Industrial Museum

smelting industry with iron works in Bersham, Ruabon and Wrexham. Other local resources, including clay for bricks and tiles, zinc ores and wool from the local sheep, soon made this area the most industrialised and populous in North Wales. Bersham was the main supplier of cannons to the British army during the Peninsular War. The iron ore eventually ran out and the Wrexham-based industry was moved north to a site near Queensferry on the Afon Dee to allow direct imports of the raw materials by sea. During 1980, however, under Government rationalisation plans for the steel industry, this major employer on Deeside finally closed its doors.

Wrexham (Wrecsam) and its environs now support a few industries, but most of those based on local resources have declined, leaving their remains for the industrial archaeologist to explore. This area of Wales is now designated as a development area by the government, and industries large and small are encouraged to move here to provide much-needed employment.

In the centre of Wrexham stands the church of St Giles, notable for its decorated tower built in 1506 and surmounted by four graceful hexagonal turrets. To the west of the tower is the grave of Elihu

The bridge and church at Bangor-on-Dee

Yale, the main benefactor of Yale University in America. It was restored by the members of the university in 1968 to mark the 250th anniversary of this benefaction. A replica of the tower of the church stands at Yale.

Virtually on the outskirts of Wrexham is Bersham, where John Wilkinson the famous eighteenth-century ironmaster made the cylinders for James Watt's steam engines and made cannons. The cannon boring mill and remains of the furnaces still survive, but are still being excavated and conserved so are not open for visitors. An industrial museum in the village concentrates on displays of the iron and coal industries.

To the east of Wrexham is an area known as Wrexham Maelor, which projects into the plains of Cheshire and Shropshire. The district was originally known as Maelor Saesneg (Saxon Maelor) and was established by Edward I as a detached part of Flint. Its character is more English than Welsh, as are many of the village names, but it has firmly remained part of Wales through the centuries, despite its vulnerable position. It finally lost its identity, and became part of Clwyd in the early 1970s. An important crossing

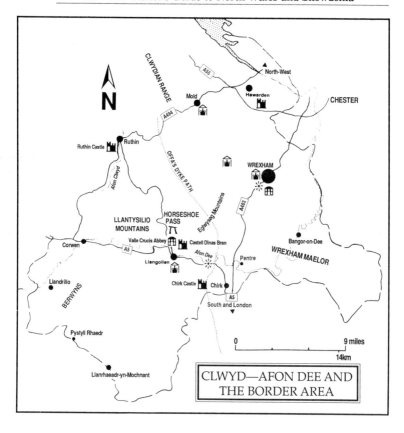

CLWYD—AFON DEE AND THE BORDER AREA

point for the River Dee in this area was at Bangor-on-Dee (Bangor-is-y-coed), with its attractive old stone bridge and church. This small village was the site of the first monastery founded on British soil about AD180. The monastery was destroyed in AD607 by Ethelfrid of Northumbria, when 1,200 monks were slain. The few survivors are said to have established the first religious community on Bardsey Island. The main Wrexham to Whitchurch road now bypasses the village.

 About one mile south of Wrexham and standing in a large estate, is the mansion of Erddig Hall, which was started in 1684 and finally completed about 1721-4 by John Meller, a London lawyer. With his nephew Simon Yorke he collected much of the fine silver and gilt furniture that can be seen here today. The property passed to Simon in 1733 and remained in the Yorke family until given to the National Trust in 1973. The family had always been good to their staff and the servants' hall has many portraits of particularly favourite staff. Visitors now enter through the stables and laundry, which, along with the restored sawmill, smithy and bakehouse, give a good idea of the domestic arrangements of an eighteenth-century house. There is a formal walled garden with old varieties of fruit trees, a dovecote complete with doves, extensive woods and parkland and a visitor centre.

Despite being the most industrial and extensively populated area of North Wales this corner of Clwyd has remained only a narrow strip. The nearby countryside is always accessible and only a short journey is necessary to leave all behind and reach the hills and valleys around **Llangollen**.

Here is a town so typically Welsh from its greystone houses to its wooded hillsides that it is hard to believe that one is only a few miles from the English border. One needs go no further than Llangollen to experience much of what Wales has to offer, and it has justifiably been a popular tourist centre for many years. George Borrow started his epic Welsh journey here in 1854 by describing Llangollen in his book *Wild Wales* as 'a small town or large village'. The town sits on both sides of the Afon Dee: the centre, with shops, cafés and hotels on the south bank of the river, is connected by a stone bridge to the thin strip of houses squeezed between the canal and the main road on the north of the river. The bridge was built originally in 1345, but it has been strengthened and improved through the centuries to cope with the increasing volume of traffic which frequently causes quite a bottleneck on a sunny summer's day. Upstream of the town is a suspension bridge for pedestrians, known as the Chain Bridge.

The town is perhaps best known for the International Musical Eisteddfod which is held to the east of the town in July every year. It attracts singers, musicians and dancers from all over the world. The town comes alive with national costumes and a true spirit of international friendship during these weeks.

The walled garden at Erddig on an Edwardian day.
Inset: *The main front*

PLACES TO VISIT
IN AND NEAR LLANGOLLEN

Chwarel Wynne Slate Mine and Museum
Glyn Ceiriog, 4 miles on scenic mountain road south of Llangollen.
Slate mine to visit, craft shop and picnic spot with nature trails.

Llangollen Motor Museum
Pentrefelin.
Collection of yesteryear's cars.

Pontcysyllte Aqueduct
Carries canal 120ft above Afon Dee, 1,000ft long. Superb position. Off Wrexham Road.

Plas Newydd
House of 'Ladies of Llangollen', beautiful black and white house in lovely gardens. South of river, well signposted.

Castell Dinas Bran
Thirteenth-century hilltop castle. Dominates the valley. Walk signposted from canal bridge on north side of river.

Canal Exhibition Centre
Llangollen.
Models and films tell the story of growth and use of canals. Horse drawn boat trips. On canal just across road from main bridge.

Llangollen Railway Society
Railway Station, Llangollen.
Passenger trains now operate to Berwyn on the former Great Western Railway's Ruabon-Barmouth line. A varied collection of rolling stock and locomotives in the station and goods yard. By bridge across the river.

Valle Crucis Abbey
$1\frac{1}{2}$ miles north of Llangollen on A542 to Ruthin.
Substantial remains in a fine setting.

Eliseg's Pillar
1,000-year-old pillar tells story of Eliseg, $\frac{1}{2}$ mile up valley from Valle Crucis Abbey.

Horseshoe Pass
On A542 Ruthin Road, 5 miles north of Llangollen.
Steep climb with good views, acquired by National Trust.

Horseshoe Falls
On Afon Dee 1 mile east of town centre. Built by Telford to provide water for canal system.

Chirk Castle
$\frac{1}{2}$ mile west of Chirk village. Large fortress partially converted to stately home. Fine furniture, tapestries and portraits. Formal gardens with clipped yews and flowering shrubs. Owned by National Trust.

Canoeing below the bridge in Llangollen

Half a mile from the town centre is the old house of Plas Newydd ⊞ (not to be confused with the National Trust house of the same name on Anglesey, overlooking the Menai Strait), once the house of two eccentric old ladies known throughout the country as the 'Ladies of Llangollen'. The ladies, the Hon Miss Sarah Ponsonby and Lady Eleanor Butler, resided at the house from 1779 until their deaths in 1829 and 1831. They were known for their rather eccentric style of dress and for the variety of their visitors — Wellington, Sir Walter Scott, who later immortalised the house in *The Betrothed*, and Wordsworth, all of whom were expected to contribute to the ladies' collection of old oak curios. Wordsworth's contribution was a rather

Plas Newydd, Llangollen

The Chain Bridge over the Afon Dee, near Llangollen

disdainful sonnet, which was not liked by the ladies — he was not invited back.

There is not much room between the river and the steeply rising hills to the north, but in that short space is squeezed a railway station, now home of the Llangollen Railway Society, a busy main road and a canal. In this limited area it is possible to study transport through the ages, for just above the station is the Canal Exhibition Centre on a spur of the Shropshire Union Canal. This is appropriate as the Llangollen Branch was one of the earliest of Britain's derelict waterways to be restored for leisure cruising. Running from Hurleston Junction on the Shropshire Union Canal it passes through beautiful countryside on its way to Llangollen.

Climbing steeply from just opposite the canal bridge is a footpath to Castell Dinas Bran, a stone castle perched 1,000ft above the town. Originally the site of an Iron Age hillfort, it later became a Norman stronghold and, finally, a little-used stone castle built in 1236 which had become a ruin by 1578. The climber is rewarded by a fine view — the long limestone escarpment of

A lifting bridge, typical of those on the Llangollen Canal

The canal basin at Trevor

The Pontcysyllte Aqueduct

Chirk Castle

Eglwyseg Rocks and the valleys radiating to the west and the north of the town. It is a magnificent place for a castle.

A narrow road rises steeply from the bridge and runs up the valley below Eglwyseg Mountain to the ford at World's End. There is parking space below the ford and a short walk can be taken along the gorge onto the moorland and forests above. If you continue along the road it takes you out onto the open moorland, mainly sheep grazing land, before finally descending to the old lead mining community of Minera.

The Afon Dee is at its wildest above Llangollen as it descends rapidly from just below the Horseshoe Falls in a series of small cataracts that tumble between the narrow banks — the venue of an annual canoe race. The Horseshoe Falls were built by Thomas Telford, the famous road and canal engineer, in 1806, to feed water into a spur of the Shropshire Union Canal running alongside and above the river before crossing 127ft above the river on the 1,000ft-long Pontcysyllte Aqueduct three miles down river from Llangollen. The aqueduct is a marvellous engineering achievement, as it

Detail of the gates at Chirk Castle

carries the canal in an iron trough supported on eighteen tall, slim stone pillars. The visitor with a head for heights can walk along the towpath across the viaduct from either the canal basin at Trevor at the northern end, or park in a small car park at Fron Cysyllte at the other end and cross the canal by one of the waterway's characteristic lifting bridges. Perhaps the most impressive view of the aqueduct is not from the top, but from below. A recently improved path down to the Afon Dee starts from the Trevor canal basin and to look up at the stone pillars soaring above one's head makes it obvious why this was regarded almost as a miracle when it was first built, and as one of the wonders of the Industrial Revolution.

Travellers from the south will miss Wrexham altogether and enter Wales close to the small border town of Chirk. To the west of the Telford A5 trunk road they will see an adjacent aqueduct and viaduct spanning the Ceiriog valley. The former carries the Shropshire Union Canal, and was built by Telford in 1801; the latter was built in 1848 to carry the railway.

Chirk owes its origins to an eleventh-century castle built origi-

The Vale of Llangollen

nally on the motte close to the church. This small Norman castle was superseded in the thirteenth century by a substantial stone castle built two miles away by Edward I to protect the English/Welsh Border or 'Marches'. Chirk Castle, now owned by the National Trust, is the only Marcher castle to have been occupied continuously since it was built. For the visitor it has the contrast of a medieval castle with towers, courtyard, steep narrow stairs, bare cold guard-rooms and a deep forbidding dungeon, with richly-appointed Adam-style staterooms. The beautiful formal gardens include notable topiary yew hedges and many flowering shrubs which are especially fine in springtime. A pair of magnificent wrought iron gates, made at Bersham in 1721, which once stood near the castle, now stand guard at the entrance to the $1^1/_2$-mile long drive.

The A5 trunk road, one of Telford's wonders, stretches from London to Holyhead and has been for more than a century and a half the main access to North Wales from England and the south. Running along the bottom of the Vale of Llangollen it provides many of the best views of the river and the surrounding hills. On the north side, the hills lean away from the road and are heather-clad in summer, but to the south the hills are heavily afforested and seem to become more so every year. Rising steeply from the very back of Llangollen the road to Llanarmon Glyn Ceiriog and Llanarmon Dyffryn-Ceiriog takes one into some of the most beautiful country-side in North Wales. The narrow lanes meander steeply up and down the deep valleys as forests and hills vie for attention. Such a large area of Wales seems seldom to be visited and it has none of the trappings associated with tourism. It is crossed by only one road — fortunately an ancient trackway unusable by anything but four-wheel drive vehicles — but what a splendid route it is, going right over the ridge between Llanarmon Dyffryn-Ceiriog and Llandrillo, crossing the pass below Cadair Bronwen.

These hills, the **Berwyns**, provide some of the best walking for many miles and can be recommended for experienced walkers as one of the quietest and least frequented parts of North Wales, but one of the most easily accessible. The long ridge walk from Moel Fferna in the north, over the Berwyns to Moel Sych in the south is well worthwhile, but a map and compass will be essential.

Much of this countryside was explored by the intrepid George

Pistyll Rhaeadr, the highest waterfall in Wales

Borrow in the 1850s, as he walked many of the lanes and visited many of the villages. One of the towns he describes with little enthusiasm is **Llanrhaeadr-yn-Mochnant**, home of Bishop William Morgan who made the first translation of the Bible into Welsh during the reign of Elizabeth I. Upstream from the village at the head of a steep sided valley is Pistyll Rhaeadr, the highest waterfall in Wales. Now largely surrounded by trees, it is difficult to appreciate the 240ft cascade from a distance. There is however a small car park by a quaint old farmhouse at the end of the lane and after a short walk one can see the full height from a bridge over the stream.

Valle Crucis Abbey

M
1-5h
**
††

The more intrepid walker can continue to the top of the falls by a steep footpath, starting from a grey gate opposite the farm, which zig zags up one side to the top, though this is a rather airy viewpoint. A walk upstream takes one into some fine country — the hills are wild, the ridge walks superb and the scenery splendid: but paths are rare, so go prepared.

To the west, the Berwyns drop slowly down to the Afon Dee as it casually meanders through the farming and forestry communities of Llandrillo and Cynwyd. Above **Llandrillo** on the slopes of Cadair Bronwen is a stone circle about 40ft in diameter. What its purpose and origin was we shall probably never know, but whoever placed it there chose the spot well for the views of the hills and the valley and the feeling of spaciousness are outstanding. It was an ideal place for religious meetings, if that was its purpose.

Joining the Afon Alwen, the Afon Dee turns east towards Llangollen, passing the market town of **Corwen** on its way. To the north the Llantysilio Mountains above Corwen are crowned by the Iron Age fort of Caer Drewyn. The heather-clad slopes run north-east to the top of the Horseshoe Pass, where the remains of the once thriving slate industry scar the landscape.

About two miles to the north-east of Llangollen on the road to Ruthin before it crosses the Horseshoe Pass, is Valle Crucis Abbey, beautifully situated in the centre of what must have been an idyllic valley. The extensive ruins of the church and some of the domestic buildings, now almost surrounded by a caravan site, give an idea of the abbey's former size. It was founded by Madog ap Gruffyd in 1201 for the Cistercian Order, dissolved in 1535, and now stands to remind us of its former beauty.

The abbey is believed to have taken its name from the pillar standing about $1/_2$ mile to the north, Eliseg's Pillar, which stands on a mound. Now well worn, it was carved with a Latin inscription in memory of Eliseg who reclaimed Powys (now Clwyd) from the English in the eighth century. Perhaps Eliseg is buried under the mound.

The mountains are crossed here by the main Llangollen to Ruthin road by way of the famous Horseshoe Pass, where the road climbs around a cirque. It is justifiably popular and there is a viewpoint at the head of the pass looking down towards Valle Crucis

PLACES OF INTEREST IN AND AROUND RUTHIN

Ruthin Castle
Norman castle with chequered history. Now a ruin and incorporated into an hotel.

Court House
Stands in main square. Lovely black and white building, was old prison with gallows, now a bank.

Exmewe Hall
Opposite Court House. Built about 1500 by Thomas Exmewe, Lord Mayor of London. Now a bank.

Maen Huail
Large stone in front of Exmewe Hall on which King Arthur is reputed to have behead Huail, his rival in love.

Church of St Peter
North-east corner of square. Fourteenth century with magnificent panelled ceiling given to the men of Wales by Henry VII.

Ruthin Craft Centre
Exhibition and workshops of many different crafts, which are worth seeing.

Abbey and Llangollen. As the friendly sheep always seem to be hungry, car doors should be kept firmly closed. The Llantysilio Mountains, which the road crosses, continue eastwards to the Eglwyseg Mountains, which curve round to the Llandegla Moors to join the Clwydian Range, which eventually terminates in the limestone quarries above Prestatyn on the north coast.

Offa's Dyke follows the line of these hills. Constructed about AD748 and running from Chepstow in South Wales, it follows roughly the present border until it crosses the Afon Dee downstream from Llangollen, before climbing up and over Eglwyseg Mountain to World's End and then heads north-west along the hills to Prestatyn. It is now a designated long distance footpath of 167 miles and, though a shadow of its former self, can still be seen in several parts of these hills. At one time its massive earth work was 20ft wide, with a bank on one side 12ft high, and was probably designed more as a deterrent than an effective barrier, though the actual hills themselves must have been a daunting prospect. Wales is probably more Welsh to the west of it than to the east, and it is on

The Old Court House (left) and Exmewe Hall (right), Ruthin

the western side that the Welsh-speaking parts generally lie.

The main road (A494) from Chester to Corwen is one of the main access routes to North Wales and cuts across this range of hills from Mold through Loggerheads, a popular area for short walks, before crossing the shoulder of Moel Famau and dropping into the Vale of Clwyd at Ruthin.

Ruthin or Rudd-Din — meaning red fortress — is built on a small hill above the Afon Clwyd. It is notable for the remains of the castle, built above a red sandstone cliff near the centre of the town. The town probably grew around the castle, which was strategically placed to watch over the river and the road which even in those days was one of the main routes from England. The original Welsh castle built by Prince Llewelyn's brother, Dafydd, was taken by Edward I in 1282 during the Welsh uprising and remained in English hands until dismantled as a Royalist stronghold by General Mytton in 1647 during the Civil War. Ruthin Castle now houses a luxury hotel.

A recently built bypass has eased the congestion in the narrow streets and open square of the town centre. Two banks occupy the notable buildings on the main square. To the south a fine old black and white building is the former Court House dating from 1401, which served as both prison and courthouse. A short beam, which was once the gallows, still projects below the eaves. On the west side is the sixteenth-century Exmewe Hall in front of which is the Maen Huail, a stone on which King Arthur is said to have beheaded Huail, his rival in love. The hall was built by Thomas Exmewe, who later became Lord Mayor of London.

The church of St Peter stands to the north-east of the square. At one time it was a collegiate church, and dates in parts from the thirteenth and fourteenth centuries. The interior has a magnificent oak panelled roof, made of 500 carved panels, every one different, which was presented to all the men of Wales by Henry VII for their help in gaining the throne for him.

The remains of Iron Age hillforts and barrows on the hilltops around the town show signs of earlier habitation. The hills here are certainly more friendly than those further west in Snowdonia: perhaps this attracted the old tribes. Today they are crossed by many roads, from which many walks can be enjoyed along the good network of footpaths, with an Ordnance Survey map.

3

CLWYD —
THE COAST AND INLAND

Clwyd was formed in 1974 during local government re-organisation as an amalgamation of the two counties of Flintshire and Denbighshire and is part of the old Welsh region of Gwynedd. It takes its most recent name from the Afon Clwyd which bisects the county, and is bounded on its eastern side by England and the Afon Dee, while its western boundary runs a few miles east of the Afon Conwy. For this chapter a more logical boundary is the Afon Conwy. The area has two main attractions for the visitor: the inland hills for walkers and sightseers, and the beautiful beaches on the northern coast for those who like a more relaxing day.

The coastlands are flat: there is a choice of roads from Queensferry, either the inland route, the A55 which is mainly a dual carriageway, or the more scenic coast road the A548, giving easy access to all the resorts. On both routes there are many reminders of the area's turbulent history, particularly of Edward I's attempts to subdue the Welsh princes in the late thirteenth century, when he built castles at all strategic points to maintain law and order. There are many fine ruins from this 'ring of steel' for the visitor to enjoy, most of them only slightly off the beaten track.

After crossing the Afon Dee at Queensferry or Chester the coastal road runs through some of the most depressing scenery in the whole of the county, as it follows for many miles the culmination

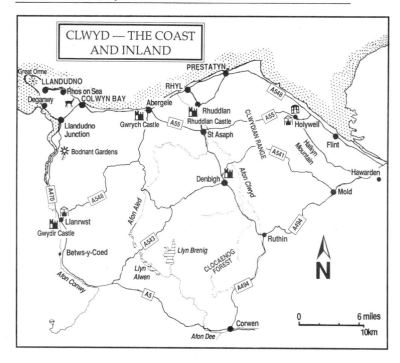

CLWYD — THE COAST
AND INLAND

of hundreds of years of industrialisation. Though the estuary is never more than a mile away, it is only glimpsed occasionally between the mammoth buildings, many of which are now redundant. Fortunately this industrial zone is limited to a very narrow belt, backing on to the estuary, and can be easily avoided by using the inland route.

Inevitably, after conquering Wales, Edward I built a fortification on the first high ground after Chester. He chose the site of an Iron Age fort at **Hawarden** and there built a stone castle with a round tower. Some parts remain today, but much of it was destroyed by the Parliamentarians in 1646. A later house, started in 1750 and still standing below the castle, was the home of one of Queen Victoria's Prime Ministers, William Gladstone, who acquired the estate when he married Catherine Glynne. He lived there for sixty years and the

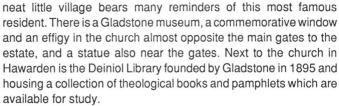

THINGS TO SEE ALONG DEESIDE

Hawarden Castle
Remains of Edward I's castle in grounds of William Gladstone's house. Close to village centre.

Ewloe Castle
Welsh castle built by Llewelyn the Last, to keep watch on

Hawarden Castle. Two miles from Hawarden on A55.

Flint Castle
On edge of estuary with interesting defensive features including separate donjon. Off main square in town.

neat little village bears many reminders of this most famous resident. There is a Gladstone museum, a commemorative window and an effigy in the church almost opposite the main gates to the estate, and a statue also near the gates. Next to the church in Hawarden is the Deiniol Library founded by Gladstone in 1895 and housing a collection of theological books and pamphlets which are available for study.

Just two miles away from Edward's castle at Hawarden stand the remains of Ewloe Castle, now surrounded by trees and barely visible from the road. It was built by Llewelyn the Last about 1260 and is typical of a Welsh stone castle, built to provide a buffer between the warring English and Welsh.

It is difficult now to imagine the importance of this area in past times; it was the main route into Wales from Chester and England, for the hills further inland were inhospitable and dangerous to cross. The coastal belt was the main highway for all invading armies from the Romans onwards. As it is also easier to supply armies by sea than over land, the area has always been strategically important.

To complement the castle at Hawarden which guarded the inland route, Edward I built a fortress at **Flint** to protect the coastal route and the estuary of the Afon Dee. The castle, built on rock on the very edge of the sands, is all that remains of a once walled town. It is just off the main square and missed by the many visitors who head each year for the beaches further along the coast. One tower

The ruins of Flint Castle

is detached from the main body of the castle and is connected by a drawbridge; it is the only example of this in the country. The tower or donjon was to be the last line of defence. The castle was the scene of the betrayal of Richard II and was immortalised in Shakespeare's play, much of which is set there. Today the castle is almost surrounded by buildings, and the Dee continues to silt up. The port that flourished until the last century no longer exists and today the town relies on modern industry for its survival.

The new county town is **Mold**, just five miles to the south of Flint. Unlike its predecessor it occupies a position of no particular geographical or historical importance, though it is a very pleasant little town. There was a small Norman castle on Bailey Hill at one end of the High Street, and the church, which is fifteenth century, has some fine stained glass windows and friezes carved with animals.

Mold was the home in the nineteenth century of Daniel Owen, a novelist and short story writer, who wrote in the Welsh language about Welsh people. He was a tailor who spent most of his life in the

---

PLACES TO VISIT IN MOLD

Daniel Owen Centre
Early Road, Mold
Exhibition centre of local arts
and memorial museum to Daniel
Owen, one of Wales' leading
novelists.

Theatr Clwyd
Three theatres under one roof,
regular programme of films,
concerts and live exhibitions.
Has its own professional
company. Close to town centre.

---

town. There is now a small museum at the Daniel Owen Centre containing memorabilia of this fine author.

Each Saturday, the main street in Mold is closed for the market, the stalls of which are set up on each side of the road. Perhaps of less interest to the visitor but more noticeable by their size are the new administrative buildings of Clwyd County Council which are about half a mile from the town centre on the Chester road. There too is the Theatr Clwyd, a centre for entertainment and arts. There are regular concerts, and the theatre has its own professional company.

L
1-1½h
*
††

On the opposite side of the town the A494 Ruthin road rises steeply to the Rainbow Inn, before dropping even more steeply down to the Loggerheads Inn at the bottom of a deeply wooded valley. There is a car park here and short walks can be taken along the valley and through the woods — a pleasant spot to spend an afternoon. There are some steep limestone cliffs above the woods which give a feeling of depth to this little valley.

M
1-2h
*
†††

Continuing along the main Ruthin road a minor road, probably the original road, turns off to the right about one mile after Loggerheads. If one takes this to the top of the pass and parks for a short while there are some breathtaking views over Ruthin and the Vale of Clwyd to the north and the sea. From the parking spot there is a good footpath leading up to the Jubilee Tower on the summit of Moel Famau. The tower was built to commemorate George III's jubilee. It is now part of a country park and on a clear day one can sometimes see the Isle of Man and the mountains of the Lake District to the north; but the closer views of Snowdonia to the west

THINGS TO SEE
IN AND AROUND HOLYWELL

St Winifride's Chapel
Holywell
Built by Margaret Beaufort,
mother of Henry VII, it houses
the Holy Well. A destination for
pilgrims for centuries.

Basingwerk Abbey
Off A548, 1 mile north of
Holywell
Praised for its beauty and
setting. Ruins fairly extensive.

Military Museum
Off the A55, $^3/_4$ mile west of
Holywell
Housed in an underground
cavern is a large collection of
military vehicles, weapons and
medals. Picnic area and café.

Maen Achwyfan
Whitford, 4 miles north-west of
Holywell
Eleventh-century carved Celtic
cross.

are more rewarding. It is a pleasant stroll, well worth doing. From the
car park the single track road descends steeply into Ruthin and
requires care.

To the north of Mold is Halkyn Mountain which runs nearly
parallel with the estuary. It is composed mainly of limestone and for
many centuries was the source of much of the wealth of the county;
it was riddled with lead and lead mines. There are many remains of
engine houses and tunnels of interest to the industrial archaeologist. The Romans mined here but it was the nineteenth-century
entrepreneurs who used their technology to sink even deeper
mines and longer tunnels. Water seepage was always a serious
problem and it was not until 1878 that a tunnel almost the full length
of the mountain drained the mines into the estuary.

Today the hill is extensively quarried for limestone, but for
walkers there are excellent views across the Dee estuary, the Wirral
and the Mersey estuary to Liverpool and the Lancashire plain.

On the northern slopes of Halkyn Mountain stands the small
town of **Holywell**, once a centre for many pilgrims. The well is said
to have curative powers and is part of St Winifride's Chapel, a
church built in perpendicular style by Margaret Beaufort, the mother
of Henry VII. Pilgrims enter the bath by steps, and kneel to pray on

St Winifride's Chapel, Holywell

the stone of St Beuno, founder of an earlier chapel on the site. The Holy Well was originally fed by a spring from the nearby limestone hills, but since the early part of this century has been fed by a small reservoir. Until the Reformation, the well was in the care of the Cistercian monks from nearby Basingwerk Abbey. The abbey, just a mile north-east of Holywell in a beautiful setting, was known for its fine building and windows. It was taken apart at the Dissolution and the present remains, which are mainly thirteenth century (though the original abbey was founded in 1132), give some idea of the extent of the building.

North-west of Holywell, near Whitford, is Maen Achwfan, an impressive early eleventh-century stone cross elaborately carved

Maen Achwfan, near Whitford, close to Holywell

with Celtic designs. Standing 11ft high it is the tallest of its type in Britain. It is signposted from the nearby village.

Modern visitors in the summer will be content to bypass the towns backing the Dee Estuary and speed west along the coast to the seaside towns and caravan sites which for many are the attractions in this part of Wales. From the colliery at the Point of Ayr the fields bordering the coastal road become a continuous mass of caravan sites and holiday camps which from Easter onwards attract visitors from all over Britain. It is a popular area for family holidays and weekend visitors, as there are many fine beaches along this northern coast which are safe for bathing and boating.

Prestatyn, the first major town to be reached, is a pleasant place with three main beaches and two large holiday camps. Ffrith beach, the most northerly, has convenient parking, a play area with motor boats, a mini-golf course and other amusements. Central

BEACHES IN PRESTATYN AND RHYL

Ffrith Beach
Prestatyn
Motor boats, children's play area, donkey rides and other attractions.

Central Beach
Prestatyn
Open-air heated swimming pool. Royal Lido Centre with bars, cafés and shops.

Barkby Beach
Prestatyn
Good for launching boats, quieter than other beaches.

Rhyl Beach
Three miles of sandy beach, backed by a promenade. Cafés, children's playground, donkey rides, cinemas and all the fun of the fair. *Bathing is not advised on the western end near the mouth of the Afon Clwyd.*

Sun Centre
On promenade, Rhyl
Super modern swimming pools, with wave-making machine, café etc, all in glass-sided building.

Ocean Beach Park and Marine Lake
West end of promenade, Rhyl. Swings and roundabouts and all the fun of the fair.

beach has the Nova Centre backing onto it, a heated swimming pool if the sea is too cold, band concerts and bars. Barkby beach is perhaps a little quieter and has access for boat trailers. Central and Ffrith beaches are the best for bathing.

The town itself is a thriving community all the year round with many residents, and does not rely solely on summer visitors for its livelihood. There is a good range of shops, cafés and hotels. Inland from the coast is Meliden. Above Meliden is a range of limestone hills with several short walks which give excellent views all along the coast. Above Prestatyn on the road out to Gwaenysgor, there is a small car park before the road climbs steeply; the signpost shows the route to Offa's Dyke Path and a walk through the woods up to the top of the hills. This is the northern end of the Offa's Dyke Path mentioned in the previous chapter. Crowning the hill are the embankments of an old Iron Age fort. Just to the south at Gop Hill

Gwrych Castle, Abergele

are some caves where remains of Stone Age man have been found. For the archaeologist this area is particularly fascinating, for there is much evidence of prehistoric man.

Rhyl is only four miles from Prestatyn, but it seems much more on a busy Sunday when the traffic moves slowly. Perhaps the most famous seaside town in North Wales, catering for many thousands of visitors each year, it differs completely from its near neighbour and is so much more brash. There is something for everybody with all the necessary seaside amusements on the promenade, and a beach which is excellent for swimming, though one must take care at the western end near the mouth of the Afon Clwyd. Most of the major attractions are along the sea front on the wide promenade. The Sun Centre dominates the Eastern Parade, a large modern structure mainly of glass containing restaurants, amusements, a swimming pool with a wave-making machine and other swimming pools.

Further along is the Floral Hall, well known for its magnificent

Colwyn Bay

opposite: *The Sun Centre, Rhyl*   *Llandudno and the Great Orme*

WHAT TO SEE AROUND ABERGELE

Abergele Beach
Pensarn
Pebble beach but sand exposed as the tide recedes. Popular for caravans.

Gwrych Castle
Mock castle built in beautiful setting. Fine furniture inside, with jousting and miniature railway in grounds. Just off A55, west of Abergele.

displays of flowers, a paddling pool, bandstand, and the Ocean beach park with its roundabouts and all-the-fun-of-the-fair. Alongside is the Marine Lake for boating.

The Afon Clwyd with its once-wide estuary and reclaimed marshland effectively forms the western boundary of the town, but the road continues parallel with the sea through the fields of caravans to **Abergele**, just four miles further on. This small town, with a busy livestock sale on Mondays, seems to be more Welsh than its neighour; at the junction of several main roads, its narrow streets are always busy. It is a market town and the old church close to the town centre contains some interesting relics of the past, with some fifteenth- and sixteenth-century glass and a dug-out chest. The churchyard has two memorials to disasters which happened in the neighbourhood, the shipwreck of the *Ocean Monarch* in 1848 and the crash of the Irish Mail train twenty years later.

Although situated about a mile from the seashore, Abergele, now joined to Pensarn on the coast, with its pebbly beaches and sandhills, is a pleasant town for a more relaxing day.

On the outskirts of the town are the long walks and great gatehouse surrounding Gwrych Castle, set below wooded hills in a large estate. It is an impressive site, though unfortunately a folly, for the castle was built in 1815 by a wealthy tycoon. It is open to the public and contains many antiques and fine furnishings. The parklands contain an amusement centre which has a miniature railway and holds jousting contests on summer afternoons. There are several short walks in the surrounding woodlands.

PLACES TO VISIT AROUND COLWYN BAY

Colwyn Beach
A long curving beach, round the bay. Good sand and safe bathing, very popular.

Eirias Park
Boating, bowls, tennis, picnic spots.

Prince of Wales Theatre
Regular variety shows, bands and plays.

Welsh Mountain Zoo
Collection of animals and birds of prey with free flying displays daily (weather permitting). Off A55 by West End Shopping Centre.

Rhos-on-Sea
Extension of Colwyn Bay, with Harlequin Puppet Theatre, open-air swimming pool (heated), and St Trillo's church on the beach.

The main road, now a dual carriageway for much of its length, speeds up and over the headland to Penmaen-Rhos with its huge limestone quarries, and then drops steeply into the back of Colwyn Bay.

Before the descent there is a fine viewpoint beside the main road where the sweep of the bay around to the Little Orme can be seen. The whole shoreline has beautiful sandy beaches with a promenade running almost the full curve of the bay.

Colwyn Bay, with its neighbour **Rhos-on-Sea**, has mushroomed in recent years to become a major holiday resort. Besides all the usual attractions along the promenade, including a pier, it has much to offer and many places of interest. Eirias Park runs south from the promenade, with picnic areas, boating, bowls, tennis and a sports area. The nearby Prince of Wales Theatre has a busy summer season with a variety of shows, while in Rhos there is the Harlequin Puppet Theatre, an open-air swimming pool just off the promenade and a golf course.

A curiosity on the seashore at Rhos is the miniature church of St Trillo built over a small holy well. The chapel is only 11ft by 8ft and is probably the smallest in Wales. The Celtic saint is believed to

Bodnant Garden

PLACES OF INTEREST IN AND AROUND LLANDUDNO

Beaches
North Shore: Good beach backed by promenade. Safe bathing, launch facilities and water skiing area.
West Shore: Shingle beach, sea goes out a long way at low tide, so bathing is only when tide is in. Lews Carroll Memorial

Great Orme
Nature trails, tramway and cabin lift to summit. Dry ski slope.

Happy Valley
Park with playground, rock gardens and open-air theatre.

Pier
With theatre and landing stage.

Rapallo House
Ffan Bach Road
Museum and arts centre with exhibits of local and national interest.

Bodnant Gardens
Beautiful gardens and woodlands, some of the finest in Europe. Especially noted for its rhododendrons in the spring. Six miles south of Llandudno Junction off A470. Owned by the National Trust.

Felin Isaf
Llansantffraid, Glan Conwy. Seventeenth-century flour mill with original machinery and methods.

have lived here for many years and local people say fishermen and sailors prayed there before a journey. Services are now held outside, and the church is open daily.

On the outskirts of the town is the famous Welsh Mountain Zoo where a wide variety of birds and animals are kept in as near natural surroundings a possible. There are many birds of prey, and weather permitting, daily flying displays of eagles, falcons, etc. Behind Rhos on Sea is the small Bryn Euryn. Although almost surrounded by roads it is nevertheless a pleasant place to stroll and to enjoy the panoramic views over the towns and bay.

L
1h
*
††

The road climbs over the shoulder of the Little Orme and then descends to follow the promenade to **Llandudno**, sheltered on a neck of land by the massive bulk of the Great Orme. The town straddles the low-lying land with the main amusement centres on

Lewis Carroll Memorial, West Shore, Llandudno

ON THIS VERY SHORE
DURING HAPPY RAMBLES WITH
LITTLE ALICE LIDDELL
LEWIS CARROLL
WAS INSPIRED TO WRITE THAT
LITERARY TREASURE
ALICE IN WONDERLAND
WHICH HAS CHARMED CHILDREN
FOR GENERATIONS

UNVEILED BY
THE RT. HON D LLOYD GEORGE O.M. M.P.
SEPT. 6TH 1933

the north-facing coast and the quieter residential areas overlooking the estuary of the Afon Conwy. The town retains much of its Victorian grandeur and gives the impression of being more conservative than its neighbours.

The promenade follows the curve of the bay and has most of the usual amusements. At the foot of the Great Orme is the Pier Pavilion. Attached is a landing stage for steamers which offer trips around the bay, along the coast and even to the Isle of Man. There are several theatres in the town attracting first class variety acts during the summer months, and it is best to enquire locally for the current attractions. Happy Valley is a public park where everybody

Bridge over the Afon Conwy at Llanrwst

should be made to smile; it has playgrounds, rockpools and an open-air theatre. From the park a cabin lift leaves for the summit of the Great Orme. Llandudno is not only an amusement centre: it has many fine shops in the main street. Rapallo House about a mile from the town centre is a museum and art gallery with many displays relating to Welsh history.

On the other side of the town, the West Shore, overlooking the Conwy estuary and Snowdonia, is generally quieter. It was here that Charles Dodgson, better known as Lewis Carroll, spent several holidays at the house of Dean Liddell, whose daughter inspired the tales of *Alice in Wonderland*. A memorial portraying the White Rabbit from those tales was unveiled there in 1933 by Lloyd George.

The Great Orme dominates Llandudno and protects it from the prevailing westerly winds. A toll road (Marine Drive) encircles the headland, giving some fine views of the cliffs, caves and coast to the south. It is possible to reach the summit café (679ft) by car, foot, tramway or cabin lift. The latter two are a continuous daily service during the summer months. There are many minor antiquities on

Bodelwyddan church

the hillsides and the Great Orme Nature Trail which starts in the Happy Valley is perhaps the best way to see them. It is also an excellent way of escaping from the hustle and bustle for a few hours and enjoying this magnificent setting.

A short distance to the south of Llandudno and standing on the shores of the Conwy estuary is **Deganwy**. With its castle, now only a ruin, it has for many centuries guarded the northern entrance to the Afon Conwy. Today, with a sheltered harbour, it is a popular resort and centre for sailing.

One of the best known attractions in this area is Bodnant Gardens, the home of Lord Aberconwy, five miles to the south of Deganwy. It is one of the finest gardens in Britain, well known for its wonderful collection of trees from all over the world. There are nearly a hundred acres of formal and informal gardens on the hillside overlooking the mountains of Snowdonia. In the spring there are magnificent displays of rhododendrons, azaleas, magnolias, camelias and a laburnum tunnel which is spectacular when it is in full flower. In the summer there are formal rose gardens and herbaceous borders.

The house here is not open to the public. The garden is laid in terraces down the side of the valley. Below the lawns surrounding the house is a large pond surrounded by mature trees and paths which lead down to a canal pond which features on many photographs of the gardens. Adjacent to this is the large area of woodland with magnificent rhododendrons. Below the wood in the bottom of the valley stands the estate watermill which Lord Aberconwy has just presented to the National Trust.

Up river from Bodnant, squeezed between the steep hills and the meandering river, is **Llanrwst**, a solid Welsh market town, It is a town little altered by tourism, that serves a wide community in the surrounding hills and forests. The Afon Conwy has many outstanding bridges, not least of which is the beautiful arched bridge here. Said to have been built by Inigo Jones in 1636, it was commissioned by the Wynn family who lived in Gwydir Castle on the opposite bank. There are other reminders of this wealthy family in the old church off the town square.

To the east of Llanrwst in the area bordered in the south by the inevitable A5 and in the north by the coast is a vast area of

PLACES TO VISIT IN AND AROUND LLANRWST

Gwydir Castle
Historic Tudor mansion, grounds with peacocks. Across the river from Llanrwst on B5106.

Trefriw Woollen Mills
Working woollen mill, showing all stages of the manufacture of tapestries and tweeds from the raw wool.

Gwydyr Forest
Extensive forests on west bank of river with many walks and nature trails. Leaflets available from Forestry Commission, Gwydyr Uchaf, Llanrwst.

North Wales Museum of Wild Life
On outskirts of town. It has a collection of game trophies and rare birds from round the world.

uncommercialised Wales. The hills to the north are gently rounded crossed by a zig-zag assortment of minor roads. There are lovely little villages and surprise views which for the car-bound visitor makes a pleasant interlude away from the bustling coastlands.

There are high moorlands with famous grouse shoots and hills that will give a good day's walking at a relatively low level. Much of the area has been afforested and once a year Clocaenog Forest echoes to screaming engines as competitors of the RAC rally tear down the forest roads on one of the many special stages through the Welsh forests.

In the centre of this area and signposted from most directions is Llyn Brenig, a reservoir opened by the Prince of Wales in 1976. Surrounding the reservoir and easily accessible for visitors is an area of unspoilt country. There are nature reserves and picnic areas around the lake and sailing and fishing on it. The information centre will provide details of the nature and history trails. It is perhaps one of the best areas in the country to look at prehistory. There is much evidence of early man with hut circles, burial mounds and enclo- sures dating from the Stone Age to more recent times. It is an area well worth exploring and within easy reach of the coastal resorts and close to a car park.

Rhuddlan Castle

PLACES OF INTEREST IN THE VALE OF CLWYD

Denbigh Castle and Leicester's Church
Interesting remains of important castle.

Llyn Brenig
6¹/₂ miles from Denbigh off B4501.
Reservoir for sailing, angling, pony trekking, has archaeological trail and visitors' centre.

St Asaph Cathedral
One of early churches of Wales, and smallest cathedral in Britain. Much added to over the years.

Chapter House. Museum with collection of religious papers.

Rhuddlan Castle
Solid looking castle on the edge of the Afon Clwyd. Historically important, but much damaged as source of local building materials.

Bodelwyddan
Near St Asaph
White 'marble' church, built in 1856. Can be seen for many miles around.

To the east is the historic former county town of **Denbigh** (known in Welsh as Dinbych), built a short distance above the river. The castle, built by Henry de Lacy in 1282 for Edward I to help maintain law and order in the region, changed hands frequently between the Welsh and the English. It was finally destroyed by the Roundheads in 1645 after an eleven-month siege; Charles I had taken refuge there after his defeat at Rowton Moor near Chester. It has a large and beautiful gatehouse and some interesting defensive ideas built in, though little now remains. Nearby are the walls of Leicester's church begun by the Earl of Leicester in 1579 to replace St Asaph's cathedral, but never completed. The remains of the town walls to the north of this ruin show how important Denbigh was in the past.

H. M. Stanley, the adventurer and the author of the remark 'Doctor Livingstone, I presume' was born in Denbigh, and Sir Hugh Myddleton, who constructed London's water supply in the reign of James I lived close by at Gwaunynog. Thomas Edwards a famous and well loved bard, and the author known as Twm o'r Nant, is buried in the parish church one mile east of the town.

Downstream from Denbigh is the cathedral town of **St Asaph**.
Though the cathedral is perhaps less famous nowadays than the
nearby white 'marble' church at Bodelwyddan it gives the place the
status of a city, the smallest (as is the cathedral) in Great Britain.
The cathedral is a squat building on the site of a church founded in
AD560 by St Mungo, who was succeeded in AD573 by St Asaph,
from whom the town takes its name. There has been a cathedral
here ever since, despite Edward I's attempts to build an alternative
at Rhuddlan. The present, much restored, building contains many
features that have survived from earlier centuries. The Chapter
Museum contains a fine collection of early religious manuscripts
and Bibles, but it is open only by request and never on Sundays.

Three miles to the north is Rhuddlan Castle, perhaps one of the
most solid-looking of all Edward's castles. It stands on the banks of
the Clwyd, which was diverted and canalised to allow ships to sail
in from the sea and berth at high tide. It guarded the main coastal
route into North Wales and stands as a grim reminder to modern
visitors of the troubled past of this land. Many people pass through
Rhuddlan each year, but few realise that the valley to the south
played such an important part in shaping the future of the Welsh
people.

4

THE MOUNTAINS OF NORTHERN SNOWDONIA

Some visitors will perhaps explore only the resorts on the northern coast, but it is the mountains west of the Afon Conwy that are the attraction to many others. Rising steeply from the banks of the river, they are some of the highest peaks in England and Wales as well as some of the oldest. They are visible for many miles, and form a jagged skyline in sharp contrast to the surrounding moorlands.

For convenience the larger towns and villages will be visited first, for the hills are to a great extent the domain of the experienced climber and hillwalker, though there are several interesting excursions on foot for the novice. All the large towns are situated on the coast and events have shown how important the routes along the coastal belt have been in the past. To the modern traveller they are equally important, for they are the normal access routes for most people approaching from the north and north-west of England. After passing through Abergele both coastal roads become one busy main road (A55), threading through Colwyn Bay and Llandudno Junction to arrive at one of the main crossing points of the Afon Conwy.

There are three bridges across the Conwy estuary: Stephenson's tubular railway bridge, Telford's beautiful suspension bridge, which replaced an ancient and dangerous ferry and is now used

The Afon Conwy

only by pedestrians, and a modern road bridge which unfortunately has turned one of the most attractive historic towns in North Wales into a bottleneck for traffic during much of the summer. The suspension bridge, opened in 1826, was a major technical achievement of its time and was built by Thomas Telford, who was associated with many major transport projects in North Wales.

Work is progressing well on a road tunnel under the estuary which should be open in 1990. This will speed traffic along the coastal route and avoid Conwy town altogether. Visitors must divert off this route at Llandudno Junction to visit the town.

The town of **Conwy** is situated on the very edge of the estuary with the superbly sited castle dominating the town from its rocky perch above the river. It is one of the most interesting, and probably one of the most visited, towns in Wales. The walls surrounding the town are almost complete and with the castle form a unique defensive work. The enclosed narrow streets are as busy as the quay and landing stage. All contribute to make the town a popular holiday and yachting centre.

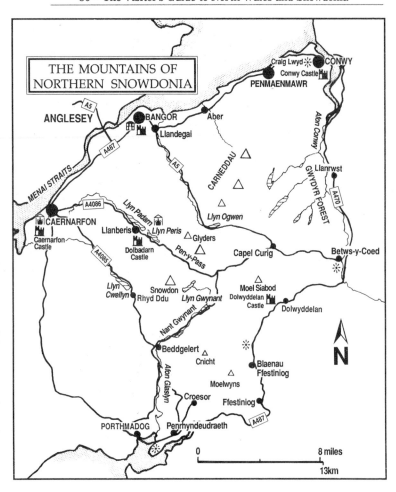

THE MOUNTAINS OF
NORTHERN SNOWDONIA

ANGLESEY

CONWY
Craig Lwyd
Conwy Castle
PENMAENMAWR

BANGOR
Aber
Llandegai

Afon Conwy

CARNEDDAU

Llanrwst

GWYDYR FOREST

Llyn Padarn

Llyn Ogwen

CAERNARFON
Caernarfon Castle

Llanberis
Llyn Peris
Glyders

Betws-y-Coed

Dolbadarn Castle
Pen-y-Pass

Capel Curig

Llyn Cwellyn
Snowdon
Rhyd Ddu
Llyn Gwynant

Moel Siabod
Dolwyddelan Castle
Dolwyddelan

MENAI STRAITS

Nant Gwynant

Beddgelert
Cnicht

Blaenau Ffestiniog

Moelwyns

Afon Glaslyn

Croesor

Ffestiniog

PORTHMADOG
Penrhyndeudraeth

0   8 miles

13km

N

The castle stands on the site of a Cistercian monastery built in the tenth century, but uprooted a hundred years later and moved to Maenan five miles upstream by Edward I, who saw the site as more suitable for defence than religion. The castle was built in only four years, a remarkable feat without modern mechanical aids, and served in part as a royal palace. During its stormy lifetime it has

The Smallest House, Conwy

regularly changed hands between the Welsh and English before finally being captured and dismantled by the Parliamentarians under General Mytton in 1646.

Modern visitors to the castle approach from Castle Square and it is from high on its walls that the best views of the nearby hills and the town walls can be seen. The walls were built at the same time as the castle and are part of an integral defensive scheme for the town; they follow the rise and fall of the land and are approximately 30ft tall with twenty-one towers throughout their length.

The quay is within the walls and has long been a port for fishing boats. Today it is becoming more important as a centre for yachts-

PLACES OF INTEREST IN AND AROUND CONWY

Plas Mawr
High Street, Conwy
Perfect example of Elizabethan building. Now houses Royal Cambrian Academy of Art.

Conwy Castle and Walls
Magnificent setting, best example in country.

Aberconwy House
Castle Street, Conwy
A good example of a fourteenth-century timber framed house. Houses Conwy Exhibition, depicting life of the town from Roman Times. Owned by National Trust.

St Mary's Church
Originally part of Cistercian Abbey but developed as a parish church over the years.

Smallest House
Britain's smallest house, on the quayside.

Conwy Mountain
Hut circles and footpaths in most directions.

Sychnant Pass
Old road connecting Conwy and Penmaenmawr.

 men and boating enthusiasts, the harbour providing a safe mooring. It is a busy place, full of hustle and bustle, though still a pleasant place to sit and watch the world go by. On the quayside is Britain's smallest house, a tiny half-up and half-down, built by a bachelor who obviously intended to remain so.

 Plas Mawr, perhaps the most visited building after the castle, is a fine example of an Elizabethan house; just off the High Street, it has many interesting features both inside and outside. Several of the rooms have associations with Elizabeth I and the Lantern Room is reputed to be haunted. There are 365 windows and 52 doors in the house, coinciding with the days and weeks of the year, a symbolic feature that the Elizabethans were quite fond of. It is now an art gallery housing the annual exhibition of the Royal Cambrian Academy of Art.

Lower down the High Street, Aberconwy is a white timber and stone house owned by the National Trust. It is the only survivor of

Conwy Castle

the type of medieval merchant's town house built in the fifteenth and sixteenth centuries which formerly abounded in Conwy.

Almost surrounded by houses and streets stands St Mary's church which occupies the site of the early Cistercian abbey. Much of the exterior structure is part of the original abbey, but the centuries have seen many additions to both inside and outside, and it is now a good example of the development of a parish church through the years. The churchyard includes the grave of two childen who are celebrated in William Wordsworth's poem *We Are Seven*, which he wrote in 1798.

Behind the town are some good hill walks with clear paths, particularly over Conwy Mountain (only 808ft high) to the Iron Age hillfort of Caer Leion. The old road crossed the Sychnant Pass behind Conwy to the coast at **Penmaenmawr**, and the head of the pass is a good place to park before enjoying one of the many short (or long) walks on the nearby slopes.

The river and the lakes upstream from Conwy are the breeding grounds for salmon. Several local families are licensed to catch the fish as they swim upstream, using nets which must not be below a particular mesh size, ensuring that only the larger fish are caught.

The modern road westwards from Conwy hugs the coast through a series of tunnels to give a smooth, quick ride through Penmaenmawr to Bangor. The old road over Sychnant Pass had a formidable reputation and many travellers preferred to walk along the shoreline than cross the pass. Frequently the road was so bad that carriages had to be dismantled to get them over the worst parts.

1-2h
*
†††

The hills to the south of the old and new roads have many reminders of the prehistoric people who inhabited the area. Just above Penmaenmawr at Craig Lwyd was a stone axe factory. Using the tough granite, Stone Age man chipped and shaped it, both for his own use and for 'export'; axes from the site have been found all over Britain. There are many other prehistoric sites, some of which have been combined into a history trail from Penmaenmawr; leaflets are available in local shops.

Modern man still finds the granite worth quarrying, the summit of Penmaenmawr, from which the town gets its name, being a major source of this material; the height of the hill is reduced annually.

Aber, a short distance further on, is a small village known for the waterfall in the hills above. One turns off the main road and parks at the car park at the end of the valley. A walk of about a mile up the valley leads to the most impressive falls, which have a vertical drop of about 120ft. To the west are the smaller cataracts of Afon Bach. The hills south of the falls are owned by the National Trust, and the mountains of the Carneddau are some of the wildest and highest in Snowdonia. Aber's car park is an ideal starting point for walks into these hills, but only experienced walkers, able to use a map and compass, should consider such an expedition.

The coast road continues south to join the A5 trunk road at **Llandegai**. This busy road from London to Holyhead was built by Thomas Telford in the early nineteenth century to speed the journey, and especially the Royal Mail, to and from Ireland. Opposite the junction is Penrhyn Castle and estate, now run by the National Trust. Until recently it was the home of the Pennant family who were the former owners of the Penrhyn Slate quarries in Bethesda. The house, which overlooks the Menai Straits, is a masterpiece of neo-Norman architecture and for obvious reasons slate has been used extensively both inside and outside.

PLACES OF INTEREST IN AND AROUND BANGOR

Penrhyn Castle
Just off the A55 north of Bangor. An elegant neo-Norman mansion on the edge of the Menai Straits; many slate artefacts in the building. Doll museum and industrial railway museum. Owned by National Trust.

Theatr Gwynedd
County centre for theatre and films with regular performances.

Bangor Cathedral
Thought to be the oldest in Britain, shows evidence of continuous development since sixth century.

Old Canonry
Bangor
Houses Museum of Welsh Antiquities, with collection of seventeenth-century furniture illustrating Welsh rural crafts. Prehistoric and Romano-British objects.

The style and ostentatious design of the building reflect the unlimited amount of money available to many nineteenth-century businessmen. Parts of the building now house a doll museum, and on the estate is an industrial railway museum with locomotives and rolling stock from the Penrhyn and other slate quarries. In the old days, most of the slate shipped from the quarries went from the quay on the estate, so that the owner and management could keep a close eye on the amount being sold and despatched.

Bangor, one of the five university towns of Wales, stands at the northern end of the Menai Straits, most of the town being squeezed between two low hills in a shallow valley. It is dominated by the buildings of the University College of North Wales which stand on the hill between the town and the Straits. The university is perhaps modern Bangor's main claim to fame, though in the past it has been a Celtic centre for Christianity; a bishopric was established here as long ago as AD546.

The cathedral is thought to be the oldest in Britain in continuous use. The building, though not remarkable, has seen continuous development since Norman times and, despite suffering much at the

Penrhyn Castle

hands of both Welsh and English aggressors, bears much evidence of the many phases of its development. Restoration was begun in 1866 under the care of Sir Gilbert Scott, who approached it with an eye to the past and was able to include much detail that had been destroyed in previous centuries. Nearby is the old Bishop's Palace, built mainly in the sixteenth century and now the town hall. Almost opposite is the Theatr Gwynedd, the centre for the performing arts in the county. The Museum of Welsh Antiquities, housed in the Old Canonry near the cathedral, contains exhibits from prehistoric, Roman and more recent times giving a good background to the development of the town, surrounding area and Wales generally. The city was a quiet religious centre until early last century. The opening of the two bridges across the Menai Straits in the first half of the

Port Dinorwig

nineteenth century resulted in increased traffic by road and rail through the town. With the arrival of the university college in 1883, Bangor finally became a municipality and busy commercial centre.

Visitors may prefer to follow the A5 trunk road out of Bangor to see the Menai Straits; there is a fine viewpoint above the suspension bridge. The Straits, which divide Anglesey from the mainland, vary between 200yd and a mile wide and are thirteen miles long. They have formed an almost inpenetrable barrier for most invaders. The bridges were constructed in the nineteenth century and will be detailed in a later chapter. They did for the first time provide a crossing that was safe and to an extent opened up Anglesey to the Victorian tourist.

After leaving the bridges behind the road south moves a little inland before passing above **Port Dinorwig**. In the heyday of the slate quarry a narrow gauge railway came down from Llanberis to load the waiting ships at this tiny port with cut slates. Neglected for many years it has taken on a new life and is now a popular centre for yachting and holidays.

PLACES OF INTEREST IN CAERNARFON

Caernarfon Castle
Finest of Edward's castles.
Polygonal towers with banded masonry make it unique.

Town Walls
Circle inner part of town, part of integral defensive system.

Segontium
Roman Fort on outskirts of town. Some buildings and a museum

showing history of the site.

Market Hall
Near town centre
Now a centre for local crafts and shops.

Museum of Royal Welch Fusiliers
Military museum inside castle, with many mementoes of the regiment's past.

At the southern end of the Menai Straits is the historic town of **Caernarfon**. It is probably the best known of all the towns in North Wales, and stands in a magnificent position at the foot of the mountains overlooking Anglesey. The castle, built by Edward I, is one of the greatest (and most attractive) castles in the country. It stands above the busy quayside as a reminder of the strategic importance of this bustling town. Traditionally the castle is where Edward II was invested as the first Prince of Wales after his birth there in 1284. The castle has in more recent times seen the investitures as Prince of Wales of the future Edward VIII (in 1911) and of Prince Charles (in 1969).

Unusually, the castle has thirteen polygonal towers and banded masonry and although outwardly perfect it is internally just a shell. Like all castles in this region it has had a stormy career, playing a significant part in the wars between the Welsh and English princes. It was twice unsuccessfully beseiged by Owain Glyndwr; in the Civil War it stood for the king, and when captured by Cromwell's troops it was ordered to be destroyed in 1660. This warrant was fortunately never exercised and it stands now as a magnificent reminder of the castle builder's craft. In the Queen's Tower within the walls is the Museum of the Royal Welch Fusiliers, with many mementoes from

A doorway in Caernarfon with a naive carving of an angel carrying a coat of arms

the history of the regiment.

As at Conwy, much of the town wall survives, built with the castle as part of an integrated defensive system. It surrounds the old parts of the town, the narrow streets forming a regular pattern within. In the north-west corner, and built into the walls, is the chantry of St Mary which utilised the adjoining tower as a vestry and bell tower. There are many fine old buildings enclosed by the walls, including the Black Boy Inn, a traditional public house with some good local dishes, and the old Market Hall which now is more a centre for local crafts than a market.

Until very recently the town, like many along the coast, was blighted by traffic, but the building of a new bypass has considerably relieved the congestion, thus allowing visitors to wander at a more leisurely pace than previously. Castle Square, which is now relatively free from traffic, has a Saturday market and is an ideal base

Caernarfon Castle

to explore the town.

The Romans also appreciated the value of the site's strategic importance, or perhaps they just found it slightly less hostile than the mountains inland. They built a fort just to the south of the present town, half a mile out, on the road to Beddgelert. Little now remains but the foundations give a good idea of the ground plan. On the site is an excellent museum covering the history of the fort and the organization of the Roman army in Britain and other related subjects. The fort, known as *Segontium*, was occupied from about AD78 to AD380 when the Roman troops withdrew from Britain. During that time a sizeable community had grown up outside the walls and on retirement many of the soldiers are believed to have settled and farmed in the area. It was a fort well integrated with local life.

The view south from Caernarfon and Bangor is of the mountains. They are not large by comparison with other European mountain ranges but they always give an overriding impression of grandeur. They form the northern end of the Snowdonia National Park and are divided into three distinct ranges, separated by deep valleys. To the east, bounded on one side by the Conwy Valley and on the other by the Nant Ffrancon Pass, are the Carneddau; in the centre are the Glyders; and on the west, the highest of all, is Snowdon with its surrounding mountains. In all there are fourteen peaks over 3,000ft, all linked by footpaths.

The mountains, originally formed more than 300 million years ago, are the worn down stumps of much higher mountains. They have been folded by earth movements to more than 20,000ft and then gradually worn by changing temperatures, water and ice to their present size. The valleys have been carved by ancient glaciers and many of the hanging valleys, called cwms, have been dammed by glacial deposits to hold lakes. The debris of glaciers is scattered around the hillsides and in moraines along and across the valleys. The alpine plants left by the receding ice in some of the high cwms provide a living link with the Ice Age and show how little these mountains have changed despite man's interference.

Snowdon is the highest mountain in England and Wales. With its sharp ridges and sombre cwms, it is inevitable that stories have grown around it. This is the land of the legendary King Arthur. Yr Wyddfa, the highest peak, is traditionally the tomb of Rhita Fawr

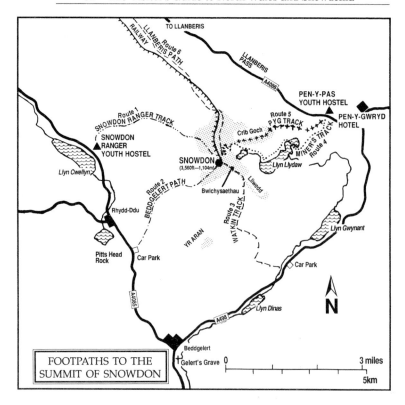

FOOTPATHS TO THE
SUMMIT OF SNOWDON

slain by Arthur. Arthur is supposed to have fought his last battle at the Pass of Arrows (Bwlch y Saethau) below Snowdon's summit; Llyn Llydaw by tradition is the lake into which Excalibur was thrown. On the slopes above is a cave in which three of King Arthur's knights rest, ready to come to the aid of the country when needed. Despite the legends, what is more certain is that several of the Welsh princes retreated into the area when defeated, for it proved a most hostile environment to the pursuing English troops.

The Snowdon Massif, known more traditionally by the Welsh as Yr Eryri, is a star-shaped cluster of peaks connected by a series of steep ridges, the highest, Yr Wyddfa at 3,560ft, is in the centre and

FOOTPATHS TO THE SUMMIT OF SNOWDON

ROUTE 1
Snowdon Ranger Track: $3^3/_4$ miles. An easy path with delightful views, zig-zags above youth hostel.

ROUTE 2
Beddgelert Path: $3^3/_4$ miles. Easy to follow, climbs gradually to summit, Steeper near top.

ROUTE 3
Watkin Track: $3^1/_2$ miles. Most interesting, but hardest walk. Good path at first up to Bwlch y Saethau, steep and loose after that. A long climb.

ROUTE 4
Miner's Track: $3^3/_4$ miles. Follows copper miners' track to lake, then rises more steeply to join PYG track to summit. Good for introduction to the mountain if you do not wish to go to the top.

ROUTE 5
PYG (Pen-y-Gwryd) Track: $3^1/_4$ miles. Good route. Climbs quickly and then contours around cwm. Zig-zags below summit. A well-made path. Recommended favourite route.

ROUTE 6
Llanberis Path: 5 miles. Follows close to railway. Starts in Llanberis and climbs gradually. Not the most interesting route. Easy but long.

generally the object of most people's attention. The main routes to the summit are fairly easy underfoot though can be arduous to those unused to hill walking. Many thousands reach the summit each year, though to enjoy the walk a certain amount of fitness is recommended.

North of Yr Wyddfa is the summit of Crib-y-Ddysgl (3,493ft) leading out on the narrow ridge to Crib Goch (3,023ft) in the north-

Snowdon and Llyn Llydaw

east. This is a splendid ridge to walk with towering pinnacles and buttresses and with superb situations, but is not for the inexperienced or faint hearted.

To the south-east is the craggy ridge of Lliwedd (2,497ft) with its steep walls overlooking Llyn Llydaw, and looking south is the long southern ridge leading out to Yr Aran (2,451ft) above the Gwynant Valley. There are good tracks across the ridges but care must be taken—the weather can be extremely inclement with gusting winds.

Many visitors are content to reach the summit by the rack-and-pinion railway which ascends the five miles from Llanberis with fantastic views en route. The railway was opened in 1896 and has a maximum gradient of 20 per cent, it was designed by Swiss engineers and uses Swiss locomotives.

For those who achieve the summit by whatever means the views, providing the weather is clear, are worth the effort. You are above every other mountain in England and Wales and can see many of them; the Welsh mountains and lakes are immediately obvious even down to Cadair Idris thirty miles to the south. Further afield to the west the Wicklow Hills of Ireland can be seen across the sea and to the north the Isle of Man and the Lake District, with the coast of Lancashire and Blackpool Tower visible. For more distant views a clear day and a good imagination is needed. There is a café and bar on the summit to reward thirsty walkers but be warned that it is only open when the train is running.

The ascent of the summit, Yr Wyddfa, has understandably been a popular achievement at least from early last century when George Borrow in his book *Wild Wales* describes how he walked up with his family in 1850 and even at that time 'there was a rude cabin in which refreshments are sold and in which a person resides throughout the year'.

There are six main routes up Snowdon, starting from car parks all around the mountain. Although some are easier and some are longer, all require much physical effort and a sound knowledge of mountain walking, for the weather can change drastically during the 5-8 hours of the walk. All the paths are well made and quite easy to follow if care is taken.

Perhaps the greatest expedition is the Snowdon Horseshoe, a traverse of all the main peaks to and from Pen-y-Pass. It involves

THINGS TO SEE AND DO AROUND LLANBERIS

Snowdon Mountain Railway
Runs a regular passenger service to the summit of Snowdon using steam powered rack-and-pinion locomotives.

Dolbadarn Castle
Home of the Welsh Princes in the twelfth century, it stands above the lake guarding the entrance to the Llanberis Pass.

Welsh Slate Museum
In the former workshops of Dinorwig Quarry, showing much of the original machinery and equipment used. Films and slides of quarry work.

Llanberis Lake Railway
Steam railway starting from the Slate Museum, running along lakeside through country park.

Padarn Country Park
On shore of the lake with native oak trees and walks through quarry remains.

Dinorwig Power Station
Information centre, hugh cavern inside mountain with guided tours (but no children under 14).

Museum of the North
Devoted to natural environment of Snowdonia and Welsh history.

steep climbing and knife-edge ridges following the rim of the cwm surrounding Llyn Llydaw and taking in the summits of Crib-Goch (3,023ft), Crib-y-Ddysgl (3,493ft) over Yr Wyddfa (3,560ft) before descending to Bwlch-y-Saethau and the steep crags of Lliwedd (2,947ft) and thence back down the Miners' Track to Pen-y-Pass. It must be stressed that this is a major undertaking and should not be attempted without a stout pair of boots, a head for heights and much previous experience; the weather and rock conditions should be checked before attempting this marvellous expedition.

H
6-7h
****
††††

Pen-y-Pass, the highest point of the Llanberis Pass, and the starting point for many of the Snowdon walks, is the site of the old Gorphwysfa Hotel, an old coaching inn converted some years ago to a youth hostel. In the early part of the century the hotel was the centre for the pioneer rock climbers who visited the many crags on the slopes of Snowdon. The road descends steeply from there down to the south-east to the Pen y Gwryd Hotel, which superseded

Lliwedd from Snowdon

it as the meeting place for climbers. Both the youth hostel and the hotel are Mountain Rescue points. To the north of Pen-y-Pass the road winds down the Llanberis Pass, between the huge rock buttresses which are the playgrounds of the modern rock climbers, to Llyn Peris and Llyn Padarn.

Llyn Peris has recently been drained and dammed to form the bottom lake of the huge Dinorwig Pump Storage Power Station. This hydro-electric scheme involves the use of two lakes, one high lake and one lower reservoir. The top lake, Marchlyn Mawr, behind Elidir Fawr to the north, stores the water until generating capacity is needed. The water is then released and drives the turbines built under the hillside opposite and flows into the lower lake, Llyn Peris. During off peak times, using surplus electricity from the National Grid, the water is then pumped back to the higher lake for future use. It is a massive project involving deep underground workings and tunnels, well hidden in the slate quarries and underground, but the entrance to the power station is visible across Llyn Peris. The electricity is fed into the national grid. There is an excellent informa-

Snowdon and Llyn Padarn from Brynrefail

tion centre at the power station and visitors can see the massive underground workings. It is a huge project and is well recommended visiting.

Llanberis, in the bottom of the valley, sits almost between the two lakes and is probably best known as the starting point for the Snowdon Mountain Railway. This is a rack-and-pinion railway carrying passengers to the summit of Snowdon; as an easy alternative to walking, it is very popular. Not far from the station is the Welsh Slate Museum, with exhibits and buildings relating to all aspects of quarry work. The old quarry railway has been rebuilt to provide a pleasant run along the north shore of Llyn Padarn through a country park of the same name. It is a narrow gauge railway and many of the original locomotives are still in use.

On a small hill above the town sits the round keep of Dolbadarn Castle built in the early thirteenth century, it is thought for Llewelyn The Great, while on the opposite side of the lake can be seen the huge tiers of the old Dinorwig Slate Mine which rise for 1,500ft up the side of the mountain. The mine now houses the aforementioned Pump Storage Power Station.

To the north of the town and above the massive slate tips rise the bulky slopes of Elidir Fawr and the Glyder range of mountains, most of which are over 3,000ft high. They are accessible on foot from the Llanberis side, but the most interesting walks and ascents are made from the north, starting mainly from Llyn Ogwen, where there are several convenient car parks. There is no village at **Ogwen** just a collection of buildings comprising a youth hostel and an adventure school — but it is easy to get the feel of the high mountains despite the busy main road. The old packhorse road runs parallel to the modern road and can be traced for much of the distance along the valley side. It makes a fine walk in magnificent surroundings and is fairly level and easy to follow. The remains of the old packhorse bridge can be seen underneath the more modern road bridge by the falls below Llyn Ogwen.

Access to the Glyders is by a footpath which climbs steeply from behind Ogwen Cottage, a Mountain Rescue Post, before levelling out into Cwm Idwal. The path then follows the shores of Llyn Idwal past the Idwal Slabs, perhaps some of the most frequently climbed rocks in Britain. It climbs steeply to Twll Du or Devil's Kitchen, a

Tryfan and Glyder Fach

narrow defile of black rock which seems to cut the mountain in half. The whole of Cwm Idwal is a nature reserve with many rare species of alpine plants and orchids found amongst the rocks. It was the early botanists who started the sport of rock climbing as they searched higher and higher for new specimens.

A pleasant afternoon can be enjoyed without leaving the cwm but the higher mountains, are steep and rocky, though in many respects totally different from their neighbours.

Climbing on past Devil's Kitchen the path comes to a small lake (Llyn-y-Cwn) and then divides. To the right the track climbs easily to the summit of Y Garn (3,104ft) then along the crest to Mynydd Perfedd and either west above Marchlyn Mawr, the top lake of the pump storage scheme, to Elidir Fawr (3,029ft) or north to Carnedd-y-Filiast and down into Bethesda.

H
2-3h
****
†††

Taking the track on the left from Llyn-y-Cwn and going south-east, the path rises steeply up the scree-covered slopes of Glyder Fawr (3,279ft) to the summit, a rather desolate boulder-strewn plateau. It continues along the ridge past the well-named Castell-y-Gwynt (Castle of the Winds) to Glyder Fach (3,262ft) and the flat

H
5+h
****
††††

The Llanberis Pass

Narrow gauge steam locomotives from the Llanberis Lake Railway at the Welsh Slate Museum

Cwm Idwal and the Idwal Slabs

stone of the Cantilever, a perched block which seems delicately balanced but has so far defied all the efforts of large and small parties to dislodge it.

The views from both these summits are some of the finest in Snowdonia, looking down on the surrounding mountains and valleys, with the summit of Tryfan seemingly only a step away to the east. The path descends steeply alongside the Bristly Ridge to the cwm and then north back to Ogwen. However the summit of Tryfan

(3,010ft), only a short scramble above, is well worth the extra effort, for this is one of the true mountains of North Wales. With a sharp profile from every viewpoint it stands separated from all others above the valley. On this ascent one's hands will be needed for extra grip, as the path to the top is steep and rocky. The summit is crowned by two great monoliths, imaginatively known as Adam and Eve. They are close together and it is said that a true Welsh mountaineer is one who has stepped from one to the other. With the steep drop below it is safer not to attempt it, but to descend by the much slower, but safer, route back to the cwm, and then north down to Ogwen Cottage.

Between the Nant Ffrancon Pass and Llyn Ogwen and the Conwy Valley is the largest range of hills, which rise steeply above the lake mainly north from Pen-yr-Oleu-wen (3,211ft) to Drum (2,529ft), then sloping more gently on the east to the foothills above Conwy. They are of a completely different character, being more rounded and grass-covered, with only occasional steep cliffs and cwms. The walking is more arduous and the route finding more difficult. As it is a large area with many access points, it is suggested that those considering mountain walking here should equip themselves with a large scale map to gain maximum enjoyment.

Despite this advice, it would be unfair not to give at least a brief description of these hills. The main path ascends from the west end of Llyn Ogwen and rises very steeply for almost 2,000ft to the summit of Pen-yr-Oleu-wen (3,211ft). Once this has been achieved, there is little further climbing for the whole length of the ridge. Circling round the very edge of one of the most perfect cwms, Ffynnon Lloer, the summit of Carnedd Dafydd (3,427ft) is soon reached; then on to Carnedd Llewelyn (3,458ft). From there a spur goes east providing some interesting and mainly downhill walking, and for those who have had enough there is a circular return route to the valley. Going north from Carnedd Llewelyn, the ridge can be followed over Foel Grach (3,196ft), Foel Fras and then down to Drum (2,529ft). This is a full day's excursion, and it is best to arrange transport at the northern end, if a long walk back is to be avoided.

The smaller hills to the south of the main range are split by a series of deep valleys, each containing a lake of individual character dammed to provide water for industry in the Conwy Valley. The

PLACES OF INTEREST IN AND AROUND BETWS-Y-COED

Waterloo Bridge
Built in the same year as the Battle of Waterloo, a superb cast iron bridge carrying the A5 over the river.

Swallow Falls
Good views of tumbling cataract just by the A5 above the village.

National Park Visitor Centre
Large and colourful exhibition on Snowdonia. Children's room, information desk, slide presentations and craft displays.

Conwy Valley Railway Museum
Housed in a purpose-built building adjacent to the station, with many items showing all aspects of railway life.

Capel Garmon
Burial chamber with remains of long barrow. North of A5, follow signs to Capel Garmon.

northernmost, Llyn Eigian, burst its dam in 1925 causing a disastrous flood; the great masonry blocks and deep fissure created can be seen just below the remaining lake. The next, Llyn Cowlyd, is set in bleak uplands, while the two smaller ones to the south, Llyn Crafnant and Llyn Geirionnydd, are in wooded valleys. The latter is a popular spot for daytrippers, yachtsmen and water skiers, though the roar of power boats upsets the serenity of this beautiful spot. All these valleys, with the exception of Cowlyd, can be reached easily by road from the Conwy Valley.

To the south is the **Gwydyr Forest** stretching from Llyn Crafnant to Penmachno and covering many of the hills and valley sides. The forests have been developed since 1921 by the Forestry Commission and are now a Forest Park with free access. They are a fine introduction to the wilder mountains beyond.

There are many footpaths through the forest, some following long forgotten roads to old lead mines and quarries, while others follow delightful little streams to quiet mountain lakes — everybody is welcome provided that they respect the forest and natural environment. As the forest has many old copper and lead mines, care must be taken when walking near the shafts.

The Afon Llugwy at Betws-y-Coed

Capel Garmon burial chamber, high above Betws-y-Coed

The small town of **Betws-y-Coed** is almost surrounded by the forest at the junction of three valleys, the Lledr Valley from the south, the Llugwy Valley from the east and the Conwy Valley to the north. It sits astride the A5 trunk road and is a frequent bottleneck in summer as most of the traffic has to cross the graceful Waterloo Bridge. This cast iron bridge was built in 1815 and carries the inscription in large letters: 'This Arch was Constructed in the Same Year the Battle of Waterloo was Fought', as well as decorative flowers in the spandrels. There are hotels, cafes and many craft shops, while near the railway station is the Conwy Valley Railway Museum. The Tourist Information Centre has descriptive leaflets of the many short walks in the locality and in the nearby forest.

The main road rises through the town and just on the left is an old stone bridge with a small cataract below it — if you are lucky you may see salmon jumping. A few miles upstream and next to the road, are the Swallow Falls, a magnificent sight particularly after rainfall. The next village, **Capel Curig**, is merely a cross roads with a few climbing and other shops and several hotels. The imposing

The Waterloo Bridge, Betws-y-Coed

H
3-4h
**
†††

mountain across the lake is Moel Siabod; from this side it is one of the easier mountain walks. Start about one mile towards Betws-y-Coed at Pont Cyfyng where a small road turns off to a cluster of cottages. The main track begins there and follows an old quarry road which at first rises easily past the slate quarries and then follows the ridge with some easy scrambling to the grass slopes below the rocky summit cairn. There are fine views over the sheer drop to the cwm below. The path along and down the ridge to the Pen-y-Gwryd Hotel gives a long walk; it is best to return the way you came for the views are always different on the way back.

❋   Just outside Capel Curig is Plas-y-Brenin, the National Mountaineering Centre, which provides courses in all grades of walking, climbing and skiing in the surrounding mountains, and canoeing on the nearby lake and river. The centre is open to the public with indoor climbing walls and at the back a dry ski slope. Many courses are introductory and even the most inexperienced can participate.

Past Plas-y-Brenin the road skirts the shores of Llynau Mymbyr and continues up the long glaciated valley with one of the finest

Plas-y-Brenin, the National Mountaineering Centre, with its dry ski slope

views of Snowdon directly ahead. Looking into the horseshoe
formed by the Crib Coch ridge to the right and Lliwedd to the left you
look directly up to the majestic summit in the centre, from here it
always looks forbidding and sombre.

Coming to the junction at the Pen-y-Gwryd Hotel continue
ahead to Nant Gwynant, the road to the right going over Pen-y-Pass
and thence to the Llanberis Pass. As already mentioned the hotel
at the junction was the training headquarters for the first successful
team to conquer Mount Everest in 1953. The main room in the bar
has the signatures of these climbers on the ceiling. It is a comfortable hotel and has long been the centre for the local Mountain
Rescue Team. Across the road on a small hillock is the square base
of a Roman fort which controlled the ancient routeways over this
pass, though a less hospitable posting could hardly be found for
men brought up on the Mediterranean coast.

The road ahead descends easily to **Nant Gwynant** passing a
viewpoint on the right. It is worth a stop for perhaps the finest view
of Snowdon and the valley. Below is Llyn Gwynant above the

The peak of Moel Siabod from the head of the Afon Glaslyn

*Entrance to the
Sygun Copper Mine*

TICKET HOLDERS
PLEASE WAIT HERE
FOR GUIDE

brooding shape of Yr Wyddfa. Continuing on you pass Llyn Gwynant, with its canoeists and windsurfers and Llyn Dinas, always quiet and peaceful and after a few miles arrive at the lovely village of Beddgelert.

Between Llyn Gwynant and Beddgelert is the Sygun Copper Mine which has recently been reopened as a visitor attraction. Visitors are taken along levels and up ladderways, rediscovering the old passageways which had been abandoned so long ago. On the surface it is possible to see the remains of some of the old buildings, reclaimed from a dense rhododendron undergrowth. There is a small café here and video-corner where details of the mine and its reopening may be seen.

Standing at the confluence of two rivers which join to become

PLACES OF INTEREST IN AND AROUND BEDDGELERT

Gelert's Grave
A short walk along the riverbank to legendary grave that gave the village its name.

Sygun Copper Mine
Guided tours around nineteenth-century copper mine and caves with views of Gwynant Valley. Visitor Centre on site. Short or long walks in beautiful surroundings, particularly along river on disused line of old Snowdon Light Railway.

The 'grave' of Gelert,
Prince Llewelyn's
faithful dog

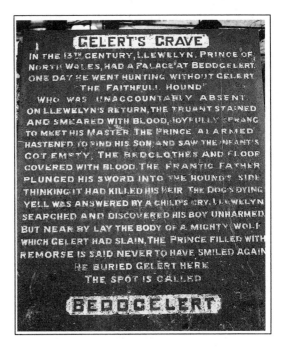

GELERT'S GRAVE

IN THE 13TH CENTURY, LLEWELYN, PRINCE OF NORTH WALES, HAD A PALACE AT BEDDGELERT. ONE DAY HE WENT HUNTING WITHOUT GELERT "THE FAITHFULL HOUND" WHO WAS UNACCOUNTABLY ABSENT. ON LLEWELYN'S RETURN, THE TRUANT STAINED AND SMEARED WITH BLOOD, JOYFULLY SPRANG TO MEET HIS MASTER. THE PRINCE ALARMED HASTENED TO FIND HIS SON, AND SAW THE INFANT'S COT EMPTY, THE BEDCLOTHES AND FLOOR COVERED WITH BLOOD. THE FRANTIC FATHER PLUNGED HIS SWORD INTO THE HOUND'S SIDE THINKING IT HAD KILLED HIS HEIR. THE DOG'S DYING YELL WAS ANSWERED BY A CHILD'S CRY. LLEWELYN SEARCHED AND DISCOVERED HIS BOY UNHARMED, BUT NEAR BY LAY THE BODY OF A MIGHTY WOLF WHICH GELERT HAD SLAIN, THE PRINCE FILLED WITH REMORSE IS SAID NEVER TO HAVE SMILED AGAIN. HE BURIED GELERT HERE THE SPOT IS CALLED

BEDDGELERT

the Afon Glaslyn, **Beddgelert** is a bustling village torn between the tourist trade and the chaos the traffic it brings can cause. It is nevertheless relatively unspoilt and at the heart of the mountains.

The village thrives on the story of the legendary Gelert, a dog belonging to Prince Llewelyn which he slew after returning from a hunting trip on finding that his son was missing and the dog was covered in blood. It was only later that his son was found safe and a wolf dead nearby, obviously killed by the dog. He buried the faithful hound and the 'grave' is just a short stroll alongside the river from the village centre. A similar story appears in other parts of the world, and it is most likely that it was introduced here by an over-zealous publican in the eighteenth century to encourage visitors. It is more probable that the Gelert referred to in the village name was an early Christian connected with a priory which once stood on that site.

Beddgelert is an ideal centre for exploring the surrounding hills, for there are some fine hotels and guest houses; though a little crowded in summer, it has a charm of its own. The old Welsh Highland Railway passed close to the village. A pleasant stroll links up with this by following the signs from the village to Gelert's grave and continuing alongside the river banks to cross the old railway bridge and then along the railway (now disused) to Aberglaslyn. Then a series of tunnels brings one to Nantmor. For a long (about 9 miles), easy, but excellent walk one continues through Nantmor on the minor road, which traces the course of an old road to the junction. Turn left and follow that road past Cae Dafydd Craft Centre and Farm (with tea shop) along the valley with its bubbling stream to pass the slate quarries and descend to Nant Gwynant. A footpath can be followed along the banks of the river and around Llyn Dinas back to Beddgelert.

A variation on this route can be made after emerging from the long tunnel on the railway. Turn left here and follow a good footpath up Cwm Bychan to some old copper mines and the remains of a bucket conveyor. The path then goes off to the left, across a small hollow, to the ridge above Nant Gwynant and then descends the old miners' track to a minor road and thence back to Beddgelert. There are many short and simple walks around the village. It is usually best to enquire locally about walks for the route very much depends on the time available.

South of Beddgelert, and downstream, is the well known **Aberglaslyn Pass** which must feature more often on calendars

Beddgelert

Cnicht and the Moelwyns

The castle folly at Llanfrothen

than any other place in Wales. It has all the components of a classic beauty spot. A steep sided valley, trees, a tumbling river and a bridge all combine perfectly and can be viewed with little effort from the roadside. At one time ships could sail right up to the bridge, but since the building of the embankment across the mouth of the estuary, the land has been reclaimed and the river is impassable from Porthmadog.

The hills to the east of Aberglaslyn are fairly easily accessible on minor roads which branch off the main road from there to Penrhyndeudraeth. The first road up the Nantmor valley has several picnic spots and small parking areas; it is a beautiful area, but the road is narrow. From the high point on that road, where there is an old slate quarry, a good little path opposite a white cottage goes up to Llyn Llagi. The path continues beyond the lake and over the shoulder to Llyn-yr-Adar and on to the ridge of Cnicht. This can be traversed with wonderful views of the estuary and descended until the path breaks off to the right at a col below a small crag. It joins an old packhorse trail which, if followed to the right, goes downhill

H
3+h
**
††††

to the road following a lovely little stream back to the quarry. Several other footpaths leave this road for other lakes, and they are all fairly easy walking but as they may be damp underfoot, it is best to go well shod.

Cnicht, sometimes called the Matterhorn of North Wales, is best seen from the south, and with Moelwyn Bach and Moelwyn Mawr it stands proudly above the estuary. **Croesor**, a small village at the end of a minor road, is the starting point for any walks on that range. The road to Croesor starts by a large gatehouse in Llanfrothen. It is narrow and high walled and passes Plas Brodanw, home of the late Sir Clough Williams-Ellis the architect, best known for the hotel and village of Portmeirion. Opposite the house a gate leads uphill to a small castle with superb views over the estuary; it is a 'folly', being the architect's wedding present from his brother officers during his time in the army. It is a short but very pleasant stroll.

From the car park at Croesor there is a well signposted track which follows the ridge to the top of Cnicht. It is an easy walk, with one difficult scrambling section just below the summit, but if care is taken it should present no problems. The walk is recommended for its ease and views.

H
3h
**
†††

Moelwyn Mawr is best tackled by following the old quarry road beyond the village to the highest quarry, which until recently had a fine collection of buildings still surviving. From the back of the quarry the footpath up and over the shoulder brings one to the top, before descending down the ridge to the south and directly to the village.

H
3-4h
**
†††

Moelwyn Bach, the smaller of the two, can be approached from the south through a small forestry plantation at the high point of the road linking Croesor and Rhyd. The path is not too clear and it is wet underfoot, but once the ridge is reached walking is drier and straightforward: the views from the summit are magnificent; for ease it is suggested that the descent is made by the same route.

H
3h
**
†††

There are many fine walks in this area and it is ideal for a good day out. There are also numerous abandoned quarries and slate mines to interest the industrial archaeologist. These hills are less frequented than those to the north, but there is still much to see and enjoy, though proper dress and equipment are essential.

5

THE LLEYN PENINSULA

In stunning contrast to the mountains of Snowdonia is the Lleyn peninsula to the west, stretching like a long finger towards Ireland. Some twenty-five miles long and between five and ten miles wide it is an area of outstanding beauty and given the more temperate weather it is accustomed to, can compare with any coastline throughout Europe.

It is a land of rolling scenery, dark hills and beautiful coves and beaches. Despite the influx of visitors in summer it has retained its Welsh charm and language. Close to the hills and well provided with facilities for the visitor it can be an ideal base for touring or for those who enjoy a relaxed holiday but occasionally like a good day on the hills. With easy access to the beaches and bays it will suit the boating enthusiast. There are cliffs for the climber, bird watcher and botanist and golf courses for those who enjoy more athletic pursuits.

Divided from the bulk of Snowdonia by a range of hills of grand stature but limited height it has much to occupy the visitor. For those who like to explore the landscape this area is steeped in history both prehistoric and from the more recent Celtic period. Walkers can enjoy the sharp hills or a coastal jaunt. All around there is a great feeling of openness, the sky seems to dominate all the scenery.

For convenience, the Caernarfon-Porthmadog road will be re-

The Nantlle ridge

garded as the eastern boundary of the area. It is a pleasant road ascending gradually from suburban Caernarfon past the old Roman fort of *Segontium* and following the course of the ancient Roman road into the heart of Snowdonia. Heading south the sharp bulk of Mynydd Mawr on the right has the profile of an elephant. Passing below the trunk and along the shores of Llyn Cwellyn and the Snowdon Ranger Youth Hostel, once famous for its 'Ranger' who led walkers to the nearby summit of Snowdon, the road arrives at Rhyd-Ddu.

Turning right, to the west, leads up to **Bwlchgylfin** which gives relatively easy access for walkers to this superb range of hills. Close to the summit of the pass is Llyn-y-Dywarchen, a diminutive lake which was once one of the wonders of Wales. It had a legendary floating island which could carry cattle across the lake; visitors came from far and wide to see this spectacle which is sadly no longer evident.

From the top of the pass, a rather gloomy place, the view to the west is one of slate waste and huge tips. What devastation man has

119

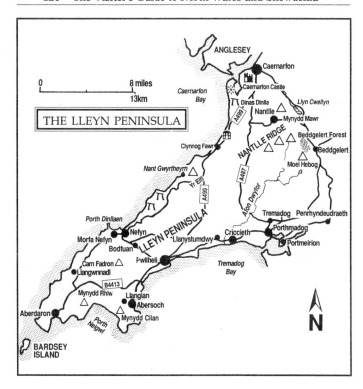

THE LLEYN PENINSULA

created in the pursuit of money! Around the village of **Nantlle** many of these huge craters have now filled with water, but efforts are being made to restore the machinery and workings of one mine above the village.

H
3h
**
††

For the summit of Mynydd Mawr go north on the path which leaves from the top of the pass and follow it from the western end of the lake near a small building. It rises easily at first through a miniature rocky pass up an easy grass slope until it narrows towards the summit with views straight down to Llyn Cwellyn. The descent is by the same route.

To the south of the pass rises Y Garn, a spur of Mynydd Drws-y-Coed, the northernmost peak of the Nantlle ridge. The traverse of the ridge is an excellent day's walking, covering in all five peaks over 2,000ft. The route is not difficult to follow with the aid of a good map and compass, but for many it will be a major expedition and is outside the scope of this guide.

H
aa
day
***
††††

South from Rhyd-Ddu stretches the **Beddgelert Forest**, covering much of the lower slopes of Moel Hebog. The Forestry Commission has done much to encourage people to use the forest; there is an excellent camp site and caravan site, a visitor information centre and shop. Available at the shop is an orienteering map of the forest — for those who have never tried the sport it is an excellent introduction and a good way to spend the afternoon, testing their navigational skills and exploring the forest, but old clothes are essential.

L
¹/₂-3h
*
†††

From the car park in the forest starts one of several paths leading up **Moel Hebog** (2,566ft). It is one of the friendliest mountains in the area, with certainly some of the finest views. The path is clear for most of the way, following the stream right up through the forest, until breaking clear just below a small crag on the left. Half way up the crag, and reached by a tricky scramble is Ogof (cave of) Owain Glyndwr. Overlooking the valley this cave is reputed to be the hide-out of the Welsh fourteenth-century leader but it is so small and damp that it hardly befits the hero's grandeur. On the same crag, but much easier to reach, is a small hollow in the cliff, which is a disused asbestos mine, though the narrow seam must have proved uneconomic.

H
3-5h
**
††††

The path continues more steeply now to the col, and at a wall one turns left for Moel Hebog and right for Moel Lefn (2,094ft), a minor summit that is worth climbing. The summit of Moel Hebog is reached after a steep climb alongside the wall. The views are magnificent: to the north lies the Nantlle ridge; to the east the Snowdon Range and in the distance Moel Siabod, Cnicht and the Moelwyns: south are the Rhinogs and Tremadog Bay; while to the west the Lleyn Peninsula is at one's feet and on a clear day the coast of Ireland can be seen.

One can descend by the same route but it is better to return eastwards down the path to Cwm Cloch farm and Beddgelert and then walk about a mile back to the forest. The route is equally enjoyable if started from Beddgelert, where the path starts just out on the road

Tremadog

Porthmadog Harbour

The Festiniog Railway at Porthmadog Station

to Rhyd-Ddu. Cross the river and go up the lane to a farm at Cwm Cloch. A signpost on the end of the barn directs one up the path which rises easily at first but becomes more steep near the summit.

South of Moel Hebog the lower hills give some pleasant rambling: but as paths are scarce one has to pick one's route carefully.

All give excellent views particularly over the reclaimed estuary of Traeth Mawr to the south. The estuary of the Afon Glaslyn, known as Traeth Mawr, was once said to be the most beautiful in the whole of Wales. It is now about 7,000 acres of reclaimed land, and is frequently flooded after heavy rain. It was created by the building of an embankment (the Cob) across its mouth in 1811 by William Madocks MP. At one time the estuary was navigable up the Aberglaslyn Bridge. Madocks' intention was to create an easy crossing point for traffic to the Lleyn Peninsula in order to open it up for the Irish trade. He also hoped to dry out the enclosed land for farming. His first intention never succeeded, the second has to a certain extent, providing grazing land only.

Madocks built the village of **Tremadog**, and later Porthmadog to be the port for his great plans. Both names have now been converted to the Welsh, so apart from a statue in Porthmadog little evidence remains of his influence on the project. He lived at Tan-yr-Allt above Tremadog and the village was laid out to please him. The poet Shelley was a frequent guest at the house and T. E. Lawrence (Lawrence of Arabia) was born in the village. The village is still of interest to architects and builders, its stone houses neatly built on each side of a square. Below the cliffs what looks like a town hall was in fact a theatre with access from the adjoining hotel on one side, with the cottage at the other end as the changing rooms; it is now a craft shop.

Behind the village, though hidden from the road by woodlands, and stretching for about one mile are Tremadog Rocks. They are a favourite area for rock climbing, particularly if it is raining further inland. The woods at the bottom are a nature reserve, much of it being natural growth with native trees.

Porthmadog was originally planned to be the lesser of the two towns but grew to pre-eminence with the opening of the port. A railway was built across the Cob to the mines at Ffestiniog, so that slates could be exported from the quay. It was intended to be a great cultural centre as well as a port, which no doubt explains why the scheme received the enthusiastic backing of Shelley. The slate trade died when the mines were closed, so that even the old slate sheds have gone — now replaced by holiday flatlets on the quayside. The railway is still running as the famous Festiniog

PLACES TO VISIT IN AND AROUND PORTHMADOG

Maritime Museum
Porthmadog
Based on the sailing ketch
Garlandstone, has displays of
ships and seamen of Gwynedd.
Slate sheds as they used to be.

Porthmadog Pottery
At the end of Snowdon Street,
off the High Street.
Demonstrations of all stages of
pottery making, visitors can
have a go themselves.

Festiniog Railway
Porthmadog
Start of steam railway to
Blaenau Ffestiniog and also
small railway museum and gift
shop on the quay

Tyn Llan Pottery
Penmorfa
Displays of crafts and pottery
from all over Wales. Snacks and
tea available, with picnic spot.
Off A487 north of Tremadog

Brynkir Woollen Mills
Dolbenmaen. East of A487, 5
miles north of Tremadog.
Weavers of tapestries, bed-
spreads and smaller items in
traditional patterns.

Welsh Highland Railway
Tremadog Road, Porthmadog.
Steam trains and workshops,
limited service but great plans
for the future.

Railway, with its terminus on the quayside. The railway, which used
the anglicised version of Ffestiniog without the double 'f', was built
in 1836 and has the distinction of being the oldest narrow gauge
railway in the world. Originally the trucks loaded with slate descended from the quarries under gravity, and the empty ones
hauled back up by horses. It was the first narrow gauge line to
introduce steam locomotives, in 1863, and the first to use the
'Fairlie' type of double locomotives which were articulated in the
middle to accommodate the very tight curves. These unusual steam
locomotives are still in use as well as a number of more conventional ones. The $13^3/_4$-mile journey rises over 700ft and there are
fine views from the train.

The port has now been taken over by yachtsmen, but because
of the silting of the estuary they must choose their sailing times by

the tide. Until recent years it was a pleasant little harbour to stroll around, but there is now little of interest, though with the opening of a Maritime Museum in an original sailing ship, efforts are being made to revitalise it. The town has a busy shopping centre with many Welsh craft shops to entice the visitor, and a pottery on the outskirts of the town where all are welcome to try their hand.

Several beaches are easily reached from the town centre; the nearest just around the headland is Borth-y-Gest, which has fine golden sands and small coves, but bathing is not too safe as the estuary is tidal. Next to it is Morfa Bychan or Black Rock Sands, much safer for bathing but more dangerous for walking. This is a two-mile stretch of wide flat beach backed by a large caravan site; car parking is allowed on the beach.

L
¹/₂-2h
*
†††

Just inland is the grand little hill of Moel-y-Gest, which is a pleasant viewpoint from which to survey the coast. There are several signposted footpaths which take no more than half an hour to the summit.

Several minor roads leave the main Caernarfon road (A4085) about two miles outside Tremadog. The first goes up to Cwm Ystradllyn past the magnificent ruin of a slate mill and then up to a reservoir. Parking is possible at the end of the road, and the hill in front is an easier alternative route to the summit of Moel Hebog. The peaceful valley may be explored by following the unmetalled road. The retaining wall below the slate tip has a superb curve.

H
2h
**
†††

The road to the north passes Brynkir Woollen Mills (open to the public) where Welsh tapestries, flannels and tweeds are woven, and continues up to Cwm Pennant. This is a beautiful little valley as it winds right into the hills with lots of tumbling streams and places to walk or picnic. It is also possible to reach this valley by turning off the main road at Dolbenmaen just past the castle mound.

Criccieth, the next town along the coast, is a popular resort with several good beaches; the one immediately in front of the town is a good place to launch a dinghy or swim. Above the harbour is the only major castle on the Lleyn peninsula and though little remains apart from the gateway it looks impressive from any angle. It is not one of Edward I's castles, being merely enlarged by him on the site of an earlier Welsh fortress. From the castle the views are magnificent and with the well developed hotel trade in the town it is an

Ruined slate mill at Cwm Ystradllyn

The seashore at Criccieth

BEACHES ON THE LLEYN PENINSULA'S SOUTH COAST

Near Porthmadog
Borth-y-Gest: Small bays and coves and tidal estuary.
Black Rock Sands: Two miles of good wide sands, safe bathing, drive your car onto the beach. Very popular and backed by caravan sites.

Criccieth
Two fine beaches divided by castle, safe bathing and launching facilities for small boats.

Pwllheli
Two safe beaches:
Gimblet Rock to south, shingle and sand;
Glandol beach to east, safe and sandy.

Llanbedrog
Sandy bay sheltered by

headland. Ideal for bathing, boating, fishing and walks on headland.

Abersoch
Popular seaside resort with miles of fine golden sands. Very popular but still quite charming. Yacht club and mooring facilities, a sailor's paradise.

Porth Neigwl (Hell's Mouth)
Open sandy beach about 4 miles long, plenty of room for everybody.

Aberdaron
Good beach with safe bathing and boating, last stop for the pilgrims on the way to Bardsey Island. Interesting old church on the edge of the beach. Good headland walks.

excellent centre for touring the peninsula and mountains. Lloyd George, the statesman and Prime Minister, knew Criccieth well, for he spent his childhood in **Llanystumdwy**, just two miles away. He was educated in the village and died at Ty Newydd, a house he owned above the Criccieth road. His grave, designed by Sir Clough Williams-Ellis, is beside the river close to the bridge. In the village is a small museum with many mementoes of him.

Shortly after Llanystumdwy, the road divides, that to the north providing a fast route across the Lleyn to Nefyn, while the main road continues to amble down the coast. About one mile after passing a holiday camp (day visitors are allowed), a small signpost directs one to Penarth Fawr, an interesting and attractive fifteenth-century

Grave of Lloyd George beside the river at Llanystumdwy

manor house. Consisting basically of one room, it is well preserved and generally fairly quiet.

Pwllheli, the administrative centre and largest town, is perhaps the capital of the Lleyn. It is an ancient Welsh borough which received its charter from the Black Prince in 1355, and although it now has little of historical interest, with its shops and beaches it is a popular centre for holidaymakers. The town and beach are separated by about half a mile and several centuries, the town being typically old Welsh and the houses along the promenade being a mixture of Victorian and modern. The harbour, protected by a hook of land which almost encloses it, is safe and, with Gimlet Rock at its entrance, easy to find.

The wide sandy bay at Abersoch

The sand and shingle beaches face south and stretch for almost five miles to Llanbedrog and its rocky point. The bathing is excellent along the whole coastline and once round the headland the beaches continue for several more miles along St Tudwal's Bay.

A few miles from Pwllheli along the road to Nefyn is **Bodfuan**, which was the abode of St Buan in the sixth century. The church has stained glass depicting St Cudfan receiving the body of the saint on Bardsey Island. Bodfuan Woods were once owned by Ann Boleyn and later Elizabeth I.

Back on the south coast, **Abersoch** is a favourite spot and the small town is now surrounded by caravan sites and holiday homes. It is a delightful little village with a small harbour, that has developed in the last twenty to thirty years as the centre for boating enthusiasts in North Wales. With two sheltered bays and wide safe beaches it is ideal for launching and sailing boats of all sizes.

Just off the coast are two small islands, no longer inhabited, known as St Tudwal's Islands, after the saint who founded a chapel there in the sixth century. Little remains of its Augustinian priory, and the islands are left to the birds and the lighthouse. Boat trips can be taken around the islands, thus also giving the opportunity to view the superb coastline from the sea.

Nearing the end of the Lleyn the villages seem to get smaller and more widely scattered. **Llangian**, near Abersoch, is of some interest as one of the best kept villages in the county and for the sixth-century stone in the churchyard carved in Latin commemorating Melus, the first mention of a doctor in Wales.

Three miles south-west of Abersoch is Mynydd Cilan, an open cliff-top area with wonderful views belonging to the National Trust. Then, crossing behind the long bay of Porth Neigwl or Hell's Mouth, the road climbs steeply over the shoulder of Mynydd Rhiw. The Plas yn Rhiw estate covers 400 acres and is criss-crossed by tracks and almost surrounded by roads. Rising to 999ft high, it has some pleasant walks with excellent views of the coastline. Early man may have appreciated the hill for the same reason, for there are several archaeological sites to be found on the hillside, including at the northern end a Stone Age axe factory. Towards Aberdaron the scenery is superb but somewhat marred by what seems like a forest of telegraph and electricity poles and their overhead lines.

Y Gegin Fawr, Aberdaron, where pilgrims ate before crossing to Bardsey Island

Aberdaron is a tiny village on the very edge of the sea, the last stop for the pilgrims on their way to Bardsey Island. A café and a souvenir shop, Y Gegin Fawr, the Big Kitchen, was formerly a hostel and resting place before the crossing, while the small church of St Hywyn, on the very edge of the shore, served their spiritual needs on the last lap. The double-naved church dates from the twelfth to fifteenth centuries. It was built on the site of an ancient Celtic oratory which was founded around the end of the fifth century by Hywyn, who is said to have come from Brittany with Cadfan, the founder of the monastery on Bardsey Island.

Bardsey Island, a mile long by half a mile wide, had various names in Welsh, but Ynys Enlli, or Island of Currents, as many a sailor and pilgrim will testify, is the most appropriate. Bardsey (a Norse name) was a refuge for monks escaping massacre by the Saxons and has been a place of pilgrimage since the sixth century, becoming so popular that many of the Welsh bishops had their

Bardsey Island

bodies transported and buried there. Little remains of the priory and the later flourishing community, but it is still a place surrounded by myths, mists and legends. Now it is an important centre for the study of birds and is owned by the Bardsey Island Trust.

Braich y Pwll, the headland opposite Bardsey Island, is a fine windswept spot owned by the National Trust. It is a superb place to appreciate the beauty and setting of the island with only the birds for company. It is the most westerly point of Wales and covers 122 acres, including Mynydd Gwyddel and Mynydd Mawr. Pilgrims embarked here for Bardsey — there was once a chapel here (St Mary's) and it is still possible to find St Mary's Well, although great care should be taken. A short way north there are walks on the common land of Mynydd Anelog, with fine views across to Bardsey and to Aberdaron Bay.

L
*
†††

Northwards the cliff scenery is magnificent and there are many fine walks, broken only by the fine coves of Porth Oer and Porth Golmon. The former is more commonly known as Whistling Sands for the remarkable little squeak given off as one walks on it or runs

BEACHES ON THE NORTHERN SIDE OF THE LLEYN PENINSULA

Whistling Sands (Porth Oer)
Beautiful bay with safe bathing and unique sands that whistle as you walk across them.

Porth Iago
Approached along farm track. Delightful cove, worth finding, a good day out for the whole family.

Porth Golmon (Penllech Beach)
Long stretch of sand with rocks and cliff walks, caves, fishing and good bathing. Interesting church in the village of Llangwnnadl.

Tudweiliog
Pleasant beach with fine sands, fairly small but private. Lovely walks along the coast.

Edern
Safe bathing, good fishing and boats for hire, power and row boats.

Nefyn and Morfa Nefyn
Excellent beaches on wide sandy bays. Popular resorts with bathing, boating and fishing. Golf course on headland. The small village of Porth Dinllaen (along beach or walk over golf course) is well worth a visit, has a pub and a lifeboat station.

one's hands through the dry sand. Apparently the quartz grains of the sand are rounded and of uniform size, and when moved, produces a note of uniform pitch. At Porth Golmon it used to be possible to see cows walking down to and along the Penllech Beach at low tide, returning again to their grazing land before the sea came up again, but this unusual practice seems now to have ceased! Near Porth Oer is Carreg Hall, once the ancient house of Welsh chieftains, but now engaged in the peaceful pursuit of serving afternoon teas.

From this section of coast the most obvious feature when looking inland is the conical hill which thrusts its way upwards. This is Carn Fadron (1,217 ft) equidistant between the north and south shores, and the views from its summit are excellent. The hill has innumerable ancient trackways with much evidence of Iron Age settlement, and its exploration provides a pleasant alternative to

L
$^1/_2$-2h
**
†††

Porth Golmon

lounging on the beach.

Near Porth Golmon is the village of **Llangwnnadl**, with its unusual church in a wooded valley running down to the sea. Founded in AD540 it boasts three naves and three altars. On the south wall is the tombstone of the patron saint (St Gwynhoedl) which is thought to date from about AD600. The chalice and paten have been in continuous use since 1574.

Nefyn and **Morfa Nefyn** are the most popular holiday centres along this coast. They both have fine sheltered beaches, ideal for boating and bathing, and, like most of the beaches on the peninsula, have superb views of the mountains, in this case Yr Eifl or The Rivals. Lacking pleasure parks and sideshows, these villages are ideal for quiet family holidays, with many guest houses and hotels and with caravan sites nearby.

Nefyn is the larger of the two and was once a major resting point for the pilgrims to Bardsey Island. **Porth Dinllaen** is a fine natural harbour and its small community can be reached only by a walk along the beach or across the golf course from Morfa Nefyn. It is a

PLACES OF INTEREST NEAR NEFYN

Tre'r-Ceiri
By the footpath, leave the B4417 at top of the hill between Llithfaen and Llanaelhaearn north of Nefyn.
Britain's oldest walled village. Built on the crown of a hill. Remains of 250 or so stone huts surrounded by several walls. Built about 3,000-4,000 years ago. Worth the effort of seeing.

Nant Gwrtheyrn
Approach only on foot, about $3/_4$ mile from car park. Turn off in centre of village of Llithfaen towards the sea, off B4417, 5 miles north of Nefyn. Accessible old quarrying village in ancient Vortigerns Valley, on sea side of Yr Eifl. An idyllic spot with small beach. Being renovated as a centre for Welsh studies.

delightful collection of beach cottages, mostly holiday homes, and a pub. A gentle stroll at low level around the headland takes one to the lifeboat station and a small sandy beach.

Nefyn, and more particularly Porth Dinllaen, was suggested during the early nineteenth century as an alternative to Holyhead as the major port to Ireland. The defeat of the motion by one vote in parliament, saved this beautiful stretch of coast for all to enjoy. North along the beach from Nefyn is Bird Rock, a craggy headland appropriately named for the many different species found there.

Continuing along the coast road from Nefyn, the ancient church of St Beuno at **Pistyll** is worth a visit. The corner stone at the eastern end of the north wall is one of only three known to exist. There is a lepers' window on the north side of the chancel and a saint is buried beneath the altar, possibly St Beuno himself. A mural on the north wall is in red ochre and represents the crucifixion, while high on the wall by the altar window is the date 1050 cut into the stone.

Towering above this stretch of coastland and visible from almost anywhere on Lleyn is Yr Eifl, anglicised to 'The Rivals' but meaning The Forks, because of its three peaks. The highest (1,849ft) is flanked on the seaward side by a much quarried summit (1,458ft), and on the inland side by the third peak (1,591ft), surmounted by the

The Nefyn coast looking towards Yr Eifl (The Rivals)

ruins of the Iron Age hillfort village of Tre'r Ceiri. This site, reached by a steep path from a stile on the Llanaelhaearn road, has the best preserved and most extensive collection of walled huts in the country. What a superb situation for a village. The site covers about five acres of the hill top. Surrounded by several defensive walls which vary in thickness from 7ft to 11ft (the inner one still has much of its parapet), it contains the remains of about fifty huts. Though never properly excavated, and unfortunately not under any obvious protection, it is well worth making the effort to see, but on account of lack of care by visitors, it has over the last few years shown a visible deterioration. A Bronze Age cairn of an earlier date can be seen at its north-eastern point.

From this site the summit of Yr Eifl is reached by an easy path which leads from the south end of Tre'r Ceiri down to a shallow valley and up to the highest peak on the Lleyn. The views are extensive — note down at the foot of the mountain perched almost on the edge of the sea a small village in a dark valley. This is **Nant Gwrtheyrn**, a tiny hamlet once dependent on quarrying, which can

PLACES OF INTEREST ON THE LLEYN PENINSULA'S NORTHERN COAST

Clynnog Fawr Church
On A499 south of Caernarfon.
One of the first churches in
Wales, dedicated to St Beuno.
The rebuilt church stands on the
site of an ancient monastery.
Contains many old relics. Close
to the church is an old burial
site, interesting because the
capstone is carved with
hundreds of cups and rings.

Dinas Dinlle
Off A499, towards Llandwrog
about 5 miles south of Caernarfon.
Oval mound with ramparts and
ditch, an ancient defensive spot
used by British and Romans.

Fort Belan
Eighteenth-century fort with
cannons, maritime museum and
old forge. Tea rooms and gift
shop with pottery. Train rides,
horse rides and even plane rides
above the mountains of
Snowdonia. Something for
everyone. As above but
continue past mound to
aerodrome and headland.

Museum of Old Welsh County Life
Tai'n Lon, Clynnog Fawr, 10
miles south of Caernarfon.
Housed in seventeenth-century
corn mill.

can be reached only by foot down a steep and winding road, There
is a convenient car park at the end of the road leading seawards
from the crossroads in Llithfaen. The descent from the car park on
foot for about a mile brings one to a village of utter peace and quiet
without motor cars. The village is simply two lines of cottages set
around a square and the inevitable chapel. After lying in ruins for
many years the cottages are now being renovated to provide a
centre for Welsh language studies. Below is a fine stretch of sandy
beach.

L
2h
*
†††

The climb back to the car park is a reminder of the plight of the
earlier inhabitants and their weekly visit to the shops. The valley is
steep-sided and sometimes sombre, the reason perhaps for its
other name, Vortigern's Valley. Legend has it that Vortigern, one
time British King, took refuge here before being struck down by

heavenly fire.

The northern side of the hills is less interesting on account of extensive quarrying around Trefor. On the road to Caernarfon the church of **Clynnog Fawr** is worthy of interest. Founded by St Beuno in AD616, it is one of the mother churches of Wales. Until the Dissolution it was a monastery, but the present church dates only from the sixteenth century. It contains many relics of the early saint and he is said to be buried there. Nearby is a much older burial site. Close to the shore and just west of the church is an ancient burial chamber with a cap stone about 6ft high by 8ft long and 5ft wide carved with hundreds of cups or depressions.

The coast continues northwards towards the Menai Straits with an ancient site, and a much more recent one to visit. Taking the road to Llandwrog and to the tip of the Straits you pass the conspicuous Iron Age fort of Dinas Dinlle. It is roughly oval with two ramparts and a ditch, and was probably also used by the Romans. Further on, at the very tip of the headland, is the eighteenth-century Fort Belan, built by Thomas Wynne (Lord Newborough) and garrisoned by a force of 400 men which he raised and equipped at his own expense. It was intended to defend Caernarfon from the French during the Napoleonic wars and as such it was a magnanimous gesture that nearly broke him. Today the fort is one of the area's newest attractions. Besides the building and many of the original features, it has a mini-railway, a pottery, a café and a gift shop. There is something for the whole family — even a light aeroplane for trips over the area and mountains.

Caernarfon is the starting and finishing point for many journeys. To the south the peninsula stretches its arm lazily towards Ireland, its coastline one of the finest in Europe.

6

ANGLESEY

Anglesey is the largest island off the coast of Wales and England. Although separated only by the Menai Straits, which vary from several hundred yards to several miles in width, it retains all the character of an island. The climate is generally milder and drier than that of the mainland nearby, making it ideal for seaside holidays. There are many sandy beaches easily accessible for swimming or boating.

Many visitors to the island will be aware of its prehistoric connections with the Druids and Celtic Christianity, for legend and fact about the past are inextricably mixed. Perhaps like modern visitors the early settlers found the climate more amenable than the mainland and the nearby mountains. There is much evidence of early man's use of the land, and visitors are today welcomed to the island by the sign *'Mon, Mam Cymru*—Anglesey, Mother of Wales'. This title comes from the island's early fertility and farming habits. It was always a major supplier of grain to the rest of Wales, for it was said that more grain was grown in Anglesey, the smallest county, than in the rest of the country. Today many of the fields are only pastureland.

Compared with the nearby mountains of Snowdonia, the island is flat, the highest point being just over 500ft above sea level. Geographically there are some fine examples of ancient rocks

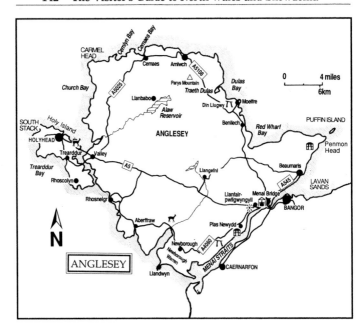

including Pre-Cambrian sandstone and limestone that come to the surface at several places. The main attraction, however, is its coastline, with its sandy beaches and quiet coves.

The Menai Straits, though narrow, are notorious for the tides that race through them and which have made the crossing until recently dangerous and fraught with difficulty. There were at one time seven ferries across the Straits all greatly overcharging for the short trip. The most common route was on foot across the Lavan Sands near Bangor and then by ferry across the remaining water to Beaumaris (Biwmares). Cattle going to market were forced to swim across, urged on by the drovers in the boats, but losses were high and life hazardous for all travellers.

 Today's visitor is more fortunate, for in 1826 Thomas Telford completed his remarkable suspension bridge as part of the London to Holyhead (Caergybi) road. Faced with the problem of bridging the Straits but allowing room for the tall fully rigged sailing ships to

Menai Straits from Port Dinorwig

Telford's road bridge over the Menai Straits

143

The rebuilt Britannia Bridge, which now carries both road and rail

pass underneath, he built the world's second chain suspension bridge. The towers of locally quarried limestone held the massive chains which were anchored into the solid rock at each end, with the road suspended below on wrought iron rods. For the first time it became possible to cross to and from the mainland with dry feet for a small toll charge, and stage coaches and mail coaches made the bridge an instant success. The graceful lines of the bridge were unfortunately not designed for twentieth-century loads and in 1936 major strengthening took place. Though not detracting from the appearance of the bridge, it has enabled it to cope with today's traffic.

The neighbouring Britannia Bridge had an equally illustrious past. Another great engineer, Robert Stephenson, built the railway between London and Holyhead for the Irish ferry. Faced also with the problem of sailing ships he solved it by constructing two parallel wrought-iron tubes high above the water between three towers, at the time a unique solution. Opened in 1850 and in continuous use

until 1970, when it was accidentally destroyed by fire, it was a tribu
to the foresight of the Victorian engineers. The re-modelled Britan
nia Bridge has one level for trains and an upper level for road traffic
and though perhaps not as graceful as the earlier bridge it has at
least lightened the load on Telford's Suspension Bridge and eased
the traffic-flow problem in summer. Much of Stephenson's original
work remains incorporated in the new bridge.

The first Marquess of Anglesey greets all visitors to the island as
they cross the Straits. From high on his limestone column he
surveys his domain and casts an approving eye over the two
bridges. Inside there are steps up to a balustrade surrounding the
top. It provides a dizzy vantage point from which to survey the
island, the Straits and the mountains of Snowdonia, but it is not for
the acrophobic. Unfortunately the marquess never saw the statue,
for he died at the age of 86, five years before it was completed. He
rose to fame as the Duke of Wellington's second in command at the
Battle of Waterloo. As Lord Paget, he had been accompanying the
duke from the battlefield when a cannon ball smashed his leg. 'By
God, sir, I've lost my leg' he shouted to the Duke. 'By God, sir, so
you have' replied Wellington, and resumed surveying the retreating
French. For his bravery at that battle he was created the First

The railway station sign at Llanfair PG

Board showing the scale of charges payable at the Llanfair PG toll house

Telford's octagonal toll house at Llanfair PG on the London to Holyhead road

Plas Newydd on the shores of the Menai Straits

The chambered cairn of Bryn-Celli-Ddu

PLACES OF INTEREST AROUND MENAI

Llanfairpwllgwyngyllogerych-wyrndrobwllllantysiliogo-gogoch
Village with the world's longest place name, also the longest platform ticket in the world, available at the railway station souvenir shop. Officially known as Llanfair PG.

Marquess of Anglesey's Column
90ft tall with statue on top commemorating the First Marquess, Lord Paget. Views from platform of mountains and Menai Straits are superb.

Plas Newydd
Off A4080 two miles from Llanfair PG.
Home of Marquess of Anglesey, on edge of Menai Straits, with many fine pictures, some by Rex Whistler, and also mementoes of the Battle of Waterloo. Beautiful grounds.

Toll House, Llanfair PG
On A5 at start of village. Last to operate, until 1895, still displays tolls.

Plas Goch Leisure Park
On side of Menai Straits next door to Plas Newydd.
Caravan site, swimming pool, picnic areas and mini golf. Many other attractions including restaurant and disco in evening.

Bryn-Celli-Ddu
$1\frac{1}{2}$ miles north of A4080 to Llanddaniel Fab, walk up farm track.
Best preserved burial mound with huge stones and passage. Probably early Bronze Age.

Brynsiencyn
There are many ancient sites in the fields around the village including burial chambers and earthworks.

Brynsiencyn Pottery
In centre of the village off A4080.

Anglesey Sea Zoo
Brynsiencyn
Aquarium with displays of marine animals from Britain's coast.

Marquess of Anglesey. With his family he lived at Plas Newydd just a mile away and despite his wooden leg he continued to have a successful career in government.

The A5 crosses the two bridges and runs by the marquess' feet.

It then turns inland to cross the island, and very soon probably the most famous village in Anglesey. Known th Britain for having the longest name is **Llanfairpwllgwyr** quite simply Llanfair PG. The name was further extended t of fifty-eight letters by a local wit at the end of the last c presumably for the benefit of tourists and became Llanfairpwllgwyngyllogerychwyrndrobwllllantysiliogogogoch. The tiny station has the doubtful distinction of issuing the longest platform ticket in the world and probably also having the longest sign.

By the side of the road on the way into the village is an octagonal toll house designed by Telford. It was the last toll house to operate in Wales, finally opening its gates in 1895, and it still bears the sign stating the tolls. This attractive building is a tribute to the genius of the engineer who did everything so well.

The A5 continues its journey to its destination at Holyhead almost bisecting the island in the process. It is not a particularly exciting drive, for the scenery is fairly plain and the road seems to stretch endlessly in front. Unless one is dashing to the ferry to Ireland or off to climb the sea cliffs on Holy Island it is infinitely more pleasant to take the less busy roads that follow the coast.

It is convenient to start from the Anglesey Column and take the A4080 which runs parallel with the Menai Straits. After about a mile is the house of **Plas Newydd** between the road and the Straits. One may take the opportunity to relax in the tranquil gardens and take in the magnificent views across the mountains of Snowdonia. Plas Newydd was the home of the First Marquess of Anglesey, and it now has a small museum devoted to his military career with some mementoes of Waterloo. It was built in the eighteenth century by James Wyatt, and there are some fine rooms, furniture and por- traits, as well as sketches, letters and more important works by Rex Whistler including his largest wall painting. This huge mural is well worth stopping to examine in detail. Fortunately a guide is nearby to explain its many features and the actual people who are featured on it. Perhaps one of its most memorable features is the perspec- tive. Whichever end of this long room you happen to be at, the painted flagstones above the sea wall appear to be laid towards you! Outside, the lawns slope down to the sea wall. During the

The wide sweep of Newborough Warren's sandy beach

Anglesey Sea Zoo, Brynsiencyn

summer a boat service from the quay at Caernarfon offers trips along the straits to the house, a most unusual approach.

Nearby is the Plas Goch Leisure Park, which seems to have something for everybody — a heated outdoor swimming pool, play and picnic areas, bars, cafés and a caravan park. All this is situated in the 200 acres of parkland surrounding the fifteenth-century Manor House. With a direct frontage on to the Straits it is also well equipped for watersports.

On the opposite side of the road to Plas Goch, and up a short lane, is the chambered cairn of Bryn-Celli-Ddu. This is the best preserved of all the burial chambers on Anglesey and is easily accessible on foot from the road. Originally 160ft in diameter and covering the whole of the area inside the fenced enclosure, little was found when it was excavated in 1928. The stone chamber dates from about 2000BC but the covering mound is a modern weather protection. From the car park is a gateway to the farm and it is a short walk along the lane to the cairn.

This southern corner of the island has many similar burial chambers, though none quite as well preserved as Bryn-Celli-Ddu. It does indicate that this was probably the most inhabited part of the island in ancient times. The sea is nearby, the land is flat and it was not as tree-covered as elsewhere. Stories of Druids are well known and give Anglesey a reputation it has never quite lived down. They were not the fearsome people we have come to expect, but the religious leaders of a particular sect, living on the island to escape persecution by the Romans. The burial chambers and cairns in the area probably even pre-date the Druids and are not, as many people imagine, the sacrificial altars of these notorious priests. Though there is in fact very little evidence of their religious monuments, it is known that this particular corner of the island was their headquarters in the early centuries after Christ.

On the edge of the Menai Straits, almost opposite Caernarfon, is the Anglesy Sea Zoo. This marine aquarium has examples of sea life from all round Britain's coast, including some species which are now quite scarce.

No love was lost between the Romans and Druids, and after a fearsome battle on the very edge of the Straits the Romans succeeded in invading the island. They destroyed everything connected with the religion and subdued the people. It was not until several centuries after the withdrawal of the Romans that Anglesey re-established itself as a religious centre with the coming of Christianity.

Newborough, formerly Rhosyr, was built to house the people displaced by Edward I during the construction of Beaumaris Castle. The area beyond the village towards the sea, is not one of the busiest parts of the island but it is certainly one of the nicest. From the centre of the village a narrow road goes out to the forest behind the town. There is a charge to enter the forest by road, which gives access to one of the finest beaches in North Wales, with car parks and picnic spots.

The forest is one vast nature reserve covering the sand dunes and salt marshes behind the sea shore. Known as Newborough Warren for the number of rabbits which used to live there — 80,000 were trapped annually — the dunes cover the old village of Rhosyr and its field system. It is hoped that the trees and grasses recently

PLACES OF INTEREST ON THE SOUTHERN SIDE OF ANGLESEY

Newborough Warren and Malltraeth Sands
Superb beach surrounded by forest with many forest trails and picnic spots. Access to car park behind dunes (small toll).

Llanddwyn
Off A4080 in Newborough village. Approach across beach from Newborough Warren. A peninsula of Pre-Cambrian rock, now a nature reserve, with old cottages, lifeboat station and lighthouse. A grand spot for views of the hills across the bay.

Aberffraw
Sandy beach with island church of St Cwfan on site of early Celtic church.

Glantraeth Zoo Garden
Off B4422 between Newborough and Aberffraw. Collection of small animals in private grounds. Ideal for children, also farm museum and restaurant.

Rhosneigr
Sandy beaches ideal for bathing and boating. Popular resort with many areas for birdwatching around the village.

Valley Airfield
Off A5 before crossing to Holy Island.
Car park near RAF aerodrome for 'plane spotters'. Jet trainers and helicopters can be seen coming and going frequently.

planted will stabilise the drifting sands. There are several paths and nature trails through the reserve and visitors should stay on the marked paths. An information leaflet is available on the site.

Besides the extensive forests there is a huge beach and foreshore with fine golden sands. It is close to the car park and is never crowded, stretching for several miles in each direction. It is a short walk across the beach to **Llanddwyn Island**, a promontory connected to the mainland by a narrow strip of rock. The island is a nature reserve criss-crossed by easily followed footpaths. Many wild flowers grow in the grass and undergrowth; visitors are asked to stay on the paths. Birds can be seen nesting around the island's cliffs, and there are superb views of the mainland hills.

On the tip of the island is a lighthouse and lifeboat station above a small bay. The lifeboatmen's cottages have been renovated as a visitor centre where there are leaflets giving an outline of the flora and fauna in the area. The adjacent cottages are furnished in original style giving a glimpse of eighteenth-century life there. There are several more miles of beach with Malltraeth sands to the north of the island, all accessible from the car park. The area is highly recommended for a fascinating day out.

Until the building of an embankment connecting Newborough with Malltraeth the estuary of the Afon Cefni almost cut the island in half. Now the low lying land is being turned into pastureland, with the estuary on the seaward side of the embankment silting up to create even more expanses of sand at low tide, teeming with wild fowl and waders.

Aberffraw, just beyond Newborough, was for many centuries the capital of Gwynedd and home of the Welsh Princes. Nothing remains today of their palaces, though a Norman arch in the church of St Beuno is traditionally said to have been built by them. The village, a busy port before the coming of the railways, is now a popular holiday centre with some fine beaches and rocky headlands. Accessible at low tide is the tiny church of St Cwyfan, built on a small island. It is thought to have been founded originally in the seventh century but was extensively rebuilt in 1893.

The bays to the north were the haunt of the eighteenth-century wreckers who lured ships on to the nearby rocks. Today they are popular with yachtsmen and weekend sailors, and some of them are particularly suitable for canoe surfing. **Rhosneigr** stands between two beautiful bays, both excellent for swimming and water sports. It was a popular Edwardian resort, and has remained an ideal family holiday town. The extensive area of gorse-covered dunes just to the north is Tywyn Trewan Common, a paradise for bird watchers and botanists.

For those who prefer to watch the creations of modern technology the nearby RAF aerodrome at **Valley** is the home of the RAF advanced jet flying school and the regional centre for the air/sea rescue service. Aircraft and helicopters are coming and going all day long, many on training flights, and there is a car park for plane spotters. The airfield was originally built in 1941 as a terminal for transatlantic crossings for the USAF. During its construction a large cache of bronze weapons and other implements was found in a

The walls of the Roman fort at Holyhead

lake. Known as the Llyn Cerrig Bach hoard, it is now in the National Museum of Wales and is thought to have been votive offerings for Iron Age religious ceremonies.

Across the bay is **Holy Island (Ynys Gybi)**, separated by a narrow strip of water from the main island, and for many centuries the religious centre of Anglesey. Thought to have been the religious stronghold of the Druids, it was settled in the sixth century by St Cybi who built a small church within the remains of the Roman fort at Holyhead. He was a formidable character who travelled the whole of Anglesey converting the people. There is still a church dedicated to him within the walls of the Roman fort at Holyhead, but it is a much more recent building with some fine carved stonework. Roman stonework is clearly seen in the walls of the churchyard. The town of Holyhead is still known in Welsh as Caergybi, Gybi's fortress.

Holyhead is a bustling town, which has grown to be the largest in Anglesey. It is basically a seaport servicing the busy Irish ferry boats and the developing trade in container ships. The town

South Stack Lighthouse, Holy Island

surrounds the harbour and is gradually spreading up the slopes of Holyhead mountain. Holyhead is also developing as a yachting centre with a pleasant shingle beach and safe mooring, protected by a long breakwater. A promenade, running along its full length, makes it also extremely popular for sea fishermen.

It has been difficult to avoid the busy A5 trunk road as it carves its way so impressively through the heart of North Wales, particularly as several of the bridges are so significant in the development of the area and are impressive features in their own right. In Holyhead the road finally reaches its destination and terminates at a triumphal arch on the quayside, just 267 miles from Marble Arch in London — a triumph of engineering in its time.

Behind the town, Holyhead Mountain rises gently to the low banks of an ancient hill fort of indeterminate age on its summit. Much of the headland is a nature reserve controlled by the Royal

PLACES OF INTEREST ON HOLY ISLAND

Beaches

Holyhead
Sand and shingle beach inside harbour breakwater (1½ mile long).

Trearddur Bay
Fine sands with rocky outcrops, ideal for bathing and many water sports.

Rhoscolyn
Sandy beaches with good sheltered bathing. Fine cliff walks.

Silver Bay
Sandy beach near mouth of channel between the two islands.

Holyhead (Caergybi)

Roman walls surrounding church of St Gybi, near town centre. Triumphal arch to celebrate completion of A5 and visit of George IV. Busy port for Irish ferries protected by 1½ mile breakwater with road along. Ideal for fishing.

South Stack Lighthouse

Steps down give magnificent views of cliffs with nesting birds and rock climbers. Lighthouse open in afternoons during summer.

Ellen's Tower

Bird observatory overlooking South Stack Lighthouse and cliffs, just below the car park for the lighthouse. All the headland is owned by the RSPB. Care should be taken when walking in the area.

Holyhead Mountain Hut Circles

By road to South Stack. Remains of an extensive settlement of second-fourth centuries. Circular and square huts, once thatched. Some have central hearths and upright slabs showing positions of beds and seats.

Feilw Standing Stones

Penrhos, 1¾ mile south-west of Holyhead.
Two stones believed to be the remains of a larger circle. There are several other standing stones on the island for those interested in these antiquities.

Penrhos

Off A5 south of Holyhead. Nature reserve with woodlands and sea birds. Nature trails.

Society for the Protection of Birds. The steep cliffs and hillsides are a favourite nesting place for many seabirds including puffins, guillemots, gulls and razorbills. During June and July the rare auk

The cliffs at North Stack, Holy Island

may also be seen there. Perhaps the best place to observe the birds is from the area around South Stack Lighthouse.

In a magnificent setting the lighthouse has a true 'Land's End' feel about it. Surrounded by steep cliffs, it can be approached down 379 steps from a car park. They are the best way to see the superb cliff faces around the lighthouse and observe the birds. The rocks offer some of the hardest climbing in Wales for many climbers from the mainland; except in the nesting season they vie with the seabirds for every little ledge and handhold. The lighthouse is on a small island at the bottom of the cliffs, approached across a small suspension bridge. It is open to the public each afternoon during the summer. For the statistically minded the lighthouse is automatic, 91ft high and 197ft above high water. Built in 1808 by David Alexander, who also built Dartmoor Prison, it is probably the most visited lighthouse in Britain.

Just below the car park and perched on the very edge of the cliffs is a squat square building that was for many years an ugly ruin. Known as Ellin's Tower, it was built in 1868 by the Rt Hon Owen

L
1h
*
††††

Stanley (MP for Penrhos) as a place to enjoy the view. Recently it has been converted by the Royal Society for the Protection of Birds into an observatory for bird watchers, for there are fine views of the cliffs. It provides a welcome refuge from the wind for ornithologists and other visitors, who are welcomed.

The whole of the South Stack area is full of interest. Alongside the approach road to the lighthouse is a fine collection of hut circles. They are the remains of twenty huts of various shapes and sizes believed to be part of a much larger settlement. Easily accessible from the road they give a good idea of how our ancestors lived, showing signs of their sleeping slabs and hearths. Now in the care of the State they perpetuate in the name Cythiau'r Gwyddelod, or Irishmen's Walls, in the belief that they were built by settlers from across the sea, although there is no evidence to substantiate this. Nearby are two large standing stones, which are thought to have been the centre stones of a much larger circle, although they now stand alone. Throughout Holy Island there are many other standing stones and hut circles, perhaps indicating that it was after all the centre of religion long before Christianity arrived.

To the south of Holyhead there are several popular holiday resorts, particularly **Trearddur Bay** which sits astride the pre-Telford road to the island. It has several fine beaches with golden sands and rocky outcrops just offshore, making it popular with skin divers and water skiers, though it can be windy. **Rhoscolyn**, on the southern tip, equally popular for water sports, is more sheltered from the wind. From the village there are some fine cliff-top walks particularly to the well of St Gwenfaen which is reputed to be able to cure mental illness. The nearby cliffs have rock formations showing the bending and folding which took place during the earth's formation.

Back on Anglesey the coast to the north with its small bays and rocky coves is very reminiscent of Cornwall. All the beaches give good views across the bay to Holy Island and Holyhead. **Church Bay** is perhaps the most visited beach on that stretch of coast. This north-west corner of the island is dominated by the hill of Mynydd y Garn, which, like any hill surrounded by flat land, appears much higher than it actually is. A road runs very close to the top leaving but a short walk to the gorse-topped summit. The views are of the

BEACHES AND PLACES OF INTEREST ALONG THE NORTH COAST OF ANGLESEY

Church Bay
Partly sand with rocky outcrops, good views across to Holy Island and Holyhead. Fine cliff walks.

Carmel Head
Rocky coves with good cliff walks.

Cemlyn Bay
Steep shelving pebble beach, now a bird sanctuary.

Cemaes Bay
Fine harbour and sandy bay. Good swimming and cliff walks to Llanbadrig and church. Overlooked by Wylfa Nuclear Power Station, which is open to visitors in summer.

Bull Bay
Rocky cove with sheltered bathing and good walks.

Amlwch
Small narrow harbour, old port for nearby copper mines of Parys Mountain. Swimming pool in town.

Parys Mountain
Eighteenth-century copper mines, now a mountain of waste. Some interesting coloured rocks to be seen and industrial archaeology remains, but care must be taken.

Llyn Alaw
Off B5112 at Llanerchymedd. Visitor centre and fishing on reservoir.

nearby coast, Carmel Head and the Wylfa Power Station. Off Carmel Head, The Skerries can be seen, a small group of islets used by breeding birds and seals. The lighthouse on The Skerries has been there since the eighteenth century and was one of the early examples that extracted a toll from every passing ship.

East of the headland the cliffs seem to get wilder until **Cemlyn Bay** is reached. The sheltered beach, once the haunt of pirates, is now a bird sanctuary owned by the National Trust. Visitors are requested to take care during the nesting season (April-June) if they use the cliff top walks around the bay and headland. Much of this northern coast, however, is dominated by the massive bulk of the

Parys Mountain   Above: *Remains of the great open-cast copper mine*

Ruins of a mine enginehouse on Parys Mountain

Amlwch harbour

Wylfa Nuclear Power Station. As the power station is in an area of outstanding natural beauty, the Central Electricity Generating Board has provided a nature trail around the headland. There is also an observation tower for looking over the power station and surroundings, while during the summer visitors can tour the site (by appointment).

Several little harbours along the northern coast are worth visiting. The nearest to Wylfa is **Cemaes Bay**; its tiny harbour and pleasant beach are well sheltered from all but the northernmost winds. The cliffs alongside the bay are National Trust property with some pleasant walks, particularly along to Llanbadrig. The church above the cliffs is dedicated to St Patrick and is believed to be on the site of one of the oldest churches in Anglesey. It is said that Patrick was shipwrecked on the little island of Middle Mouse just a short distance from the headland. He established a church here as thanksgiving for his salvation before leaving to convert the people of Ireland.

Amlwch, a little further east, has a fine little harbour, built of unmortared rock placed vertically rather than horizontally. It is small and narrow, owing its fame to the nearby Parys Mountain copper mine. During the heyday of the mine, it became the main port for the export of copper and the remains of the old quays can still be seen. Ships were built at the port after the decline of the copper industry and the remains of the old slipways can be seen. It has now become a major oil port. At the Anglesey Marine Terminal two miles offshore, crude oil tankers of more than 500,000 tons can moor and discharge their cargo. It is pumped directly ashore and through an underground pipeline to Stanlow, seventy-eight miles away in Cheshire, where it is refined. The harbour has had a new lease of life servicing the terminal and has been expanded.

Inland from Amlwch are the scarred remains of **Parys Mountain**. Once the biggest open-cast copper mine in the world, it produced 80,000 tons of ore per year until the early nineteenth century. In the eighteenth century the output was so great as almost to cause the collapse of the whole of Cornwall's great copper mining industry. Visitors must beware of the dangerous shafts and waste heaps around the scattered workings. Efforts are being made to work the mine again, and to show visitors life and conditions in its heyday.

Further inland, behind the mountain, is Llyn Alaw, a fairly new reservoir much favoured by trout fishermen. The church at nearby **Llanbabo** has three grotesque carved faces above the door, while inside is a finely carved slab believed to date from the fourteenth century. There are also several standing stones and burial mounds around the lake. One in particular, known as Bedd Branwen (Branwen's grave), is traditionally the burying place of Branwen mentioned in the Welsh folk legends *The Mabinogion*.

The eastern side of the island is extremely popular for family holidays. Most of the beaches are well sheltered, with good stretches of fine golden sands and safe bathing. Behind, the countryside is more rolling than elsewhere, with trees more noticeable than on the windy north and west coasts.

Traeth Dulas to the north is a quiet estuary and land-locked bay. Quite out of place are the remains of the old brickworks established in the heyday of Parys Mountain, presumably to cash in on the lucrative building projects. The nearby beaches of Traeth Lligwy are

BEACHES AND PLACES OF INTEREST ON THE EASTERN COAST OF ANGLESEY

Traeth Dulas
Land-locked bay with sandy beach. Also remains of old brickworks from heyday of nearby Parys Mountain.

Traeth Lligwy
Sandy beach backed by dunes and fields. Nearby is Iron Age village of Din Lligwy, a short walk across fields to walled village with remains of hut circles, a pleasant stroll. Also Capel Lligwy, a church standing above headland. Nearby is a Neolithic (New Stone Age) burial chamber with massive capstone. All are just by the road $1/_2$ mile north of Llanallgo church.

Moelfre
Boat hire, sailing and water skiing. Pebble beach.

Benllech
Long sandy beach, with donkey rides, deckchairs and cafés. Very popular.

Red Wharf Bay (Traeth Coch)
Wide bay with long walk to the sea when tide is out. Good sand and good bathing at high tide.

excellent, backed by sand dunes.

On the approach roads to the beaches overlooking the bay are several antiquities well worth visiting. They are all signposted from the main road and all can be seen at any time with only a short easy walk. The largest is Din Lligwy, probably the fourth-century fortified residence of a native chieftain. Now surrounded by woods it is a fine example, with much of the floor plan and walls evident. On the same walk is Capel Lligwy, a church of obscure origin but in a superb situation. Just a short distance along the road is the Lligwy Burial Chamber, with an impressive cap stone of solid limestone about 15ft square and 3ft thick, supported on a ring of upright rock 'posts'. It was probably erected in the early Bronze Age, about 2,000BC.

Moelfre, out on the headland, has boats for hire, and, a pebbly beach which is good for water skiing and sailing. The lifeboat station has been involved in many famous disasters; perhaps the best

Penmon Priory and dovecote

known is the *Royal Charter* which went down nearby with the loss of 452 lives in 1859. To the south, the beaches of **Benllech** and **Red Wharf Bay** are the most popular on the island. They are long and sandy, and at low tide Red Wharf Bay is an extensive estuary. Benllech has donkey rides, deck chairs and sea front cafés. There are several caravan sites along this section of coast.

Stretching out towards the main land is **Penmon Head**, with Puffin Island just offshore. Although the coast is scarred by the remains of old limestone quarries, used during the building of both Telford's and Stephenson's bridges across the Menai Straits, the headland is a pretty spot. It can be approached through Penmon Priory whose remains, mainly eleventh century, are adjacent to the road and there is a fine dovecote. Much of the priory is still in use, the abbot's house is still inhabited and the attached church still a parish church. Just behind the buildings is the well of St Seiriol, an early Celtic saint active on the island at the same time as St Cybi. Around the well are a few small buildings and the remains of an oval hut, possibly the early saint's cell.

For a small toll you can drive to the coastguard station and café

Beaumaris Castle, surrounded by its moat

at Trwyn Du or Black Point just opposite **Puffin Island**. It is a grand spot and with the mournful toll of the bell on the lighthouse one can easily conjure up thoughts of shipwrecks. The island, also known as Priestholme or Ynys Seiriol, once had a small monastery, later moved to Penmon Priory — and of course many puffins. The bird population declined on account of the popularity of pickled young birds in the early nineteenth century. At the point, there are some small sandy beaches and excellent views across to the mountains of Snowdonia, particularly the Carneddau. On the south is the entrance to the Menai Straits and across the bay are the Lavan Sands, once the main route to the island.

It was to command this route into Anglesey that Edward I built a castle at **Beaumaris**, almost on the edge of the Straits. It is small compared with its two near neighbours at Conwy and Caernarfon, but around it are the remains of a moat which once connected the castle to the sea. Because of its lowlying situation it does not at first sight seem impressive but it is in fact one of the most complete and best designed castles built during Edward's reign. Despite its solid

PLACES OF INTEREST ALONG THE MENAI STRAITS

Penmon Priory and Dovecote
On road from Beaumaris to
Puffin Island.
Medieval monastery still partly
in use as house and church.
Dovecote is sixteenth century
with room for 1,000 nests. Good
solid stone building with domed
roof.

St Seriol's Well
Penmon
Holy well close to priory with
some stone walls possibly of
the original saint's cell. About
sixth century. Short walk from
priory.

Puffin Island
Along road past Penmon Priory
(small toll).
Just off Black Point (Trwyn Du),
lighthouse with melancholy bell,
coastguard station with café
and pebbly beach. A lonely
spot.

Church of St Tysilio
On island in Menai Straits
accessible by causeway from
Belgian walks.

Tegfryn Art Gallery
Cadnant Road, Menai Bridge.
Exhibitions by Welsh artists.

Belgian Walks
Menai Bridge.
Constructed by Belgian

refugees during World War I as
a promenade. Give good views
of Telford's suspension bridge.

Museum of Childhood
Water Street, Menai Bridge.
Fascinating collection of toys,
games and other things that
have held children's interest
throughout the ages. Suitable
for all ages.

Butterfly Palace (Pili-Palas)
Hundreds of butterflies from all
over the world. Exotic plants,
nature shop and picnic sites at
Menai Bridge.

Beaumaris Castle
Last of Edward I's mighty forts,
once accessible by sea, now
well preserved and not aggressive looking. Children's
playground next to it.

Beaumaris Courthouse
Oldest courthouse in the country
still in use. All the original
furniture and fittings still intact,
very interesting if you are
unfamiliar with such buildings.
Opposite castle.

Beaumaris Jail
Built in 1829 and still as it was,
with treadwheel and cells. All
the work rooms, exercise yards
and punishment blocks are
complete.

defences it has seen little trouble, a short occupation by the Welsh during Owain Glyndwr's uprising in 1404 probably being the high point of its career. Nevertheless it is a charming little castle, with a children's playground against the outside wall.

Opposite the entrance to the castle is the courthouse built in 1614. Still in its original state and still in use, it is furnished as it was built with the coat of arms of James I over the bench and the public area separated by massive iron bars. Until the last century it was the main Assize Court for the county, but since 1971 it has been only a magistrates' court. It is the oldest courthouse in the country and it is said that the notorious Judge Jefferies once held an Assize

here. An equally fascinating place for those unfamiliar with the ways of justice is Beaumaris Jail. Built in 1829, it still has all the cells, the punishment cell and a treadwheel unique in Britain. There is much of interest and one is reminded of the harshness of our early penal system.

The town has several other interesting buildings in its narrow streets, including the Bull's Head Hotel, a favourite with visiting judges and believed to have played host to General Mytton, Cromwell's general during his Anglesey campaign, Dr Johnson and Charles Dickens. The church of St Mary and St Nicholas is almost as old as the castle and has many interesting features. Above the town is the obelisk memorial to the Bulkeley family, once the biggest landowners on the island, whose home at Baron Hill is now an overgrown ruin.

Beaumaris plays host each August to the Straits Regatta, a major yachting event organised by the Royal Anglesey Yacht Club. The town has something for everyone: bowls, tennis, fishing, many elegant buildings and excellent views.

By comparison, **Menai Bridge** seems a busy little town crouching below Telford's suspension bridge. To suit children of all ages, including grownups, is the Museum of Childhood near the town centre, with some fine displays of toys, games and furniture. The Tegfryn Art Gallery has regular shows by Welsh artists. Along the Belgian Walks, built by refugees during World War I, there are several pleasant walks to Church Island, out in the Straits, which is easily reached by a causeway.

With the building of the two bridges, much of the importance of the towns along the Straits was removed. Holyhead became the biggest and most important town and Llangefni, almost in the centre of the island, took over the role of administrative centre from Beaumaris. **Llangefni** is a bustling market town with wide streets (market day Thursday), situated on the Afon Cefni by which it could once be reached by boat. There are some easy walks in the vicinity of the town. However, most visitors to the island come to see the coastline and the beaches, and will probably spend little time in the interior. There is something for everybody on Anglesey and there is always the probability of warmer weather than on the mainland, so go prepared for a relaxing time.

7

BLAENAU FFESTINIOG, BARMOUTH AND BALA

The area of country bounded on the north by the Lledr Valley and the Vale of Ffestiniog and to the south by Llyn Tegid and the Mawddach Estuary contains some of the best, and at the same time the least known, mountains of Snowdonia. The ranges to the north with fourteen peaks over 3,000ft are well known and well visited, but how many people are aware of the quieter slopes of the Rhinogs, the Arenigs and the surrounding hills?

Visitors to this area, either walking or touring, can expect some pleasant surprises. It is a large area crossed by few roads. The hills and moorlands are high, divided by long valleys bearing the inevitable main road; but the character of the country is such that there are few of these. On the side facing Tremadog Bay are twenty miles of beautiful golden sands with some of the best bathing in North Wales.

It must be said that to gain the most from this compact highland area, you must be prepared to get off the beaten track a little. The area abounds with lakes and reservoirs, some easily accessible, others up tiny minor roads that wander uphill far into the mountains. Walkers will be at an advantage here. The hills are rough and craggy, and with many ancient trackways into and across them, their efforts will be well rewarded. It is a wonderful area to explore, but do be prepared to be adventurous.

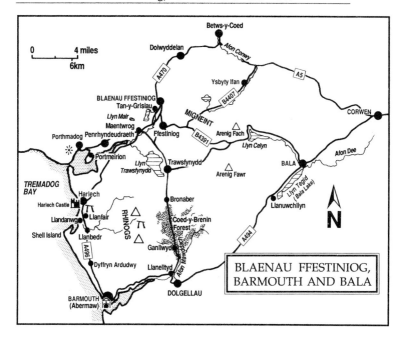

BLAENAU FFESTINIOG, BARMOUTH AND BALA

The towns in the area are small, reflecting much that is Welsh — not for them the bright lights and noises, but honest down-to-earth service, and the main language of the area is Welsh.

When the National Park was designated, **Blaenau Ffestiniog**, almost in the centre, was excluded. As an industrial town with huge slate tips towering above it, the grey terraces of houses blending in to give a gloomy view particularly in the rain, it was considered to be a blot on the landscape. Now, thirty years after that decision, the quarries no longer produce slate in any quantity and the once ugly town is ironically a popular centre for visitors. It is the slate they come to see, and slate artefacts they come to buy.

There are many sorts of mining and quarrying in North Wales, but it is slate for which the region is best known: until recently most buildings had a slate roof. Now with clay or concrete roof tiles, and even imitation slates, there is very little slate mined in the area. Several other towns have been dominated by slate, including

View from the Llechwedd Slate Cavern

Llanberis and Bethesda, but in Blaenau Ffestiniog everything is slate. It has been the life and breath of the community for two hundred years, though now most of the quarries are quiet and the drainage pumps switched off.

Slate underlies most of Snowdonia and appears frequently on or near the surface. Where it does appear it can be quarried, but around Blaenau it was found easier to mine it. Many of the seams are forty or fifty feet thick and tilted at an angle of forty-five degrees; so the caverns created when the slate was removed are enormous, large enough to contain an average size house.

Undoubtedly life in the quarry was hard: men, usually all from the same family, worked in small groups. They were paid according to their production, and there was no time for idling: they worked underground by candlelight. One man did the drilling to blast the rock loose, sometimes working high above the ground suspended only by a rope around one thigh. The others would break up and reduce the blocks to more manageable sizes, ready for removal. Outside they would be shaped and dressed as required. Each size

Typical slate mining ruins at Rhosydd, high up in the Moelwyn hills

of roofing slate had its own name: countess, princess, wide lady and many more.

Two mines are open to the public in Blaenau Ffestiniog, on opposite sides of the A470 before it crosses the Crimea Pass to Dolwyddelan. On the north side is Gloddfa Ganol, the largest slate mine in the world, and on the south, the Llechwedd Slate Cavern; both have visitor centres and guided tours down the caverns to experience the miners' conditions. There are shops for souvenirs and one can watch slates being trimmed and cut in the old way. Justifiably, they are both very popular and can be well recommended.

For the walker it is possible to visit many of the older disused mines in the hills surrounding Blaenau though care must be taken and shafts avoided. A short distance from the town is **Tan-y-Grisiau**, a small community surrounded by remnants of its slate-mining past. A steep track rises from the back of the village up to Llyn Cwmorthin and an old chapel; beyond are the barracks and sheds of the old quarries. The path uphill past the chapel continues

M
4-5h
***
††††

PLACES OF INTEREST AROUND BLAENAU FFESTINIOG

Llechwedd Slate Cavern
Trips inside the slate caverns by tram, and to the deeper caverns by special railway. Demonstrations of slate working and photos of life in quarries. Slide and photographic displays.

Gloddfa Ganol
Displays of massive machinery used in the slate industry and visits to the mines wearing helmets and miners' lamps. Collection of old steam engines.

Ffestiniog Power Station
First pumped storage scheme in Britain. Tours of the power station and the top lake are available. Book at the information centre at Tan-y-Grisiau.

to the old Rhosydd mines, the highest in Wales. It is easy to imagine the hardships of the miner as he walked this path to work at the beginning of each week. Here all the slate was mined, and the tunnels (or 'adits' as they are known) stretch up and through the hillside.

This is the back of Moelwyn Mawr and a walk up the old inclines or the old tracks through the Rhosydd quarry leads to two great holes from which the slate has been extracted. Just behind these and over the shoulder is a terraced track which can be followed easily around the hillside to the south to above Llyn Stwlan, the top lake of a pump storage scheme. From there a road leads back downhill to Tan-y-Grisiau. The lower reservoir is a favourite place for trout fishermen. The adjacent power station can be visited by appointment, and there is a visitors' information centre, open daily during the season.

The Festiniog Railway, one of the 'Great Little Trains of Wales', runs between Blaenau Ffestiniog and Porthmadog. Operated now mainly by volunteers, this narrow gauge railway was originally built to carry the slate from the mines in Blaenau to the quay at Porthmadog. Now it provides a regular passenger service for most of the year. The scenery en route is superb, as the track drops from

The Festiniog Railway as it climbs towards Blaenau Ffestiniog

the hills down the beautiful Vale of Ffestiniog before skirting the estuary of Traeth Mawr and crossing the Cob (or embankment) to Porthmadog. It is more usual to catch the train at Porthmadog and do the return journey to and from the terminus near Blaenau Ffestiniog. The little engines are original and excellently maintained. A connecting bus runs up to the slate quarries for visitors. (See also chapter 5, pages 124-5).

Near neighbour to Blaenau Ffestiniog is **Ffestiniog**, a quiet little

Llyn Mair behind Plas Tan-y-Bwlch,
the Snowdonia National Park Study Centre

village, standing at the head of the valley to which it gives its name and with superb views of the surrounding mountains. Below, the Vale of Ffestiniog is justifiably said to be the most beautiful in North Wales. The steep sided slopes are covered in many places with the original oakwoods that once covered most of Wales. The Afon Dwyryd meanders lazily along the valley bottom to an ancient stone bridge at **Maentwrog**, a pleasant little village that takes its name from a prehistoric stone in the churchyard — *Maen* (stone) of Twrog. Now isolated from the sea, the village was once a busy little port for the slate from the surrounding hills.

Across the valley is Plas Tan-y-Bwlch, the Snowdonia National Park Study Centre. Set in beautiful woodlands, the house once belonged to the wealthy Oakley family, owners of the quarries of Blaenau Ffestiniog. The centre runs many courses open to the public on all aspects of the countryside and the National Park. A

Portmeirion

nature trail starts from the car park by the house and wanders up through the woods to Llyn Mair, a small reservoir above, returning eastwards close to the railway and back to the garden. A second trail starts at the lake and circles through the woodland for about three-quarters of a mile.

The lake, Llyn Mair (Mary's Lake), is an idyllic spot and can easily be approached by the steep road (B4410), past the Oakley Arms Hotel; there is a picnic area and car park and the rhododendrons are magnificent when in bloom. Just above is one of the stations for the Festiniog Railway which curves and winds its way through the woods of Tan-y-Bwlch.

The river meanders slowly down to **Penrhyndeudraeth** where it is crossed by a toll bridge and then out to sea by **Portmeirion**. This small private village with its tiny harbour was designed and built by the late Sir Clough Williams-Ellis, the Welsh architect whose intention was to create a place free from careless building and advertising. The cottages, mainly in the Italian style, are grouped around a small bay and contain many features collected from other

PLACES TO VISIT IN THE VALE OF FFESTINIOG

PlasTan-y-Bwlch
Maentwrog, on A487
Snowdonia National Park Study
Centre, runs courses for visitors
on countryside and aspects of
the national park.
Nature trail to Llyn Mair.

Portmeirion
Off the A487 at Minffordd.
Beautiful Italianate village
conceived by Sir Clough
Williams-Ellis. Gardens, café
and craft shops. Where *The
Prisoner* was filmed.

buildings and saved for posterity. The hotel, the centrepiece of the
village, was sadly destroyed by fire in 1981, and, with it, many of Sir
Clough's drawings and records. The village has craft shops and
restaurants, and many of the cottages are available to rent. During
the 1960s the cult TV series *The Prisoner* was filmed here and there
is a small display of memorabilia in one of the cottages. It is on a
private estate but visitors are welcome, though charged; access is
off the A487 at Minffordd.

Across the sandy estuary from Portmeirion the hills rise steeply
to the lofty summits of the Rhinog range. It is a rugged range of hills
stretching twenty miles to the south, dotted here and there with little
lakes and woodlands, penetrated, but never crossed, by single-
track mountain roads. It follows the magnificent sweep of Cardigan
Bay right down to Barmouth (Abermaw).

At the northern end of the range the coastal land of Morfa
Harlech is wide, backed by huge sand dunes from which the sea
has retreated. The town of **Harlech** stands pinched between the
sea and the hills with the castle perched high on a rocky outcrop

dominating the surrounding area.

Built by Edward I in 1238 on the very edge of the bay the castle
must have served as a strong reminder to the Welsh of the power
of the king, for it is visible for many miles around. The sea has now
retreated, but it is nevertheless striking. It came under attack many
times from the Welsh before being taken in 1404 by Owain Glyndwr.
It served for some time as his capital before being re-taken by the

PLACES OF INTEREST IN AND NEAR HARLECH

Harlech Castle
Fine castle in superb situation. Scene of many bloody battles and inspiration for the march *Men of Harlech*.

Muriaur Gwyddelod, Irishman's Walls
Situated in fields south of Harlech.
Remains of early Iron Age settlements possibly Irish.

Llanfair Slate Caverns
2 miles south of Harlech on A496.
Walk-in caverns of old slate mine and see the real conditions.

Beaches
The whole of the bay in front of Harlech has beautiful golden sands with lots of room for everyone.

English in 1408. During the Wars of the Roses the Lancastrians held out there for eight years before fleeing overseas. One survivor, a twelve-year-old boy, went on to become Henry VII, and it is said that this siege inspired the march *Men of Harlech*. It was the last Welsh fortress to be captured during the Civil War, but since then has been left to become a ruin, a grand ruin however, with an inner courtyard surrounded by two mighty walls surmounted by narrow walkways. There are magnificent views over the estuary, the mountains to the north and the Lleyn Peninsula. The castle is approached from the town side to gain a full appreciation of the difficulties faced by an attacker.

A short distance to the south of the town in the fields above the road is Muriaur Gwyddelod or Irishman's Walls, believed to have been built by settlers from Ireland between 1,000 and 2,000 years ago. The walls are a circular enclosure about 4ft high and subdivided into 'rooms'; there are several similarly named sites in North Wales, but we can only guess their true origin.

The beaches along the bay below Harlech are some of the finest; they are backed by sand dunes and are wide enough for the most energetic game of football. Stretching from Harlech Point in the north almost to Barmouth in the south, they are safe for bathing

Harlech Castle with the mountains of Snowdonia in the distance

PLACES OF INTEREST AROUND LLANBEDR

Llandanwg Church
Signposted from A496.
Ancient church on beach nearly
buried by sand dunes.

Shell Island
Turn off A496 in Llanbedr
opposite the youth hostel.
Connected by causeway covered at high tide. Sand dunes and
excellent beach with café and
bars. Millions of shells to collect.

Roman Steps
Turn off at Victoria Hotel in
Llanbedr.
At head of Cwm Bychan,
footpath leads from lake to the
steps. Remains of ancient
packhorse trail with well
preserved steps. Picnic spot at
lakeside.

Maes Artro
Adjacent to A496 just south of
Llanbedr.
Village containing workshops of
craftsmen including weavers,
potters, clockmakers and gold
and silversmiths plus many
more. You can watch them at
work and buy if you wish.
Aquaria, playgrounds and cafés,
something for everyone.

and never crowded. Access to the beaches is from the A496 and is signposted. The Royal St David's golf course lies behind the dunes.

South of Harlech at **Llandanwg** (there is a car park right behind the dunes), an interesting medieval church lies buried by sand nearby. At **Llanbedr** the road to Shell Island is directly opposite the youth hostel and goes across a causeway which is covered at high tide. There is a charge to reach the island for day visitors, but, as may be guessed, it is a great spot to collect shells and enjoy the sea,

and is ideal for children. Also in Llanbedr is Maes Artro, a commune of craftsmen and artists making everything from candles to gems. It is an imaginative scheme giving an opportunity to visitors to see many local craftsmen at work. There is a playground for children, an aquarium with specimens of locally found fish, and a restaurant, all pleasantly laid out in a small area of woodland.

It is thought that in prehistoric times this particular section of the coastline was the main landing spot for trade with Ireland. There are

The church at Llandanwg, almost buried in the sand dunes

Part of a Welsh village in traditional style, at the Maes Artro craft centre

many old tracks and roadways leading into and across the hills from Llandanwg and Llanbedr. Several tracks can be traced continuously into England. Many of the old tracks, now metalled roads into the hills, are steep and narrow but lead to some fascinating places.

One such road leaving Llanbedr beside the Victoria Hotel divides after a mile and a half. The right fork goes up to Cwm Nantcol, a beautiful isolated valley below Rhinog Fach and Rhinog Fawr and a good spot from which to ascend these mountains. The left fork follows the narrow wooded valley of the Afon Arto to the head of Cwm Bychan, where there is a parking spot by the lake; from here the famous Roman Steps can be followed. The footpath leads across the stream and through the woods to the start of the steps which lead over the shoulder of Rhinog Fawr before descending to the valley beyond. The steps are an interesting walk, particularly if at the highest point you turn left and walk into the hills to the north; the rock scenery is superb, with hugh perched rocks (glacial erratics) sometimes the size of small houses deposited on the glacier-polished granite. The steps are man-made, but there is no evidence that they are Roman. It is more likely that they were a medieval packhorse trail, though the route could very easily be the same as an earlier prehistoric track which can be traced and followed right through the hills to Bala.

Perhaps the finest road into the hills leaves the coast road from the village of **Llanfair**. It climbs easily for a mile or two, with several large standing stones beside the road, to the highest point with magnificent views over Harlech, the estuary and the Lleyn Peninsula beyond. The metalled road then dips down to the left around the hillside but directly in front is a rocky track, leading first to an Iron Age hillfort that crowns the hill Moel Geodog, and then continuing north into and across this range of mountains. There is a possibility that at one time this track was the main road to England from the coast and Ireland, for, though overgrown now, it is terraced into the hillside and paved across the marshes. There are many hut circles and standing stones along the route indicating its importance. If time allows, it makes a good (fairly easy) walk.

The metalled road, which can be followed more easily, runs at a high level parallel with the coast for about five miles to a small lake. From here a road to the left drops steeply down to rejoin the coast

The 'Roman Steps' at the head of Cwm Bychan

PLACES TO VISIT AROUND BARMOUTH AND THE MAWDDACH ESTUARY

RNLI Maritime Museum
On quay in Barmouth.
Lifeboat and other ship models,
old photographs.

Barmouth Estuary
Footpath across the railway
bridge over the estuary gives
good views of the estuary and
Cadair Idris to the south.

Old Country Life Centre
Off A496 at Tal-y-bont
Glimpses of bygone days in the
country with traditional tools,
crafts, fashions and other
aspects. Old mill now houses
restaurant and gift shop.

Weaver's Loft
Jubilee Road, Barmouth
Weaving shop producing
tapestries and tweed.

**Coed-y-Brenin Forest and
Visitor Centre**
Off A470 at Pont Dolgefeiliau.
Displays of forest fauna and
flora, and gold mining machinery. Plus many tracks of interest
in the forest and environs.

**Rhaedr Mawddach and
Pistyll Cain**
In the forest to the east, follow
the footpath from the picnic spot
at Pont Dolgefeiliau. Map obtain-
able at visitor centre as above.

road; or it is possible to continue on this minor road for several more miles and return by the same route. This is a splendid drive though care must be taken as the road is single track with few passing places; it can be joined at several points by climbing steeply from the coast road.

South from Llanbedr the busy road follows the wide coastal plain to **Dyffryn Ardudwy**; here again there are significant prehistoric remains: signposted to the east is Dyffryn Cairn, which when new was estimated to be 100ft long and 54ft broad. The visible remains are those of the burial chambers. Joining the A496 just after the village is a minor road to the east which leads to further burial chambers and several old drovers' routes across the hills. There are many fine old trackways crossing these hills; almost certainly the road south around the estuary was hazardous and only since the coming of tourism and the railways has access to the coast been opened up. Keen walkers with a map and compass can be guaranteed a splendid day out on these hills, simply by following any of these trackways. They can have the hills to themselves all day with some of the finest scenery in the whole of Wales.

The main seaside resort along this coast is **Barmouth, (Abermaw)** squeezed tightly between the hills and the sea. It owes much of its popularity to the railway and the Victorian penchant for sea bathing, much of the architecture reflecting that era. The railway still plays an important part in the life of Barmouth, approaching the town from the south by an 800yd-long bridge across the estuary. There was a danger that the bridge, which is built on wooden piers, would have to be closed, as it was badly damaged by seaborne rot. Fortunately this has been arrested and for the time being the line has been saved. It has also been passed as fit to take occasional steam trains, which makes a magnificent sight as they cross in this fine setting. The bridge can be used by pedestrians for a small toll and is a recommended way to see the superb views around the estuary.

Today Barmouth is still a popular town in a beautiful setting; it has some fine beaches and whether approached by sea, road or rail, the scenery is breathtaking. The estuary of the Afon Mawddach is similar to a Norwegian fjord with its steeply wooded slopes and surrounding mountains. The road (A496) from Dolgellau, clinging in many places to the very edges of the shore, is particularly scenic with views across to Cadair Idris high above the opposite bank.

A few years ago a large multi-national mining company proposed to dredge the sand and silt of the estuary to extract the particles of gold that had been washed down from the surrounding hills. Although extensive tests and trials showed that gold did exist, its price at that time made the project unviable, and fortunately the idea was abandoned.

At the head of the estuary is the very Welsh market town of Dolgellau, a compact little town with narrow streets that seems to be the dividing line between North and Mid-Wales. Despite its position and its sixteenth-century bridge, it has figured little in Welsh history. The views to the south are commanded by the mighty summit of Cadair Idris (2,927ft). It is a good centre for exploring the

The hills on the northern side of the Mawddach Estuary have a number of abandoned gold mines

The neighbouring waterfalls of Pistyll Cain (right) and Rhaeadr Mawddach (below) with its small reservoir once used for the nearby gold workings

surrounding hills and valleys with a number of easy walks in the locality, details of which are available from the Tourist Information Centre.

Dolgellau will be described in detail in the next chapter. Meanwhile, retrace your steps slightly to the small village of **Llanelltyd** to the north-west. Now merely a junction of two major roads it was once the major crossing point of the Mawddach and it was perhaps for this reason that in 1199 a Cistercian abbey was founded on the eastern bank. Little remains of Cymmer Abbey nowadays — a few walls and some of the thirteenth-century church — but it must have been a magnificent setting in its early years.

North from the abbey the steep-sided valley of the Mawddach is followed on the west by the A470 and on the east by a minor road. Both have their merits as they wind up the wooded valley following this renowned trout river. The 'A' road first reaches the highly recommended Tyn-y-Groes Hotel, well known to anglers, while the minor road can be followed into the hills and forests (though a map should be taken to avoid getting lost), where there are some wonderful panoramas. The A470 can be rejoined at **Ganllwyd**.

This small hamlet is in the heart of the Coed-y-Brenin Forest, the Forest of Kings, the oldest and most extensive forest in North Wales. It is also in the heart of the gold prospecting area and though little is found nowadays, at one time the hills and valleys around were akin to the Klondyke.

The best place to learn more of both is to visit the Forestry Commission's Maesgwm Visitor Centre north of Ganllwyd, signposted off the road at the ancient bridge of Pont Dolgefeiliau. It is most interesting, explaining the forest, the wildlife, and for those interested in the history of the area, the goldmining. The displays are well done and explanatory. There is also a splendid display of equipment used in the refining of gold. While there do pick up a leaflet on the forest walks and spend some time exploring. There are marked tracks and picnic sites, many just off the main road. It is a lovely area to visit, but allow plenty of time as there is much to enjoy in the forest.

The map available details over fifty miles of roadways and footpaths, but thoroughly recommended is the walk from the car park by the bridge to the twin waterfalls of Pistyll Cain and Rhaeadr

Cymmer Abbey, Llanelltyd

Mawddach. These are not accessible by road but are well worth the effort. Between the two falls is the site of the gold smelting works and above the Mawddach (about half a mile) is an occasionally-worked gold mine. It is really a splendid area to explore. There are 16,000 acres of forest, mainly firs and spruces but much of the original woodland of old Welsh oaks is intermingled with the new. It is a place of peace, good walking and not too many people.

The road (A470) continues north through the forest and on to the high moorlands, a straight and easy drive allowing plenty of time to enjoy the views before reaching the village of **Trawsfynydd**. The village has achieved dubious fame by being the site of Britain's first inland nuclear power station. Standing on the shores of the nearby lake, the large square structure seems to fit well into the scenery, in many ways enhancing the nearby hills.

A short distance beyond the power station a small road goes off to the right under a railway bridge and between steep banks to a wood. Here by a gate are the mounds of a small Roman amphitheatre, unique in Wales. It was part of the camp of Tomen-y-Mur, visible as a small mound across the field. It must have been an isolated posting for a legionary born and bred on the Mediterranean coast, especially when the north westerlies blew in the winter. Nevertheless it was in a fine position and perhaps he could take comfort from the beauty of the surrounding hills.

The main road now drops sharply back into the Vale of Ffestiniog, or turns right through Ffestiniog and Blaenau Ffestiniog to cross the Crimea Pass. The descent into the Lledr Valley is steep, but gives some splendid views of the southern slopes of Moel Siabod. Pass through Roman Bridge, which has no Roman connections, to **Dolwyddelan** and its small castle. Built about 1170 as the home of Llewelyn the Great, the castle has several interesting features, but is small compared with Edward's fortresses on the coast.

The road winds through the Gwydyr Forest to meet and cross the Afon Conwy close to Betws-y-Coed. A short distance upstream from the bridge is the Fairy Glen and Conwy Falls, easily approached by a pleasant path along the river bank. Above the falls, the river divides into the Afon Machno which turns south-west along the lovely Cwm Penmachno. The Afon Conwy continues up the valley for several more miles before turning south-west near Pentrefoelas.

Leaving the busy main road (A5) the Conwy turns towards its source, followed closely by a minor road. Halfway up the valley is the community of **Yspytty Ifan**. It was a hospice run by the Knights of St John for the pilgrims on their way to Bardsey Island, but there are now few traces of its past. Four miles to the south is Llyn Conwy, source of this famous river. The surrounding moorland was until the Dissolution a sanctuary and, despite the many passing pilgrims, was known for its lawlessness. Today the area is equally notorious; known as the Migneint it is a marshy plateau with few tracks, crossed only by the roads from Yspytty Ifan and Penmachno. Close to the junction is an old decorated well which has associations with the pilgrims.

To the south stand the two peaks of Arenig Fawr and Arenig Fach. The taller, Arenig Fawr, stands to the south of its smaller sister, separated by a road, stream and railway. The now disused railway was the main line from Ffestiniog to Bala and then into England. Running high above Cym Prysor from Trawsfynydd and

Memorial stone to the drowned Quaker village at Llyn Celyn

crossing a high viaduct which now seems quite out of place in these wild moorlands, it was a magnificent journey under full steam. The Afon Tryweryn runs towards Bala but was dammed early in the 1960s to form Llyn Celyn which now supplies water to Liverpool. Beneath the waters of the lake was the small community of Capel Celyn, a mainly Quaker village, from where many families left to settle in America with the Pilgrim Fathers. A small chapel and carved rock on the northern shore commemorate the village. Below the dam the river is used for international canoe races, the water level being controlled from the reservoir; it joins the Afon Dee at Bala.

The town of **Bala** was famous before the Industrial Revolution for its woollen stockings. It takes its name from the Welsh *bala* meaning outlet, for there the Dee starts its journey to the sea from the nearby lake. Despite its central position in Wales, at the junction of many old roads, Edward I seems to have found it strategically unimportant. There is a small mound or motte in the town believed

Statue of the Reverend Thomas Charles, founder of the British and Foreign Bible Society, in the main street, Bala

to be of Norman origin though there are doubts even about that.

It is a grey stone town with a wide main street and was for many years the home of the Reverend Thomas Charles (1755-1814), founder of the British and Foreign Bible Society and a pioneer of Methodism in North Wales; his statue stands in the main street. It continued as a Methodist stronghold when the Reverend Lewis Edwards started an academy in 1837 on the outskirts of the town for young Methodist ministers. Many other Methodists left the town to start a colony in Patagonia in 1865, founding the town of Trelew where the families still live and farm, using Welsh as their first language.

Modern Bala is something of a holiday centre, reflecting little of its Methodist upbringing. It stands at the head of Llyn Tegid or Bala Lake, the largest natural lake in Wales, a favourite spot for yachtsmen as the occasional strong south-westerly wind can give exhilarating sailing. Known also for the fishing, both fly and coarse, the lake yields a unique species called the gwyniad believed to be a survivor from the Ice Age. It is a small fish resembling a herring that spurns the rod and is only occasionally caught by net. There are several specimens in the White Lion Hotel in the town.

The roads on each side of the lake make this shoreline accessible for most of its length, with several pleasant picnic and parking areas off the minor road to the south. A comparatively recent addition along the southern bank is the Bala Lake Railway, a narrow gauge railway following the old main line which has steam and diesel engines running the full length of the lake. The main station is at **Llanuwchllyn** at the south end of the lake. The locomotives once worked the old North Wales slate quarries and ensconced in an open or closed carriage one can enjoy the magnificent mountain and lakeside scenery.

On the northern side of Llyn Tegid the main road A494 speeds between Bala and Barmouth, but for those with more time several metalled tracks across the hills towards Trawsfynydd provide an interesting and adventurous trip. Starting from Llanuwchllyn the recommended route follows the course of the Afon Lliw over to Bronaber and Trawsfynydd. Two miles up the left-hand side above the road is Castell Carndochan, possibly a Norman motte, but more likely the home of an unknown brigand. Nearby are the characteristic white spoil heaps from a nineteenth-century gold mine. The road climbs steeply into the very heart of the mountains following the course of an ancient highway before descending through the forests to Bronaber on the Trawsfynydd to Dolgellau road.

It is a wild mountain road passing through some beautiful countryside and forests. Walkers should be armed with the necessary Ordnance Survey maps, either sheet 124 or 125, and a compass. There are few tracks and fewer walkers, and one must be prepared. Please remember also that, though all the hills and countryside are within the Snowdonia National Park, most of the land is privately owned. Walls and fences should not be damaged.

H
all
day
***
†††

Lake Bala (Llyn Tegid)

─── 8 ───
SOUTHERN SNOWDONIA

Many visitors to the Snowdonia National Park tend to regard the northern mountains as the only area within the park boundaries. It does in fact stretch quite extensively down to the south of Dolgellau and Bala, taking in the superb ranges of hills of the Arans and Cadair Idris, the beautiful estuary of the Afon Dyfi and the steep coastline north of Tywyn to the Afon Mawddach.

Apart from the coastline with its beaches and resorts, which are always busy in the holiday season, the mountains and the whole inland area tends to be less frequented and less popular than northern Snowdonia. Visitors who do tour the area will be well rewarded. It is a compact area with steep hills and deep tranquil valleys. The towns and villages are small and typically Welsh; the mountains, which seem to dominate every view, have been described as some of the most beautiful in the country. Certainly this description would fit the Arans, which loom high above the southern end of Bala Lake. The visitor who likes to get a little off the beaten track will have ample opportunity; there are many fine mountain roads that cross high cwms and visit out-of-the-way lakes and valleys. There are nature reserves, quiet rivers and mountain walks. Once into the area the hills are all around, seemingly rolling on forever.

At the northern end of the area is Bala Lake and the small town

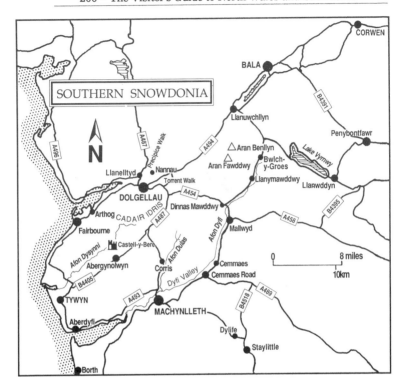

 of Bala (see chapter 7, pages 195-7), which stands at the outflow of the lake into the Afon Dee. The lake, also called Llyn Tegid, is roughly four miles long by half a mile wide and lies pleasantly though undramatically below rolling green hills with the ever present Arans commanding the southern view.

The A494 trunk road to Dolgellau follows the northern shoreline before ascending two miles south of the lake to the old farmhouse of Pont Gwyn right on the watershed. It is said that a raindrop on one side of the roof runs to the Dee and the Irish Sea and one on the other flows south to join the Afon Wnion and thence to the Maw and Cardigan Bay. The Wnion flows down a beautiful narrow wooded valley, a land of forest-clad hills and rocky precipices. The road hugs the steep side of the river and the now defunct railway (closed in 1965) fights for space between road and river. It is a lovely journey — British Rail must be sadly regretting closing some of their more picturesque lines. Towards Dolgellau the valley widens marginally and Cadair Idris comes into view over the hilltops, its rampart-like ridges giving it an appearance of strength towering above the valley. After twenty miles the river descends to the flood plain and finally joins the broad estuary of the Afon Mawddach and so to the sea. It has been a tossing, tumbling journey through some of the finest scenery in Wales.

An alternative road leaves Bala's main street and crosses the northern shores of the lake, ideal for photographers, and then traverses round the quieter southern lakeside to Llanuwchllyn, home of the Bala Lake Railway which, utilising the old trackway, has regular trips along the lakeside.

A single track road leaves Llanuwchllyn heading almost due south. Signposted Dinas Mawddwy it climbs gradually past the lower slopes of the Arans up the beautiful Cwm Cynllwyd to the summit of the pass. This is the infamous Bwlch-y-Groes, the highest road in Wales at 1,790ft. At the summit is a rather dismal parking area close to the peat hags. It is a bleak spot on a cold day, further spoilt by the signs refusing access to the nearby mountains. To the west can be seen the craggy ridge of the Arans. In times gone by the moorlands were famous for the peat gathered for fuel. Apparently some of the best in the land, it was hauled downhill by pony and sledge.

In 1850, when George Borrow was taking his leave of his host in Bala to traverse this same route, he was warned that his journey that day 'would be very rough over hills and mountains which constituted upon the whole the wildest part of all Wales'. This is still true today — the journey, though more comfortable, is just as awe inspiring in these superb hills.

The Arans, two magnificent peaks, rise sheer to the west, almost twins in shape and height. Formed of a volcanic ridge which runs between Dinas Mawddwy and Bala Lake they are the focus of one of the finest mountain walks south of the Snowdon massif. Aran Benllyn, the northernmost at 2,970ft and Aran Fawddwy, slightly less at 2,901ft, are best done as a complete traverse to appreciate

The notorious Bwlch-y-Groes descending to Pennant

H
5-6h
****
††††

their finer qualities. It is easier to start from the northern end close to Llanuwchllyn, where the gradual climb opens expanding vistas with each step. The summit views are unrivalled in Wales: the Berwyns to the east and Arenigs and even Snowdon to the north, Cadair Idris to the west and to the south a never ending view of rolling hills. The descent recommended would be to follow the ridge south to Cym Cywarch, though this does require extra transport; alternatively, return north to where you started the walk.

Motorists journeying south from the Bwlch-y-Groes will find their trip equally enjoyable and exciting, though the descent is a trifle worrying for the nervous. Close to the summit is a small, single track road signposted Lake Vyrnwy leading off to the east. This is a fine mountain road that gently follows a small stream. There is limited parking but some fine picnic spots in lovely settings. Eventually the bumpy road descends to the lake.

The lake is in fact a reservoir, opened in 1888 to supply water to Liverpool. It was formed by building a massive dam on a natural ridge across the end of the valley. The old village in the valley,

The dam and overflow at Lake Vyrnwy

PLACES TO VISIT IN SOUTHERN SNOWDONIA

The Arans
Two magnificent peaks between Dinas Mawddwy and Bala Lake which provide one of the finest mountain walks south of Snowdon.

Bwlch-y-Groes
The summit of the highest road in Wales at 1,790ft. Bleak on a cold day, and no access from here to the nearby mountains, but the climb up Cwm Cynllwyd to the summit is beautiful.

Llyn Vyrnwy
Reservoir in a beautiful setting. Largest nature reserve in Wales, administered by the RSPB, with visitor centre, marked trails and picnic spots.

Ffrwd Fawr Waterfall
Near Dylife
The most spectacular fall in Wales, but difficult to get a good view, and the descent to the base on foot is hazardous.

Pistyll Gwyn
A fine waterfall a mile to the west of Llanymawddwy along a pleasant track.

Merion Woollen Mill
Dinas Mawddwy
Huge craft shop and display of weaving traditional tapestries.

Plas Machynlleth
Machynlleth
House originally built in 1653 in fine grounds. Houses local government offices and exhibition of Welsh crafts.

Centre for Alternative Technology
Machynlleth
Fascinating centre demonstrating the possibilities of living on a small share of the earth's resources. Much of interest, bookshop and restaurant.

Corris Railway Museum
Corris
Collection of memorabilia and

Llanwddyn, was first rebuilt below the dam, then the earlier houses and church were demolished and the villagers evacuated to the new village. Nowadays it is a beautiful setting — the lake formed is roughly four miles long, contains 12,000 million gallons of water and covers 1,100 acres. The area surrounding the lake is a nature reserve, the largest in Wales, and is administered by the Royal

material relating to the slate quarries and their railways.

Foel Friog Picnic Site
Aberllefeni
An idyllic and peaceful spot, ideal for children. Several waymarked tracks into the Dyfi Forest nearby.

Tal-y-Llyn Railway
One of the 'Great Little Trains of Wales'. Travels inland for seven miles, skirting the hills and valley of the Afon Fathew.

Castell-y-Bere
Dysynni Valley
Stands on large promontory rock near the head of the valley. Begun in 1221 but eventually captured by Edward I and destroyed in 1294. Fine ruins, with original layout still evident.

Fairbourne and Barmouth Steam Railway
Rebuilt engines from all over the world. Regular service along the coast to the Mawddach Estuary in summer.

Butterfly Safari
Fairbourne Station
Collection of free-flying butterflies from Africa, America and Asia. Also small mammals.

Creggennen
Twin lakes at about 800ft, in a shallow depression below Cadair Idris. Small car park and free access to banks of lake.

Precipice Walk, New Precipice Walk and Torrent Walk
Near Dolgellau
Three fine walks with magnificent views.

Penmaenpool Wildlife Centre
Near Dolgellau
In former railway signal box alongside Mawddach estuary, run by RSPB and North Wales Wildlife Trust. Information centre and observation point.
Also Morfa Mawddach Railway Walk along disused railway line on the south side of the estuary.

Society for the Protection of Birds who have converted an old Calvinistic chapel close to the dam into a visitor centre. There are many marked trails and maps are available of recommended routes.

L
1-2h
*
†††

A narrow road circumnavigates the lake with several picnic spots. Visitors are encouraged, though as the water is for drinking

Bunant Fawr, a beautiful spot on the moors above Lake Vyrnwy

The Vale of Dyfi north of Machynlleth

they must beware of causing any form of pollution, so boating and swimming are forbidden. From most viewpoints the Gothic-style draw-off tower gives an almost fairly tale impression to the surroundings. Many of the hillsides have been planted with mixed woodlands, further enhancing the scene and creating natural cover for wildlife and birds.

The lake can also be approached from the village of **Penybontfawr** in the Tanat Valley. It must be said that no matter what approach is taken, the roads are narrow and care must be exercised.

Returning to the Bwlch-y-Groes, the descent south into the valley is not for the faint hearted. The road is in a superb situation, terraced down the hillside. The hills, craggy and rough with deeply incised streams, give an air of grandeur to this fine cwm. It is a steep and narrow road with few passing places so care must be taken.

M
$^1/_2$-1h
**
††††

Shortly before the valley bottom is reached there is a sharp bend in the road. If you can park here or close by, a small path leads uphill following a fence to Llaethnant (Milk Valley) at the very head of the valley. Presumably the name relates to the beauty of the setting. The infant Dyfi flows from the high cwm below Aran Fawddwy over a series of small waterfalls and pools before starting its more leisurely flow to the sea. Some of the pools are ideal for paddling — the valley is sheltered and delightful on a warm sunny day.

Until very recently an enterprising local farmer had a small hydro-electric generator at the head of the valley providing electricity to the local farms and the nearby village of Llanymawddwy. He was the last private supplier in Wales; now it is operated by the local electricity board.

L
1-2h
**
†††

At last the road levels out and wanders easily along the valley bottom, first through **Llanymawddwy**, a hamlet on the Afon Dyfi. Close to the village are some fine waterfalls, notably Pistyll Gwyn, a mile to the west along a pleasant little track which starts by the church. The river is often known as the Royal Dyfi but whether it is because of the magnificent setting or the trout fishing is open to speculation; it is certainly a king of rivers.

There are many tempting places to stop along this tranquil valley before reaching **Dinas Mawddwy**. This small town, which had a fearsome reputation, lies in a lovely amphitheatre below wooded

The Merion Mill, Dinas Mawddwy

hills; during the flowering season much of the hillside is coloured by a breathtaking display of rhododendrons. The quiet little town, no longer fortified as its name would indicate, huddles along a wide main street and was once the centre for the nearby lead mining industry. In the sixteenth century the area was notorious for the red-haired thieves of Mawddwy who terrorised North Wales in the sixteenth century, plundering, pillaging and killing throughout the land until eventually they were caught in 1555 when eighty of the bandits were condemned to death.

Their reputation still lingers however, and amongst this wild scenery it is easy to conjure up the past. The local pub, The Red Lion, has a Brass Room full of old horse brasses and other collectable brass items. It is also known locally for its excellent restaurant.

Close to the Dyfi bridge just below the village is the terminus of the railway which closed in 1950. The old engine sheds now house a woollen mill open to the public with a huge craft shop and a display of weaving traditional tapestries; the station building is a café.

Mallwyd church with a whale rib hanging above the porch

The imposing clock tower at the end of the main street in Machynlleth

To the west of Dinas Mawddwy the busy A470 trunk road climbs up and over the Bwlch Oerddrws, with fine views of the southern hills and Cadair Idris before descending to the old coaching inn of Cross Foxes and then down to Dollgellau. It provides one of the main access roads into Wales from Shrewsbury and is a lovely journey through some of the best Welsh scenery.

Mallwyd just to the south of Dinas Mawddwy has a Brigands Inn, named to commemorate the Red Robbers. The church, close to the pub, has a whale's rib hanging in the porch (which is dated

1641), dug up locally in the nineteenth century. Its early history is vague, but how it came to be in the area is open to speculation.

Still following the Afon Dyfi the valley begins to open out and the hills become less dominant, the road winding easily now through the small villages of Cemmaes and Cemmaes Road before arriving at Machynlleth. To the north of this route is the huge expanse of the Dyfi Forest, which seems to cloak the upper slopes and even the summits of the hills.

Machynlleth, pronounced Ma'hun'hleth, is a smallish market town serving a very widespread population. It has an open atmosphere and a wide main street, at the end of which stands a large decorative clock tower. Built in 1872 to commemorate the coming of age of Lord Londonderry's heir, it is an elaborate structure which would no doubt cause the planning authorities a headache in this present age. The Londonderrys lived in a large house, Plas Machynlleth, just off the main street, which has been developed since its original foundation in 1653. It stands in fine grounds and was latterly donated to the town by the family, now housing local government offices and an exhibition of Welsh crafts. The gardens consist of a pleasant park open to the public.

Across the main street is the Owain Glyndwr Institute, a Tourist Information Centre and library, and adjacent is an older building known as Parliament House which is reputed to be the place where Owain Glyndwr held his first parliament in 1404. It was at this gathering that he first laid down his plans for an independent Wales with its own laws and universities. Sadly for him he never saw his dream come to fruition, though many Welsh people would still seek to achieve his goals.

A small mountain road signposted Dylife leaves the eastern end of the main street to follow an ancient trackway the route of which has changed little. It crosses a golf course to Forge before following the narrow valley of the Afon Dulas and climbing steeply to pick its way along a series of ridges giving splendid views of the rolling hills all around. To the south is Plynlimon, source of many rivers including the Severn. There is evidence of prehistoric man at the high point of the road, and just above is Bryn-y-Fedwen with some ancient burial mounds.

From the summit the road descends to the now almost deserted village of **Dylife**, once a bustling township in the eighteenth and nineteenth centuries when over 1,000 people lived here, mining the lead and sending it by horse drawn wagon to Machynlleth. There were three or four inns, several chapels, a church and a school to provide for their needs; there is one pub, The Star Inn, and a few isolated houses left. During its working life the mine is said to have had some of the best working conditions in the country, but now only a rather ugly site remains.

Below Dylife and just by the road is the Ffrwd Fawr waterfall. It is difficult to get a good view and the descent on foot to the base is hazardous but it certainly is the most spectacular fall in Wales. The difficulty of access has ensured that it remains relatively undisturbed. The water drops clear into a deeply incised rocky canyon before pouring over a series of cataracts to the gentler valley below. There is a small viewing platform close to the road but do take care.

Above Dylife is a small Roman fortlet which sits atop a rounded hill, again an indication of the antiquity of this roadway and its importance in the past. Penycroben hilltop is accessible by a footpath that starts close to the road junction in the village, a right turn along the ridge brings you to the summit and the Roman camp. Little remains to be seen; the walls of the fort were originally turf banks. During excavations in 1960 Roman pots were found, but no evidence to prove that they were aware of the lead ore to be found M locally. The name means Gibbet Hill, as later it was used for public 1h executions until the early nineteenth century. The trackway crosses ** the summit before a right turn returns you to the village. ††††

There are many small mountain roads in this area for those who prefer to get off the beaten track and explore a little but it is also worth returning to Machynlleth and heading north to the Dyfi Bridge, built originally in 1533 but later strengthened, to the road junction. The road to the west follows the Dyfi downstream to Aberdyfi and its estuary. For the moment however, take the northern route up through the valley of another Afon Dulas. This, like most of the roads hereabouts, winds up a narrow wooded valley with steep-sided hills on each side. A minor road runs parallel along the opposite side of the river and gives access to perhaps the most unusual visitor centre in Snowdonia.

Tucked away in a magnificent old slate quarry is the Centre for

A demonstration of solar panels at the Centre for Alternative Technology

Alternative Technology. It is a demonstration centre showing the possibilities of living on only a small share of the earths resources with a minimum of pollution and waste. It creates its own energy with windmills and solar panels, it grows much of its own food organically and shows the possibilities of re-cycling much of the waste we create in everyday living. It demonstrates a more economical way of life both in monetary cost and the saving of the earth's resources. It is altogether a fascinating place with much to offer the visitor in its displays and mode of life. There is a restaurant and bookshop with free parking; allow plenty of time for your visit — you will be truly surprised by the alternatives offered to 'normal' lifestyles.

L
1h
*
††

If you can tear yourself away, the Dulas valley still has much in store. There is a pleasant little picnic site at **Tan-y-Coed** which is the start of a waymarked walk which can be extended to the high moorlands ridge beyond. **Corris**, a small village standing at the confluence of the Dulas and a small tributary and dominated by tips from the surrounding slate workings, is the home of the Corris Railway Museum. It houses a collection of rolling stock (especially

Corris and the surrounding Dyfi Forest

their almost unique slate waggons), memorabilia and material relating to the nearby slate quarries and their railways. A length of track has been reinstated.

L-M
$^1/_2$-2h
**
†††

A minor road follows the Afon Dulas north to **Aberllefeni** giving access to the Dyfi Forest. Just short of the village is the Foel Friog picnic site, ideal for children and an idyllic spot far from the madding crowd. Close by are several waymarked tracks into the forest. Guides to the walks and the forest can usually be bought at local shops — it is a vast area so do take care not to get lost.

Take the main road from Corris to come first to the junction with the Tal-y-Llyn valley at Minffordd and then climb steeply over the rugged shoulder of Cadair Idris to descend to Cross Foxes and so to Dolgellau.

The alternative route from Machynlleth and Dyfi Bridge follows the Afon Dyfi, first across the wide river valley and then tightly along the very side of the estuary sharing the narrow bank with the main line railway. The estuary to the south is an important site for the study of wildfowl and migrant waders; the marshes across the estuary are part of the Dyfi National Nature Reserve and contain much, beside wildfowl, of scientific interest. Most of the area has restricted access and is maintained by the Royal Society for the Protection of Birds.

Aberdyfi is a small coastal resort hugging the side of the estuary. It is a colourful little town huddled along the quayside. A venue for yachtsmen and holidaymakers it still manages to retain its very Welsh feel. The quay is a busy little place catering for the Outward Bound School of Wales who provide courses in sailing, canoeing and climbing locally. Close by is a wide sandy beach which stretches some way up the coast.

The town is immortalised in the song *The Bells of Aberdovey* from Charles Dibdins' opera *Liberty Hall*, based on an old Welsh legend that below the sea lies an old village and church, drowned many years ago, but the bells of the church still peal. The legend first appears in the thirteenth century, but became popular with writers in the romantic period of the eighteenth and nineteenth centuries.

The road and railway continue to follow the coast past the well known golf course to **Tywyn**, a rather bleak town that has become a popular seaside resort with a wide sand and shingle beach.

*The Dolgoch viaduct
of the Tal-y-Llyn
Railway*

Perhaps its main claim to fame is that it is the terminus for the Tal-y-Llyn Railway, one of the 'Great Little Trains of Wales'.

 The railway opened in 1865 to serve the slate quarries in the Tal-y-Llyn valley. It starts at Tywyn Wharf station, where there is a museum with many exhibits from the heyday of narrow gauge railways. Saved from closure by volunteers the line travels inland, skirting the hills and valley of the Afon Fathew for just over seven miles. There are several stations en route and at **Dolgoch** the railway crosses an impressive viaduct to the station. A scenic walk to the Dolgoch waterfalls makes a pleasant excursion, with a not too steep climb up through the woods. The line continues to **Nant**

Aberdyfi and the estuary

L
$^1/_2$-2h
*

†††

Gwernol, where there are extensive forest walks above the terminus at **Abergynolwyn**.

The narrow valley can also be followed by car, though the journey may be more fraught for the road is narrow and busy in summer. The walks to the falls can easily be reached from the roadside, as can those in the forest above Abergynolwyn, from convenient car parks at both points. From the village a trackway can be followed to the south up to the old Bryneglwys slate quarry for which the railway was originally built.

Continuing up the valley will bring you to Tal-y-Llyn (lake), a pleasant spot with many places to picnic and relax along its shoreline. In fine weather the lake is ideal for swimming and there are two hotels close by. The steep southern slopes of Cadair Idris rise sharply from the lake to dominate the surrounding countryside. The finest ascent of this mountain starts in the valley just north of the lake close to Minffordd, which will be described later.

Parallel with the valley of the Tal-y-Llyn, accessible on the minor road north-west and signposted from Abergynolwyn, is the Dysynni

Tal-y-Llyn

Valley; more open and with wider views it has a charm of its own. Dominated by the great mountain to the north it is peaceful and more rural, in sharp contrast to its past when it was swept by the great glaciers descending from the north.

In this isolated valley, now far from the mainstream of Welsh political life, Llewelyn the Great built what was to be one of the most important of Welsh castles, Castell-y-Bere. Carefully designed and ornately constructed, it stands on a large promontory of rock near the head of the valley. Begun in 1221, it saw many Welsh rulers, some optimistic some despairing, before Edward I crushed so many hopes in 1277. Dafydd, brother of Llewelyn and the last Welsh prince, established himself at the castle and continued his forays against the English. The enraged Edward sent his armies after Dafydd and the castle became the last point of resistance for the Welsh people. Eventually captured, the castle fell to Edward and was finally destroyed in 1294, its short but turbulent history over. The ruins are rather grand on their rocky crest, and the original layout is still evident with three ruined towers and a rectangular keep. It is difficult to imagine that this peaceful valley played such a significant part in Welsh history.

Looming large above the lower reaches of the valley is Craig-y-Aderyn, Bird Rock, a sharp crag that is a remnant from the days when this low lying valley was an arm of the sea. It is still a breeding place for cormorants and is protected by the RSPB.

A fine road, which in the South of France would be described as a corniche, follows the coastline north. High above the sea it hugs the steep hillside with some fine views across Cardigan Bay before reaching **Borth** and later **Fairbourne**, two coastal resorts that are more in the English style than Welsh. They are a collection of caravan sites and holiday bungalows that, though busy in summer, lie dormant for much of the year.

Fairbourne, like its close neighbour Tywyn, is the home of a narrow gauge railway. The Fairbourne and Barmouth Steam Railway is a major award winner and visitor attraction; it has has been reconstucted to a 12$\frac{1}{2}$in gauge and the trains are pulled by scale replicas of famous narrow gauge locomotives based on both British and foreign prototypes. During the summer a regular service operates along a two-mile stretch of the coast north to the Mawddach estuary, where an adjoining ferry will take you across the waters to Barmouth before returning. The stations on the line are re-created in Victorian style and much of the equipment is manufactured in the railway's own workshop.

A recent additional attraction at the station is the Butterfly Safari. Housed in a purpose-made building are free flying butterflies from Africa, America and Asia. An adjacent collection houses a range of small mammals such as racoons, lemurs and wildcats. Regardless of the weather, the atmosphere is carefully controlled and it can be an ideal family day out. Tickets are available at the station to cover both attractions.

A short distance to the north of Fairbourne, close to the wide marshlands of the estuary, is the small village of **Arthog**, its terraced houses hugging the roadside; a single track road climbs steeply from the village past Arthog Hall and waterfalls. Following the stream it rises quickly to reach the twin lakes of Cregennen at about 800ft. It is a lovely spot, the scenery so different from that of the coast a short distance away. It can also be much cooler. The

Eldon Square, Dolgellau

lakes and the countryside around them were given to the National Trust in 1959 by Major C.L. Wynne-Jones in memory of his two sons who had been killed in the war.

Cregennen sits in a shallow depression below the steep flanks of Cadair Idris; there is a small car park and free access to the banks of the lake. A large log cabin on the shore of the lake was imported from Canada in the late nineteenth century and erected here by the Wynne-Jones family. It can be booked for holidays from the National Trust.

An impressive looking hill, Bryn Brith (1,256ft) stands to the north of the lakes, which can be ascended easily by the wide footpath up the ridge. Cadair Idris, which dominates the whole scene, can be climbed from this side, though it must be quite a daunting ascent as the slope here is at its steepest.

M
1-1½h
*

†††

Past Cregennen the road wanders around the contour of Cadair giving some fine views of the mountain and also access to several footpaths which lead upwards towards its summit. Passing the small but pleasantly situated Gwernan Lake and hotel, it finally

Cadair Idris and the Cregennen lakes

descends easily to Dolgellau.

The main centre and market town for a much of the surrounding mountain district, **Dolgellau** can be very busy in summer. Several main roads meet here and at one time all used to pass through the centre of the town, but a bypass now alleviates at least some of this traffic. It is a very Welsh town, despite its popularity with visitors, clustered around its central square with its grey stone and slate buildings.

Despite being the major town in the old county of Merioneth and at the main crossing point of the Afon Wnion it seems to have figured little in Welsh history. In 1405 Owain Glyndwr is said to have held the last Welsh Parliament here, though the house in which it was reputed to have been held was dismantled in 1882 to make way for a shop and removed bodily to Newtown.

Within a short distance of the town are several shorter walks that have been popular since Victorian times. Perhaps the most famous is the Precipice Walk, a three-mile walk which circles Foel Cynwch just to the north of the river. The start is best made from near to the

Cadair Idris

M
1½-2h
*
††††

entrance of Nannau Park on the Dolgellau to Llanfachreth Road, where there is a car park and picnic spot. The route is clearly signposted and follows a terraced route around the hill. It is a delightful stroll, giving some of the best views across the Mawddach estuary and to Cadair Idris in the south. The walking is easy and though airy is safe for children. There are no major climbs involved and if care is taken the path is safe.

M
2-3h
*
†††

Another fine circular walk is the New Precipice Walk, which can be completed in about three hours. From **Llanelltyd** take a path to the right over a hump-backed bridge, bear left until you reach a lake, then head towards a house high on the mountainside. This path leads to a mountain road which drops down to the main road at Penmaenpool. This walk also has spectacular views.

L
1-2h
*
††

The Torrent Walk follows the deep glen of the Clydewog, starting at the junction with the Afon Wnion about one and a half miles east of Dolgellau. Approach down a minor road which leaves the A470 about a mile out of Dolgellau, or alternatively there is a small car park just after turning off to Brithdir, in which case the walk will be downstream. The well made path follows the narrow river as it tumbles down deep clefts and cataracts. It is a lovely walk at any time.

A couple of miles downstream from Dolgellau, where a toll road crosses the Afon Mawddach over a wooden bridge, is the Penmaenpool Wildlife Centre in a former railway signal box with an information centre and observation point. The wildlife centre is owned by the Snowdonia National Park, but is administered jointly by the Royal Society for the Protection of Birds and the North Wales Wildlife Trust, who provide telescopes and binoculars for public use.

When the railway line closed down in 1965 the National Park purchased the section from Dolgellau to Morfa Mawddach and converted it to a walk along the south side of the estuary. For those who like guided walks the RSPB lead groups along the Railway Walk during the summer, as well as walks through their bird reserve at Coed Garth Gell at the northern end of the Penmaenpool toll bridge.

Throughout this area Cadair Idris dominates the view. It is a huge mountain that seems to loom above the surrounding countryside no matter where you are. It is one of the great Welsh mountains

Penmaenpool toll bridge and former signal box

and though not quite as high as the earlier mentioned Arans it seems to have much more presence. After Snowdon it is perhaps the most climbed mountain in the National Park.

Cadair Idris, the 'Chair of Idris', is named, according to legend, after the giant Idris who was at once astronomer, poet and philosopher. His 'chair' is reputed to be the precipitous hollow between the summit and Llyn-y-Gadair, his observatory, a chamber formed by massive rocks. Whoever spends a night in his chair is said to awake as a poet or a madman. It can only be hoped that Idris is a friendly giant, as the mountain is very popular with walkers; its summit is marked by a huge cairn amongst a chaotic jumble of rocks and the views are superior to those of any mountain in Wales, those to the north being the best. On a clear day it is possible to see the Rhinogs range running south to north, and beyond them most of the mountains in the Snowdon massif. To the north-east are the Arenigs and the Arans and further east are the hills of Shropshire, the Long Mynd and the Wrekin; to the south are the Radnor forest and the mountains of central Wales. The whole of the coastline from

The sign which is to be seen at the boundaries of the Snowdonia National Park

the Lleyn Peninsula in the north to St Davids Head in the south should be visible on a clear day, and you may be very lucky and see across the sea to Ireland and the Wicklow Hills. It is certainly a magnificent prospect.

The ascent of this great hill can be made from most points of the compass. Some paths are famous, others less favoured, but all will bring you to the summit with a little effort. Go prepared on this mountain, as there is no railway or summit café to reward your efforts. The paths are reasonably well signposted where they leave the road and are quite well worn as they ascend; it is possible in some cases to reach the summit by one of them and descend by an alternative. Those contemplating climbing Cadair Idris should arm themselves with the Ordnance Survey Outdoor Leisure Map No 23 *Cadair Idris Area*, which is excellent and can only increase the enjoyment of their day. They should also allow for at least four hours walking to appreciate the mountain, and go prepared for cooler weather on the summit.

The mountain is in fact a long ridge, precipitous and craggy on its northern face, but more gently sloped to the south. The summit is Penygadair at 2,927ft. It stands on a narrow section of the ridge high above the cwm or seat of Idris. Llyn-y-Gadair lies to the north and the great bowl of Llyn Cau is to the south.

Two famous ascents start from the northern side of the mountain. In Victorian and Edwardian times the Foxes Path was popular, starting from Dolgellau and walking along the road, though nowadays most people would opt to park at Gwernan Lake and take the footpath opposite which climbs quite steeply to the Llyn-y-Gadair then more steeply up a jumble of boulders to reach the summit.

The Pony Path commences close to a car park at Ty-Nant about a mile south of Foxes Path. It climbs in a more leisurely way at first, but more steeply as it nears the ridge. Here it meets the path coming up from the south and turns east to climb steeply to the summit. The Foxes Path could be taken as an alternative means of descent.

The very fit might like to contemplate doing the whole ridge, starting at Cross Foxes Hotel in the north and heading south over all the summits to finish on the coast near Fairbourne. It would be a superb walk.

On the southern side of the mountain one of the more popular climbs is the Minffordd Path, beginning pleasantly in the valley just to the north of Tall-y-Llyn (lake). A path leaves the roadside close to Minffordd and climbs quite steeply up to Llyn Cau, a haunting spot, a dark lake set in a deep craggy cwm. You can rest awhile now, as the path follows the edge of the lake and is relatively flat before climbing very steeply out and onto the ridge below the summit. An easy but steep ascent leads to the cairn and refuge shelter. This is the best though steepest ascent, full of interest and with some fine situations.

Llanfihangel — a trackway — is the longest ascent, but also the least steep. Starting at the head of the valley north of Castell-y-Bere, it ascends easily alongside the Afon Cadair and along the flanks of the hills to meet the Pony Path on the summit ridge. Turning to the east it climbs to the summit. The early part of the trackway follows the line of the ancient packhorse trail which continued over the ridge to Dolgellau.

Many keen walkers will doubtless be able to find alternative routes to those suggested. Whichever way you decide to go, it is certain that you will have a memorable day with, weather permitting, one of the best views in the country as your reward.

The whole of the southern section of Snowdonia is in sharp contrast to the rest of North Wales. The scenery is superb, the villages are smaller and more homely and you must to a greater extent be prepared to explore to get the most from the countryside. There is something for everyone, and the effort required is always worthwhile. Every area has its own particular character, each slightly different from its neighbour, but all can be appreciated in their own right and in their own special way.

USEFUL INFORMATION FOR VISITORS

ACCOMMODATION

There is a great range of accommodation available in North Wales, everything from caravans and guest houses to luxury hotels. Many visitors will have booked their stay in advance, but for those who cannot, or are content to tour without prior booking, many Tourist Information Centres offer a bed booking service. This service is designed to give information on type, style and prices of accommodation and recommends the most suitable for your requirements. If you prefer to scout about for your own accommodation the Tourist Information Centres can generally supply a list of hotels, guest houses and other beds available in the locality.

Youth Hostels

Throughout North Wales there is a chain of Youth Hostels. These are ideal for all ages, and are not restricted to young people. They are cheap to stay at and are generally in beautiful situations. The dormitory accommodation is excellent and meals can usually be provided.

There are hostels at:

Clwyd
Chester
Colwyn Bay
Corris
Cynwyd
Llangollen
Maeshafn

Gwynedd
Bala
Bangor
Betws-y-Coed
Bryn Gwynant, Beddgelert
Capel Curig
Ffestiniog
Harlech

Idwal Cottage
Kings, Dolgellau
Llanbedr
Llanberis
Lledr Valley, Dolwyddaelan
Penmaenmawr
Pen-y-Pass near Snowdon
Rowen
Snowdon Ranger

For further information and leaflets covering all aspects of youth hostelling in North Wales contact the regional office:
YHA Area Office
12 Wynnstay Road
Colwyn Bay
Clwyd
LL29 8NB
☎ (0492) 531406

ARCHAEOLOGICAL SITES

North Wales has many sites that may be of interest to visitors who are keen on history and prehistory. There are trackways, burial sites, hill forts and many standing stones and hut circles. Most are marked on Ordnance Survey maps and most are documented in separate guidebooks, which can only add to your tour of Wales and provide some good short walks and excursions. Here are a few of the major sites:

Clwyd

Elisegs Pillar
Llangollen
1,000-year-old carved pillar relating tale of early Welsh Prince Eliseg in field west of Valle Crucis Abbey.

Maen Achwyfan
Whitford
1 mile west of village
Eleventh-century wheel cross with fine carvings.

Offa's Dyke
Linear earthwork that runs parallel with English border. Bank and ditch now not too evident. Also a long-distance footpath.

Gwynedd

Capel Garmon
Neolithic burial chamber in fine situation on hills above and to east of Betws-y-Coed. Easily accessible on foot.

Harlech
The area behind Harlech, accessible by mountain road, has some fine hut circles and standing stones. There is also an Iron Age hillfort at Moel Coedog. South at Dyffryn Ardudwy are good examples of burial chambers.

Muriau'r Gwyddelod
Just off road south of Harlech. Huts, circles and enclosures possibly of early Irish settlers. Sometimes known as Irishman's Walls, they also occur in other locations.

Roman Steps
At Cwm Bychan, inland from Llanbedr, there is a line of steps going over the mountain pass. They are unlikely to be Roman, but are still very old.

Tomen-y-Mur
Near Trawsfynydd
Roman amphitheatre and encampment with later motte on same site.

Tre'r Ceiri

North of Nefyn on the Rivals (Yr Eifl). Superb remains of Iron Age fortified township with stone walls. Steep climb from road but worth it. Unprotected and now getting vandalised.

Anglesey

The island has a wealth of prehistory, evident particularly in the southern corner and on Holy Island.

Bryn-Celli-Ddu

Near Llanfair PG
Chamber and small mound now remaining of much larger construction.

Caer Gybi

Holyhead
Roman fort almost intact with high walls and towers. Later St Gybi's church built within walls.

Din Llugwy

Near Moelfre
Fortified village of variety of huts, well preserved in fine setting with other antiquities in vicinity.

Holyhead Mountain Hut Circles

Close to car park on South Stack road.
Some hut circles remaining of large farming village occupied from neolithic to Roman times.

BUS SERVICES

Sherpa Service

A regular bus service operating around Snowdon during summer for walkers and visitors. Runs from Caernarfon, Llanrwst or Porthmadog from May-September. Timetable from Tourist Office or Bus Station.

At least twenty different bus companies operate within the regions. Many have a smart new livery of red at the front and bear a sign 'Bws Gwynedd' for the western regions and 'Bws Clwyd' to the east of the area.
Timetable enquiries for Bws Clwyd should be directed to the Clwyd County Offices,
☎ 0352 2121, Ext 4035
In Gwynedd timetable leaflets are available for most individual regions and will be available on the buses or from Infomation Centres.

CASTLES

The heyday of castle building in North Wales was in the twelfth and thirteenth centuries and the introduction of masonry walls at that time has ensured the survival of at least some remains. Iron Age hillforts, Roman enclosures and the later mottes from before this period can be seen throughout the area, but apart from the earthworks associated with these fortifications little remains of their above-ground structures.

Many of the smaller medieval castles were constructed originally by the Welsh princes in their struggles to defend the country, at first from Norman invaders and later from the succeeding monarchs' attempts to conquer the country.

In 1272 Edward I came to the

throne of England and started a campaign to subdue the Welsh princes. By 1283 he had quashed the revolt and set about building his massive 'Ring of Steel' to subjugate the Welsh. He built new castles which could be supplied by sea and strengthened strategic Welsh fortifications.

Many of the remains seen today date from this period; some examples show the ultimate in castle building techniques and overall must constitute the finest remains within any area of Europe.

The major fortifications are generally dominant in the town or village so no addresses have been given. Most are open throughout the year, some contain small museums; some have an admission charge but the smaller sites are usually free of charge.

Beaumaris
Fine castle on low-lying site with moat.

Caernarfon
The peak of the castle builders art. Traditionally associated with the Prince of Wales.

Castell Dinas-Bran
Llangollen.
Ruins high on hill overlooking the Vale of Dee.

Castell-y-Bere
Close to Tywyn.
Beautiful setting, significant in Welsh history.

Conwy
Masterpiece of engineering, complete with town walls.

Criccieth
Welsh castle extended by Edward I.

Denbigh
Thirteenth-century, with violent history in later centuries.

Deganwy
Small Welsh fortification, on Conwy estuary.

Dolbadarn
Welsh royal castle with surviving keep close to Llanberis.

Dolwyddelan
Birthplace of Llewelyn the Great — little left.

Ewloe
Pleasant site close to English borderlands.

Flint
First of Edward's castles, on the edge of the Dee. Separate Donjon.

Harlech
Commanding position; massive walls; significant in later history.

Hawarden
Old castle with little remaining. Later mansion on site was home of Gladstone, Prime Minister to Queen Victoria.

Rhuddlan
Fine remains of significant castle. Treaty of Rhuddlan in 1277 saw surrender of Llewelyn to Edward I.

Ruthin
Baronial castle now part of hotel. Permission needed to visit.

Segontium
Roman fort on outskirts of Caernarfon.

CHURCHES AND RELIGIOUS MONUMENTS

Western Wales was influenced greatly by the Celtic saints who in the sixth and seventh centuries converted the natives to Christianity. If they had churches, little now remains. However, many are associated with wells which can be visited. In other cases it is likely that present day churches occupy the sites of earlier temporary buildings and there is little doubt that this religious connection is extremely longstanding. All abbeys or monasteries were razed to the ground on the order of Henry VII and few walls remain. More recently Welsh religion has swung towards Methodism, and most villages have a fine, sometimes almost Palladian, chapel. This information is by necessity limited to the major religious sites or ruins.

Bangor Cathedral
Monastic community founded in 525 by St Deiniol and in continuous use since then.

Basingwerk Abbey
1m north-east of Flint.
Known to have been the finest monastery in Britain. Little now remains.

Clynnog Fawr
South of Caernarfon on Pwllheli Road.
Thought to have been the Mother Church of Wales founded in 616 by St Beuno and used ever since. Other ancient sites in vicinity.

Cymer Abbey
2 miles east of Dolgellau, just off road to Barmouth.
Not a lot remaining but a lovely place.

Penmon Priory
Just north of Beaumaris, Anglesey. Remains are twelfth-century and still occupied. Dovecote and well reputed to be St Seriol's. Close to Puffin Island.

St Asaph Cathedral
Said to be the smallest in Britain with library and collection of Welsh and other religious papers.

St Winifride's Chapel and Well
Holywell, Clwyd.
A place of pilgrimage with curative powers. A fine example of Perpendicular work donated by Margaret Beaufort, mother of Henry VII.

Valle Crucis Abbey
$1\frac{1}{2}$ miles west of Llangollen. Remains of Cistercian abbey in beautiful situation.

FISHING

In a country so well endowed with rivers, lakes and the sea there is obviously a wide variety of fishing available. It is necessary though to have the required permits for each stretch of inland water. Each small river, stream, lake, reservoir or canal falls within the boundary of the Welsh Water Authority. You must first obtain a licence from them to fish in these waters, then you must obtain a permit (usually available locally) to fish in the relevant stream or lake. Remember the rights to fish any stretch of water belong to the owner of the adjacent bank.

Welsh Water Authority Offices

Gwynedd River Division
Highfield, Caernarfon, Gwynedd
☎ (0286) 2247

Dee and Clwyd River Division
Shire Hall, Mold, Clwyd
☎ (0352) 2121

Some lakes for fishing:
Llyn Trawsfynydd
Llyn Tegid (Bala Lake)
Llyn Alaw, Anglesey
Tan-y-Grisiau Reservoir, Blaenau
    Ffestiniog
Llyn Brenig, near Denbigh
Lake Vyrnwy

Sea fishing is widespread right around the coast of North Wales, providing many varieties of fish and fishing. There are sands, piers and jetties and even rocks to provide a variation for the sea angler. Boats can be hired at several centres for the more adventurous.

The keen angler will probably already have a copy of the excellent publication by the Welsh Tourist Board. The Wales *Angling Guide* available nationally will tell you all you need to know about

the inland and sea fishing available throughout Wales

GUIDED WALKS

The Snowdonia National Park offers a full range of guided walks throughout the season. They also offer many courses on subjects of interest such as local history, wildlife, mines and quarries, birdwatching, photography and painting. Many are for weekends or a full week. The programme of courses and walks is subject to revision each year. Details of both can be obtained from:

Snowdonia National Park Offices
Penrhyndeudraeth
Gwynedd LL68 6LF
☎ 0766-770274
or from any of the National Park visitor centres.

HOUSES AND GARDENS OPEN TO THE PUBLIC

Generally open daily between April and September.

Aberconwy House
(National Trust)
Conwy, junction of High Street and Castle Street.
☎ Conwy 2246
Open: daily, April-September, 10am-5.30pm.
Exhibition of Conwy history

Bodnant Gardens (National Trust)
Tal-y-Cafn, Colwyn Bay

Off A470, 5 miles south of Conwy
Beautiful gardens, some of the
best in Europe.
Open: daily, March-October,
10am-5pm

Bodrhydan Hall
Rhuddlan
3 miles south-east of Rhyl.
Open: June-September, Tuesday
and Thursday afternoons

Bryn Bras Castle
Llanrug, Caernarfon
A4086 between Caernarfon and
Llanberis
Open: Sunday and weekday
afternoons May-September; late
July and August 10.30am-5pm.
Romanesque castle in extensive
grounds

Chirk Castle (National Trust)
Off A5, $1/_2$ mile west of village
Open: April-September daily
except Monday and Saturday.
Early fortress which later became
an elegant household. Fine
wrought iron gates

Erddig House (National Trust)
Wrexham
Off A438, 1 mile south of Wrex-
ham.
Open: April-October, 12noon-
5.30pm, closed Monday.
Agricultural museum, restaurant

Gwydir Castle
Llanrwst
Off B5106 close to Llanrwst
Open: daily in summer except
Saturdays.
Historic Tudor mansion with
peacocks

Gwyrch Castle, Abergele
1 mile south-east of town centre.
☎ Abergele 825007
Open: each afternoon mid-May to
mid September. Café, walks and
amusements

Hafodty Gardens
Betws-Garmon, Caernarfon
4 miles south of Caernarfon on
A487
Open: daily, no charge but charity
collection box

Penrhyn Castle (National Trust)
Bangor
A5, one mile east of Bangor
Open: every day beginning April
to end October. April, May and
October 2-5pm; June-September
11am-5pm
☎ Bangor 53084
Magnificent neo-Norman hall,
Railway Museum and Doll
Museum.
Restaurant

Plas Mawr
Conwy
High Street.
Fine sixteenth-century house now
home of Royal Cambrian
Academy of Art

Plas Newydd (National Trust)
Llanfair PG, Anglesey
1 mile south-west of Llanfair PG
on A4080
Open: daily mid-April to end
October except Saturday,
12noon-5pm
☎ Llanfair 714795
On edge of Menai Straits, home
of Marquess of Anglesey. Military
Museum, restaurant

Plas Newydd
Llangollen
1 mile south of town centre.
Open: May-September

Plas-yn-Rhiw
On Lleyn Peninsula south of Pwllheli, on the road to Aber-daron.
Open: April-September daily except Saturday.
Small seventeenth-century manor house in beautiful setting

Portmeirion
Porthmadog
Near Minffordd, 2 miles east of Porthmadog
Open: daily Easter-October
Italianate village in fine setting and gardens

Smallest House
Conwy
On the quay.
Open: daily during summer

Ty Gwyn
Barmouth
On harbour front
Open: summer season
☎ 0341-422341
Medieval Tower House where Tudor plotted to seize the throne of England

Ty Mawr (National Trust)
Wybrnant, Gwybernant
3¹/₂ miles south-west of Betws-y-Coed
Open: April-October daily except Saturday, 12noon-5pm.
Birthplace of Bishop Morgan.
Nature trail

LEISURE CENTRES

Most have pools, squash courts, badminton and other facilities.

Aberconwy Centre
Llandudno
☎ 0492-79771

Amlwch Leisure Centre
☎ 0407-830060

Buckley Sports Centre
☎ 0244-546458

Caernarfon Leisure Centre
☎ 0286-76451

Colwyn Bay
☎ 0492-63323

Deeside, Queensferry
☎ 0244-812311

Flint
☎ 03526-3677

Holyhead
☎ 0407-4111

Holywell
☎ 0352-712027

Mold Sports Centre
☎ 0352-56116

Plas Arthur Centre
Llangefni (Anglesey)
☎ 0248-722966

Plas Madoc Centre
Porthmadog
☎ 0978-821600

Prestatyn:
Nova Complex
☎ 07456-88021
Sports Centre
☎ 07456-5632

St Asaph
☎ 0745-583368

Wrexham:
Plas Madoc
☎ 0978-821600
Queensway
☎ 0978-355826
St Davids
☎ 0978-353792

MILLS AND CRAFTS

Many towns have a craft shop or two in the main street, while tourist attractions also usually have an associated craft shop selling locally made artefacts, so it is not feasible to list them all here. This list has therefore been restricted to places of manufacture that can be visited. There are many artisans working in North Wales who make a variety of products, and the local information office will be able to give the most up-to-date information. Below are listed some of the places to visit.

Potteries

Cae Dafydd
Llanfrothen, close to Beddgelert
Also has rare breed centre.

Conwy Potteries
Tyn-y-Coed Farm,
Glan Conwy, Colwyn Bay

Cwm Pottery
Trefor, near Caernarfon
Glazed pottery made in splendid location.

Dolwyddelan Pottery
The Old School, Dolwyddelan

Throwing, casting handling always in progress.

Llanbedrog Pottery
near Pwllheli
See a variety of processes.

Piggery Potteries
Y Glyn, Llanberis

Porthmadog Pottery
Snowdon Street, Porthmadog
Throw your own pot.

Woollen Mills and Knitwear

Bodeilio Weaving Centre
near Llangefni, Anglesey
Open: daily during summer

Brynkir Woollen Mills
Golan, near Porthmadog
Open: all year during working week

Holywell Textile Mills
Holywell
Open: all year Monday-Saturdays

Llangollen Weavers
Llangollen
Open: all year

Meirion Mills
Dinas Mawddwy

Penmachno Woollen Mill
near Betws-y-Coed
Open: all year during working hours and weekends in summer

Trefriw Woollen Mills
Llanrwst
Open: all year during working week and Saturdays and Sundays in summer.

Flour Mills

Felin Isaf
Llantsantffraid, Conwy Valley
Open: April-October, Tuesdays-
Saturdays and Sunday 2.30-
5.00pm.

Slate Products

Gloddfa Ganol
Blaenau Ffestiniog
See slate work direct from quarry
face.

Inigo Jones
Tudor Slateworks, Groesion, near
Caernarfon
Exhibition and workshops, clocks,
lettercutting and old skills.

Llechwedd Slate Products
Blaenau Ffestiniog
Underground tours of mines and
various products manufactured.

Other Crafts

Maes Artro
Llanbedr, near Harlech
Open every day during season
and some parts throughout the
year. Sells and manufactures a
wide range of products.

Ruthin Craft Centre
Lon Parcwr, Ruthin
A purpose-built craft complex with
fourteen different craft workers.

MUSEUMS AND ART GALLERIES

Some museums are run by the
local councils and are open all
year round. Privately owned ones
are generally open only during
summer months. Most have
giftshops and cafés.

Canal Exhibition Centre
The Wharf, Llangollen
☎ 0978 860702
Open: Easter-end September
Museum of life on the narrow
boat, horse drawn rides along the
canal.

Conwy Valley Railway Museum
The Old Goods Yard, Betws-y-
Coed
☎ 069202 568
Displays covering all aspects of
railways.

Daniel Owen Centre
Earl Road, Mold
☎ Mold 4791
Art gallery as well as memorabilia
of Welsh author

David Windsor Gallery
High Street, Bangor
Closed Wednesdays, Saturdays
and Bank Holidays
Displays of paintings and
porcelain from all over the world

**Encounter, North Wales
Museum of Wildlife**
School Bank Road, Llanrwst
Open: summer: Monday-
Saturday, 9.30am-6.30pm; winter:
Monday-Friday, 10.30am-6.30pm
Collection of big game trophies
and rare birds both local and from
around the world

Geological Museum of Wales
Bwlch-gwyn, Wrexham
Adjacent to A525, $1/_2$ mile west of
Bwlch-gwyn.

Exhibition of industrial relics and mining. Marked trail

Grange Cavern Military Museum
Holywell
Off A55 at Holway, near Holywell
Open: summer, 9am-6pm, winter, 9am-5pm
Collection of military vehicles and militaria in limestone caverns

Holyhead Maritime Museum
Rhos-y-Gaer Avenue, Holyhead
Open: daily May-September except Mondays. Open Bank Holidays

Llandudno Doll Museum
Masonic Street, Llandudno
Open: Easter-end of September, Monday-Saturday
Collection of old dolls and toy railways

Lleyn Historical and Maritime Museum
Old St Marys Church, Nefyn
Open: July-September

Lloyd George Museum
Llanystumdwy, near Criccieth
Open: May-September, 10am-5pm weekdays
Mementoes of this great man

Maelor Arts Centre
Rhosddu Road, Wrexham
☎ Wrexham 2351
Visiting exhibitions and displays

Mostyn Art Gallery
12 Vaughan Street, Llandudno
Open: April-September, 11am-6pm; October-March, 11am-5pm
Wide range of contemporary arts

from Wales and abroad

Motor Museum
Pentrefelin, Llangollen
☎ 0978 860324
Working cars and garage

Museum of Childhood
Water Street, Menai Bridge, Anglesey
☎ 0248 712498
Open: Easter-October, Monday-Saturday, 10am-6pm, Sunday, 1-5pm
Collection of everying to do with children over the last 150 years

Museum of Old Welsh Country Life
Felin Faesog, Tai'n Lon, Clynnog Fawr
East of A499, 10 miles south of Caernarfon
Open: April-October, daily 10am-5pm
Folk museum in old corn mill

Museum of the North
Llanberis, Gwynedd
☎ 0286 870636
Open: May-September
New building devoted to natural environment of Snowdonia and Welsh nation

Museum of Welsh Antiquities
Fford Gwynedd, Bangor
Visiting exhibitions of painting and sculpture

Porthmadog Maritime Museum
The Harbour, Porthmadog
Open: daily April-September
Interesting display of harbour life 100 years ago. Slate quay re-created with sail ketch to explore

Rapallo House Museum and Art Gallery
Ffern Road, Llandudno
Open: April-November, Monday-Friday
Collection of paintings, sculptures, armour and weapons

The Royal Cambrian Academy of Art
Plas Mawr, Conwy
Annual summer exhibitions of Welsh artists

Segontium Roman Fort and Museum (National Trust)
1 mile south of Caernarfon on A4085
Open: mid-March-mid-October, Monday-Saturday, 9.30am-6.30pm; Sunday, 2-6.30pm; Mid-October-mid-March, Monday-Saturday, 9.30am-4pm, Sunday, 2-4pm
Archaeological finds and foundations

Seiont II Maritime Museum
Victoria Dock, Caernarfon
Open: daily Easter-September
Visit working steam boat.

Welsh Slate Museum
Llanberis
☎ 028 682 630
Open: daily, Easter, 9.30am-5.30pm; May-September, 9.30am-6.30pm
Shows how the slate was won, with original machinery and buildings

NATURE TRAILS AND RESERVES

There are innumerable nature trails and town trails throughout North Wales. Many are run by local authorities, the Forestry Commission or CEGB (at power stations). Most produce individual leaflets containing details of routes, etc. It is therefore wise to enquire locally for these.

The Welsh Tourist Board publishes a booklet available in most shops and information centres, called appropriately *Walking*, it covers most nature trails and town trails in the area.

The following bird reserves are owned or run by the RSPB or NWWT and welcome visitors. They are usually always open.

Aber Oguren
Near Penrhyn Castle.

Coed Garth Gell
Off A496 near north side of Penmaenpool toll bridge across Mawddach estuary.
Reserve and nature trail
☎ 0341 250650

Great Orme Country Park
Llandudno
Other nearby reserves at Little Orme, Rhos Point and Pensarn Beach.

Point of Air
On the Dee estuary east of Prestatyn.

Llyn Brenig
Clwyd
Off B4501 south-west of Denbigh.

Llyn Penrhyn
Anglesey
Near RAF Valley.

Lake Vyrnwy
Information centre off the B4393
Llanwddyn-Llanfyllin road.
☎ 069173 278

Penmaenpool Wildlife Centre
On A493 west of Dolgellau on
south side of toll bridge across
Mawddach estuary. Information
centre in old railway signal box.
Open: daily late May to September
☎ 0341 250650

South Stack Cliffs
Anglesey
Telescopes and remote-controlled
cameras at Ellin's Tower Information Centre.
☎ 0407 3043

OTHER PLACES OF INTEREST

Jails etc

Beaumaris Courthouse
Opposite castle entrance
Open: all year
Oldest and most original courthouse still being used in Wales

Beaumaris Jail
Church Street, Beaumaris,
Anglesey
Open: May-September, daily
11am-6pm.
Grim but interesting reminder of
prison life in the past

Fort Belan
Near Dinas Dinlle, Caernarfon
Open: May-September, daily
10am-5.30pm.
Old fort in fine setting, museums,
gift shop and flights over Snowdonia

Mines

Chwarel Hen
Llanfair, near Harlech
Open: Easter-October
Small but old mine, walk-in with
helmet and light

Chwarel Wynne
6 miles east of Chirk on Glyn
Ceiriog road, B4506.
Tours of slate mine and visitor
centre with films. Picnic site and
nature trail.

Gloddfa Ganol Slate Mine
Blaenau Festiniog
Open: Easter-October, daily
10am-5.30pm
Machinery and mill in world's
largest slate mine. Walk around
the caverns

Llechwedd Slate Caverns
Blaenau Ffestiniog
Open: March-October, daily
10am-6pm
See a quarry as it was 100 years
ago and visit the deepest caverns

Sygun Copper Mine
Close to Beddgelert
Open: daily March to September.
Guided tours of old mine shaft
with audio visual presentations
explaining early processes.

Power Stations

Dinorwig Power Station
☎ Llanberis 363
Hydro-electical pumped storage
scheme built inside a mountain.

Information centre and guided
tours, Easter-September

Ffestiniog Power Station
Open: Easter-October
☎ Blaenau Ffestiniog 465
Pumped storage scheme with low
and high reservoirs

Trawsfynydd Power Station
☎ Trawsfynydd 331
Nuclear power station set amidst
mountains. Parties only allowed to
visit.

Wylfa Power Station
Cemaes Bay, Anglesey
☎ Cemaes Bay 710471
Tours at 10.15am and 2pm
Monday-Friday, June-September
Observation tower open daily
Nuclear power station set on
rugged coast

Zoos

Anglesey Sea Zoo
Brynsiecyn, Anglesey
☎ 0248-73411
Largest aquarium in Wales. Ideal
for children with unique collection.
Seafood centre and tea room.

Pili Palas
Porthaethwy close to Menai
Bridge.
Butterflies from around the world
in natural habitat. Relax in exotic
surroundings.

**Welsh Mountain Zoo and
Botanical Gardens**
Off Kings Road south of Colwyn
Bay town centre.
☎ 0492-2938
Open: summer 9.30am-8pm,

winter 10am-4pm
Collection of birds of prey and
animals in magnificent setting

RAILWAYS

There are several narrow gauge
railways in North Wales and two
lines operated by British rail that
offer exciting scenery

Bala Lake Railway
Llanuwchllyn, Bala
Daily service April-September
☎ Llanuwchllyn 666
    or Bala 520226
Steam railway alongside lake,
with magnificent scenery

Conwy Valley Railway Museum
Betws-y-Coed station
Open: daily 10.30am-5pm
Steam miniature railway and
historical rolling stock and railway
items

**Fairbourne and Barmouth
Steam Railway**
Narrow gauge with Victorian-style
stations. Runs along coast to
meet ferry to Barmouth. Butterfly
Safari on station.
Open: Late March-October
☎ 0341-250084

Festiniog Railway
Runs from Porthmadog to
Blaenau Ffestiniog
Operates every day April-
September and thereafter a
limited service
☎ Porthmadog 2384
Superb run on most famous
narrow gauge steam railway

Great Orme Tramway
Llandudno
Continuous daily service in
summer from town to summit

Llanberis Lake Railway
Runs alongside Llyn Padarn
through country park
Daily service April-September
☎ Llanberis 549

Llandudno Cabin Lift
Open: daily Easter-September,
weather permitting
Swiss-style trip up the Great
Orme

Llangollen Railway
Has short trips daily, on the hour,
alongside Afon Dee. Collection of
rolling stock. Special events.
Open: April-September.
☎ 0978-860951

Snowdon Mountain Railway
Llanberis to Snowdon summit
Daily service April-October,
conditions permitting
☎ Llanberis 223
Rack and pinion steam railway to
highest summit in England and
Wales

Tal-y-Llyn Railway
Wharf Station, Tywyn
Narrow gauge, with steam
locomotives, 14 mile round trip
from Tywyn to Nant Gwernol.
Museum at station.
Open: March-November.
☎ Tywyn 710472.

Welsh Highland Railway
Railway, closed in 1937, now
being restored. Short run in fine
scenery. Train sheds and
workshops.
Open: weekends, April, May,
June and September; daily in July
and August.
☎ 0766-513402

British rail operate regular
passenger services along the
North Wales coast and Holyhead.
Two branch lines are worthy of
mention because of the magnificent views and situation of the
lines:

Cambrian Coast Line
Aberystwyth to Pwllheli
Regular daily service
Follows coast across estuaries
with sea and mountain views. Can
be joined at any station en route

Conwy Valley Railway
Conwy to Blaenau Ffestiniog
Regular daily service throughout
the year
Superb run along valley and
through mountains. Can be joined
at any station en route

SWIMMING POOLS

There are public swimming pools
in many of the larger towns.
Opening times will vary, so check
before setting out.

Bangor
☎ 0248-370600

Blaenau Ffestiniog
☎ 0766-830484

Buckley
☎ 0244-544469

Connah's Quay
☎ 0244-819561

Conwy Valley
☎ 0492-640921

Corwen
☎ 0490-2600

Denbigh
☎074571-3958

Harlech
☎ 0978-780576

Llandudno
☎ 0492-78838

Ruthin
☎ 08242-3880

Wrexham
☎0978-263795

Rhyl Sun Centre: Pools, Wave
machine, family fun.
☎ 0745-31771

TOURIST INFORMATION CENTRES — GANOLFAN CROESO CYMRU

Many towns in North Wales now have tourist offices either run by the local council or the Regional Tourism Council. They are able to provide up-to-the-minute information on what is going on in the area, local timetables and places to visit, plus leaflets on local nature trails and accommodation. The staff are extremely helpful and anxious to see that you get the maximum benefit from your visit to Wales. Most offices are open throughout the summer and are generally easy to find in the town or village, being well signposted.

There are information centres in the following towns:

Aberdyfi
☎ 065-472321

Bangor
☎ 0248-352786

Betws-y-Coed
☎ 06902-426

Blaenau Ffestiniog
☎ 0766-830360

Caernarfon
☎ 0286-2232

Chester
☎0244-40144 & 49026

Colwyn Bay
☎ 0492-530478

Conwy
☎ 0492-592248

Dolgellau
☎ 0341 422888

Harlech
☎ 0766-780658

Holyhead
☎ 0407-2622

Holywell
☎ 0352 780144

Llanberis
☎ 0286-870765

Llanfair PG
☎ 0248-713177

Llangollen
☎0978-860828

Menai Bridge
☎ 0248-713923

Mold
☎ 0352-59331

Porthmadog
☎ 0766-512981

Prestatyn
☎ 07456-2484

Pwllheli
☎ 0758-613000

Rhyl
☎ 0745-55068

Rhos-on-Sea
☎ 0492-48778

Ruthin
☎ 08242-3992

Tywyn
☎0654-710070

Wrexham
☎ 0978-357845

Many of these offices can book
beds in the area for you.

USEFUL ADDRESSES

British Mountaineering Council,
Crawford House,
Precinct Centre,
Booth Street East,

Manchester MI3 9RZ
☎ 061 273 5835

British Tourist Authority,
64 St James Street
London SW1
☎ 01 499 9325

Camping and Caravanning Club
of Great Britain and Ireland
11 Lower Grosvenor Place
London SW1W 0EY
☎ 01 828 1012

Cyclists Touring Club
69 Meadrow
Godalming
Surrey
☎ Godalming 7217

Forestry Commission (Information)
231 Corstorphine Road
Edinburgh
EH12 7AT

National Mountaineering Centre
Plas-y-Brenin
Capel Curig
Betws-y-Coed
Gwynedd
☎ Capel Curig 214280

National Trust
36 Queen Anne's Gate
London SW1H 9AS
☎ 01 222 9251

National Trust
North Wales Regional Office
Trinity Square
Llandudno
Gwynedd LL30 2DE
☎ 0492 860123

North Wales Wildlife Trust
376 High Stree
Bangor
Gwynedd LL57 1YE

North Wales Tourist Board
77 Conway Road
Colwyn Bay
Clwyd

Outward Bound Trust
14 Oxford Street
London W1
☎ 01 637 4951

Rambler's Association
1-5 Wandsworth Road
London SW8 2LJ
☎ 01 582 6768

Royal Society for the Protection of
Birds (Wales Office)
Bryn Aderyn
The Bank
Newtown
Powys SY16 2AB

Snowdonia National Park
Information Office
Penrhyndeudraeth
Gwynedd
☎ 0766 770274

Wales Tourist Board
PO Box 151
Cardiff CF5 1X5

Welsh Water Authority
Cambrian Way
Brecon
Clwyd

Youth Hostels Association
Trevelyan House
St Albans
Herts AL1 2DY
☎ St Albans 55215

VISITOR CENTRES

The Forestry Commission and the
Welsh Water Authority have
visitors' centres within the region.
They generally have interesting
exhibitions of the locality, its
wildlife and history and they also
provide picnic spots and marked
trails for short walks with leaflets
available detailing the route and
what to look out for. They are well
worth visiting to discover more
about the area.

Forestry Commission Centres

Bod Petrual
In centre of Clocaenog Forest, 7
miles west of Ruthin on the B5105
road to Cerrig-y-Drudion. Story of
forest past and present told in
lovely setting.

Maesgwm Visitor Centre
In heart of Coed-y-Brenin (Forest
of Kings) between Dolgellau and
Trawsfynydd. Excellent centre
with history of gold mining in the
area and natural flora and fauna
found in the forest. Lots of walks
in miles of forest.

Y Stablau (The Stables)
In centre of village of Betws-y-
Coed with information on
Snowdonia National Park and the
nearby Gwydyr Forest.
Open: daily during Easter week
and from Spring Bank Holiday to
autumn.

Other Forestry Commission areas
worth visiting are:

Beddgelert Forest Park Campsite

Details of walks and wayfaring course within forest available from campsite shop.

Llyn Geirionydd

Off A5 between Betws-y-Coed and Capel Curig.
Picnic site at lakeside. Idyllic spot and start for walks or a cold swim.

Newborough Warren

On Anglesey, off A4080 from Llanfair PG
Superb situation looking across sea to mountains. Miles of beach. Forest located on dunes.

Tan-y-Coed

In Dyfi Forest, just off A487, 4 miles north of Machynlleth.
A picnic site in fine setting with lots of forest walks all around.

Water Authority Centres

Lake Vyrnwy, Clwyd

Close to dam, signposted from Tanat Valley and Bwlch-y-Groes. Pleasant little centre, with history of dam and local wildlife. Nature reserve around lake. Map of walks available from centre.

Llyn Alaw

Anglesey
Between A5 and Amlwch.
History of lake and the surrounding area. Fishing is available, and there are picnic spots.

Llyn Brenig, Clwyd

Signposted south of Denbigh on B4501.
Exhibition and information centre. Nature and history trails. Fly fishing, canoeing and sailing are allowed with permit. Lots to do in lovely setting.

INDEX